'A truly dark, ...
cracker of a thriller. The ending ...
come. Absolutely fantastic and very highly reco...
Bloomin' Brilliant Books

'Beautifully told and perfectly paced . . . a brilliant read. I haven't read her first novel *Unravelling Oliver* but I will definitely be seeking it out on the back of the fantastic *Lying in Wait*' Adrian Dooley on *Goodreads*

'I loved #LyinginWait – my tea went cold and my Wispa shockingly uneaten. Just bloody brilliant' @aineltoner

'From start to finish it was gripping. Kept guessing the ending and then bang . . . oh no, she didn't!' Amy Howlin, the Rick O'Shea Book Club

'An absolute stormer of a read . . . this psychological chiller will definitely stick in your mind once you've turned the last page' *Mini Adventures*

'I loved #LyinginWait! Deliciously dark!' @AnahitaMody

'I read this book in one day . . . a beautifully written novel, with superbly flawed characters' Andy Wormald on *Goodreads*

'Just started *Lying in Wait* last night, Liz Nugent! Totally hooked from the first sentence!' Carolann Copland, the Rick O'Shea Book Club

'Liz Nugent, I read *Lying in Wait* in 24 hours! Absolutely fantastic!' Claire Barry, the Rick O'Shea Book Club

'Just finished reading #LyinginWait and I need to lie down it was so good! Lydia is Mummy Dearest with a sprinkle of Ted Bundy' @ClaireyLove

'Dark, disturbing and brilliant, I just loved it. And that ending!' *My Chestnut Reading Tree*

'Oh my GOD!!! Liz Nugent! What have you done? Two days after finishing *Lying in Wait* I kept glancing at the cover in total awe of what I had read. I mean, words escape me when I think of that book – just read it! The best week of reading I ever put in!' Denise Scally, the Rick O'Shea Book Club

'Read *Lying in Wait* by @lizzienugent on my holidays in two days flat. The pages just turned themselves' @eithneshortall

'Beyond brilliant from start to finish . . . I still can't get it out of my head. I lay in bed the night after finishing the book and couldn't sleep, so much was running through my head concerning the storyline. I had heard nothing but good things about this book and normally when this is the case and I go on to read said book I am left disappointed and wondering did I read a different book from everyone else? That's happened to me quite a bit this year but *Lying in Wait* deserves every bit of praise heaped upon it and it went way beyond my expectations. The quote on the cover from Sophie Hannah says "a stunningly talented writer" and Liz certainly is and has confirmed it with a read that will get deep inside your head and leave you breathless as you race through the pages' Emma Crowley on *Goodreads*

'Just finished *Lying in Wait* . . . absolutely brilliant, I was gripped from the first few pages!' Emma Maguire, the Rick O'Shea Book Club

'I came to the last page, I closed the book with a shudder of disgust as well as an acute desire to read the next Liz Nugent novel asap! Brilliant, mesmerizing and truly disturbing'
Laura Bambrey Books

'I loved this book in every way' *Swirl and Thread*

'In *Lying in Wait* Liz Nugent firmly cements herself as a skilled storyteller, whose monstrous creations are all the more effective for their outwardly normal facades'
From First to Last Page

'A thrilling, dark read . . . a twisted ending I didn't see coming' Inishowen Cailín on *Goodreads*

'Unbelievably brilliant . . . nothing prepares you for the ending! A one-sitting read, I promise!' Ipsita Banerjee on *Goodreads*

'So without giving anything away, I finally got to finish #LyinginWait. All I can say is, I was NOT expecting that!!!'
Jenny Tuohy, the Rick O'Shea Book Club

'Finished @lizzienugent's #LyinginWait last night – if you like dark and twisted, you'll love this! Couldn't put it down!'
@JillyMcDonough

'I was so caught up in this horrifically dysfunctional family that the pages practically turned themselves . . . dark, disturbing and brilliant, I just loved it. And that ending!'
Joanne Robertson on *Goodreads*

'Just perfect' *Book Addict Rambles*

'Well, I read Liz Nugent's *Lying in Wait* in record time this evening, I *even* let a beer go warm. Now that's serious. I adore words but the only one I can come up with now is "WOW". Lydia will stay with me for a long time to come. An enthralling, captivating, thought-provoking and disturbing read. Excellent plot, mesmerizing characters, I LOVED it'
Karen Breathnach Uí Chuinn, the Rick O'Shea Book Club

'I finished *Lying in Wait* just a few minutes ago. What an ending! But I wish it didn't have to come to an end!'
Laura Hughes, the Rick O'Shea Book Club

'Liz Nugent's writing is beautiful, the voices of the three narrators perfectly pitched, the quirks and tics we might expect in their speech beautifully translated to the written form. From the opening page, Nugent holds the reader in the palm of her hands . . . An incredible novel, *Lying in Wait* is a lightning-fast read that should be an essential item for anyone packing for a holiday. It cements Liz Nugent's place as one of Ireland's finest living novelists' *Reader Dad*

'This book should come with a warning. "Only start if you can finish in one sitting." Gripping, from start to finish. Each character so complex and believable right to the end. Loved her style. Unembellished, straightforward storytelling. Most enjoyable book I have read in a while'
Lucia Gannon on *Goodreads*

'Talk about a dysfunctional family – Lydia reminded me of the fabulous Bette Davis in *The Anniversary*. A cruel and clever matriarch ruling her family without them even realizing they are being ruled . . . needless to say a brilliant opening line deserves an outstanding ending and Liz Nugent doesn't fail to deliver . . . a deliciously dark and constantly surprising story – I loved it' Michelle Ryles on *Goodreads*

'One of my favourites of the year so far' *Behind Green Eyes*

'One of the best thrillers I've read in a long time'
Nurse Fancy Pants

'Psychological writing at its finest . . . disturbing, enthralling and utterly brilliant' *Linda's Books Bag*

'Pulled me in from the start and I couldn't stop reading it!'
Saint Sophie

'Not a book that will easily be forgotten. Just brilliant!'
Sarah Kenny on *Goodreads*

'Was Lying in Wait myself all year for Liz Nugent's second book because I enjoyed *Unravelling Oliver* (her first book) so much. This DID NOT disappoint. But now I have to wait for her NEXT one . . .' Sheena Lambert on *Goodreads*

'Spine-shivering in its subtlety' *Bleach House Library*

'OMG what a brilliant, dark and twisty book'
Sue McQuaide Kitt on *Goodreads*

'A great, compelling read! I cannot stop thinking about this book. I cannot remember disliking a character as much as one in this book, which obviously means a great character has been developed! An ending which I certainly did not expect!'
Susan Hunter on *Goodreads*

'This is the easiest five stars I've ever given . . . you'll find yourself slotting characters into "good" and "bad" boxes. You'll be prepared to feel a certain way about every character before every preconceived notion comes crashing down with the turn of a page' *Go Book Yourself*

'Tightly plotted and excellently paced, *Lying in Wait* is absolutely gripping. The writing is excellent, the surprises never stop. It is unnerving and irresistible, dark with a devastating twist. Absolute genius. I loved every single word'
Random Things Through My Letterbox

'I have read so many positive reviews about this book and I really did try to savour each chapter and make this book last, but today I was so swept along by the voices of Lydia, Laurence and Karen that I just had to find out what happened. I so did not see that ending. Loved it, really loved it'
Tom Scullion, the Rick O'Shea Book Club

'Twisty and chilling with an ending that leaves the reader astounded' *Handwritten Girl*

'I downloaded *Lying in Wait* this morning and finished it this afternoon. Wow! It's brilliant. I don't remember ever enjoying a book as much' Una Reynolds, the Rick O'Shea Book Club

'Liz Nugent take a bow! Folks, if you haven't read *Lying in Wait* yet you're missing out. Oh, my god, what a read. Fantastic' Yvonne Swords, the Rick O'Shea Book Club

Lying in Wait

LIZ NUGENT

PENGUIN BOOKS

PENGUIN BOOKS

UK | USA | Canada | Ireland | Australia
India | New Zealand |South Africa

Penguin Books is part of the Penguin Random House group of companies
whose addresses can be found at global.penguinrandomhouse.com

Penguin
Random House
UK

First published by Penguin Ireland 2016
Published in Penguin Books 2017
001

Set in 12.5/14.75 pt Garamond MT Std
Typeset by Jouve (UK), Milton Keynes
Printed in Great Britain by Clays Ltd, St Ives plc

A CIP catalogue record for this book is available from the British Library

ISBN : 978–0–241–98507–6

www.greenpenguin.co.uk

MIX
Paper from
responsible sources
FSC® C018179

Penguin Random House is committed to a sustainable future for our business, our readers and our planet. This book is made from Forest Stewardship Council® certified paper.

For Richard, with all my love

The cold earth slept below,
Above the cold sky shone;
And all around, with a chilling sound,
From caves of ice and fields of snow,
The breath of night like death did flow
Beneath the sinking moon.

Percy Bysshe Shelley

PART I

1980

1. Lydia

My husband did not mean to kill Annie Doyle, but the lying tramp deserved it. After we had overcome the initial shock, I tried to stop him speaking of her. I did not allow it unless to confirm alibis or to discuss covering up any possible evidence. It upset him too much and I thought it best to move on as if nothing had happened. Even though we did not talk about it, I couldn't help going over the events of the night in my mind, each time wishing that some aspect, some detail, could be different, but facts are facts and we must get used to them.

It was the 14th of November 1980. It had all been arranged. Not her death, just the meeting to see if she was genuine, and if not, to get our money back. I walked the strand for twenty minutes to ensure that there was nobody around, but I needn't have worried. The beach was deserted on that particularly bitter night. When I was satisfied that I was alone, I went to the bench and waited. A cruel wind rushed in with the waves and I pulled my cashmere coat around me and turned up the collar. Andrew arrived promptly and parked not far from where I was seated, as instructed. I watched from thirty yards away. I had told him to confront her. And I wanted to see her for myself, to assess her suitability. They were supposed to get out of the car and walk past me. But they didn't. After waiting ten minutes, I got up and walked towards the car, wondering what was taking so long. As I got closer, I could hear raised voices. And then I saw them fighting. The passenger door swung open and she tried to get out. But he pulled her back towards him. I could see his hands around her throat. I watched her struggle, mesmerized momentarily, wondering if I could be imagining things, and then I came back to myself, snapped out of my confusion and ran to the car.

'Stop! Andrew! What are you doing?' My voice was shrill to my own ears, and her eyes swivelled towards me in shock and terror before they rolled back upwards into her head.

He released her immediately and she fell backwards, gurgling. She was almost but not quite dead, so I grabbed the crook lock from the footwell at her feet and smashed it down on to her skull, just once. There was blood and a little twitching and then absolute stillness.

I'm not sure why I did that. Instinct?

She looked younger than her twenty-two years. I could see past the lurid make-up, the dyed black hair, almost navy. There was a jagged white scar running from a deformed top lip to the septum of her nose. I wondered that Andrew had never thought to mention that. Her jacket had been pulled off one arm during the struggle and I saw bloodied scabs in the crook of her elbow. There was a sarcastic expression on her face, a smirk that death could not erase. I like to think I did the girl a kindness, like putting an injured bird out of its misery. She did not deserve such consideration.

Andrew has always had a short fuse, blowing up at small, insignificant things and then, almost immediately, remorseful and calm. This time, however, he was hysterical, crying and screaming fit to wake the dead.

'Oh Christ! Oh Jesus!' he kept saying, as if the Son of God could fix anything. 'What have we done?'

'We?' I was aghast. 'You killed her!'

'She laughed at me! You were right about her. She said I was an easy touch. That she'd go to the press. She was going to blackmail me. I lost my temper. But you . . . you finished it, she might have been all right . . .'

'Don't even . . . don't say that, you fool, you idiot!'

His face was wretched, tormented. I felt sympathy for him. I told him to pull himself together. We needed to get home before Laurence. I ordered him to help me get the body into the boot. Through his tears, he carried out my instructions. Infuriatingly, his golf clubs were in there, unused for the last year, taking up most of the space, but luckily the corpse was as slight and slim as I had suspected, and still flexible, so we managed to stuff her in.

'What are we going to do with her?'

'I don't know. We have to calm down. We'll figure it out tomorrow. We need to go home now. What do you know about her? Does she have family? Who will be looking for her?'

'I don't know . . . she . . . I think she might have mentioned a sister?'

'Right now, nobody knows she is dead. Nobody knows she is missing. We need to keep it like that.'

When we got home to Avalon at quarter past midnight, I could see by the shadow from his window that the bedside light was on in Laurence's bedroom. I had really wanted to be there when he got home, to hear how his evening had been. I told Andrew to pour us a brandy while I went to check on our son. He was sprawled across the bed and didn't stir when I ruffled his hair and kissed his forehead. 'Goodnight, Laurence,' I whispered, but he was fast asleep. I turned out his lamp, closed his bedroom door and went to the bathroom cabinet for a Valium before I went downstairs. I needed to be calm.

Andrew was trembling all over. 'Jesus, Lydia, we're in serious trouble. Maybe we should call the guards.'

I topped up his glass and drained the bottle into my own. He was in shock.

'And ruin Laurence's life for ever? Tomorrow is a new day. We'll deal with it then, but we must remember Laurence, whatever happens. He mustn't know anything.'

'Laurence? What has it to do with him? What about Annie? Oh God, we killed her, we murdered her. We're going to prison.'

I was not going to prison. Who would look after Laurence? I stroked Andrew's arm in an effort to comfort him. 'We will figure it out tomorrow. Nobody saw us. Nobody can connect us with the girl. She would have been too ashamed to tell anyone what she was up to. We just have to figure out where to put her body.'

'You're sure nobody saw us?'

'There wasn't a soul on the strand. I walked the length of it to make sure. Go to bed, love. Things will be better tomorrow.'

He looked at me as if I were insane.

I stared him down. 'I'm not the one who strangled her.'

Tears poured from his cheeks. 'But maybe if you hadn't hit her . . .'

'What? She would have died more slowly? Or been permanently brain-damaged?'

'We could have said that we'd found her like that!'

'Do *you* want to drive back there now and dump her, ring an ambulance from the phone box and explain what you are doing there on the strand at one o'clock in the morning?'

He looked into the bottom of his glass.

'But what are we going to do?'

'Go to bed.'

As we ascended the stairs, I heard the whirr of the washing machine. I wondered why Laurence had decided to do laundry on a Friday night. It was most unlike him. But it reminded me that my clothes and Andrew's really needed to be washed too. We both stripped and I set aside the pile of laundry for the morning. I washed the sand off our shoes and swept the floors we had passed over. I deposited the sand from the dustpan in the back garden, on the raised patch of lawn beyond the kitchen window. I studied the ground for a moment. I had always thought of having a flower bed planted there.

When I slipped into bed later, I put my arms around Andrew's trembling form, and he turned to me and we made love, clawing at and clinging to each other like survivors of a terrible calamity.

Andrew had been a very good husband until just a year previously. For twenty-one years, our marriage had been solid. Daddy had been very impressed with him. On his deathbed, Daddy had said he was relieved to be leaving me in good hands. Andrew had been Daddy's apprentice in Hyland & Goldblatt. He had taken Andrew under his wing and made him his protégé. One day, when I was about twenty-six, Daddy had telephoned me at home and told me that we were having a special guest for dinner and that I should cook something nice and get my hair done. 'No lipstick,' he said. Daddy had a thing about make-up. 'I can't stand those painted trollops!' he would say about American film stars. Daddy's views could be extreme. 'You are my beautiful daughter. No point in gilding a lily.'

I was curious about this visitor and why I should dress up for him. I should have guessed, of course, that Daddy was intent on matchmaking. He needn't have worried. Andrew adored me right away. He went to enormous lengths to charm me. He said that he would do anything for me. 'I can't stop looking at you,' he said. And indeed, his eyes followed me everywhere. He always called me his prize, his precious jewel. I loved him too. My father always knew what was best for me.

Our courtship was short and very sweet. Andrew came from a good family. His late father had been a consultant paediatrician, and though I found his mother a little contrary, she raised no objections to our relationship. After all, when Andrew married me, he would get Avalon too – a six-bedroom detached Georgian house on an acre of land in Cabinteely, south County Dublin. Andrew wanted us to get a house of our own when we got married, but Daddy put his foot down. 'You'll move in here. This is Lydia's home. Don't look a gift horse in the mouth.'

So Andrew moved in with us, and Daddy gave up the

master bedroom and moved to the large bedroom on the other side of the corridor. Andrew grumbled a little to me. 'But, darling, don't you see how awkward it is? I'm living with my boss!' And I admit that Daddy did order Andrew around quite a lot, but Andrew got used to it quickly. I think he knew how lucky he was.

Andrew did not mind that I did not want to host parties or socialize with other couples. He said he was quite happy to keep me to himself. He was kind and generous and considerate. He usually backed away from confrontation, so we did not have many arguments. In a heated moment, he might kick or throw inanimate objects, but I think everyone does that from time to time. And he was always terribly contrite afterwards.

Andrew worked his way up through the ranks until finally all his time on the golf course paid off and three years ago he was appointed as a judge in the Criminal Courts. He was a respected member of society. People listened to him when he spoke, and quoted him in the newspapers. He was widely regarded as having the voice of reason on matters legal and judicial.

But last year, Paddy Carey, his old pal, accountant and golfing partner, had left the country with our money. I thought that, at the very least, Andrew would be careful with our finances. That was the husband's job, to be a provider and to look after the economic well-being of the household. But he had trusted Paddy Carey with everything and Paddy had fooled us all. We were left with nothing but debts and liabilities, and Andrew's generous salary barely covered our expenditure.

Had I married badly after all? My role was to be

presentable, beautiful, charming – a homemaker, a companion, a good cook, lover and a mother. A mother.

Andrew suggested selling some land to developers to raise capital. I was horrified at the suggestion. Nobody of our status would do such a thing. I had spent my whole life in Avalon. My father had inherited it from his father, and it was the house in which I was born. And the house in which my sister died. I was not going to compromise on selling any part of Avalon. Nor was I going to compromise on the money we needed to pay the girl.

But we had to take Laurence out of the hideously expensive Carmichael Abbey and send him to St Martin's instead. It broke my heart. I knew he was unhappy there. I knew he was victimized because of his class and accent, but the money simply wasn't there. Andrew quietly sold some of the family silver to pay our debts, and we kept the wolf at bay. He could not risk being declared bankrupt, as he would have been forced to resign from the bench. We had never lived extravagantly, but the few luxuries that were normal to us began to disappear. He gave up his golf club membership but insisted that he could still pay my store account at Switzers and Brown Thomas. He always hated to disappoint me.

But now, this? A dead girl in the boot of the car in the garage. I was sorry she was dead, but I can't honestly say I wouldn't or couldn't have strangled her myself under the circumstances. We just wanted our money back. I couldn't stop thinking about the scars on the girl's inner arm. I had seen a documentary about heroin addicts on the BBC, and reports of a heroin epidemic were in our newspapers. It seemed obvious that she had injected our money into her bloodstream, as if our needs and wants hadn't mattered.

As Andrew slept fitfully, whimpering and crying out occasionally, I made plans.

The next morning, a Saturday, Laurence slept late. I warned Andrew to say as little as possible. He readily agreed. He was hollow-eyed, and there was a tremor in his voice that never quite went away after that night. He and Laurence had always had a fraught relationship, so they were not inclined to be conversational. I planned to get Laurence out of the house for the day, send him into town on some errand or other while Andrew buried the girl in our garden. Andrew was shocked that we would bury her here, but I made him see that, this way, she could not be discovered. We were in control of our own property. Nobody had access without our permission. Our large rear garden was not overlooked. I knew exactly the spot where she could be buried. In my childhood there had been an ornamental pond under the plane tree beyond the kitchen window, but Daddy had filled it in after my sister's death. Its stone borders, which had lain under the soil for almost forty years, were conveniently grave-like.

After Andrew had buried the body, he could clean out and hoover the car until there would be no trace of fibres or fingerprints. I was determined to take all precautions. Andrew knew from his job the kind of thing that could incriminate a person. Nobody had seen us on the strand, but one can never be too sure of anything.

*

When Laurence arrived at the breakfast table, he had a noticeable limp. I tried to be cheerful. 'So how are you today, sweetie?' Andrew stayed behind his *Irish Times*, but I could see his knuckles gripped it tightly to stop it from shaking.

'My ankle hurts. I tripped going upstairs last night.'

I examined his ankle quickly. It was very swollen and probably sprained. This scuppered my plans to send him into town. But I could still contain my boy, confine him to quarters so to speak. I strapped his ankle and instructed him to stay on the sofa all day. That way, I could keep an eye on him, keep him away from the rear of the house where the burial was to take place. Laurence was not an active boy, so lying on the sofa watching television all day and having food delivered to him on a tray was no hardship to him at all.

As dusk fell, when everything had been done, Andrew lit a bonfire. I don't know what he was burning, but I had impressed upon him the need to get rid of all evidence. 'Think of it as one of your court cases – what kind of things betray the lie? Be thorough!' To give him his due, he was thorough.

However, Laurence is a smart boy. He is intuitive, like me, and he noted his father's dark mood. Andrew was snappy about wanting to see the television news, terrified, I suppose, that the girl would feature. She did not. He claimed he had the flu and went to bed early. When I went upstairs later, he was throwing things into a suitcase.

'What are you doing?'

'I can't bear it. I have to get away.'

'Where? Where are you going to go? We can't change anything now. It's too late.'

He turned on me then for the first time, spitting with anger.

'It's all your fault! I'd never have met her if it wasn't for you. I should never have started this. It was a crazy idea to begin with, but you wouldn't stop, you were obsessed! You put too much pressure on me. I'm not the type of man to . . .' He trailed off because he was exactly the type of man to strangle a girl, as it happens. He just didn't know it until now. Also, my plan had been perfect. He was the one who ruined it.

'I told you to pick a healthy girl. Didn't you see the marks on her arms? She was a *heroin addict.* Don't you remember that documentary? You must have noticed her arms.'

He broke down into sobs and collapsed on the bed, and I cradled his head to muffle the sound. Laurence mustn't hear. When the heaving of his shoulders had subsided, I upended the contents of the suitcase and put it back on top of the wardrobe.

'Put your things away. We are not going anywhere. We will carry on as normal. This is our home and we are a family. Laurence, you and I.'

2. Karen

The last time I saw Annie was in her bedsit in Hanbury Street on Thursday the 13th of November 1980. I remember that, as usual, the place was immaculately clean. No matter how disordered her life was, Annie was always madly tidy since her time in St Joseph's. The blankets were folded neatly at the end of her bed, and the window was wide open, letting the freezing air into the room.

'Would you not close the window, Annie?'

'When I finish my smoke.'

She lay back on the bed, smoking her short, untipped cigarette, while I made a pot of tea. The mugs were lined up neatly on the shelf, upside down, handles facing front. I poured two scoops of tea leaves from the caddy into the scalded pot and poured on the boiling water. She looked at her watch.

'Two minutes. You have to let it sit for two minutes.'

'I know how to make a cup of tea.'

'Nobody knows how to make it right.'

That's the kind of thing that always drove me mad about Annie. She was so stubborn. There was her way, or the wrong way.

'It's freezing.' She wrapped her long cardigan tightly around her, the sleeves dangling below her hands. When the two minutes were up, she gave the nod and I was allowed to pour. I handed her a mug of tea and she emptied her ashtray into a plastic bag which she carefully folded over before placing it in the bin.

'Are you sure it's sealed?' I was being sarcastic.

'It's sealed.' She was serious. She reached over and closed the window and then sprayed the room with one of those rotten air freshener cans that filled the room with a smell that would choke you.

'How's Ma?' she asked.

'She's worried about you. So is Da.'

'Yeah, right,' she said, her lip curling sideways.

'You didn't stay long on Sunday. You're always rushing off somewhere. He does worry about you.'

'Sure.'

My sister and me were always very different. I like to think I was a good child, but maybe that was just in comparison to Annie. I was quick at school, but things have always been easier for me. If we were in a shop together, the assistants would ignore her completely and serve me. People want to help me and do things for me. Annie always said it was because I'm pretty, but she never said it in a jealous way. We looked alike to a certain extent. As children, we were referred to as 'the carrot tops' on account of our flaming red hair, but we were different in one obvious way. Annie was born with a harelip. She had a botched operation when she was a baby, and her top lip was stretched and flattened at the front. She had a scar stretching down from her nose to her mouth. My mouth turns upwards at the sides, so I look kind of smiley. I think that's why everyone says I'm pretty. I'm not really. I look in the mirror and I just see carrot-top Karen.

When we were small children, Annie regularly went missing. We'd be playing with the neighbours out the front of our house, and Ma would come out and say 'Where's Annie?' and we'd all be sent off to look for her. She'd be in a street beyond the patch we were allowed to play in, and once, she'd hopped on a bus into town and Mrs Kelly who lived in number 42 had spotted her and brought her home. Annie was just curious, I think. She wanted to know what was around every corner. Back then, Da and her were close. She used to climb up on his shoulders and he'd piggyback her around the house and she would scream with laughter, but I was smaller and afraid to go up that high. By the time she was a teenager, though, Da and Annie were at war.

My sister had a reputation. Ma said she kicked her way out of the womb feet first and she hadn't stopped kicking since. In secondary school, Annie was in trouble all the time for giving cheek to the teachers, stealing, vandalism, mitching, and beating up other girls. She was smart for sure, but couldn't settle to learning. She was slow to read and slower to write. I am three years younger, but by the time I was seven my reading and writing were better than hers. I tried really hard to help her, but she said the letters didn't always make sense to her. Even if I wrote down a sentence and asked her to copy it, the words would come out as a jumble. She'd been moved to two different schools by the time she left at fourteen. She could just about write, but her main hobbies by then were smoking and drinking. Ma tried reason, talking to her, bargaining with her, but when that didn't work, Da tried violence. He beat her and locked her in our room, and I know it killed him to do it.

'Jesus, Annie, look what you have me doing!' and he'd go quiet and not speak for a few days. But that didn't work either, and eventually the worst thing that could happen in a family back then happened. We didn't know until she was four months gone.

All hell broke loose. She was only sixteen. The father was a boy her own age who, of course, denied all responsibility and said the baby could be anyone's. He and his family moved away shortly after that. Da called the parish priest, and he and a guard took Annie away to St Joseph's in a black car. I didn't see her again for nearly two years.

When she returned, she was completely altered. That was where all her tics and cleaning obsessions started. She had never been like that before. Her appearance was a shock. Her fiery red hair was gone because her head had been shaved. She was painfully thin. On her first night back, in the room we shared, I asked her to tell me what it was like to be locked up in a mother and baby home, and she said it was a living hell that she wanted to forget. She told me about the day the baby was born. It was the 1st of August. She called her Marnie. 'She was perfect,' she said, 'even her mouth was perfect.' When I asked what happened to the baby, she turned her face to the wall and cried. For the first two months after her return, she used to hide food under her bed. She jumped at the slightest noise. Neither Annie nor my parents ever mentioned the baby. We tried to be normal and Annie tried to settle. Da got her a job cleaning in the bakery he worked in. Her hair grew back, but she dyed it black. A really harsh blue-black. It was her rebel statement.

A few months later, on the 1st of August, I bought Annie a gift in the Dandelion Market, an identity bracelet. I had the bracelet engraved with the name 'Marnie'. I'd been saving up for a while, but it wasn't real silver so it tarnished quickly. She never took it off after that, though. Da commented on it one day.

'What's that thing you have on?'

She stuck her wrist in his face, but he couldn't make out the word on the bracelet.

'It says "Marnie",' she said, 'your granddaughter's name if you must know.'

Gradually, Annie went back to her old ways. She was fired from the bakery by Da's boss because her work was shoddy. After that, the frostiness between her and Da was unbearable and she moved out of the house. I admit that I was glad when she moved out.

Though she was always a rebel, when it came to my schooling, Annie leaned hard on me to do my homework and stay out of trouble.

'You've got brains *and* beauty, Karen,' she said. 'You need to use both of them.'

I am clever enough, I suppose, and I liked school, but I worked hard to remove the stigma she had tainted me with. My teachers recognized this. 'You and your sister, chalk and cheese!' said Miss Donnelly one day, scoring me a B in an English test. When I meant to leave school at fifteen and try for work in the Lemons factory, Miss Donnelly spoke to Ma and Da and told them that I could stay on to do the Leaving Certificate. Nobody in our family had ever done the Leaving Certificate. My parents were thrilled and Annie was over the moon. 'You'll take the bad look off me!' she said.

I wasn't a natural genius, but I studied hard to justify Ma and Da's pride. Then, when I got reasonably good results, there was talk about going to university. I knew that keeping me in school had been a strain on my parents when I should have been out earning, and I could probably work my way through college, but I couldn't decide what I would study. English and Art were my best subjects, but if I studied English in college, I would have to do a three-year arts degree and then a year's HDip just to be a teacher, and if I did Art I'd have to go to an art college and Ma said there were no jobs for artists. Anyway, I had the wrong accent for university.

Ma thought I should do a secretarial course. There were still some jobs for typists, though they were few and far between. I liked the idea of that a lot better, and AnCO were running six-week courses for girls who had got good Leaving Certificate results. Annie was disappointed in me. 'You could have gone to college, you could have got a grant.' She didn't understand my reluctance. I was not curious like she was. She loved that I had stayed in school, but when she was drunk, she mocked me when I used big words that she didn't understand.

Annie got bits and pieces of cleaning work here and there, but most of the time she was on the dole, living in a bedsit not too far away. Ma gave her money sometimes on the sly. On her Sunday visits, Da would try and pretend he was glad to see her, but I think he was ashamed of her, though he denied it later. He couldn't understand why she was so different to the rest of us. Ma and Da and me all worked hard for what we got. We were quiet and tried to avoid trouble. Annie went looking for it.

After I did the course, I got a job in a dry-cleaning company, typing up invoices and doing a bit of bookkeeping as well. I can't say I loved it, but I met Dessie Fenlon there. Some of the men I dealt with were sleazy, passing comments on my figure or making smutty remarks, but Dessie was different. Just respectful, like. One day, I saw him giving one of the young lads a clip around the ear for the way he'd talked to me. Dessie was one of the van drivers. He was quite shy, and it was six months before he got up the courage to ask me out. I think he thought the age difference was too much. He was twenty-six, almost nine years older than me. The best part of the job was when he'd come in to do pick-ups or drop-offs, because we'd be giggling and flirting like mad. We started going out properly then. He said he couldn't believe his luck that I'd said yes to a date. When it was clear to everyone else in the shop that Dessie Fenlon and I were an item, the comments stopped. Dessie was quiet, but he could be fierce too if you crossed him. He had a reputation as a scrapper and had thrown a few punches in his time.

The job was dull and I was bored most of the time, but I was earning enough to move out of home too. I said to Annie that we could get a flat together, but she wasn't too keen on the idea. I was disappointed. I mentioned it to Ma, who told Da. He said, 'Don't move in with Annie, she'll drag you down to her level.' I wonder whether, if I had moved in with Annie, things would have been different. I wonder if Da remembers saying that. If it haunts him. I don't want to remind him. He's already suffering. We all are.

On that last day I saw her, she was agitated but excited about something. She said she was going to buy me a proper painting set because she knew that I still loved sketching and painting. I should have been excited about the promise of a gift like that, but I knew Annie too well. She was annoyed that I wasn't jumping up and down with happiness, but Annie was always swearing to buy me things or to do things with me, and they rarely ever happened.

'A proper set. I saw it in Clark's window, paints in tubes in a big wooden box with all kinds of brushes. All watercolours and inks, not oils. You see? I remember everything you told me about your art stuff – I know you don't like oils. It's gorgeous. The box is really old-fashioned-looking, but it's brand new and there's loads of things in it. I'm buying it for you on Saturday morning. I really am. I promise. Come round on Saturday, in the afternoon.'

'Where will you get the money for that?'

'Never you mind, I'll have the money.'

'Yeah.'

'I *will*. Do you not believe me, Karen?'

It was easier to play along, but I knew it was never going to happen. Like the time she said we'd go for dinner in Sheries in Abbey Street a few weeks before that, and I'd waited half an hour outside in the cold but she never showed up, and when I rang her about it, she'd said she was busy and we'd go another time.

Despite all this, I loved Annie. She wanted the best for me, wanted me to learn from her mistakes. She warned me off fellas, told me I was too good for the lads round our way and that I should keep myself for someone special. I didn't always obey her. Nobody could make me laugh like she could, and although her time in the mother and baby home turned down her brightness, the old spark was beginning to re-emerge by the time she vanished into thin air.

'Promise, you'll call on Saturday? About three, yeah? I can't wait to see your face when you open it.' So I promised, not daring to hope that she'd keep her word but never imagining that I wouldn't see her again.

'Sure,' I said. 'I'll bring Dessie.'

Her face clouded over. They'd got on well to begin with, though he thought she was a bit wild. He didn't like how drunk she'd get and, like Da, he didn't like me spending too much time with her. When I told him about Annie's pregnancy and her time in St Joseph's, his attitude to her worsened.

'She's one of them slappers?' he said. 'Who was the father, or did she even know?'

I was disgusted by his reaction. I ignored him for weeks then and avoided talking to him in work, but he didn't give up and eventually he won me over again with a bunch of flowers and a written apology. He said that he shouldn't have called my sister names. But if Dessie, who was basically good and kind, thought that way about Annie, so did everyone else. He was never comfortable in her company after that, and Annie wasn't stupid.

'What's wrong with your fella?' she said once in the Viking. 'He's always in such a hurry to leave.'

'He just doesn't like this pub much,' I said, which was true. The Viking was a rough enough spot, in a semi-derelict part of town. Teenage glue-sniffers hung around the area. Dessie had often given out about the fact that we had to meet her there, but Annie was a creature of habit. 'It's full of alcos,' he said, but I pointed out that could be said about most pubs in Ireland. Annie was clearly a popular character in the bar and was one of the youngest regulars. Late in the night, a sing-song would start and Annie, worse for wear, would sing 'Do Ya Think I'm Sexy' or 'I Will Survive' in a loud voice. Dessie hated that. 'She's making a show of herself,' he'd say, and though sometimes I agreed, she could still carry a tune and had full recall of the lyrics. I wasn't going to stop her enjoying herself.

When I called to her flat on Saturday, I'd decided not to bring Dessie along. I wasn't all that surprised when she wasn't there. That evening I rang her, and the girl who answered the phone in the hall said she'd take a message.

At Ma and Da's on Sunday, Annie didn't show up. Lunch after twelve-thirty Mass was the only family ritual we held on to, and Annie still turned up most of the time.

'Did she ring you, Ma, to say she wasn't coming?'

'She did not, the strap,' said my da, who took her feckless behaviour as a personal insult. I played it down.

'She might have the flu – the flat was freezing when I saw her on Thursday.'

'Did she not have the gas fire on?'

'She did, but you know she always opens the window when she smokes.'

'She gets the smoking from you,' my mother said to Da.

'That's all she got from me, Pauline, I can tell you.'

I changed the subject, asked Da if he was going to the greyhounds on Thursday.

The next day, Monday, I called round again with Dessie and there was no answer from her flat but I caught another girl on her way out. There were three bedsits in the two-storey house with a shared bathroom. I asked her if she'd seen Annie. 'Not since Thursday or Friday, now that you mention it. I thought she was away. It's usually her radio that wakes me.'

That was the first time I felt a bit worried. Annie wouldn't have gone away without telling me. Besides, where would she have gone?

'With some fella?' Dessie suggested, but clammed up again when I gave him a sharp look.

We'd usually be in touch twice or three times a week, but on Wednesday I still hadn't heard from her. I called to Ma's, but she hadn't heard from her either.

'Did she say anything to you about going away?'

'Not a thing. It's weird.'

I was still there when Da got home from the bakery.

'She's probably off on the piss somewhere. She'll turn up.'

'She's never disappeared for so long before. It's been nearly a week.'

'When last did you see her?'

'Last Thursday. She told me to call round on Saturday. She promised me she'd be there.' I didn't tell him about the painting set. There was no point.

'She promised, did she?' he said sarcastically.

*

On Friday when we still couldn't contact her, we all knew something was wrong. Da and me went to her flat together while Ma rang round her friends and some of the girls she used to work with. At Annie's flat, one of the other tenants said she hadn't been there all week. We called the landlord from the phone in the hall and he came round, a large sweating man with a big nose, complaining about being disturbed after 6 p.m. He let us into her bedsit with his enormous set of keys. Everything was as neat as a pin as usual, but all the clothes I knew she had were still in the wardrobe, except her grey herringbone coat, the woollen sleeveless dress Ma had bought her for her birthday and the knee-high purple boots. I didn't want to go rifling through all her stuff, but a quick glance told me she hadn't gone on a trip. Her long holdall bag was still under the dresser. A single mug sat in the sink with a spot of mould in the bottom of it.

'She'd never have left that there, Da, if she knew she was going away. Maybe for a few hours, but that's got to have been there for days.'

The landlord said, 'Her rent is due next week you know. I won't be left out of pocket.'

'Would ya shut up!' said my da, and inside I cheered because he was standing up for Annie and it was a very long time since I'd heard him do that. The landlord told us to leave, and said that if he didn't get his rent the next week, he'd be putting Annie's stuff in a bag on the doorstep.

When we got home with our news, Ma was worried sick. None of Annie's friends had seen her in over a week, and said she hadn't turned up for two cleaning jobs in the city centre. That alone would not have rung alarm bells, but my timid mother had bravely gone into the Viking after dark. The regulars there all knew Annie, but they said she hadn't been in for over a week.

'Do you think she got herself knocked up again and went back to St Joseph's?' said Da, a tone of concern creeping into his voice.

'She'd never go back there, Da, not in a million years. I know she wouldn't.' Ma agreed with me. 'And even if she was pregnant, why would she go anywhere without her clothes, or a bag?'

'I'm ringing the guards,' said Da on Friday the 21st of November 1980.

3. Laurence

I heard him say it quite clearly.

'The weekend of the 14th of November? Let me think . . . hold on now . . . let me see – ah, yes, I was here with my wife. Why do you ask, Garda?'

'The whole weekend? You didn't leave the house?'

'Yes, well, I got home from work on the Friday about six o'clock and didn't go out again.'

It was a lie.

'And was it just you and your wife here? Nobody else?'

'My son was out that Friday. But I think he was home before midnight. What is this about?'

'Well, sir, it's just that . . . a car was seen visiting the home of the missing woman over recent months, sir . . . Like yours, sir . . . the old Jaguar.'

The guard's tone was nervous, subservient. Too many 'sir's. It was clear he had drawn the short straw when sent to question my dad. Or Judge Fitzsimons, as he was more recently known.

'And may I have your name?' my father asked, and although I couldn't see him, I could hear the air of superiority in his voice, coupled with a strange tremor that was new. The kitchen door behind me was only slightly ajar, and I strained to hear what followed on the doorstep.

'Mooney, sir. I'm sorry to be having to ask, like –'

'And what exactly is your rank, *Mooney*?' He lingered on the 'oo' in Mooney.

'I'm a detective, sir.'

'I see. Not a detective sergeant or a detective inspector, then?'

I knew that tone. Dad could be rude or dismissive with strangers and he could fly off the handle. He intimidated me sometimes. I'm not sure that he meant to. He just did.

At the other end of the table, my mother was looking at me quizzically.

'Is that your fifth potato, Laurence? Go on, quick, while your father isn't looking.'

I hadn't been counting.

My mother got up, muttering about the draught. She closed the door behind me and turned on the radio and began to hum along tunelessly to the song playing. I said nothing, but now I couldn't hear what was being discussed at the front door.

My father had just deliberately lied to the guards. I admit I was taken aback by his lie. He was being asked about his movements almost two weeks earlier. I remembered that Friday night very clearly indeed because I was having my own adventure. I had also lied about my whereabouts. I had told my parents that I was going to the cinema with school friends, when actually I was losing my virginity to Helen d'Arcy, who lived in Foxrock Park, just twenty minutes away.

I had not intended to have sex with Helen on our first real date. I did not find her physically attractive. She had very nice silky blonde hair, but her frame was both wide and too thin. Her face, which was unnaturally big, sat on top of a scrawny neck. My own skin was flawless in comparison, perhaps because it was stretched.

I went to Helen's house simply because she invited me. I did not get many invitations.

She had caught up with me as I was returning from school a few weeks earlier. It was raining, as usual. School was awful. I had only started in St Martin's Institute for Boys the previous January because of Bloody Paddy Carey. I tried very hard not to let my parents know how much I was bullied in my new school. There was a particular group of four or five boys, all brawn and no brain. They did not often attack me physically after the first month, but my books were stolen or defaced with disgusting slogans, and my lunch was taken and replaced with items too revolting to mention.

Helen's school was one of the fee-paying ones a little closer to town, but she lived near our school. I had overheard stories about her from other boys in my class. I felt a kinship because the bullies in my class seemed to have as much contempt for her as they did for me.

I heard her before I saw her. 'What's your name?' she asked. I turned. Her green uniform skirt, made of some hairy fabric, was worn to baldness in places and the hem had come down on one side. I could see the inside of her collar was threadbare at the neck.

'Laurence. Fitzsimons.'

'Ah yeah, I've heard of you. Why do they call you the Hippo? You look normal to me.'

I warmed to her immediately. 'I *am* normal. They just don't like me.'

'Well, who gives a fuck what they like? Do you live on Brennanstown Road? I've seen you around.'

I lived in Avalon, a large detached house with a well-kept garden at the end of the road, but I wasn't sure if I should tell her. She didn't seem to mind whether I responded to her questions or not. We ambled companionably onwards. When we passed Trisha's Café, she suggested that I buy her a Coke. I hesitated.

'OK then, I'll buy *you* one,' she said as she pushed the glass door open. It would have been rude not to follow her. Unfortunately, the bullies were already there, sitting near the counter.

'Oink, oink!' one of them shouted in our direction.

'Fucking eejits,' said Helen, 'ignore them.'

We very rarely had bad language in Avalon, but now, in the same five minutes, I'd heard *fuck* and *fucking*. From a girl. I used bad language too sometimes, but never out loud.

Helen strolled coolly to the counter and returned with two Cokes.

I shoved two 10p pieces towards her to pay for them.

'You don't have to. Just because I paid, it doesn't mean you have to ask me out.'

Ask her out?

'I want to pay. It's fair.'

'Fine,' she said. There was a lull in conversation as we sucked our Cokes through thin straws. And then she said, 'You'd be quite good-looking if you weren't fat.'

It was not news to me that I was fat. My mother said it was puppy fat and that I'd shed it soon enough, but I was seventeen. My father said I ate too much. My scales said fifteen stone. I hadn't always been big, but over the last year, since I'd moved schools, my eating habits had gone completely out of control. The more nervous and miserable I was, the hungrier I felt. I love food, and mostly the fattening stuff. But this was the first time that a non-parent had said I was fat without a look of disgust.

'Your hair's nice,' I said, to return the compliment. She looked very pleased.

'I love food too, I probably eat more than you,' she said. Helen obviously had no idea just how much food I could put away.

'If you could give me about three stone, we'd both be perfect.'

Helen and I met a few times in the weeks after. We took it in turns to buy the Cokes. Then one day Helen said, 'Do you want to come to my house tomorrow night?'

'For what?'

'To visit me? To kick off the weekend?' she said, as if it was completely normal to be invited to girls' houses. 'My mum has made this amazing cake that's going to get thrown out if it's not eaten.'

We had only known each other a few weeks, but already she knew which buttons to push. An arrangement was made for after school, an address written down on the inside cover of my jotter.

At home that evening, I tried to be casual and breezy. 'I won't be in for dinner tomorrow, I'm going to the cinema with some of the lads,' I lied, as casually as I could. I focused on my copybook with fierce concentration. My dad perked up: he was delighted.

'Well, isn't that great now, great altogether. Going out with pals, eh? What are you going to see? There's a new *Star Wars* one, isn't there?'

We had been to see *Star Wars* together as a family. Dad and I had enjoyed it, but Mum had put her hands over her ears during the explosions, jumping at every clash of a light sabre. After that, she swore she was never going to the cinema again.

'*Herbie Goes Bananas*,' I said confidently, trying to ignore the crimson creep from my collar.

'I see,' said my father, slightly deflated and puzzled. 'Well, that'll be good, won't it, going out with friends?' He looked meaningfully at my mother, pleased no doubt that I finally had friends, but she was concentrating on cutting me a slice of cheesecake. I tried to nudge her hand a little to make the slice bigger, and she did so with a sigh and shake of her head.

'I'll take that one,' said my dad. 'Give the boy a smaller bit.' Nothing got past him.

'Just be home by midnight.'

'Midnight?! But we don't even know who these people –'

'No more about it, Lydia.' Dad closed the subject.

Midnight. Janey Mackers, I was amazed. I'd never had a curfew before. I hadn't needed one, but midnight seemed generous. Thanks, Dad. But now I had to go through with the date with Helen. I was pretty sure it was an actual date. In less than twenty-four hours. I was partly looking forward to it and partly terrified.

Preparing for a first date was tricky. I knew this from the cover of *Jackie* magazine in the newsagent's. There were ten steps to it, apparently. I could guess two of them: fresh breath and flowers.

After some thought, I decided that, while there might be ten steps for a girl, there could only be two for a boy. I was on top of the fresh breath. After we left Trisha's, I had bought myself a new toothbrush and some Euthymol toothpaste, even though it practically took the mouth off me. I figured that if it was that painful, it must be more effective.

Flowers. It was November. There were, however, some nice pink and white carnations blooming in my father's greenhouse that I raided late that night while my parents watched the *Nine O'Clock News*. I wrapped the stalks in some tinfoil and put them gently on top of my school-books in my satchel.

On that fateful Friday, my father gave me £2 after breakfast and told me to enjoy myself. Money was a huge issue in our house at that time. Dad's accountant, Bloody Paddy Carey (it was the only bad language I ever heard my father use), had absconded with our money a year previously. Dad was furious about it. We weren't allowed to tell anyone. The accountant had been a close friend, or so my father thought. Carey had several high-profile clients who had been badly burned, and the story had been all over the media. So far, my father's name had not been mentioned publicly. He was extremely stressed about this; he was mortified that Bloody Paddy Carey had made a fool of him, and that he might not be able to keep my mother in the style to which she was accustomed. We had had a full year of shouting and slamming doors, and endless talk of tightening our belts. So to get £2 out of my dad without even having to ask was most unexpected. I thought that maybe I could buy shop flowers now, but since I already had some, it would be a waste. I wasn't sure what I should spend the money on.

By the time the final bell rang in school, I was almost sick with anticipation. Even the idea of an alternative to the usual Friday night ritual – homework, dinner, watch *Bonanza* and *The Dukes of Hazzard* on television by myself, then the *Nine O'Clock News* and a chat show with Mum, a snack and then bed – was exhilarating. Dad usually went for dinner and drinks with colleagues on a Friday. Mum didn't like socializing and was always at home. But this morning, Dad had made rather a big deal of the fact that, since I was going out, he would spend the evening at home with my mother. The significance of this only became clear much later, after the policeman's knock on the door. For me, at the time, it meant that I could not back out of my arrangement with Helen. It would require too much explanation, and I couldn't bear to see my father's disappointment.

At last I stood on the doorstep of Helen's home. It was in a housing estate with a communal green area in front of the houses. I wondered what it would be like to have neighbours that you probably saw every day, coming and going. The wooden gate swung listlessly on one hinge, the white paint flaking off it. My father would never have allowed Avalon to fall into disrepair; anything broken or damaged was fixed or replaced immediately, regardless of our changed circumstances. Appearances were important to him. Helen's family were slovenly, I decided. They did not have a long driveway and land like we had, but a short front garden and a gravelled area for a car. There was no car.

I got quite a surprise when she answered the door. We had both just got out of school, but Helen had found the time to change her clothes, curl her hair (her straight, silky hair was the one thing I really did like about her) and apply make-up. The lipstick was a dark purple and had stained her teeth. Her black leather-look jeans were not tight enough on her bony legs to achieve what I assume was the desired effect (Sandy in *Grease*). Helen looked like a proper grown-up. I was immediately at a disadvantage. In my tight school blazer, I was still, painfully, a schoolboy.

'S-sorry,' I stammered. 'I didn't have time to change . . .'

But Helen was delighted to see me. 'Come in!' Her welcome was effusive. Had she worried that I wouldn't come?

The house reeked of cigarette smoke and was overwhelmingly floral. Rugs, curtains, upholstery, table mats, carpets, cushions and wallpaper. I could have been in the Botanic Gardens. And there were scribbled words everywhere, on walls and mirrors. There were sheaves of paper and books of every size and description on every surface.

'Oh yeah, my mam's a poet,' said Helen by way of explanation. 'She's out for the night and my little brothers are staying with Auntie Grace, so we've the place to ourselves.'

This information was given casually, but meaningfully. There was now nobody who could stop whatever it was that was going to happen. Judging by Helen's demeanour, at the very least *kissing* was definitely going to happen.

'Is your dad at work?' I asked, not without a little hope.

'My dad? I haven't seen him in years.'

I wondered when The Kissing would begin.

'We can have dinner now – there's pizzas I can just throw in the oven. They're only small. How many do you want?' She produced a bag of frozen discs from the freezer. I wanted four. No, five.

'Two, please,' I said. I was aware that my appetite was a source of great amusement to some, and I had not forgotten the promise of her mother's cake, though I was slightly concerned there was no sign of it.

'Have three,' said Helen, 'they're only small.'

I warmed to her now, as she tore the cellophane with her teeth.

'Do you like gin?'

'Does your mum let you drink, then?'

'What she doesn't know won't hurt her.'

Helen poured us some drinks. I remembered the carnations in my satchel, which I'd left at the front door. I had meant to present them to her on arrival. It seemed to me like the moment had passed. If we were now to drink gin, then The Kissing was imminent and the flowers were no longer necessary.

I knocked back the gin and tonic she had poured for me. I winced at the sharp taste. I then realized why my parents sipped at their alcoholic drinks. Nevertheless, I managed to drink two more gin and tonics in quick succession.

Dinner was pleasant enough, I suppose, though I know I ate four of the pizzas, leaving Helen with one. I recall enquiring after her mother's cake, and hiding my disappointment on finding myself presented with what I would describe as a sliver of plain sponge cake on a floral plate. Helen poured us more gin. When The Kissing started, I was very pleased. We had sort of inched towards each other on the living-room sofa. Her hand stroked my thigh. I am not sure who started it, but there were teeth and tongues and sucking and slopping noises.

I admit that I quickly became aroused. Helen did not fail to notice, and suggested that we go to her bedroom. I baulked. I hadn't planned on SEX. Of course, my underpants were clean (Mum was strict about that), but I was sure sex meant getting naked, and even in my drunken state I was not looking forward to displaying my flab. I never did it in school. I regularly forged notes from my mother to the games teacher about my bad knees. My knees would not have been bad if they hadn't such a huge burden to carry.

After one more very quick drink, we went up two flights of stairs. I stumbled a bit and then decided it would be a great idea to jump the last few steps. By this stage we were howling with laughter, and it was hilarious when I toppled over and twisted my left foot. It was a bit sore and there was quite a gash on my ankle, but I didn't make a fuss. I wondered how she was going to explain the blood on the stairs to her mother, but she implied that her mother mightn't notice. I was pretty curious about Helen's mother.

Then we entered Helen's room. 'I changed the sheets this morning,' she said, as she unbuttoned her grandfather shirt. I turned away to give her privacy, but then realized how silly that was and turned back to face her. She stood before me in nothing but a pair of underpants that featured a tennis racket motif on her hip. I didn't know she played tennis. Downstairs, I hadn't dared to squeeze her breasts, and I knew she was thin and I really should have anticipated the reality, but I had expected *some* breasts. She had definitely had breasts when fully clothed. Where had they gone? Mine were significantly larger than hers, and I immediately felt my physical deflation. I began to feel nauseous and hot.

'Get in, then!'

She was lying under the covers with her arms behind her head.

'There isn't much room,' I said truthfully.

'Well, you're going to be on top, so it's fine.' She was very bossy. 'You'll have to take your clothes off.' A pause. 'I seriously don't mind about you being fat, you know.'

I hardly cared myself now. I just needed to get it over and done with. My school uniform dropped bit by bit to the floor, but taking her example, I kept my underpants on until I was in the bed. Then began an amount of unseemly grunting and squealing from the two of us, and copious sweating from me, as we discarded our pants and I tried to negotiate my way up the correct corridor. Helen handled things, so to speak, and guided me in the right direction. It was absolutely brilliant for the first three minutes, but after that it was a struggle not to vomit. I tried to think about Farrah Fawcett, but it was no good. I don't wish to go into further detail about The Sex. Suffice to say that I didn't enjoy it. It was uncomfortable and messy, humiliating on my part, and I was glad when Helen said she'd had enough. Pregnancy was not something we had to worry about.

'You haven't done this before, then?'

'No.'

'Me neither.'

I was surprised. I took some solace from her admission.

Helen and I parted on awkward terms.

'You won't tell anyone, will you?' she said anxiously as we lay in bed after The Sex. She expressed my concern exactly.

I rootled around the bottom of the bed for my Y-fronts, squashing Helen and pinching the tiny amount of flesh on her skeleton in the process. She winced in pain.

'Never,' I said, a little too vehemently, as I clambered out of the bed, noting as I did so that my ankle was extremely painful.

'You'd better go. Mam will be home soon.' It was clear we both wanted to draw a line under the encounter.

'My ankle is swollen,' I said as I pulled up my elasticated trousers, trying desperately to suck in my belly.

'How can you tell?'

I thought that was a bit much. Coming from a girl who could potentially be my girlfriend.

I was sick into a hedge on the way home. My watch registered five past eleven as I hobbled up the driveway to Avalon, and I knew I was in for some sort of inquisition. The lies I had prepared about *Herbie Goes Bananas* and my 'friends' seemed feeble now. I hadn't anticipated explaining vomit stains on my trousers and a busted ankle.

To my surprise, the garage doors were wide open and

there was no car in the driveway, which meant that my father must have gone out after all.

When I let myself in the front door, the house was silent and in darkness. Mum had obviously gone to bed. Relieved, I pulled off my clothes in the laundry room and stuffed them into the washing machine with the rest of the pile from the basket, then stopped for a full glass of water in the kitchen. I climbed the stairs as quietly as I could, crept past my parents' bedroom door and crawled into bed.

As I lay there, I wondered if this was how I was supposed to feel, now that I had had sexual intercourse. I had expected that I would feel strong, masterful and virile. In fact, I felt tearful, resentful and sick. Maybe it was the gin. I'd never had that before either.

Anyway, that's what *I* was doing on Friday the 14th of November 1980, the night my father murdered Annie Doyle.

4. Lydia

The eleven days after the girl's death were the most stressful, waiting for the axe to fall. We bought all the newspapers and listened to every news bulletin, waiting for a report on her disappearance, but nothing happened. Andrew went to work, and I did my exercises, went out to the shops, made dinners, tended to our son and the house, and from time to time I would lock myself into my bedroom and put on my mother's scarlet lipstick. It had been decades since I had used it, and though it had completely dried out, the pigment was as vivid as ever and I would use some Pond's cream to smooth it on to my mouth, and look in the mirror and see her peering back at me.

Sometimes, I would wake and wonder if Annie's death had all been an awful nightmare, but every night when Andrew came home, one look at his increasingly grey face told me that it was no dream and that we would never wake up. From the kitchen window, I could see the freshly dug grave. I had asked Andrew to buy some plants to take the bare look off it, and now, at the end of a cold November, it was an obscene riot of colour.

I hoped, though.

'Nobody is looking for her,' I said. 'Maybe she won't even be reported missing. I mean, if Laurence went missing, we'd be calling the guards within a few hours, wouldn't we?'

'*You* would,' said Andrew. 'I'd be inclined to let him have some breathing space.'

'But . . . this girl. Obviously, nobody cares about her.'

'It's only a matter of time until the alarm is raised. You're fooling yourself if you think otherwise.'

On Tuesday the 25th of November, our doorbell rang during dinner. Andrew went out to answer it while I took over carving the ham. I heard the beginning of the conversation and realized that it was a guard. I could see Laurence was listening intently, so I closed the door and turned up the radio while forcing myself to remain calm.

When Andrew returned to the table, I could see that his face was ashen. I didn't dare ask him what had happened in front of Laurence, so instead I engaged him in a conversation about the boiler in the hot press that needed lagging. He nodded curtly and withdrew behind the *Evening Herald*. Laurence was staring at his father's hands. Large hands, more weathered than one might expect for a member of the judiciary. Andrew snapped the paper to smooth the pages, which momentarily startled me. He put his newspaper down. 'What time were you home, that night you went to the cinema with your friends?' he said to Laurence.

'Oh, em . . . before twelve anyway. You said I could stay out till then . . . ?' Laurence said, and I noticed his cheeks flushing.

'Good, good, never heard you come in. We were fast asleep, weren't we, Lydia?'

I didn't know what to say. What had the guard said? Had we been seen on the strand after all? Andrew was clearly lining up Laurence as an alibi. It was a clever move, but he was being too obvious.

'I suppose –' I said.

'Fast asleep,' Andrew repeated.

Laurence looked baffled. I winked to reassure him that everything was fine.

He was not reassured.

'What did the guard at the door want?' he asked.

'Oh, was it a garda?' I said, keeping my voice casual. 'Is there something wrong, Andrew? Something to do with a case?'

As a judge in the Special Criminal Court, Andrew had presided over a trial of IRA members two years previously. He had even been subject to some non-specific death threats. There had been talk of a sentry box being installed at the end of our driveway for a security guard, but Andrew wouldn't countenance it. 'I refuse to live in a fortress,' he had said, and I agreed. Senior gardaí visited us on a semi-regular basis to discuss his safety and protection, but were usually invited into the library to talk matters through with my husband in private. Andrew rarely mentioned his work to us.

He paused before answering. 'Nothing to do with any of my cases. A young woman has gone missing. The guard was just making routine enquiries. I told him I stayed in that entire weekend, two weeks ago.'

I was watching Laurence's face and I saw flickers of confusion.

'Oh, that's dreadful! Where was she last seen? Around here? Why was he making enquiries *here*?' I feigned concern, but I needed to know. Why did they come to our door?

Andrew took up his paper again, obscuring his face while he said, 'They think a car like mine was seen recently near the girl's home.'

That car. A vintage navy Jaguar, and Andrew's pride and joy – he insisted on doing all the running repairs on it himself – it drank fuel and cost a fortune to run. He had been trying to sell it since Paddy Carey had sunk us, but couldn't find a buyer. Why hadn't he been discreet enough to park it away from her door?

'Well, isn't that just ridiculous? They had the nerve to question *you*? You need to have a word with someone about that, Andrew. The *nerve*.'

'Well, it is an unusual car, Lydia. They're just doing their job.' There was a hard edge to his tone.

Laurence was looking from one to the other of us. Andrew excused himself from the table and left the room.

'Mum . . . was Dad . . . didn't he go out that Friday night? His car wasn't in the driveway when I came home.'

I was surprised that Laurence had such a good memory about a night nearly two weeks previously, but he was right. I didn't want to have to contradict him. My poor boy was so confused. 'No, darling, it *was* there.'

But I had to protect myself too. 'I had a migraine on Friday and went to bed very early, and your father must have come upstairs before you came home, I suppose. You just heard him yourself – he was home and so was the car.'

'But were you awake when he came to –'

'Laurence!' I laughed now. 'Why all the questions? Would you like another slice of brack?' I knew how to distract my son.

*

The phone rang in the cloakroom. I was glad to get out of the room and desperate to talk to Andrew to see how much the guard knew. I answered the phone to a girl who asked to speak to Laurence. I was surprised. Nobody had rung for Laurence in months, and certainly no girls.

'It's for you,' I told him, 'a girl called Helen.' He blushed to his roots as he went to take the call.

I found Andrew upstairs, pacing the bedroom. 'We're going to be arrested. The guards know. They know!'

'What do they know? Exactly what did you say to them? Tell me.'

'Her family reported her missing on Friday. The guards questioned the others who lived in her house, and one of them said that she'd been visited by a man in a car like mine.'

'What type of car? Was she specific? Why did you park at her door? Fool!'

'They know it's a dark-coloured vintage car. He said she thought it was a Jaguar or a Daimler. Oh, Jesus.'

'And does she have a description of you? Did she see you?'

'No, she couldn't have. I *thought* I was being really careful. I always wore that old trilby hat of your father's with a scarf pulled up around my chin. Nobody around there ever saw my face. I didn't want to be recognized, you know?'

'Where is that hat?'

'What?'

'Where is the hat? Right now?'

'In the cloakroom . . . Oh, Christ. They might come back with a search warrant.' He began to tremble.

'Stop it. Don't fall apart, I can't bear it. How many of those old cars are there in Dublin? Ten . . . fifteen maybe? The guard is just crossing you off a list. Nobody saw your face. I'm your alibi. You were here, home with me.'

'But I think Laurence knows . . .'

'He doesn't know anything. We can convince him of that. Don't give him any reason for suspicion. Throw some water on your face and come downstairs and join us in the drawing room.'

I flew downstairs into the cloakroom, where I found Laurence still chatting on the phone, sitting on the wooden stool directly under the old trilby. I thought it had been on the same shelf for thirty years. I remember Daddy wearing it. I hadn't wanted to throw it out. But now it had to go.

'What do you want, Mum?'

'Nothing. It's fine.'

I would retrieve the hat later.

Laurence joined us in the drawing room. I was trying to keep things breezy to distract him from his father's shaken demeanour. 'So who's this Helen?' I said, but Andrew hushed me and turned up the volume on the TV. The news was on. It wasn't the top headline, but maybe the third or fourth item.

'*Concerns are growing for the whereabouts of a 22-year-old Dublin woman who went missing eleven days ago. Annie Doyle has not been seen since the evening of Friday the 14th of November, at her home on Hanbury Street in Dublin's inner city.*'

There was a grainy photograph of the girl. Dark, thin, lots of make-up, clad in a denim jacket, grinning at someone behind the photographer with a beer glass in her hand. She was caught unawares, it seemed, the deformed top lip revealing crooked front teeth. I glanced over at Andrew. He was staring intensely at the television.

'That must be the woman they were asking you about earlier, Dad.'

'Shhhhh!' Andrew said furiously.

A Detective Sergeant O'Toole, leading the investigation, was speaking: '. . . *a dark-coloured luxury vehicle was seen in the vicinity of the woman's home in preceding weeks. We believe that the male driver was a regular visitor to Miss Doyle's home. We are asking anyone who noticed anything suspicious to notify the gardaí immediately.*'

Then they moved on to another story, about fuel shortages. Laurence was looking at Andrew, no doubt wondering why he was being so intense. I had to break the atmosphere. 'I hope they catch whoever it was. That poor girl,' I said.

Neither Laurence nor Andrew said anything.

'Who'd like a cup of tea?'

Laurence shook his head, but Andrew was clutching the arms of his chair. I needed him to snap out of this trance.

'Darling?' I said a little sharply.

'What? No,' he barked. He was very pale. He noticed Laurence looking at him. He flinched a little, and then said, 'So, who is Helen?'

'She's my . . . my girlfriend.'

'Girlfriend!' I whooped, delighted to have the chance to break the tension in the room. 'Did you meet her at the cinema that night? When you went to see *Herbie* with your friends?'

Because of what happened, I'd never really asked him about that night, but I should have been suspicious that he was going out with 'friends'. He found deception difficult, like his father, and now the truth came spilling out.

'I didn't go to the cinema with friends. I went to Helen's house. She asked me over. We ate pizza and watched *The Dukes of Hazzard*, and that's all I'm telling you.' He looked to Andrew for a response. 'Dad?'

'That's great, Laurence, great.'

There was clearly more to Laurence's date than he was prepared to tell us. I was unsettled by this. I recalled the washing machine going that night. Laurence and I did not, as a rule, keep secrets from each other. Not until now. But I had to take control as Andrew left the room again without a word. I took Laurence's hands in mine.

'Laurence, do not interrupt me now. I don't know what you got up to with this Helen, and I don't want to know, but you lied to your father and me. You came home with a sprained ankle and gave us a cock and bull story about where you were going, and I don't know what you were doing in the laundry room that night, I'm not even going to ask. Your father gave you two pounds to enjoy yourself at the cinema, so I'll have that back, thank you. We are an honest family and we do not tell lies to each other. Is that clear?'

Although none of us mentioned the dead girl again at home, her name, Annie Doyle, was impossible to avoid in the two days after that first news report. Her photograph was on the second page of Andrew's *Irish Times* the next day, the same photo with the crooked-toothed deformed smile. She had last been seen that Friday afternoon, entering her home. There were unconfirmed sightings of her around the inner city that morning, and the guards appealed to anyone who might have come into contact with her that day.

A photograph and an interview with her parents appeared in the newspapers the day after that. I studied the photograph. A detective stood behind the remaining three members of the family. You could tell straight away that they were poor. Annie's father's face was strained with pain, and his eyes were glassy with exhaustion. He looked rough, unshaven and stocky. His wife was unremarkable. There was another daughter with them in the photo, with her head down and her face hidden behind a mane of hair. Annie's mother was quoted as saying that she was a good girl really, a very intelligent girl, she said, very bubbly and popular growing up. They appealed to the public to look out for her. They just wanted Annie to come home. Reading it, I couldn't feel the mother's anguish. I tried, but I couldn't imagine it. I wondered what Annie's father would say if he knew what his darling daughter had been up to. He might actually be relieved to discover that she was dead. And yet I was more sympathetic to him than his wife. The press report went on to detail what Annie had been wearing when she was last seen: a herringbone coat, purple boots and a silver-plated identity bracelet. Unremarkable, cheap stuff that half the young girls in the country might be wearing. They noted that her red hair was dyed black.

I relaxed after that. A week later, more salacious reports about Annie Doyle hinted at an unfortunate history of institutionalization and shoplifting. They didn't say it outright, but they implied that she was a prostitute. I was disgusted. Andrew swore he'd had no idea, but admitted she had agreed to the plan far more readily than he had expected.

'I should have known, I should have guessed,' he said.

Still, fortunately for us, she was the kind of girl to put herself in the way of trouble and the last person the guards would link with a family like ours. They had nothing to go on except a vaguely similar car. They never came back with a search warrant. I had burned Daddy's trilby in the fireplace the first chance I got. They would find nothing unless they literally went digging, and we gave them no reason to.

The new flower bed in the back garden initially unsettled me. Naturally it brought up memories of my sister. But I find you can get used to anything eventually.

Shortly before Christmas, Andrew and I went out to dinner together. I very rarely went on nights out, and they had been even less affordable since Paddy Carey, but I thought he needed a little treat. We had been through so much. Besides, I wanted to talk to him in a public place where he would not be able to overreact. I made sure the maître d' found us a corner table where we could not be overheard.

I waited until the main course before I broached the subject.

'You love Laurence and me, don't you, darling?'

'What . . . yes . . . why are you asking me that? Of course I do.'

'It's just that . . . if anything should happen . . . if anything were to be discovered –'

'Christ, Lydia.' He dropped his cutlery.

'I mean, it's all fine, I'm sure we're safe now. The fuss has died down. Nobody is looking for her any more, but just *if* . . .'

'What?'

'Well, I hope that you would think of Laurence.'

'What are you talking about?'

'If they caught you, *if*, for some reason, they found evidence and could arrest you, and there was no way out of it, well, you could say you did it on your own.'

He looked at me, open-mouthed, and I was glad I had chosen this quiet restaurant, because I knew that if we had been at home he would have shouted and thrown things around. I have always known how to manage my husband's temper.

'You see, darling, if Laurence lost both of us, in such awful circumstances, his life would be ruined. But if they got you, you could say that it was just a transaction gone wrong. A lovers' tiff. You could tell them that she was trying to blackmail you, and that would be true! But I could say I didn't know anything about it, and Laurence and I could go on afterwards and rebuild our lives. Isn't that what you would want for us, darling?'

His lower jaw quivered, and when he eventually spoke he sounded, ironically, as if he were being strangled.

'I was a fool to go along with your crazy plan. I did it

because I loved you. I will do whatever you want. You get your own way, yet again. You always do. But don't pretend you are doing this for Laurence.'

Andrew never understood the strength of a mother's love.

5. Laurence

I hated the way they said 'disappeared', as if Annie Doyle had vanished into thin air when clearly something had happened to her, something bad. The idea of my father being involved in a woman's 'disappearance' would have been absolutely preposterous before that day. He was a respectable guy and, reading between the lines of the *Sunday World*, she had been a junkie and a prostitute. He had never even had an affair – not that I was aware of, anyway. But he knew something about it. I was sure of that.

First, he lied to the guard about having been home that night, and then he tried to tell me that he'd been in bed when I knew he was out, because his car wasn't there when I got home. Mum went to bed early with one of her migraines and he must have sneaked out afterwards. That was suspicious enough, but when I read about the silver-plated identity bracelet in the newspaper, I was really alarmed. The report detailed things that Annie Doyle had been wearing when she disappeared.

Two days before that, my mother had asked me to replace the hoover bag. She hated dirty work and it was always my father or I that did this chore. When I had removed the bag, something shiny was poking a tiny hole through it. I pulled it and a filthy, dust-covered string came out. When I blew off the dust, I could see a thin metallic chain attached to a narrow bar. The bar was inscribed with the name 'Marnie'. The clasp was stained a deep red. There were no links at the other end of the bar – half of a bracelet, I guessed. I casually wondered who Marnie was, and put it in a kitchen drawer, assuming it belonged to my mother. I thought it might have been hoovered up by mistake, but I forgot to mention it to her.

Now, having read the latest on Annie Doyle, I understood its significance and realized that Mum would never have worn such a bracelet. Mum wore only gold antique jewellery. A silver-plated bracelet would have been too modern and cheap for her. When I got Dad on his own in the kitchen, I showed him the bracelet that I'd found.

'I found this in the hoover. It's not Mum's, is it?'

'Give it to me.' It was an order. 'It's just some rubbish.'

He threw it into the bin and promptly left the room without any explanation. I fished it out of the potato peelings and the pieces of fat cut from the previous night's meat. When I had rinsed it under the tap, I wrapped it in tissue and put it in my pocket. I didn't know what I was going to do with it, but I knew it was evidence of something. I dreaded to think what, but it seemed important that I should hang on to it.

And then, a few days later, I was coming home from school when I noticed a squad car pull up outside our gate. I almost started to hyperventilate. Were they here to arrest Dad or was it just one of their routine visits? A heavyset guy got out just as I turned into the driveway. I recognized him from the television news. It was the man in charge of the missing-person investigation. Another man sat in the back seat and a uniformed guard was the driver.

'How'r'ye, son. I'm Detective Sergeant Declan O'Toole, and that there' – he nodded towards the back seat – 'is Detective James Mooney. Do you live in there?' He pointed towards our house.

'Yeah.'

Detective Mooney got out of the car and stood behind O'Toole. 'And what's your name?'

'Laurence Fitzsimons.'

'And is your father home?'

'I don't think so. He doesn't normally get home until after six.'

Detective Mooney nodded and walked back towards the car, but O'Toole told him to hold on. He had a sly smirk on his face. I didn't like him.

'So you're the son of Judge Fitzsimons, are you?'

'Yeah.' I wanted to run away up the driveway, but the guard put his hand on my shoulder to keep me there.

'Well, aren't you a fine big lad.' He was trying to be my friend. I said nothing. 'Tell me something, Laurence, do you remember the weekend of the 14th of November, two weeks ago now.'

'Yeah, why?'

'Were you home that weekend yourself?'

I wondered if I should ask to have a lawyer present, but the detective was keeping it all very casual. He wasn't writing anything down. But I was terrified.

'I was in my girlfriend's house that Friday night. You can check with her.'

'Ah here, no need to be defensive, sonny. I'm not accusing you of anything at all, it's just a routine thing I'm doing here, y'know?' He was much more confident than

Mooney, who I had heard questioning my dad. He was . . . jolly.

'Why are you asking me about that weekend?'

He ignored my question. 'And tell me now, was it a late night like, that Friday? What time did you get home to your own bed? Or did you?' He nudged and winked at me as if we were a comic double act.

'I had a midnight curfew. But I was home just after eleven.'

'A curfew, eh? And were your mam and dad waiting up for you to get a full report?' He winked again.

'Yes,' I said.

'You're sure now? Both of them?'

'Yes.' I kept my voice as still as possible, though I could not control the flush in my cheeks. The lie came so easily, it surprised even me.

'And did your dad go out again that weekend at all?'

'No. We all stayed in.'

'Don't you have a great memory?'

'I remember it because I sprained my ankle and Mum and Dad were home the whole time, fetching me stuff.'

'Grand, that's all I needed to know, sonny. I'm just crossing people off a list. It's a dirty job, but sure, someone has to do it, ha?' He winked again and went to get into his car.

'Are you not going up to the house?' I said, nodding towards Avalon.

'No need, no need at all.'

Detective Mooney, who had stood silently all this time, whispered urgently into O'Toole's ear. O'Toole waved him away, annoyed, but said, 'Oh, one more thing, does your dad ever wear a hat? A trilby-type hat?' He pulled a photograph of a hat out of his pocket. 'This shape,' he said, pointing at the photo. I heaved a huge sigh of relief.

'No. Never. He doesn't have a hat.' O'Toole looked at Mooney with smug satisfaction on his face.

'Good, good, that's it then, I'll be on my way.'

'But why are you asking about that weekend, and my dad and a hat?'

He tapped the side of his nose. 'Ongoing investigation, but you've nothing to worry about now, off you go!' He tooted the horn and drove off.

They were looking for a different man, a man who wore a hat. I needn't have lied at all. Dad was guilty about something, though – maybe he had gone out that night for another reason. I was almost relieved to think that he might be having an affair, and the bracelet belonged to his fancy woman, Marnie. None of the reports had mentioned the name on the bracelet, and one would assume that it would be the woman's own name, Annie. So Marnie must be Dad's floozie. That was better than . . . whatever had happened to a missing prostitute. The knot in my stomach loosened.

Mum was cutting fabric on the kitchen table when I came in.

'Mum,' I said jovially when I got in the front door, 'Dad's off the hook. They're looking for a fella in a hat!'

She didn't look up. 'What *are* you talking about, darling?'

'There were two detectives outside just now, and one of them was asking me about that night, the night he questioned Dad about, but they're looking for a guy in a hat.'

She smiled sweetly. 'Good heavens, a guard asking you questions. What did you tell him?'

'I told him Dad and you were here when I got home from my night out and that Dad didn't even own a hat.'

She laughed. 'So ridiculous, questioning a schoolboy.'

'I hope they catch him.'

'Who?'

'The fella in the hat!' I foraged in the fridge for some cheese and cut two slices of thick bread from the loaf.

'Leave room for your dinner,' said Mum. As if.

I was relieved that I no longer had to think about this girl. After the newspapers had been thrown out, I had retrieved them from the bin and cut out the articles about the missing woman. Unusually, Dad had recently been buying all of the newspapers, including the ones he had claimed to despise. We were not a house that would ordinarily take the *Sunday World*. At first, there was just information about where she had last been seen, a description of what she may have been wearing, but the later reports suggested that she was leading a sordid life. I had been poring over them nightly, looking at her snaggle-toothed grin, her misshapen mouth, desperate to rule out my father's involvement. I had raided the desk in his study, looking for evidence of an affair he was having, but really looking for some link between him and Annie Doyle. I don't know what I expected to find – a photograph? A legal case file that named her? It was ridiculous and I knew it. Prostitutes did not give receipts or hand out business cards.

I had had nightmares in which I was having sex with Annie in Helen's distorted bedroom, and others in which

I was stabbing her viciously with my father's silver letter-opener and then I'd see my mother's face, and I'd wake up, drenched in sweat and guilt-ridden. Now I was free of all that.

Until two days later, when I noticed a gap on the shelf where my grandfather's old trilby hat had been for as long as I could remember. I asked Mum where it had gone. 'Oh, I think your father finally threw it out,' she said absent-mindedly, and all the fear and anxiety swept back up into my heart. I nervously asked Dad if he had thrown out the hat.

'Why do you want to know?' was his first question, before he claimed that he didn't know what had happened to it, his voice quivering as he spoke.

I knew. I knew for sure he was lying.

I didn't do anything with this knowledge. I was scared of what it meant. I had lied to the guard now, so I could go to jail too. What had he done with the woman? I know we were broke, but if he was going to kidnap someone, shouldn't he have chosen someone rich? He wasn't that desperate, surely. And where were the ransom demands? The IRA had kidnapped a man but everyone knew it was the IRA, and they kidnapped a rich guy, a foreign industrialist. My father was not a stupid man. That led me to the idea that maybe Annie Doyle had been in trouble with the IRA or some criminal gang, and Dad had given her the money to move away abroad with a new identity. Dad was helping a young woman in trouble. Wasn't that more likely? But if that was the case, why were the police not involved? Maybe the guards were not being told because the case was so sensitive that it had to be entrusted to a judge. I tried to believe that version of events because, as unlikely as it seemed, the alternatives were too dreadful to contemplate.

I did my best to avoid spending time with Helen in the following weeks, but she phoned regularly, ostensibly to check that I hadn't told anyone about the sex.

'I don't want them to think that I'm a slut.'

I didn't tell her that the boys in my class already called her a slut, even before we'd had sexual intercourse.

She continued, 'It's just something I needed to get out of the way, you know? To see what all the fuss was about.'

I could feel her disappointment. I guessed if she had wanted to offload her virginity, I would probably not have been her first choice. As hurtful as this dawning realization was, I wondered if other boys had rejected her before she chose me. And then I wondered how likely it was that a boy in my class would have refused sex from any girl. So she did choose me. Poor Helen.

'Sorry,' I said, when we first talked on the phone after that night.

'God, no, I'm sorry, I shouldn't have . . . it was just . . . let's never mention it again.'

'Sure.'

There was a pause and then I had to ask because I needed to know. 'So are you my girlfriend or anything like that?'

'Do you want me to be?' She was slightly incredulous. How the hell was I to answer that?

'Well, I suppose . . .'

'Great, that's great.' Her voice brightened. I wasn't sure what to say.

'. . . Are you still there?'

'Yes.'

'It's OK then? To call you my boyfriend? And we don't have to . . . you know . . . ?'

'What? Ever?'

'Well, maybe . . . sometime, but not soon . . . OK?'

'OK . . . well, goodnight.'

'See you tomorrow?'

'Yes, probably.'

'Goodnight.'

I should have been celebrating the fact that I had a girlfriend, even if it was just Helen, but I was afraid to have a confidante. If I voiced my fears, that would legitimize them and make them real. Helen got upset and clingy. She was paranoid and claimed that I had obviously just been using her for sex. She swore that if I told anybody we'd done it, she'd tell them what a small penis I had, and that even if it was huge, the flab of my belly would have hidden it anyway. I had really struck gold with my first girlfriend.

Helen visited Avalon, often uninvited. 'Jesus! Look at the fucking size of your house!' she said the first time she came over. I shushed her, asking her to be polite in front of my parents. She just about curbed her language, but I could tell that she didn't really care what people thought of her. I knew that Mum and Dad were unimpressed by her. Mum was cold and stiff in her presence, made awkward polite conversation and then left the room. Dad caught her siphoning vodka from a bottle in the drinks cabinet into a small lemonade bottle one time. I had taken the blame and said it was my idea. Normally he would have been incandescent at something like that, but he just shuffled away, muttering. I'm sure he thought Helen was a bratty teenager, but maybe he was relieved that I had a girlfriend. As far as I knew, he didn't tell my mother about the vodka. Helen didn't care.

Christmas holidays came finally on the 19th of December. It was a mixed blessing to be out of school. On the one hand, I didn't have to face the bullies, but on the other hand, the courts were closed and my dad was at home a lot more. I was nervous around him. Also, there was the small matter of my school report. Since the night the guard had come to our door, I had given up doing my homework or revising. I was not concentrating on schoolwork at all, preoccupied as I was by the fact that I was living with a liar and a murderer, probably.

I thought about forging the report. I wasn't bad at forgery. In my old school I used to do it for friends, but in St Martin's I had quickly offered up this skill to avoid beatings. I forged sick notes from parents, school reports, train tickets. There was one attempt to have me forge £10 notes, but then they'd beaten me up when it proved unsuccessful, as I'd told them it would be. I decided to be honest about the report, but I worried about my father's reaction.

I had already disappointed him by not being athletic and not loving rugby or golf. One time, he had forced me to endure eighteen holes of golf in his company. I never knew how to have a conversation with him, and I couldn't hit the ball more than three yards. On that particular trip, I embarrassed him in front of his friend. It was a 'father and sons' outing, suggested no doubt by his friend, who belonged to a posher golf club than Dad's one. The other son was a good bit younger than me, but I disgraced myself by fainting at the fourth tee and had to be rescued by a golf buggy and carted back to the clubhouse. When Bloody Paddy Carey had done his worst, Dad had to cancel his golf membership, claiming that he just didn't have the time. Every cloud.

But I had always managed to maintain top grades. He didn't need another reason to go ballistic. And I wasn't sure if I'd be able to control my own reaction if he did. Mum would try to play it down and point out that Bs and Cs were still very good.

I handed the blue envelope over to my dad on the first day of the holidays, thinking I just needed to get it over and done with. He opened it absent-mindedly as I waited nervously, but as he scanned through it, he didn't seem angry at all. 'Where are all the As? You've slipped,' he said.

Mum picked it up then. 'Oh God, Laurence!' she said after she'd read the whole thing. 'It's not a disaster, darling, but what has happened to you?' And before I could answer, she said, 'It's that girl. She's a distraction. Not a tap of work is being done while she's around.'

'Her name is Helen,' I muttered.

'Don't talk back to your mother,' snarled the suspected murderer/kidnapper, but he left the room then and didn't mention it again.

Mum gave me a lecture: she was going to keep a closer eye on me, she said, and I could catch up on the lost As over the Christmas holidays. 'Of course, it's all my fault, I could tell that girl was trouble the moment I heard about her. I should have put a stop to it then.'

I managed to ring Helen and tried to tell her that we needed to cool things down a bit.

'Fuck that,' she said, 'are you a man or a mouse?'

I didn't answer the question.

Mum worried as Dad began to look old and ill. I tried not to think about it, but I couldn't settle. Mum said we should just be gentle around him and try not to make any demands on him. She confided there were serious financial worries that he refused to discuss with her. I played along with her concerns, insisting that my too-small blazer was fine and there was no point in getting a new one for the last five months of school. She admitted we simply couldn't afford to buy what we needed.

I had never known my dad to be beaten by stress before. Stress and depression were my mother's weaknesses. As he became more frail, I realized that I was possibly the only person who knew the real reason for his decline.

I turned eighteen on Christmas Day. Helen and I exchanged gifts the evening before, when she called to Avalon. Helen said I was a cheap date because she'd only had to get me one combined birthday/Christmas gift. It was a *Star Wars* T-shirt (we'd seen *The Empire Strikes Back* by then), but I didn't dare try it on in front of her. I told her it would be great for the summer. As I suspected, it was too small. I got her a pair of earrings made of pieces of coloured glass. She said they were lovely and that she'd been meaning to get her ears pierced anyway.

I was angling with Helen to try sex again, but she said I'd put her off. My hand was red from being slapped away. That is my abiding memory of that Christmas Eve – me wheedling, her slapping.

The big day started out as the usual family affair. We ate in the dining room instead of the kitchen. The table was set with linen and crystal, and Dad, for the first time since, well, since *that* time, made an effort to be on good form. He faked jollity and merriment and read the same lame jokes we'd heard every year from the Christmas crackers. He complimented the food, and although I could see how much it irked him, he ignored the amount I heaped on to my plate. I decided to take advantage of the birthday/ Christmas Day amnesty and ate an entire box of Quality Street. Neither of them commented.

We opened our presents. Among other things, I got a Rod Stewart *Greatest Hits* album that I really wanted. I had bought my mother a charm for her bracelet. I got her one every year. It was a tiny figurine of a ballet dancer. Mum had done ballet when she was young and could have studied it in London as a teenager but refused because she was scared of being homesick. Mum never went on holidays. She couldn't bear to be away from Avalon for more than a day. As a twelve-year-old child, she had been painted doing exercises at the barre in the manner of Degas, and the large rosewood-framed canvas hung over the mantelpiece. She still practised her steps and did stretching exercises for hours every morning in front of the mirror in the dance room upstairs. She loved her new charm, but then I knew she would. I gave Dad a *Rumpole of the Bailey* book. He liked the television series, liked to complain how unrealistic it was, but would never miss it.

'Thank you, son, very thoughtful.' He seemed to be genuinely moved, and I began to feel a glimmer of *something* for him, and to wonder if all would be well. And then I thought of Christmas Day in Annie Doyle's house, and her mum and dad and sister staring at the empty space at their Christmas table. I knew they were not having a good day.

Dad wanted to make a fuss about the fact that I was eighteen, and gave a nice speech about how I was a man now and that soon I'd be out in the world, in charge of my own decisions, and that he knew I would make them proud. Mum tutted at the bit about me being out in the world, but poured me a small glass of wine, my first legitimate glass of alcohol, and then presented me with an extra gift, something specifically from her, she said. It looked like a jewellery box, but when I opened its hinged lid there was a solid gold razor inside, nestled in a velvet mould. It was a family heirloom and had been her father's.

I knew this was momentous for her and that she wanted it to be so for me, but my father couldn't help himself.

'For God's sake, Lydia, that's ridiculous! Laurence doesn't even shave yet,' he said with a sneer. 'He's a late developer, aren't you, boy?'

It was true that I did not yet need a razor, but I was fully developed in every other way and was sorely tempted to tell him I'd already had sex. Mum was hastily trying to calm things down. Her refereeing skills were second to none. 'Maybe he doesn't need it quite yet, but he soon will!' she said brightly, putting her hand firmly on my father's arm.

My father squirmed for a moment and said rattily, 'Yes, yes, of course he will.' He gave me a manly playful punch on the shoulder. I tried not to wince, not from the pain but from the insincerity of it.

'Cheers! Happy birthday!' said my mum as she raised her glass, and we all clinked glasses.

I met my father's eyes and I could see that he was trying to look at me in a genuine way just for that briefest moment, trying to see who I was. I held his gaze. A moment of understanding passed between us in which I could see some decency and he could see his son beneath the layers of flesh. The moment faded though, when the phone rang. Mum went out to answer it.

'It's that girl!' she called from the hallway. I could hear the heavy sigh in her voice.

Dad threw his eyes to heaven in exasperation. 'It's Christmas *Day*!' As if there was a law that you couldn't use the phone on Christmas Day.

'It's my birthday,' I reminded him. He remembered and smiled indulgently at me. I felt again the knot of anxiety in my stomach. He looked so damn benign, but I knew the truth.

The phone call from Helen was brief.

'Happy birthday! And Christmas! What did you get?'

I listed the gifts I'd received.

'Is that all? I thought you would get more than that.' Helen thought that a big house equalled rich equalled extravagant. It is rarely the case.

I could hear the yelling of her brothers and loud pop music in the background.

'Mum looped the fucking loop and got Jay and Stevo a

drum kit. The mad bitch.' Jay and Stevo were six and eight years old respectively. Then all I could hear was a deafening clash of cymbals, and Helen and two other voices roaring, 'Shut up!'

My mother put her head around the cloakroom door and gave me her 'Get off the phone' look. Conversation was more or less impossible at Helen's end anyway because of the cacophony, so I bade her farewell. As I approached the kitchen, I could hear the clatter of them clearing up in there. Dad said, 'What kind of moron rings on Christmas Day?'

'Andrew, I don't like her any more than you do, but for God's sake can you just try and be nice to him for one day? It's his birthday!'

'What does she even see in him? The size of him. She's no oil painting but –'

'He is your son! Can't you please –'

I coughed. I wanted them to know that I'd heard them. They both looked uncomfortable, and my father at least had the grace to be embarrassed. I had never heard him express his opinion about me so blatantly before. By now I felt hot and restless. I was all too aware of this scornful, sour, superior presence standing at the kitchen sink, looking out of the window, pretending Annie Doyle didn't exist and wishing that I didn't either. I hated him. I wished *he* were dead.

6. Karen

After Da had reported Annie's disappearance to the guards, we expected news within a day or two, but it didn't happen quite like that. We went to the station that Friday night, the 21st of November. Detective Mooney seemed to take our concerns seriously. We gave him descriptions of the clothes missing from her wardrobe.

'Any distinguishing features?' he said. I pointed to her mouth in the photograph. 'And she wears an identity bracelet that she never takes off.'

'So her name is on the bracelet?'

'No, it just says "Marnie".'

'Is this Marnie a friend?'

Da glared at me. 'Never mind about that. Marnie is someone she used to know. The name isn't important.'

I know that the next day they interviewed the girls who lived in the house with Annie. I went to Clark's Art Supplies to ask if my sister had bought a painting set on the previous Saturday. I showed the girl behind the counter a photo of our Annie. Annie was pretty drunk in the photo, but it was the best one we had. It had been taken the year before at my uncle's fiftieth birthday party. In all the other photos she had her hand over her mouth, obscuring her most notable feature. The guards had rejected all of those, but I knew Annie would be furious that we were putting out the photo she had tried to tear up. 'I look like a bleedin' mutant!' she had said.

The girl in the art supplies place remembered Annie coming in weeks previously, examining the painting set and talking about coming back to buy it. She said she had suggested that Annie could leave a deposit, but she had said she would be back with the full price. It wasn't surprising that Annie had never turned up. I was annoyed with myself for even hoping that she might have.

I wondered if she had travelled to London for an abortion. If she'd been pregnant, there is no way she would have risked being sent back to St Joseph's. But if she'd gone to have an abortion, she would have packed a bag, and she would certainly have been home by now. In desperation, I spent a morning on the phone to all the hospitals in Dublin. None of them had any record of her or of anyone matching her description. Detective Mooney told me he had covered the same ground with the same results.

Ma spent all her time in the church, praying for Annie's return, but Dessie and me took time off work to go out looking for her. We talked to the locals in the Viking. I thought they'd be more likely to talk to me than to Ma. We knew some of them to see. They all knew Annie, smiled when talking about her. 'She's some demon for the Jameson's,' said the barman, who, no doubt, had never refused her cash. They had wondered where she'd been. I asked if she'd ever been there with a boyfriend. One of her 'friends' looked a bit cagey then. 'A few,' she said, and Dessie got that mortified look and left the pub.

We went to her boss at the cleaning agency too. The

guards had already talked to him by the time we got there, and he refused to talk to us, saying he'd already told the guards all he knew. 'She's a pain in the arse' was all he said. 'I was going to fire her anyway.'

Three days after we had reported Annie missing, the guards got in touch with the landlord right before he was about to clean out her flat. He was furious apparently and ranted about lost rent. They searched it from top to bottom. And I think that's when they began to take a different kind of interest in Annie.

On Wednesday the 26th of November, Detective Sergeant O'Toole rang and asked us to go to the station, Ma, Da and me. We all exhaled with relief. We convinced ourselves they'd found her.

At the station, Detective Mooney brought us into a small windowless room. There were only two chairs in it, and somebody went to get three more so that Da and I could sit down too. They wanted us all to be sitting down before anything was said. Ma got nervous then, clutching her rosary beads. 'What's all the drama for? Can you not just tell us where she is?'

Detective Sergeant O'Toole had been the person we'd been in touch with over the phone in the last few days, but none of us had met him. He was mid-thirties, a stocky build, but he had a shaving cut on his chin and one just under his left ear. I noticed these small things to distract myself from what I now knew was going to be bad news. I realized that if there had been good news about Annie, we would have been told over the phone. Mooney sat beside Detective Sergeant O'Toole on one side of the table and the three of us sat on the other. The table was old and battered, the size of a teacher's desk. It looked like chunks had been carved out of it with penknives, and it had been graffitied with doodles of topless women and scrawls of 'fuck the pigs' and suchlike in pens and markers.

The detective had a file open in front of him. I couldn't see what had been written down, but I could see the photo of Annie. We had put it up everywhere we could – on lamp posts and in shops, pubs and church porches.

Detective Sergeant O'Toole introduced himself as Declan and asked our first names. He looked me over a bit too long in a way that made me slightly uncomfortable.

'Did you see me on the television last night? We're taking this very seriously.'

Ma had seen him interviewed, and treated him like a famous person. Me and Da had missed it because we'd been out looking for Annie.

'Well now, to be honest I thought we'd get a better response, but I must say at the outset that we have not found Annie.' A sob escaped from Ma. The tension was driving us all crazy. He ignored her distress and continued: 'But we have made a few discoveries that I'm not sure you are aware of.' He looked at me and said, 'Did you know that your sister is a heroin user?'

'She isn't. I mean, she likes a drink but she wouldn't go near drugs.'

'Oh, Jesus,' said Da.

'When we searched her flat, we found certain items under the mattress that lead us to believe that she is a regular user.'

'Like what?' asked Ma.

'Syringes, foil wraps, a ligature.'

I was shocked. I knew about heroin addicts. You'd see them sometimes around our neighbourhood. They were all hopeless cases, living on the streets, begging for their next fix. I'd seen them with my own eyes. Annie wasn't one of them. Ma said nothing but cried quietly.

'She's not like that,' said Da, 'she can be trouble all right, but she's too smart for drugs.'

'Gerry,' said O'Toole, ignoring my ma's distress, and I didn't like the condescending way he said it, 'did you know that Annie has been caught shoplifting three times in the last year? She's been up in court. The last time, the judge said he'd lock her up if she came before him again. She is not living a good life.'

Da went quiet then, but I was shocked and furious. 'Why are you saying that? Annie's not a thief! And she wouldn't have the money for drugs. It's not true, and even if it was, where is she? Have you done anything about finding her?'

Mooney looked towards the ceiling, in embarrassment I think, while O'Toole continued.

'She got the money from items she stole and then sold on to a third party . . . and' – he coughed, but it was a fake exaggerated cough – 'from other sources.'

He reached out, put his hands flat on the table and addressed himself to Ma. 'Pauline, we all have to be calm now. I admit that we don't know where she is, but it seems that she had regular gentlemen . . . clients . . . over the last few months, and they might also have paid for her habit.'

It took a few moments for the impact of what he was

saying to sink in. Ma was still bewildered, but Da leaped up, sending his chair crashing backwards.

'Are you saying my Annie is a prossie? Is that what you're saying? Because I'll break your face if that's what you're after hinting.'

I pulled Da by the sleeve as O'Toole jumped out of his chair and pushed Mooney in front of him. Mooney moved behind Da, put a calming arm on his shoulder and spoke quietly. 'Now, sir, we're just dealing with the facts here to help us find your daughter.' Da was breathing heavily, clenching his fists together, then pulling at his hair.

'Da, please stop! Sit down.'

He slumped back into his chair. O'Toole nodded at Mooney, who stood sentry beside Da. O'Toole leaned forward and spoke quietly.

'I understand that it's upsetting for you to hear this, but we looked into Annie's background. We know that she spent two years in St Joseph's. You sent her there yourself, Gerry.'

Da put his hands over his face.

'Now, I have to ask you a question and I want you to think hard before you answer it. Do you think there is a possibility that Annie might have taken her own life?'

I didn't have to think hard at all. 'No, absolutely not.' It had already crossed my mind, but Annie was optimistic on the last Thursday I'd seen her. She was upbeat and hopeful of getting money from somewhere. She had left no note. There was no body. Annie would not have done that to us. Despite the constant arguing with our da, there had always been some sort of a bond between them. She wouldn't even have done it to him. Ma and Da readily agreed with me.

'Not our Annie,' Ma said.

'Well, we can never rule it out and I'm happy to proceed with the investigation. However, as you might guess, the news coverage so far hasn't proved very . . . fruitful. But I know a few people in the press who might be interested in the human angle of the story. Would you be prepared to talk to them this afternoon, if I was able to get them down here to the station?' O'Toole was excited by this, I could tell.

'Just me?' said Da.

'All of you.' He nodded towards me. 'Sure, it's no harm to put a pretty face forward.' He winked at me. I was disgusted.

'And tell them that my Annie is a drug addict and a prostitute?'

'Well, of course, there would be no need to reveal any of those more . . . troubling details. I'm just talking about a straightforward appeal for your daughter to come home. We have no evidence that any harm has come to her, but she may be in the company of some, shall we say, unsavoury types. It would just be you three talking to a few reporters, no big deal. None of the other . . . information would be released to them.'

Detective Mooney looked at Da gravely. 'I think it's your best chance of finding her, Gerry.'

We argued about it. Ma wanted to do it, but Da was reluctant. They had a massive row in front of O'Toole, and I was caught in the middle.

'You were always ashamed of her,' Ma said to Da.

'Can you blame me, Pauline? I'm hardly going to be boasting about my junkie whore daughter, am I?'

'So you'd be happy if she was dead in an alley somewhere, would you? You'd be happy if you never saw her again?'

'No! I'm not saying that. I just worry about what happens next time she goes off on a bender. I'm worried sick, if you must know.'

'She's your flesh and blood. We have to find her.'

'I agree with Ma. What if she's in some bad situation? She's not on a bender. If the people she's with know that the guards are looking for her, they might send her home.'

'We don't even know that she hasn't gone off somewhere –'

'We *do* know, Da. All her stuff was still there. She wouldn't have taken off and left her stuff behind.'

We went back to the garda station in the afternoon. Dessie came with us, though he sat at the back of the room. I'd told him about the drugs and prostitution. He was utterly shocked. 'Jaysus,' he said, 'I never knew she was *that* bad.' He shook hands firmly with my dad, as if it were a funeral. 'I'm sorry for your trouble.'

Da just glared at him. Da was still unenthusiastic about meeting the reporters, and Ma was really nervous. O'Toole said, 'Don't worry if you break down and cry when you're talking about Annie,' and I thought that was a strange thing to say because he was almost hinting that we *should* cry. Detective Mooney told us, 'Just be honest, tell Annie that you want her to come home.' Da said, 'I *do* want her to come home,' as if the guard was challenging him. 'It's OK, Da,' I said.

We were brought into a bigger room with a big conference table and sat on one side of it with O'Toole. I couldn't call him Declan. I noticed that he had had his hair cut since that morning. I guessed he didn't give a damn about Annie and just wanted to be in the papers. He'd been so pleased with himself about being on the telly. When a photographer requested our photo, O'Toole jumped up and stood between us with his arms out, like Jesus in a holy picture of the Last Supper. A few men scribbled into jotters and clicked their cameras as Ma and Da talked about Annie. O'Toole looked meaningfully at me, urging me to say something, but I just sat with my head down and said nothing. I didn't want to cry in front of strangers.

I had information too that I had not shared with my parents; it would have hurt them too much. Earlier, before the press conference, O'Toole had taken me aside. He put his arm around my shoulder in a way that was supposed to be comforting, but I felt like gagging from the smell of his overpowering aftershave.

'Karen,' he said, 'if there's anything I can do, you know? I hate to see you suffering, like.'

'Don't you have any leads on where she went? Any clue as to what might have happened to her?'

'Afraid not, but we've tracked down her pimp. He thinks she was seeing fellas on her own for the last few months. She wasn't on the streets like she'd been before, but she seemed to have money for heroin. Sometimes, you know, a girl is better off with a pimp because he'll offer her some protection.'

'And did you arrest him?'

O'Toole seemed perplexed. 'For what?'

'For being a pimp! Isn't it illegal?'

He actually laughed at me. 'Now, don't be getting upset, a pretty girl like you. Pimps are useful to us in other ways.'

I was livid. 'I bet they are.'

He released me from his grip then. 'I'm on your side, you know. I wouldn't bite the hand that feeds you, if I were you.'

I was shocked by how threatening he was. I needed to play along with him or he wasn't going to help us.

'I'm sorry, it's just that . . . I'm worried . . . we're close, me and Annie.'

'I suppose it hurts that she kept secrets from you.' He rifled through his desk and pulled up a copybook, like an old school jotter. 'We found this with the syringes under the mattress. It's not of any use to us, but maybe you'd like to keep it?'

I reached out to take it from him, but he held it aloft. 'What do you say?'

'Thank you, Detective Sergeant.' I smiled sweetly.

'*Declan*.'

'Declan.'

'She's not great at writing, is she? Did she go to school at all?'

I tried not to glare at him.

'There's some large cash amounts listed in there. We don't know what they refer to. If you can shed any light on them, let us know? Prostitutes would never make that amount. The going rate averages at ten pounds for full sex,' he said. He suggested that she must have been providing 'very special services' for the amounts listed in the notebook. It took me a few moments to understand what he was getting at. I thought of my sister, who I had shared a room with throughout my childhood. I was still trying to take in the fact that she might be a prostitute. He insisted that the addresses and phone numbers had all been checked and led to nothing.

He wrote his own phone number on a piece of paper. 'Ring me any time. Any time you want to talk.'

'About Annie?'

'About anything.'

I recognized Annie's scrawl at once. It was a diary of some sort. Her handwriting and spelling were terrible. But it was so . . . Annie, and when I read the contents, I felt sick. Sick about reading her personal stuff, but heartbroken for what she'd written. The first entry was a letter, dated shortly after she came home from St Joseph's four years earlier.

Dear Marnie

I bet theve givin you a new name but youll allways be Marnie to me couse of that film. she was gorgues in that film and I think youll be gorgues like her wen you grow up. Your the mort buetifull thing I ever seen. I hope your new family are treeting you good. They wouldent tell me were you was going and I dint want to leave you but they said that Id be looked up their for ever if I didt sign the papers I wish I could have stayed and bawrt you home with me but my Da wouldn have it. He said i was a discrase to the famly. I dont want to be a discrase to you. I will come looking for you some day soone. I wish i new wher you are because I really miss holding you in my arms and cuddeling you. My sister asked me about you but i cant say anything becuse i am the bad one who left you behinnd and now I wish Id stayed and they hadnt sent you away. I am sorry with all my haert and i promise ill find you.

There was a lock of soft, downy, almost yellow hair stuck to the page with Sellotape.

As well as writing, there were things like cinema tickets pasted to the pages like a scrapbook, and random phone numbers, cash amounts and badly spelled hotel addresses. Some recent entries were listed with a 'J' on one side of the page and '£300' on the other. I could make no more sense of it than O'Toole.

After the reporters printed our interview, information came flooding in. Annie had been spotted in five different pubs and two restaurants in Dublin, working in a café in Galway, a hotel in Greystones, an office in Belfast. Countless possible sightings. Detective Mooney kept us updated, but even he admitted that they didn't have the resources to follow up on every single call. Not properly. Me and Dessie chased up a lot of them ourselves. We took the bus and went to hotels and pubs and shops with her photo, but it was infuriating. It seemed like some of the people who had 'spotted' Annie just wanted to be part of the excitement of a missing-person's case. Their stories didn't hold up, or they were contradicted by their friends. Often they were just people with problems of their own that wanted some attention. Each new lead excited us for a time, but none of them checked out.

A week after our press interview, the muckraking began. New headlines appeared: 'Missing Annie's Heroin Addiction' and 'Annie Doyle's Secret Teen Pregnancy'. There were vague references to gentlemen callers, and anyone with a brain could see what they meant.

Da and Ma were distraught. Da and I went straight to see O'Toole. 'How did they know? You said you wouldn't tell them any of that private stuff!'

O'Toole played the shocked innocent. 'We're launching a full investigation into how those details were leaked, Gerry. I can assure you, we're just as upset as you are.'

Detective Mooney, I could tell, was furious. His eyes blazed at O'Toole. I knew it was O'Toole who had done the leaking. After the press conference, I saw him and some of the reporters laughing and joking together. He posed for photographs with them. I was sure he would not hesitate to provide any dirty details they wanted. Maybe he told them to hold off for a week, so that the articles couldn't be connected to him.

To me, the tone of these reports seemed to imply that Annie deserved whatever she got, and if she was dead in a ditch, she had nobody to blame but herself. Even Dessie was upset by all the coverage. 'It's as if she doesn't matter,' he said.

Within three weeks, everything stopped. No leads, no investigation. Gradually, the name Annie Doyle disappeared from the headlines. I guess nobody cared enough to really investigate the vanishing of someone like Annie. If she had been a posh rich girl without a 'troubled' history, they would not have given up so quickly.

I couldn't stop thinking of that first entry in Annie's copybook. It had been written four years earlier, but the pain in that letter was obvious. What if she had travelled to St Joseph's in Cork to find out where her baby had gone? What if something happened to her in Cork?

I rang O'Toole.

'Did you ask St Joseph's?'

'What?' He didn't appear to know what I was talking about.

'St Joseph's in Cork, where Annie was forced to give up her baby.'

'Oh yeah, I did, yeah.'

'And what did they say?'

'They didn't have any information that would be helpful.'

'But did they say she had been there? Had she gone down to find out where the baby was?'

'Karen, a beautiful girl like you, all this worry is doing you no good. You have to leave this investigation to us. We're doing everything we can.'

'Like what?'

'Pardon?'

'Like, today. What are you doing today?'

There was a pause before he said, 'You know, Karen, patience is a virtue.'

'I'd just really like to know what you're doing to find my sister.'

'Would you like to discuss it over a drink?'

I hung up.

I rang St Joseph's in Cork. I didn't know who I should speak to. The place was run by nuns. The woman who answered the phone identified herself as Sister Margaret.

'I'm trying to find out if my sister visited in the last five weeks, please? Her name is Annie Doyle.'

'And why would she visit here?'

'She . . . she had a baby there in 1975. The baby's name was Marnie. I have her date of birth, if that helps? She stayed there until December 1976, when she gave up the baby.'

There was a rustling of papers then.

'I see. Do you know what her St Joseph's name was?'

'No . . . I . . . what do you mean?'

'All the girls who come here are given new names.'

'Her name is Annie Doyle. She's missing. I think the guards were in touch with you?'

'Not that I recall. If you can't give me her house name, I can't help you.'

'Wait, but don't you keep records? Where did you send her baby? She might have gone looking for her.'

A long silence followed.

'I don't know who you are talking about. Perhaps she went away because she was ashamed.'

Ashamed. I bit my tongue.

'Lots of girls in her position go away.'

'Away? Where?'

'Just . . . away.'

'Can I come and see you? I can bring a photo. It's been in the papers. The guards are looking for her.' I couldn't hide the desperation in my voice.

'We don't talk to the papers. Nobody who leaves here ever comes back voluntarily.'

This one was a right bitch.

'Can I find out where her baby is, at least? She could have gone looking for her.'

‘If your sister was here for two years and left without her baby, it means that she took a while to make up her mind, but she must have eventually signed the adoption papers. The whereabouts of the child is privileged information and will not ever be released. The baby will have been placed with a good Catholic family. I can’t help you. Goodbye.’

I reported what I had discovered to my parents. Ma cried. Da broke down too, which wasn’t like him. ‘I should never have sent her there. We could have kept her here. She wouldn’t be the first on the street to have a bastard child.’

Ma reared up on him. ‘Bastard child? That was my grandchild, and yours too. She might have been all right if we’d kept her at home, but you were always too bloody proud for your own good. I let you beat her and I let you send her away and now, I think . . . I think she’s . . .’

Ma didn’t finish the sentence, but we all knew what she was thinking. I left the house and went back to my own flat. I couldn’t accept it. Annie, my big sister? Annie was larger than life, people said. She couldn’t be dead.

Ma and Da had always been a team. I hadn’t known till now that Ma had wanted to keep Annie and her baby at home. The cracks in their relationship began to appear then. On a later visit home, I noticed Ma had moved into my old room.

My relationship with Dessie strengthened. He had been really kind and helped me put up posters in shops and bars near where Annie had lived and in buildings she had cleaned. O’Toole fobbed us off with excuses and didn't return Da's calls. I tried to believe that no news was good news.

But by Christmas, Annie had been gone for six weeks. I rang O'Toole myself. On Christmas Eve, I met O'Toole – *Declan* – for a prearranged drink in O'Neill's on Suffolk Street. I had tried to arrange a meeting with him in the station, but he had refused and insisted on a drink instead. 'Less formal, you know what I mean?' I knew what he was playing at, but I had no other way of speaking to him. He was already drunk by the time I joined him. I told him the nun in St Joseph's had no recollection of anyone from the guards ringing there about my sister. He didn't care enough to deny it. He just shrugged his shoulders and smiled awkwardly.

'You need to forget about her. All this worry will give you wrinkles and you're a beautiful girl.'

'What? I'm not just going to forget about her.'

'We could go back to my flat and open a bottle of vodka and I could help you forget?'

He put his hand on my thigh. I knew he was sleazy, but I hadn't thought he would be so obvious.

'No, thank you,' I said, removing his hand, unable to keep the disgust out of my voice. 'You've met my boyfriend, Dessie?'

'Don't be a fucking ice queen. You're better-looking than your sister, you know. You could charge more.'

I threw my glass of Guinness in his face. He jumped up, and as I hurried out of the bar, he roared after me, 'You stupid fucking bitch! She's dead. Everyone knows it but you.'

7. Lydia

All the pressure got to Andrew in the end, I suppose. My relationship with him was strained, to say the least. I was used to being the one who was looked after, but now I'd find him weeping in the shower and uncommunicative for days at a time. He stopped socializing completely, took sick days from work and stayed in bed. I urged him to see a doctor, but he said he was afraid of what he might say. He didn't want to be anywhere near me. One evening, I found him in bed in one of the spare rooms.

'What are you doing?'

'I don't want to share a bed with you any more.'

'But, darling, why? What have I done?'

He looked so exhausted. 'Nothing. You managed everything really well. I just hate that you were able to.'

I ignored the implication of what he was saying. 'Come back to our room. Laurence would be so upset if he thought we were fighting. And we're not fighting, are we, darling?'

He allowed himself to be led back to our bed. I offered him one of my tranquillizers, but he refused. 'You and your pills,' he said. I kissed him gently on the mouth, but he turned his head away, unable to respond. I hoped that he would snap out of this humour soon. Apart from anything else, it was tedious.

I should have taken it more seriously. My poor husband had physically aged a decade in a month, his movements had slowed down, and he started shuffling around like an old man. I should have realized that the strain of keeping our secret on top of the financial trouble would be too much for him, but when I look back on it now, I am so sorry that Laurence's birthdays and Christmases were ruined for ever. The twenty-fifth of December will never be a good day for us.

The day started off relatively well. I made a special appeal to Andrew to get out of bed and be in good spirits for Christmas Day and Laurence's birthday. We gave him our birthday gifts, and we all exchanged Christmas presents. It was almost how it used to be. Andrew's mother, Eleanor, was due to come over after she had dined at Andrew's brother's house.

After dinner, Andrew and I were in the kitchen, cleaning up. He was moaning about Laurence's weight and his uncouth girlfriend. He was being quite cruel about the idea of them being a couple. I did not like her either, but my intuition told me it was a passing fancy. Helen's mother was Angela d'Arcy, a poet of note, so status-wise she was just about acceptable, but Andrew, so quick to be irritated these days, said, 'What does she even see in him?' and then I saw Laurence. He had been standing at the kitchen door and heard Andrew's whole tirade. We had allowed Laurence to have a little wine with dinner to celebrate the fact that he was eighteen, but I don't think the drink suited him, because he had this really aggressive, hostile expression on his face when he looked at Andrew, as if he despised him.

'There are worse things to be than fat,' Laurence said insolently.

'Oh dear, please let's not fight,' I said, trying to broker a truce, but Andrew ignored me.

'What are you trying to say?'

'Nothing,' said Laurence, sullen.

'I'm sorry you heard me say those things. I know I haven't been very . . . well recently . . .'

Laurence left the room abruptly, slamming the door behind him, not allowing his father a chance to apologize.

Andrew turned to me. 'He *knows*.'

'Don't be silly, darling. He doesn't know anything.'

'But the way he looks at me . . . he won't even be alone in the same room as me any more –'

I cut him off. I was determined the dead girl wasn't going to ruin Christmas for us. 'We are not talking about that. You should speak to Laurence. Let him know that you actually care about him.'

'For God's sake, Lydia, of course I care about him, but I don't intend to smother him like you do. He's eighteen. He'll have moved out of the house by the end of next summer.'

'Don't say that. He can live here as long as he likes.'

'Well, if I was him, I'd be gone like a shot. You indulge him like he's a little boy. You need to let go.'

'I would have been able to let go if you hadn't destroyed our plan by *killing that girl*.' I whispered it.

'So now it's OK to talk about it, is it? When it suits *you*? Her name was Annie.' Andrew's temper flared. I knew to stay quiet. He would brook no interruption in this mood. He whispered furiously, 'You carry on as if nothing has happened, and I'm living a waking nightmare, in dread of every knock on the door. You have it all arranged. If anything happens, I go to *prison* and you and Laurence go away and live a very nice life without me. Can you imagine how a judge might be treated in prison?'

I moved the glass and decanter out of his reach because he was very angry, angry enough to smash something, but he barely noticed.

'Have you ever loved me the way I love you? Really? I actually liked Annie. You chose her, remember? I didn't mind that she was a plain-looking girl, because it was less of a betrayal of you. She was different of course, but she was sweet and funny . . .'

I put my hands over my ears, but I could still hear him.

'. . . but it was only ever you, and now I have to look at her fucking grave out the kitchen window every day! I did it all for you –'

I wanted to speak up then about the violence of his language, but he put his hand up as a warning to me.

'And no, of course you didn't ask me to kill her, but you kept on and on at me – "Don't let her make fools of us", "Get the money back from her", "You should never have trusted her", "Why did you believe her?" – on and on and on until the pressure was unbearable. And when Annie threatened to blackmail me, I snapped. And she was a living human being. I'm on a knife edge, Lydia, don't you see?'

He clutched at his chest and I thought he was being overly dramatic but then he gasped for breath. I watched in horror as he tried to steady himself against the table. I reached out to stop him falling and he grabbed my hand.

'What is it? What's wrong?' I said, like an idiot, because

any fool could see he was having an attack of some kind. He slipped downwards, and I tried to hold him up. His eyes were open, pleading and desperate. He could no longer speak, but I could see that he was begging me to help him. I pulled at his shirt collar, but he had taken off his suit after Mass and was wearing a loose open collar and no tie. I tried to hold on to him, but he was too heavy. He fell through my arms and slumped past me, across the table, displacing the turkey carcass from its serving platter, and then he was face down across the table, his hair in the turkey grease.

I looked at the turkey, which had dropped off the end of the table and slid along the slight slope in the kitchen floor to rest at the skirting board beside the door. I had ordered a big turkey, even though there were only three of us. Daddy had always said a small turkey looked mean, and we could make sandwiches and stews from the leftovers, and all these thoughts about the turkey and how many ways I could prepare it went through my head as my husband died, there and then, in front of me. I stood in shock in those ten seconds while he fought to breathe, until he was entirely still. I looked from him back to the turkey on the floor, trying to believe what I was seeing. And then I tried to shake him. I turned him over and blew into his mouth, but nothing I did worked. I screamed for Laurence. He came immediately and took in the scene at once. My poor brave boy.

Without saying anything at all, Laurence picked up the turkey and put it in the swing-top bin, forsaking the sandwiches and stews. He went to the cloakroom to call for an ambulance and returned with a brimming glass of brandy for me. He mopped the floor and then moved Andrew carefully on to it and put one of the kitchen cushions behind his head. He wiped the grease from the side of Andrew's face and his hair with a tea towel. I wanted to close his eyes, but there was a kind of empty innocence in them and I needed Laurence to see that. He went to ring Andrew's brother, Finn, who could relay the news to their mother, Eleanor.

Perhaps because it was Christmas Day, the ambulance took an hour to arrive, or maybe it was because Laurence had told them that Andrew was already dead and therefore it was not an emergency. Eleanor, Finn and his wife, Rosie, were there by then. Finn was shocked but stoic about his younger brother's passing. They were not close.

Rosie swung into action, making phone calls and filling glasses while Eleanor just cried silently in Andrew's leather armchair. I resented her sitting there. Andrew was her baby. Eleanor and I tolerated each other most of the time, but she never pulled her punches. Her role as the family matriarch entitled her to say whatever she wanted, and it was usually critical. She could never refrain from commenting about Laurence's weight. Andrew usually visited his mother alone, and when she came to visit us I sat on my hands and bit my tongue. In our grief on this saddest of days, we did not make any attempt to comfort each other.

I think I went into shock after that. Finn and Laurence found my tablets and fed them to me. I was put to bed and woke up hours later, screaming for Andrew. Laurence came and sat with me, rubbing my arm, assuring me that everything was going to be OK and that he would look after me now. It seemed so stupid to me, a little boy saying he was in charge. The pain of this loss was so much worse than all of the miscarriages.

In the few days before the funeral, I stayed in bed, leaving all the arrangements to Finn and Rosie and my son. I lived in a tranquillized haze. There was some fuss over the clothes that Andrew was to be laid out in. Laurence had chosen Andrew's favourite mustard-coloured corduroy slacks and burgundy cardigan, and Eleanor was horrified that he wasn't in his best suit. I was beyond caring.

The funeral happened without my input. I felt as if I were underwater in a swimming pool and everything was happening above my head, beyond the surface of the water. I watched, absorbed, but could not engage. I stood in a receiving line, shaking hands with hundreds of people: politicians, broadcasters, coroners and lawyers. Laurence, by my side, kept me upright and supplied me with tissues. My emotions broke through when I watched Laurence carrying the coffin that contained his father's corpse. I began to scream, and everyone stood away from me in horror until Rosie and one of her sons hustled me out of the church into the waiting black Mercedes. She found some pills in my bag and I was glad to take them. Eleanor got into the car and told me that I must conduct myself with dignity, and I wanted to slap her, but the pills began to work so I looked out of the window on the way to the graveyard, watching people carrying shopping bags, waiting at bus stops, chatting over hedges, as if nothing had happened. When the coffin was later lowered into the ground, Laurence held firmly on to my arm.

Back at Avalon, Rosie and her brood handed out

sandwiches to the forty or fifty people who milled around our reception rooms. I recognized two or three of the women from some outings I had endured in the distant past, and I wondered who had invited them all. The wives of Andrew's former colleagues filled our freezer with stupid, useless casseroles and pies, all labelled neatly. They marvelled at the size of our home. A few boys from Laurence's old school came, and that girl Helen was there, clinging on to Laurence every chance she got, but Laurence was taking care of me. A wizened priest wanted me to pray with him, but I couldn't bear to be in the room with him, and Laurence led him away towards Eleanor, who was more accepting of his condolences.

In the wake of Andrew's death, I found it impossible to climb out of the fog. I spent most of my days in bed, and when I ventured downstairs I stared at the television, trying to ignore the empty armchair beside me. I simply could not stop crying. Laurence would bring food on a tray and feed me like I was a baby, and I would eat mechanically, without tasting.

When my mother-in-law and Finn and Andrew's friends telephoned to see how I was coping, I did not go to the phone but asked Laurence to take messages. I let the condolence cards pile up without opening them. I swallowed tranquillizers to blot out the pain, but really they just took the edge off it and stopped the rising panic that threatened to overwhelm me. I was forty-eight years old. Laurence was all I had now – my boy who was growing up way too fast. And I was terrified he would not want to be my baby for much longer.

*

After Laurence was born, I had nine miscarriages. They devastated me, every one of them, the pain and the loss and ultimately the fear. I carried one as far as four months, and we really thought we were safe then. I'd never held on longer than ten weeks before that. It was the glorious summer of 1977. We celebrated by having dinner in our favourite restaurant, Andrew, Laurence and I. And then, right after our dinner plates were removed, I felt that dreadful and familiar tearing in my womb and I doubled over in agony. Within seconds, pools of blood seeped on to the velvet-upholstered seat beneath me. Andrew realized quickly what was happening and carried me out to the car, leaving a dribbled trail of my insides on their plush carpet as we went. Fourteen-year-old Laurence was white-faced and crying, but even he knew. 'Is it the baby, Mum? Is it?'

Usually, after the miscarriages, it took me a week or two to return from the dead place I occupied with my lost foetuses, but that time it was much longer.

Doctors could do nothing to help me. Three different adoption agencies turned us down. I assumed it would be a matter of making a generous donation, but there were all sorts of interviews where Andrew and I were grilled separately and then together. The questions were deeply intrusive. I told Andrew to use his status, but it didn't seem to do any good. He pulled every string available to us, and although the first two agencies were not prepared to give their reasons for denying us a child, the third agency gave us a written report. They said that they thought I had not dealt properly with issues in my childhood, and they regretted that I might not be able to meet the needs of a new baby. They said it was strange that I had no close friendships and that I rarely left my family home. When I got that report in the post, I went straight into the agency and screamed blue murder at the woman on reception until she called security. Andrew came to take me home, and after that he insisted we couldn't apply to any more agencies.

We had never given up on trying for our own baby, even when we had planned that Andrew would get that girl pregnant and pay her for the child. He had been supposed to find a young healthy girl who was poor enough to go along with it. The plan was that once she was pregnant he would visit the girl once a month and pay £200 per month of pregnancy and £500 on the baby's arrival. A lot of money for a poor girl. A lot of money for us. Though the idea was straightforward, I had to plead with Andrew to go through with it. I had to beg him.

'Doesn't Laurence deserve a sibling? We'll tell him that we were finally accepted by an adoption agency.'

'If it ever came out, we would be disgraced,' he said. I reassured him: who would believe that we would do such a thing? He still refused. 'We can't afford it,' he said.

I sold the Mainie Jellett painting that Daddy had sworn would be worth something one day. I always thought it hideous, but Daddy was right about its value. Andrew still threw objections in the way. 'How will I know I can trust a girl who would do something like this?' he said.

I wish I had put more thought into the question of trust. It's not like Andrew could march her into a doctor's surgery for a pregnancy test. He was too well known. He suggested that I deal with her once she was pregnant, but that was out of the question. I did not know how to talk to those people. He was the one who saw them every day in the courts – 'the dregs of society' he called them. He only eventually agreed to it when I stopped eating for a week. But the plan was merely theoretical until we found the right woman. That was a lengthy process. It's not something he could casually raise as a suggestion in the Four Courts. We couldn't ask anyone for recommendations. Andrew had approached a few women, but he said they were either disgusted when he suggested dinner, or else they were interested in beginning an affair. Besides, they were the wrong type of women. Middle class or too old.

Then, one night out of the blue, he told me about a young woman he had caught red-handed lifting his wallet as he bought a newspaper at a kiosk on the street that afternoon. She begged him to let her go, said she'd do anything he wanted. She cried and pleaded with him. She said she needed the money to buy medicine for her sick little sister. He took pity on her, gave her £5 and drove her home.

'You believed her?' I asked him.

'Not really, but she seemed desperate.'

When he said the word 'desperate', it all fell into place for me.

'What age was she? Did she look healthy?'

Andrew immediately understood my questions, and shook his head. 'Please, Lydia, I know where you're going with this and I don't like it.'

'Are you shaking your head because she didn't look healthy?'

'No, she's young and fit, but –'

'Does she know who you are?' I asked.

'No.'

'Do you think the place you dropped her off was her real home?'

'I doubt it, unless she lives above a pub called the Viking.'

'You have to find her. She sounds like a perfect candidate.'

He argued against it. He said that he didn't want the mother of his child to be a thief.

'I will be the mother of the child. Find her.'

He found her easily enough within a few weeks. She was leaving the Viking. He asked her to get into his car and she did.

It had been a perfect plan, but as it turned out, Annie Doyle was an addict and a prostitute with a harelip who slept with my husband four times and then said she was pregnant. But she wanted more money than he was offering. She demanded £300 per month, and £600 when the baby was born. After five months and £1,500, he admitted there was no sign of a bump. The girl couldn't or wouldn't produce any document to confirm that she was pregnant. So I forced him to confront her that night, and of course the stupid little thief admitted that she wasn't pregnant at all, and said that she'd go to the papers with her story of how a high-court judge had paid her for sex and tried to buy her baby. She was utterly shameless. I couldn't believe that she would be so dishonest and so cruel, but I didn't know then that she was a heroin addict and a prostitute.

Not until she was dead. I have since read that nearly all prostitutes are heroin addicts, and addicts are capable of anything.

I never got the baby I wanted so badly, and the stress of it all killed Andrew. I hold Annie Doyle entirely responsible.

8. Laurence

Wishing my father dead, and then having him actually die minutes later, made me feel very strange, powerful and guilty at the same time. As if I had made it happen.

I had never been to a funeral before. Everyone told me to 'stay strong' and that 'you'll get through it', but I felt fine. I accepted condolences on behalf of my zoned-out mother, kept Granny Fitz supplied with tissues, and carried the coffin down the aisle with Uncle Finn and the paid pall-bearers. It was a lot heavier than I expected. My shoulder ached for days afterwards. The worst part was having to restrain Mum at the graveside and keep her and Granny Fitz apart.

Dad's friends and some neighbours came back to the house afterwards. Helen was there. I was glad to see her, and she held my hand in the kitchen when the priest came to say goodbye. She pointed out that we had even more in common now that we were both fatherless. I questioned what she meant by 'more'.

'Ah well, you know, the way we're both freaks,' she said. 'Fatherless freaks.'

It had a certain ring to it.

'At least you know your father's dead. I'm not even sure who mine is!'

She told me I was very brave and that she didn't think it was unmanly to cry at one's father's funeral. I got the impression that she wanted me to cry so that she could make a display of comforting me and being a girlfriend. I accepted her hugs and squeezes gratefully, but I had no need of comfort.

Two boys from my class came. I don't remember speaking to them before, but they hadn't particularly bothered me in school. They shoved Mass cards into my hand but didn't stay long because they were on their way to Funderland to meet girls. A few boys from my old school, Carmichael Abbey, came also and we made unspecific plans to meet up again in an undefined number of weeks' time.

Afterwards, when everybody had departed, Helen and I washed up and put all the linen and silver away, and Helen helped me put my mother to bed.

We came downstairs then and opened a bottle of whiskey.

'It's really OK to cry, you know,' said Helen again. 'Your dad's just died and you're acting like nothing's wrong.'

'I'm fine.'

'You think you are, but it will hit you later.' She gave me a consoling hug, but I wanted sex and suggested we go upstairs since Mum was knocked out on sleeping pills.

Helen refused. 'You're some weirdo, you know that?' she said.

Afterwards, I tried to think about my father the way he had been before the money troubles, before my weight gain and before Annie Doyle. He had not always been a bad father to me, and it was clear that he adored my mother. Although he could sometimes be impatient with her, I think he felt he didn't deserve her. I often caught him simply gazing at her as if she were a prize painting. He did every single thing he possibly could to make her happy. Even after Bloody Paddy Carey, he didn't cancel her Switzer's account, though she swore she could easily give it up. I think he was jealous of my mother's love for me. He hated how close we were. She loved him too, but I think not as much as she loves me. A strange triangle.

My mother took his death very badly. It was like before. After her miscarriages, my mother had had to be sedated for days. Her inability to conceive after my birth broke her heart, and Aunt Rosie's constant pregnancies and eight children depressed her. For weeks after the funeral, I renewed her tranquillizer prescriptions, and soon my mother was calm and distant and, just as in the past, she was no longer a mother, or a widow, or a daughter-in-law, or even a woman, but just a shadow. However, this time she showed no signs of recovering.

I was managing reasonably well. I got Mum to sign cheques that I cashed at the bank and, as far as I could see, we weren't destitute yet. The new school term had started and, while I missed a few days here and there, I was capable of preparing my uniform and lunches, and I could cook oven chips and sausages (my favourites), and the mourners' shepherd's pies and beef casseroles had stocked our freezer well. I marked their efforts out of ten, grading for taste, texture and presentation. I also did additional general shopping.

After three weeks, Mum had stopped communicating altogether and slept almost all the time. Eventually, I rang an old friend of Dad's who was a doctor. He'd been at the funeral and told me to call him if I needed anything.

I wish people wouldn't say that when they don't mean it. I ended up having to beg him. He very reluctantly agreed to come to the house, a big tall man with a sinister death-rattle cough of his own which he used to punctuate every sentence, and which only underlined the gravity of what he was saying. He examined her in her room. Then he came down and started asking me questions about how I was managing, *cough-splutter*, what I was eating, *splutter-hack-phlegm*, as if *I* were the patient. He suggested that my mother needed residential psychiatric care, that she needed to 'go in somewhere for a rest'. I thought this was a mistake and said so. I suggested that all she needed were stronger tablets and time. Dr Death-Rattle insisted she needed professional medical supervision. My mother, even in her drug-induced stupor, screamed at the thought of going into a mental hospital.

Dr Death-Rattle broke the Hippocratic oath and told my uncle that my mother was in a terrible mental state and that I was coping alone. I sincerely regretted getting a family 'friend' involved. An enormous fuss ensued, and despite my insistence that I could look after myself, that I was *eighteen*, an *adult*, Granny Fitz declared she was moving into Avalon 'to look after the boy' while my mother was committed to St John of God's. I didn't get a say. The doctor had informed my school, who immediately pretended to be very concerned for my welfare. The headmaster expressed grave concerns about my unexplained absences, my undone homework and my free-falling grades. They hadn't given a shit when I was beaten up every day in my first month there.

'It's what your father would want,' said Granny Fitz,

arriving with a large suitcase, as if that settled everything. Aunt Rosie, Uncle Finn, the doctor and the headmaster agreed. My mother was taken to St John of God's one day while I was at school. When I got home, Granny was sweeping up broken glass, so I guessed that my mother had not gone without a fight.

Granny Fitz was seventy-seven years old, physically fit and mentally sharp. When I was a small child, she had doted on me. I was her first grandchild and she couldn't spend enough time with me. She lauded all my early achievements and boasted about me to her friends. Mum and she fought over me like I was a puppy. But where Mum indulged my every whim, Granny was stricter. She was appalled by how much weight I had gained over the last year and had berated my mother for feeding me so carelessly. With Mum now out of the way, she ran our home like an army camp. I hated it, hated the fact that she was there, treating me like a child. I was desperately worried that my mother would never be well enough to come home. I escaped to Helen's house as often as I could, partly for the company and the kissing and the possibility of more, but largely because I ran the chance of a decent-sized meal and some proper TV shows. I could always scrounge a mini-pizza or a Vesta curry. I met her floral famous-poet mum. She looked like Helen, not even that much older really. She was a hippy who chain-smoked and spoke in a deep voice. She drank beer from the bottle. When she wasn't writing, she worked as an editor for a literary journal and hung out with long-haired, denim-clad men, who would be there from time to time. I had met Helen's little brothers by then; they were raucous and foul-mouthed like Helen, but were welcoming and friendly. 'Jesus Christ, look at the size of you!' said the oldest boy the first time I met him. The younger one sniggered behind his hands. It was worth it if it meant a mini-pizza or a slice of toast with the obligatory cup of tea.

Granny Fitz didn't like Helen. She said she was 'uncouth' and 'common'. I concede she was probably uncouth, but she definitely wasn't common. There were not too many girls like Helen. She and I met up in a pub a few times, but Granny smelled alcohol on my breath and tried to ground me. She belittled my outrage and insistence that I was an adult and could legally drink now, challenging me to earn the money to pay for it. She didn't know about the cheques my mother had signed. Granny insisted that I needed to study and that I should put Helen 'on ice' until after the exams. I agreed that I would only see her at weekends, but I lied and said I was going to the library when I went to see Helen during the week.

Under Granny's regime, there was four months of food rationing, restricted pocket money and enforced labour. After the first six weeks, we kind of got used to each other. We lived in an atmosphere of mutual intolerance, but as time went on we became almost cordial. I put it down to Stockholm syndrome. The IRA hunger strikes were in the news. I wondered if my grandmother was making some kind of political point with our tiny meals. There was nothing that drove Granny Fitz to distraction more than seeing me seated, particularly in front of the television. I was allowed only to watch *Little House on the Prairie*, *The Waltons* and *The Angelus*. Everything else was off-limits. The only other time I was allowed to sit down was to study.

I don't know why I could no longer study, but I had just lost interest. There didn't seem to be any point to it any more. I was anxious about my mother, and Annie Doyle was still haunting my dreams. So when I was sent to study, I mostly just wrote mad fantasy stories in which I was saving Annie Doyle, or going for dinner with Annie Doyle, or having sex with Annie Doyle. I kept the Marnie bracelet under my pillow. If only Granny had known. She invented jobs to keep me on my feet. She had me digging up hedges through permafrost in February, carrying rubbish from the attic to the shed at the end of the garden, and then back up again. She offered me as a dog walker to a dotty old neighbour.

Granny Fitz made no secret of the fact that she thought my mother was weak and selfish. Granny had lost a son, her 'flesh and blood', and 'you don't see me languishing in an institution, leaving a poor child to fend for himself'. I suppose I must give her some credit for acting in what she thought were my best interests. She must have known that I despised her by my permanently surly mood and scowling expression, but she ignored my bad attitude and put a lock on the fridge. Once or twice I heard her sniffing or crying, but when I came into the room she would quickly dab her eyes and bark an order at me. I realized that she was mourning her son.

I visited Mum every week and complained bitterly about Granny, but my mother wasn't really able to respond in any meaningful way, not for ages. I would try to remind her of happier times and point out all the charms on her bracelet to remind her of the significance of each one, but there never seemed to be any visible improvement. I worried that she might never recover. She would sit beside me and stroke my face and smile at me like a blind person might. The medication was doing its thing, I suppose, allowing her mind to heal.

Eventually, she began to engage a little bit, talking about the stories in the newspapers and the TV shows she watched. She was growing painfully thin and complained of not being able to sleep because of her new medication. She gradually began to notice me again. She wanted to get better. She was terrified of being locked up for ever.

One day she told me, 'At least there'll be no more miscarriages. Now that Dad's gone.' Her eyes brimmed.

'I'll look after you, Mum,' I promised.

Her eyes brightened and warmth returned to her face, and I began to hope that she might soon be back to her old self.

One day, I returned from school to find that my grandmother had bought me a whole new set of casual clothing. Her choices were surprisingly fashionable: proper jeans, jackets, T-shirts, sweatshirts, pullovers. I was used to elasticated waists and plus-size jumpers.

'Don't you ever look in the mirror?' she said.

The answer was no. Usually I avoided the mirror, or else only took in isolated parts – the recurring spot on my chin, the bruise on my knee where I'd been pushed against the wall at school, the tuft of hair behind my left ear that refused to be flattened by Brylcreem or comb.

'Go up and try them on,' she said. 'I can return anything that doesn't fit.'

I went up to Mum's room because there was a full-length mirror in there. Even as I passed the mirror to lay the clothes on the bench, I got quite a surprise. The person looking back at me was unfamiliar. I won't exaggerate, I was still fat, but I had certainly lost some chins and a few rolls of flab around my stomach. My face had structure and I could see the rounded top of my cheekbones. With the increased physical activity and tiny portions, I should have expected to be losing weight. I had noticed that my collars had loosened up, but the elasticated waistbands had obviously adjusted by themselves. Helen had said something about how she was glad that I was making an effort for her, but I hadn't understood until now what she meant. Most of the new clothes fitted well. I looked, for the first time in over two years, merely chubby, as opposed to obese. Maybe my *Star Wars* T-shirt would fit now.

I stood back and did a twirl, and when I turned again to face the mirror, Granny Fitz was standing in the doorway, looking at me with pride and satisfaction.

'You're almost there. That's what you're supposed to look like. I know I've been hard on you, but I needed you to see what you could be, without making you self-conscious about it.'

I was tongue-tied. If this had been a film, I would have run over and hugged her, but it wasn't. My grandmother was not the tactile type. We had never exchanged hugs or kisses. We stood smiling awkwardly at each other.

'Your mother is coming home on Tuesday. She is better than she has been since Andrew's death,' she sniffed. 'I'm sure she cares about you, but you mustn't allow yourself to get into that condition again. You could be a very handsome young man. Look!' She indicated the mirror.

I looked hard and saw the man and not the boy. But the boy in me was excited. Mum was better! I couldn't wait for things to get back to normal, whatever the new normal was going to be, without Dad. I beamed at Granny, and for a moment there was a truce. And then she ruined everything by turning me to face the mirror and saying, 'See? You are just the image of your father.'

The Saturday morning before my mother's homecoming, we were in the kitchen and Granny pointed to the flower bed beyond the window. 'That's still a mess. Would you go out and fix it up? When was it planted?'

I couldn't remember exactly, but I knew it hadn't been there for that long before Dad died. I grumbled and delayed, but Granny insisted. 'I can't believe Andrew left it like that with random plants just dumped into the earth. Go on out and dig the whole thing up. There's some dahlia tubers ready to go in the potting shed. It all needs to be replanted. Go on now, it will be a nice surprise for your mother. You can do it on your study breaks.'

It was April now, almost Easter, and it was still whip cold outside, though there had been no frost that week. I wrapped up in a woolly hat and cardigan and Dad's wellington boots, and fetched the shovel and rake from the shed. As I began to dig at the edge of the raised bed, I discovered a granite border about six inches below the surface. I remembered old black-and-white photographs of an ornamental pond at this spot with a bird bath at its centre, and it occurred to me that maybe it would cheer up Mum if I could restore the pond to its former glory.

I consulted with Granny and she was fully encouraging. I didn't have the first clue how to go about it though, so before I dug any further, I took myself off to the library and borrowed *A Complete Guide to Garden Ponds.* Granny and I pored over the right way to approach it, and I had to go back into town to buy some rubber sheeting with which to line the pond.

On Sunday, having spent the morning pretending to study, I started digging again in earnest. I was excited by how pleased Mum would be. Reinstating the pond would take a few weeks, but it was a project that she might take an interest in. She would be proud of my efforts and see that she didn't need Dad to do everything around the house. My mother always liked to have Avalon perfectly preserved, exactly how it was in her childhood. A few modern conveniences had been acquired over the years, like a dishwasher and washing machine, but Mum would have nothing to do with them until the cleaners had to be let go after Paddy Bloody Carey had done his worst. I thought that the restored pond would delight her. The stone bird bath had lain wrapped in hessian in the corner of the shed since long before I was born. I didn't want to get too ambitious, but I thought that later, in the summer, with a bit of expert advice, I could re-install that too.

The instructions in the pond manual suggested that I needed to dig down quite deep, about four feet, because a brick layer had to go under the rubber sheeting, to allow for earth shifting and ground stability. But then my spade hit something odd, and I could see some kind of fabric under a half-torn piece of black plastic, peeking through the soil. I brushed the earth back with my father's boot, curious and irritated at the same time. I didn't immediately recognize the herringbone pattern. I bent down to pick it up. And then the stench hit me.

I shouted out loud in horror and disgust, and, unable to look away, pushed the plastic upwards with the tip of my boot. Above the herringbone cloth, a tuft of unnaturally black hair was visible, while creatures of many legs and none slithered and crawled through the cavity behind part of an exposed lower jawbone. The crooked snaggletooth was unmistakable, though the flesh around it was blackened and bloated. I quickly shovelled all the soil back on top of Annie Doyle, my tears blinding me as I did so.

Granny rapped at the kitchen window, calling through the glass that it was getting dark, that dinner would soon be ready and that I should come in and shower and change. I returned the gardening tools to the shed and went into the house, stopping in the dining room for a swig of brandy straight from the decanter. I went upstairs and showered. In the bathroom cabinet, Mum's Valium bottle stood on the shelf. I had never taken one before, but I knew how they were effective in lessening her panic, so I put my mouth to the tap and swallowed a tablet.

I don't remember much of our dinner conversation, just that I fought to stay awake and Granny commented on how quiet I was. She prattled on about this and that, and when I could no longer keep my eyes open, she said that maybe digging out the pond was a bit much for me and that she would do a bit of digging herself tomorrow. I struggled then to be aware, insisting that I was fully capable and would get back to it during the week after school.

'Well, if you're sure?'

I went straight to bed, and slept the best night's sleep I'd had in many months, without dreaming, until my alarm went for school the next day. The horror took hold of me once again.

At breakfast, Granny was peering out the kitchen window. 'I thought you were digging out the pond? It looks like you've filled it all in.'

I made up some nonsense about having to weigh down the rubber sheeting to settle it before I removed the earth again. She looked doubtful, but was happy enough to assume that I knew what I was doing.

I was a small pebble being washed out to sea by an enormous, storm-force wave and there was nobody I could turn to for help. School that day was . . . I have no idea. Helen was waiting for me at the bus stop when lessons were over.

'May I come to your house for dinner?' I asked, trying to keep the desperation out of my voice.

'What about Granny?'

'Fuck Granny.'

'Ooooh, Lar, what has she done this time?' Helen was used to my giving out about Granny.

'Nothing, I just want to go to your place.'

Helen took this as a compliment, but really it was nothing to do with her. I wanted to be surrounded by her and her noisy brothers and her gravel-voiced mother. I wanted there to be chat and squabbles and music and television, clamour and distraction. I didn't want to go home and look out my kitchen window.

Perhaps because of the contrast, that evening in Helen's was one of the most enjoyable I'd ever had. Her mother was pleased to see me, in her perceptive way: 'Oh, Lar, look at you – you look great – but a little pale.' She didn't mind when Helen and I cracked open cans of beer at the dinner table, and I found my voracious appetite had returned as I forced more and more food into my maw.

'I think you've had enough,' said Helen as I scraped the last crumbs of an apple pie on to the side of my fork. Helen and I went upstairs 'to study' and fumbled with each other in an ungainly fashion, and I got further with her than any time since we'd had full intercourse, but not quite there.

'Jesus, you're persistent tonight,' she said, 'but you'd better go home. It's nearly eleven and Granny will have the guards out looking for you.'

When I got home, Granny was livid. 'I'd made a special dinner for you as it is my last night, and you didn't even have the decency to ring to let me know. It shows a complete lack of consideration. What was I supposed to think? I suppose you were in that girl's house?'

I apologized. I should have rung her, but I knew she'd have forbidden me from going to Helen's on a school night. Mum would be home tomorrow. How was I going to tell her what I had found? She had been through so much already. But I would have to tell her eventually. I cursed my father for what he had done, not just to Annie Doyle, but to us too. What would happen to us now? I didn't think my mother would be able to handle it.

PART 2

1985

9. Karen

In the beginning, being married to Dessie was great. We had our wedding the summer after Annie went missing. It was a quiet, small affair, partly because of money and partly because it didn't seem right to celebrate without Annie. For the first few years, Dessie was really affectionate and considerate, but I didn't want to have kids yet and he was in an awful hurry. He'd always said that the age difference shouldn't come between us, but I was afraid now it might. I was twenty-four. I thought there was loads of time, so I was always pretty careful. He said he wanted to have a son before he was too old to kick a ball around a field with him.

'What if it's a daughter?' I said.

'Sure, we'll keep going till we get one of each.' He laughed but he wasn't being funny, and I knew that sooner or later I really was going to have to sit him down and have a proper conversation.

I hadn't told him yet about Miss La Touche and her offer. She used to come into the dry-cleaner's a lot, and sometimes when the others were on lunch I'd do the counter service. She was in her mid-forties, I guessed, always very well groomed, with immaculate hair and painted nails. She was tall and slim, walked in a particular way, hips forward, head straight, and she was always neat and tidy-looking. She was really particular about her clothes, and she must have been minted because nearly every stitch was dry-cleaned, and it was all fur, velvet, silk, satin and jewel-coloured fabrics with labels in foreign languages. I recognized some designer names. You couldn't work in a dry-cleaner's without taking some interest in clothes, and just occasionally me and the girls used to try stuff on if Mr Marlowe was out, even though I was the assistant manager by then. There would have been war if we were ever caught, but we were careful. The other girls would comment on how everything always looked so good on me, and I have to admit, I loved Miss La Touche's luxurious dresses.

One day Miss La Touche had come in to collect an Yves Saint Laurent silk coat that had been for Special Attention Cleaning, and as I handed it to her in its plastic wrapping, I had to say it to her: 'That's the most beautiful thing we've ever had in here.' She peered at me over her glasses, and looked me up and down before she responded.

'What height are you?'

'What? Uh, five foot seven, I think?'

She peered over the counter to look at my flat shoes.

'Pity.'

'Sorry?'

'Have you ever done any modelling?'

I laughed, pointing to my hair. 'With this? No way.'

She reached out and took my chin gently in her hand, turning my face up to the light. Her accent was almost English. 'Your hair is your best asset, dear. Don't underestimate it. Good bone structure too. You're too short for catwalk, but product shots are a distinct possibility. You could be the rare Irish girl that goes international. The

Italians love redheads.' She pulled a card out of a wallet. 'Give me a call if you're ever interested.' And then she glided out of the shop, as smoothly as she had entered.

I had only seen a business card once or twice before, but this was a work of art in itself. On a background of very pale pink roses, in a curly script, there was her name in embossed gold:

Yvonne La Touche
The Grace Agency

Ireland
Telephone: 01-693437

I kept the card in my purse for a few weeks. I'm not sure why I didn't tell Dessie, but I think I was afraid he'd accuse me of getting notions about myself. He often gave out about actresses and models in the magazines I was reading: 'Look at the state of her, half-dressed. I bet her father's proud.'

It hurt me when he said those things, because it reminded me of Annie and my father, and the girls in the magazines weren't even doing anything like the guards had said Annie had done.

We didn't talk about her any more. My family hadn't heard a single thing from the guards since my encounter with O'Toole nearly five years earlier. I had written to his superiors to complain about his behaviour, but they never wrote back.

Dessie could be fairly judgemental about what I wore and how I dressed, but when he bought me things that were a little more buttoned-up than I would have chosen, I knew it was because he wanted to protect me. I had become a bit well known after the publicity around my sister's disappearance. I had overheard one of the suppliers referring to me as 'yer wan, the ginger wan who's the prossie's sister'. I had been upset, and Dessie was furious on my behalf. I had to restrain him from giving the fella a thick ear. I couldn't blame him. He said it made him look bad too.

Ma and Da had separated. Ma blamed Da for driving Annie away, and Da blamed himself and hit the bottle a fair bit. Ma eventually moved back to her sister's house in Mayo on the other side of the country. She begged my forgiveness for going, but I knew she'd be better off there in the end. Da stayed in the house in Pearse Street, but things were bad for him at work. People were being laid off, and he thought he'd soon be let go.

We never said it, but at Christmas times, and on our birthdays especially, we scoured through every card, looking for a few lines from Annie. Her signature would have been enough. There was never anything. But none of us wanted to say it. 'Maybe next year?' Ma would say, though the hope had faded from her eyes. And yet I saw Annie, or thought I did, in pubs, on street corners and in supermarkets, and I would run up behind her, about to scream at her for leaving us, and then I'd see the perfect lips that made her someone else.

It was mean of Dessie to say those things about the girls in the magazines. I thought it would be easy money to get your photo taken, and surely if you didn't want to wear a bikini in a photograph, they couldn't force you to.

I rang Miss La Touche two months after she gave me the card. 'Call me Yvonne,' she said. I met her in a large attic office in a building on Drury Street. I had dressed carefully in an A-line green dress I'd bought for Christmas in Mirror Mirror. My hair was washed and blow-dried and tied into a straight ponytail. My shoes were high and made of plastic that looked like patent leather.

I'd never been in a room like this before. It was long and vast, but surprisingly warm. Miss La Touche was alone in there. Free-standing mirrors and rails of clothing were everywhere, and piles of shoes all over the floor. Overstuffed filing cabinets ran the length of the wall behind her desk. Another long wall was covered with photographs of beautiful girls with golden hair and long limbs. I immediately felt like a fake. Yvonne was pleased to see me. But I was shocked when she asked me to strip down to my underwear.

'I . . . didn't think . . .'

'Don't worry, dear, you'll never be a lingerie model, your bust is too small, but I need to get your statistics.' She laughed, though not unkindly. She was efficient as she proceeded to measure my hips, waist and bust. Then she stood me on a weighing scale.

'Do you lose and gain weight easily?'

'I . . . I don't know. I never really weigh myself.'

'You are one of the lucky ones. Still, you should drop about three pounds and try to maintain that weight.'

I wasn't sure if that meant an extreme diet.

'Nothing drastic,' she said, reading my face. 'Cut out bread and potatoes and you'll be there in no time.'

She set up a very bright lamp against a white sheet at

the back of the loft and took Polaroid photographs of my face from every angle. She took garments from a rail, and shoes from a rack, and sent me to a small booth to change into them. She had me comb my hair out straight, and pile it on top of my head, and tie it into bunches on each side of my face, and all the time I'd hear the click and whirr of the camera as it spat out print after print of me in every pose – hand on hip, arms behind my head, eyes closed, reclining on a sofa, jumping in the air. Afterwards, she gestured me to sit in the chair opposite hers.

'I think you're worth investing in. Would you like me to represent you?'

I didn't know what she meant. Yvonne patiently explained.

'Darling, you're a very beautiful girl, with a natural smile. You are like a young Shirley MacLaine. Perfect skin tone and bone structure. I don't understand why it took you so long to ring me. Any other girl your age would have chased me out of the shop.'

I didn't know what to say.

She sighed. 'Why do redheads have such low self-esteem? You must remember that what might have been carrot-orange in your childhood is what we now call a Titian auburn. Do you know how much people pay to have their hair dyed that colour?'

I shook my head, self-consciously running a hand through my hair.

'My clients will pay to have you model their clothing, hair products and skin products, or it could be groceries and washing machines, who knows? But I intend to pitch you to the high-end magazines. I make twenty per cent of whatever you make, but I get you the jobs. In the meantime, at my own expense, I will send you to classes for deportment, etiquette, make-up and fashion. You need to know how to move and dress like a model. Never wear polyester again, do you hear me?'

I was mortified. My best dress was not good enough.

'From now on, wear just cotton and wool until you can afford better. It shouldn't be long!' She grinned at me. 'When can you start?'

I was gobsmacked, and flattered of course, but all this information was a lot to take in. 'I . . . I'll have to talk to my husband first.'

'Husband? Good Lord, what age are you?'

'Twenty-four.'

'Really? My God. Well, not any more. If anyone asks, you're nineteen. And you are *not* married. It is perfectly acceptable to have a boyfriend, but a husband already? You should have waited until you were thirty. Fenlon is your married name? What is your maiden name?'

'Doyle.'

'That's worse. We'll keep it as Karen Fenlon. It has a certain charm.' A thought struck her. 'Oh God, please tell me you don't have children?'

'No.' I could be firm about that, at least.

'Good. About your accent . . .'

'Yeah?'

'Best not to speak unless you're spoken to. Most of my girls come from . . . educated backgrounds.'

I shrank back into the chair.

'Nevertheless, my clients will be paying for what you look like, not what you sound like, but we don't want to put them off unnecessarily.' She paused. 'I'm from the Liberties, you know. La Touche isn't even my real name.'

That shocked me. People from the Liberties sounded more like me than her.

'Elocution lessons, darling. Nobody would take me seriously in the fashion business if I sounded like . . . you.'

'I can't . . . change the way I talk.'

She laughed. 'With your looks, you probably won't have to. Now, let's talk about your lifestyle. Drink? Drugs? Wild party girl?'

'Pardon?'

'If you are as successful as I hope, journalists might want to know more about you, your background. Is there anything we need to worry about?'

'No, nothing. I'm very ordinary.' It wasn't a lie.

We spent the afternoon discussing my future. She assured me that I was unlikely to be asked to do underwear shoots, unless I went international, and only if I chose to do so. I smiled at the thought of that. International.

But there were obstacles. While Yvonne would pay for my classes, there were things I'd have to pay for too. I needed a photo book done by a professional photographer. I needed a range of make-up, hair accessories, hats, scarves, stockings of all colours, shoes of all heights. She advised that I could pick up a lot in second-hand shops, but the photographer would cost a week's wages. Dessie and me were saving for a house of our own. I was happy enough in the flat above the funeral home in Thomas Street, but Dessie had been saying we'd need a garden for the kids.

*

I braced myself to tell Dessie when I got home. He thought I'd been to see my da, and I hadn't exactly put him straight. Dessie and me were a team, and I didn't usually go off making decisions on my own. I needn't have worried, though, because when I told him everything, and that I could be getting £50 a day, he was delighted.

'For wearing clothes? There's some eejits in this town, eh?' and he wrapped his arms around me and told me he was proud and lucky to have married such a stunner. 'And you don't have to be in your knickers, like?'

Two months later, I'd had my photos taken and done the course on make-up and all that. I'd given up my chewing-gum habit and my job at the dry-cleaner's. I'd taken up occasional smoking and lost five pounds in weight. My first modelling job was coming up. Da was OK, but Ma was less happy about it.

'You need to remember where you're from. That's what sent Annie wrong, you know. She was always curious. She wanted more than we knew about.' Her voice down the phone line from Mayo was full of regret.

'Maybe she's got it now, Ma,' I said, keeping Annie in the present tense.

I went to meet Da, who was on his customary bar stool in Scanlon's. When Ma lived at home with him, he might go to Scanlon's once or twice a week for a swift one before he came home to his tea, but now that he had nobody for company I was more likely to find him there than in the house. He was delighted. 'And you'll be in magazines, you think? I'm proud of you, girlie.'

I set off for the photo shoot. It was for a new brochure for a very expensive hotel in town, the type of place I wouldn't dare go into. I had to dress up in all these different outfits and have my photograph taken with other girls on plush sofas in the tea room, and then on a bar stool at the bar, with my head back, laughing at this model fella as if what he was saying was hilarious, and then in bed in one of the swish rooms, with my head on the pillow, my hair combed out behind me, and the soft blankets brushing my shoulders. The other models were gas fun, though they were all a bit hoity-toity. The photographer was a fairly grumpy fella, and there was a lot of hanging around so there was plenty of time to chat to the other girls. Everybody smoked. The girls said that cigarettes stopped your appetite and kept you thin. The one male model was gay, they said, which was a shame because the blonde one, Julie, really fancied him, but it turned out that the photographer was his boyfriend.

That day, I came home with £70 in cash, which was just slightly more than I made in a week at the dry-cleaner's. Dessie was thrilled and said he'd lodge it in the post office the next morning. I told him all about the day and the other girls and the gay male model. 'A queer?' He laughed. 'Well, that's a relief, I wouldn't like to think of you hanging out with good-looking normal men!'

Three weeks later, I made £190 on three different assignments. Yvonne said the clients loved my look and that I should prepare myself for the big time. She told me that I was in great demand and that she was turning down clients whose brand was 'not of sufficient quality'. I thought she was mad. But gradually, over the course of a month, the jobs started coming in and the money was getting bigger. Everything looked great. Dessie and I would soon have a deposit for a house.

And then the brochure for the hotel was published and I was amazed by it. It looked like a glossy magazine you might find in the hairdresser's. I really thought for the first time that I looked beautiful, though I knew that I hadn't got there without make-up artists and hairdressers and fashion stylists. I couldn't wait to show Dessie when he got home. I left it on the table just in front of the door where the bills and letters usually stacked up. I thought it would be a lovely surprise for him. I sat in the kitchen, waiting for his reaction. I heard the door click and heard him stop at the table, and then he called out, 'Karen?'

'Yeah?'

He appeared around the kitchen door. His face was red with fury. I was astonished, thinking there must have been a row at work, but he held up the brochure and threw it with force into my lap. 'You never told me that they photographed you in bed.'

'What? I'm sure I did –'

'You did not. Do you think I want people looking at pictures of my wife in bed?'

'I don't . . . what do you mean? But sure, I'm covered up by the quilt.'

He was being completely ridiculous. The photo had me covered up to my armpits in the bedclothes. My eyes were closed and my hair was splayed out over the pillow in a perfect circle around my head. I had one arm raised, bent at the elbow, hand facing palm outwards. My shoulders were covered in a white linen and lace nightdress. The area about two inches below my neck and my exposed lower arm were bare. There was nothing sexy about it whatsoever.

'For Christ's sake, Karen, did you not think? There you are, in a *bed,* in a *hotel room*?'

I had no idea what he was talking about.

'Like a *prostitute*.'

I was so utterly shocked. 'I don't believe –'

'What do you think it's been like for me, with people whispering about Annie all the time, goading me?'

'What people?'

'They might not say it to your face. You don't have to listen to their sly jokes.' He was shouting now.

I had never realized. Nobody had even mentioned Annie in the last few years, so I assumed it was old news. I had never thought how Annie's reputation affected Dessie.

'What do they say?'

'I wouldn't repeat it. Disgusting stuff. About you. I landed one fella in hospital over it. I was nearly fired.'

'Oh God.'

'You see, that's why I'm saying, look, you just can't do stuff like this.' He stabbed the page of the brochure so violently that it tore. I started to cry and he realized that he had rattled me. He took me in his arms then and rubbed my back. 'I'm just trying to protect you, love.'

That was the first time I felt a stab of resentment towards Annie. Whatever had happened to her, her behaviour had ripple effects that were still causing upset and grief nearly five years later. Of course, I still loved her, but I wanted her in the room so that I could yell at her.

I told Yvonne the following week that she had to be more selective about my assignments.

'Darling, what are you talking about? That shoot was really tame, if not demure. It's early days now, don't throw it all away out of prudishness.'

'I'm not a prude.'

She was steely. 'If you want to continue in this career, you have to be reasonable. I have invested in you already. Do not let me down.'

'You don't understand.'

'Then why don't you explain it to me?'

My voice choked and I tried to stem the tears.

'What is it?'

'You're going to be so furious with me. I'm so sorry.'

'What have you done?' Yvonne was alarmed.

'When you asked me about my lifestyle . . .' I told her everything, about Annie, her drugs, her 'clients' and her disappearance, about Dessie, about how it had destroyed my parents' relationship.

Yvonne sank into her armchair. 'Oh my God, I remember that case. My son was working on it.' Her eyes dropped to the desk.

'Your son?'

'Yes, he was a detective, James Mooney – you must have met him.' She took a photo out of her wallet. I had only ever seen him in uniform, but I remembered Mooney well. He was O'Toole's sidekick. He always seemed vaguely embarrassed by O'Toole.

'Yes.'

'They never found her body, did they?'

'Well, there's no proof that she's actually dead.'

'I thought they had a suspect?'

'What?'

She got flustered then. 'Oh, don't mind me, I'm probably thinking of another case he was on.'

'You think they had a suspect? For her murder?'

'Well, yes, the odd time he'd talk about cases, but honestly, they all get jumbled in my mind and I get them confused.'

Yvonne was not the type of person to get confused about anything. She was incredibly sharp. Her son had told her something about Annie's case, something that had been withheld from us, Annie's family.

'Please, Yvonne, you have to tell me, if you know something? If James knows something?'

'I . . . can't.'

I was frantic now and almost hysterical. 'You think she's dead! You have to tell me. You have to. She's my sister. I'll go to the garda station and find James myself.'

'You can't. He died in a car accident two years ago.' She reached for a file and raised it in front of her face, but I could see her hands were trembling a little. The wind was taken out of my sails. I sank back into my seat, ashamed.

'Oh no, Yvonne, I am so sorry, how awful! I thought he was really good, and decent. He treated us with respect.'

She lowered the file and dabbed her eyes with a tissue. 'Thank you for saying so. He was my only child. I miss him every day.'

'I felt like he was the only one who cared about Annie. The rest of them didn't help. They didn't even look that hard. They wrote her off.'

'James didn't.'

She stood up and turned her back to me for a moment.

I thought she was going to tell me to leave, but then she grabbed her bag and her coat.

'Let's go for a drink.'

We went to a hotel off Grafton Street. 'I don't do pubs,' she said. On the way, she chatted about the new fashion lines, her doubts about shoulder pads – 'too masculine' – her belief that cheesecloth was 'over'. I said nothing. In the hotel, we sat in armchairs in a wide lobby and she ordered us gin and tonics. I leaned forward in anticipation, but she downed half her drink and placed the ashtray between us. She gave me a cigarette and I took it.

'I don't have a name for you. But I can tell you what James told me.'

'Please, everything.'

'There *was* a suspect, somebody well known and respectable.'

'Who?'

'That's what I'm saying – I don't know. James never told me.'

'Suspected of . . . killing her?'

'Well . . . that's what James thought, but he couldn't get his boss to take him seriously – that buffoon, what was his name?'

'O'Toole?'

'Yes. O'Toole didn't believe James, but James thought the man was definitely worth investigating. He might have been a senior guard or a politician or something like that. His car was unusual – a vintage Jaguar, I remember that. It had been seen outside your sister's flat. James went to question him in the early days of the investigation, but the man was very defensive and pulled rank on him. James went back with O'Toole to see him, but they only got talking to his son, a young boy, who provided an alibi, but James didn't believe him. I can't recall . . . There was something about a hat, a trilby hat. I'm sorry, I just don't remember the details. I know the investigation stopped very quickly after a few weeks. I don't know why. James moved on to another case, and he never mentioned that one again. It was strange because normally he would be quite dogged. O'Toole was lazy. James wasn't the type to give up.'

I racked my brains to remember exactly what had been said during the search. There had been mention of the car, but no suspect was ever mentioned. Not to me.

'Do you know if he, the suspect, was a . . . if he used prostitutes?'

'I think that's what stumped James. He talked to some street girls that worked the same area as your sister, but they didn't know him and she hadn't done street work for months before she disappeared. I don't know why James was so convinced about that man. He accepted that they had no evidence.'

'Do you remember any more details? Where he lived or worked?'

'I'm sorry, Karen. James only told me that much because he was so frustrated with the O'Toole fellow. He would never have been deliberately indiscreet. But, Karen . . .' She took my hand in hers and grasped it. '. . . he was convinced that Annie was dead.'

I had been in denial for so long, but I knew she was right.

'I'm sorry.'

'I'm sorry about James.'

She exhaled a long plume of smoke. 'We can't let these tragedies stop us living. We'll never forget our loved ones, but they would want us to be happy, darling. Your career is beginning. Let's keep this to ourselves. Tell Dessie to be a man. You have to be allowed to move on. With or without him.'

I was shocked by her words. None of this was Dessie's fault. It was this man, this suspect that James had identified, who had caused all the anguish and fear. I was going to find him, with or without the guards.

10. Lydia

The time after Andrew's death when I was forcibly removed to a psychiatric institution was not the first time I had been taken from my home against my will. I spent nearly a year in an aunt's house directly after my ninth birthday. It was because Daddy didn't want me in Avalon after the accident.

It was just two years after Mummy had caused a scandal by running off with a plumber. She wanted to take us with her, but Daddy forbade it. He said he should never have married beneath him and that he would never get over the humiliation that Michelle, my mother, put him through.

Eventually, we all got used to her not being there. For the first year, I cried myself to sleep every night, wishing and hoping she would come home. Diana called me a baby and said that Mummy didn't love us, but it wasn't true. Mummy did love me once. I remember the feeling.

Mummy was very beautiful. I recall her quite well, even though all the photographs were destroyed. When I look in the mirror now I can still see traces of her, despite the fact that I am much older than she was the last time I saw her. She died sometime in the 1960s, alone and abroad apparently. I got a card from her on my wedding day, but I did not get to keep it. Daddy threw it in the fireplace. My twin sister, Diana, looked totally different from Mummy and me. Where I was fair, she was dark; my eyes were blue, hers were brown. My brow was high and she had no chin. She wasn't pretty, but while she had not inherited Mummy's looks, she had Daddy's breeding. She was more refined than I. I remember Daddy saying that it was impossible to teach me any manners.

I clung to Diana after Mummy left, and I adored her with all my heart. We belonged to each other. But I valued our twin-ship more than she. It was annoying, to be frank, the way that she tried to go off and do things on her own and how she wanted to dress differently from me. She loved me, of course she did – one has to love one's sister, especially if one is a twin – but as we got older there were times when I began to think that she did not *like* me. She would look at me sometimes with disgust if I forgot to chew with my mouth closed or if I licked my knife by accident. She rubbished my favourite books and said she preferred the classics. If I ever did something to upset her, she could go whole days without speaking to me. She said that she couldn't wait until we grew up so that she could have her own house; I did not like to imagine a house without her in it, and cried at the thought. But I always forgave her quickly.

I wonder, if she had lived, would we be friends now?

For a while after Mummy left, Daddy withdrew into himself and spent long periods locked in the library, drinking brandy. Then he would emerge, drunk. He mostly ignored me because I reminded him of his wife. But he would take Diana on to his knee, telling her stories, giving her sweets and tickling her, giving her all the attention that used to be divided equally between the three of us. I was left to the care of our nanny and housekeeper, Hannah, who smelled of mothballs and snuff. Gradually, he began to love me again, although I could sense his suspicion that I would somehow betray him, and I suppose I did, though I spent the rest of my life making it up to him.

It was 1941, and Diana and I were to have a ninth birthday party, the first party since Mummy's departure. We were terribly excited. We hadn't even been to a party in the intervening years, I assumed because Daddy had forbidden it. All fifteen girls from our class had been invited, and Daddy had ordered us new dresses and ribbons for our hair. He had pulled string to get extra coupons. It was May, an unusually hot one, and trestle tables had been set up outside in the garden, laden with dainty sandwiches, jellies and trifles all covered with netting to keep the bees away. Bottles of cold ginger ale stood at the end in ice buckets. Bunting was strung between the apple trees. Daddy had decided the mourning period for my mother was over, and this was the first outward sign that he intended to re-engage with the world. He had invited his sister, our Aunt Hilary, and some friends too, a couple who laughed at everything he said and wore matching tank tops. The lady gave us a shilling each and professed how generous she was for the next hour. At the time appointed for the guests' arrival, Diana and I were kneeling up on the chaise in the drawing room, our faces pressed to the window to see who would be first to arrive. Amy Malone came first and we knocked her over with our enthusiasm, leading her out to the garden, showing off the pond and the luncheon spread and the bunting and the large rocking horse that Daddy had presented us with that morning. We took turns and played for a while until it dawned on me that nobody else had knocked on our door. Where were they all? Daddy and the couple were talking at the far end of the garden as we ran in and out of the house to make sure that Hannah was listening out for the knocks on the door.

Half an hour later, nobody else had arrived and our friend Amy began to look embarrassed and uncomfortable. We sat on the edge of the pond, trailing our bare feet in the water.

'Where are they? Why didn't they come? Didn't they want to?' said Diana.

Amy shook her head and bit her lip. She looked like she was about to cry. It was clear she knew something. Diana grabbed her arm and twisted it behind her back. 'What is it? Why aren't they here? Is it because of Mummy?' She whispered it menacingly into Amy's face.

I didn't understand what Diana meant.

'It . . . it's because of your mother being . . . a loose woman,' Amy said.

'That's not our fault,' said Diana.

'What do you mean?' We had stopped mentioning Mummy a long time ago.

Amy said that the other parents thought that we might be a bad influence, but that her father, Dr Malone, had said that it would be cruel to punish us for something our mother had done.

I realized now that it wasn't Daddy who had forbidden us to go to other children's parties. We hadn't been invited to them. I remembered how our classmates were often distant with us, though Diana and I were always so thrown together that I did not notice it as much as I might have, had we not been twins. I was shocked. Diana looked at me as if I was stupid.

'Stop crying, you idiot. You'll probably do the same thing yourself when we're grown up. Everyone says you're just like her. You're not like Daddy and I. You're common. You're the one they're afraid of. Not me!'

'I am not common.'

'Yes you are, Daddy can't even look at you. You're the exact same.'

It seemed like the most natural thing in the world to push Diana back into the pond. I didn't snap. I was perfectly calm. I simply didn't want her to say those things. She was being so unfair. I heard a crack as she smacked her head under the water, and when she struggled to surface, I sat on her chest to stop her. Right in that moment, I wanted Diana to drown. I wanted Diana to drown because if she was dead, she could never say those things again. Amy's nervous laughter turned to tears.

'Please let her up, Lydia, *please*. She'll drown!'

I didn't care. Amy became hysterical and ran off to get my father, who had disappeared into the greenhouses with his guests, no doubt to show them his melon-growing experiment. I was saturated now, as Diana thrashed around in the water beneath me, and soon she stopped struggling and became still. She had learned her lesson.

'That's better,' I said, as I stepped out of the pond and pulled her up by the arm, but Diana crashed back into the water when I let her go and I was confused. I had wished really hard for Diana to be dead in that moment, but I hadn't really meant it. She was going to be furious with me, and I would be in trouble for ruining the party. Daddy would be livid about our ruined dresses, covered with frogspawn and moss.

I pulled her up again, by the shoulders this time, but she wouldn't lift her head and then I saw the blood seeping down the back of her neck. Daddy and his friends and Amy were running across the lawn and they were all shouting at me. Aunt Hilary ran indoors to get Hannah to telephone for an ambulance, and Daddy had pulled Diana out and laid her on the lawn, but she still wasn't moving. He clamped her mouth open, but it was full of pondweed and he pulled it out in one long string of mess and saliva. He turned her upside down and held her up by her feet with one hand. Her dress fell down and everyone could see her knickers and I was shocked. Daddy thumped her on the back with his free hand. Daddy was crying and so were Amy and Daddy's friends, the Percys.

All the time I was thinking, 'What is *wrong* with everyone? She'll be *fine*.' I waited for her to shout at me and complain to Daddy about how awful I was. I knew it would take her a very long time to forgive me this time. But she still wasn't moving. Had I gone too far?

Everything changed. The upheaval was far greater than after Mummy went away. I never returned to school. That night, while everyone was at the hospital, Hannah packed a trunk for me. Aunt Hilary told me Daddy had instructed her to take me to her home in Wicklow. I wanted to wait for Daddy and Diana to come home, but Aunt Hilary would brook no argument. I didn't want to go, but not even Hannah would look at me as Aunt Hilary carried me into the car while I kicked and screamed. I did not speak for a week. I desperately missed Diana and Daddy and couldn't understand why I could not return home.

Aunt Hilary lived with a friend – a thin woman with bony fingers and long loose grey hair, Miss Eliot. She was a retired schoolteacher and agreed to give me daily lessons. Early in that first week, I determined to eavesdrop on their conversation. I lay on the landing with my nightgown drawn down over my feet and my ear to the floor. It was clear from what they said that Miss Eliot, unlike my Aunt Hilary, was at least prepared to give me a chance.

'She's just a child,' said my tutor. 'She has no idea what she has done, she's too young to realize.'

'There's just something about her. How could she do it? I can't wait for Robert to take her back. I can't keep her for ever.'

'He needs time, Hilary. First Michelle abandoning him and the girls, and now this? He has to keep her out of the way to contain another scandal. Nobody knows that the girls were fighting at the time. As long as everyone thinks Diana just tripped and fell in, it will be dismissed as a terrible domestic accident.'

'In barely three feet of water? But that Malone girl, Amy, she said that Lydia *sat* on her in the water. That sounds deliberate. It's not something that should be ignored.'

'Children say all sorts of fanciful things. And people drown in shallow water all the time. Anyway, Robert said Amy's father is a good sort. All the other parents had boycotted the party because of Michelle. He was the only one to send his child to the party in the first place.'

'I'll bet he regrets it now. Oh Lord,' said Aunt Hilary, 'it's too, too awful.'

'I know, but we must do what we can to help. That child upstairs will be scarred for life, we must make her realize that it wasn't her fault.'

Aunt Hilary made a snorting noise, but Miss Eliot said, 'You can't seriously blame her, she's a child!'

It dawned on me then that I had killed my best friend, my worst enemy, my twin sister.

At the end of that first week, Miss Eliot explained that my sister had died but reassured me that it was an accident, nobody's fault, and that it was an unavoidable tragedy. Dry-eyed, I asked her how it had happened. She turned her head to one side and fixed me with a look.

'Don't you remember? You and Diana were . . . playing in the pond?'

'Yes?'

'And Diana banged her head. Do you remember?'

'Yes.'

I wrote Daddy lots of letters to say that I was very sad and missed him and Diana. I begged him to come and visit me or bring me home. He did not reply. Miss Eliot said he was very busy and there were fuel shortages because of The Emergency and nobody was allowed to drive. I suggested he could have cycled, but Miss Eliot said I was being silly.

I saw Aunt Hilary at dinner times. She would watch me warily and correct my table manners. At bedtime she would come to my room and ensure that I had said my prayers and asked for God's forgiveness. I said my prayers with gusto, although I could hardly believe any longer in a God who would allow my mother to run away or let me kill my own sister. Aunt Hilary remained distant with me, but I determined to give her no cause for complaint whatsoever. Even at the height of summer, the small house was cold. As autumn turned to winter, it was absolutely freezing. Its setting was idyllic, but we lived in the permanent shadow of a mountain. We stayed in the kitchen as much as possible, where the range was located. Food was being rationed, and awful, disgusting things appeared on our dinner plates, but I ate every morsel without so much as a grimace. I remembered my manners and never raised my voice or stamped my foot. I tried to be ladylike at all times. Just like Diana.

Christmas came and went without a visit or a note from my father. Aunt Hilary and Miss Eliot tried to be jolly with me, but the forced merriment was transparent as water.

By the time I returned to Dublin after ten months, I was fizzing with excitement and had quite forgotten that things could never be the same. I travelled in a jaunting car with Miss Eliot, who left me at the door with my trunk. 'What a fine house,' she said. 'I had no idea.' Everyone said that when they first saw Avalon. We said our goodbyes and I promised to write. 'Everything will be all right, little one. You are not a bad girl.'

There was only one bed now in our bedroom, and the wardrobes contained just one set of clothing, most of which had become too small for me. Hannah had been replaced by Joan, a good deal younger but almost mute. Diana was missing. And whereas, at Aunt Hilary's, I had missed her sorely like an inexplicable sadness, on my return it felt like an amputation. I ran through the house, up and down the stairs, looking for signs of life. I went to the hole in the wall behind the writing desk under our bedroom window and retrieved the scarlet lipstick that I had hidden there since my mother's departure. Diana had laughed at me for keeping it, but I had found it under the skirting board in Daddy's room, and for the first year after she left, it still smelled vaguely of her perfume. I sniffed it now, but the scent was gone.

Downstairs, I stopped short at the kitchen window and noted that the pond had been drained and filled with soil. The silence ate into my bones and I went to the piano and played and played until I heard Daddy's footsteps in the hall.

I ran full pelt at him and grabbed him around his waist, pushing my head into his upper stomach, trying to reach his heart. At first, he held his hands outwards, not wishing to touch me, but I would not release him and then I felt the warmth of his large hand on my skull and his other hand slowly enveloped my shoulder. He pulled my face upwards and looked into my eyes. 'We must start again, you and I. We are all we have.'

It was easier not to talk about Diana after that, though she smiled at us from the framed photographs on the mantelpiece.

A new home tutor was appointed and Daddy chose all the subjects that I should study: Latin, music, art, literature, sewing and such like. I worked very hard and excelled at everything. Daddy said my posture needed attention and a ballet instructor was brought to the house, a tiny French woman. We had plenty of space, so a barre was installed upstairs, and there, in the newly named dance room, I jetéed and pliéed and walked en pointe until my toes bled. I loved Madame Guillem. She treated me like her own child, although she never mentioned whether she had children. She took me under her wing and explained everything when my body began to change. She told me that I should be mixing with girls my own age, but I didn't want to. Madame Guillem told Daddy that I was the best student she had ever taught. When I was sixteen years old, she suggested that I apply to the Sadler's Wells Ballet School in London. I was horrified and terrified at the thought of being sent away again. Daddy thought it would be a good idea, but by then I had begun to notice the way he sometimes looked at Madame Guillem, and I didn't like it. One day, I saw him help her to put her coat on and he held on to her arm the way he used to with Mummy. She smiled up into his face. Was she planning to get me out of the way? I have learned that you can never trust anyone. I gave up eating until the idea of ballet school was abandoned and Madame Guillem had been dismissed. I still practised to stay toned and supple. There was a mirrored wall behind the barre upstairs, and I liked to think that the girl in the mirror was Diana and that this time we were identical twins, dancing a duet.

Many years later, when I met Andrew and he enquired about the girl sitting beside me in the old photographs, Daddy explained that my sister Diana had drowned tragically when we were children, and abruptly changed the subject. When Andrew and I became more intimate, he questioned me about the incident and I lied and said it had happened on a day at the beach. He hugged me tightly to console me on my loss.

I became pregnant with Laurence over three years after our marriage. Andrew and I were so happy when I finally conceived, and Daddy opened a bottle of vintage wine to celebrate the news when I told him.

'About time,' he said.

I wasn't quite sure what to expect, having no sister or mother to advise me. My sister-in-law, Rosie, the queen of fecundity, descended upon me with advice and booklets and potions and lotions, but I preferred to work things out for myself. The pregnancy was uncomfortable and exhausting, and childbirth was excruciating, but when the midwife placed my newborn child at my breast, I felt complete for the first time since Diana's death. Laurence being born on Christmas Day was fate intervening. My most treasured gift. I adored my little boy. He was mine. Andrew left us to our own devices, certainly for the first few months, but I wept when he was ten months old and Andrew insisted that we move the cot into the bedroom next door to us, which had been carefully prepared as a nursery. 'We must have our own room back.' Daddy agreed with Andrew, and the matter ended there.

In the summer time, I would bring Laurence's pram outside. It soothed him when he was teething to be outdoors. He would stop crying then. I would lie on a rug on the lawn beside the pram and listen to his soft gurgling, feeling like I didn't deserve such happiness.

When Laurence was nearly a year old, Daddy died, on the same day as John F. Kennedy. He had been sick with cancer for many months. Still, Daddy's death shocked me as much as the American president's. Andrew was of course sympathetic, but I had lost Mummy, Diana and Daddy, and now I clung to Laurence, the only one left of my blood.

I wanted to home-school Laurence, but Andrew put his foot down again, arguing that our son needed to be socialized. I kept him home as long as I could, so that when Laurence did eventually start school, he was one of the oldest boys in his class. That first week, I stayed outside the school every day, trying to spot him through the classroom window. Other mothers tried to inveigle me into conversation when the school bell rang, but I didn't want to talk to anybody except my cherub. I swooped him up into my arms and carried him all the way home.

Gradually, Laurence began to talk about other children and his teachers, and I felt the first pangs of jealousy. As he grew into an independent little boy, I got used to it, but the deep bond we had shared was fading. Shortly after his seventh birthday, Laurence refused to sit in my lap any more, encouraged by Andrew. 'You are far too attached to that boy. Let him off.' We had been trying for another baby. I told Andrew that I wanted to have five children. He baulked at five but thought a sibling or two would be good for Laurence. We tried, and failed, and failed, and failed, and continued to fail. Laurence was to be my only child.

Forty years after Diana's death, I echoed my father's words to my son. 'We must start again, you and I. We are all we have.' The poor boy has had so much to deal with, and he has handled it all with such consideration and discretion. And he has done it all for me.

The months following my confinement after Andrew's death were strange times. I let Laurence take charge of everything. It took quite some time for me to realize that we had no money. Laurence went to deal with the bank manager and the solicitors. I wasn't able for it. The news was grim. Andrew had at some stage mortgaged Avalon to make investments with Paddy Carey. Although thankfully Andrew's death meant that the mortgage was redeemed, there really was very little left over. Carey had told Andrew that he was investing his money in a gilt-edged fund, but it turned out that he had been siphoning it off into his own pet projects, hoping in vain for a hit to cover his losses. Because Andrew had been a judge for only three years, his state pension was small, and the portion of it that I was entitled to as his widow was even smaller. The payments that Andrew had made into a private pension plan and life insurance over twenty years had been gambled away by Paddy Carey. There was a delay with Andrew's will going through probate, because Andrew had been in the process of suing Carey when he died. The solicitor had told Laurence that suing Carey would be a futile exercise. He'd tried to persuade Andrew not to bother. Carey himself had gambled with the stolen money and was now rumoured to be destitute somewhere on the west coast of America.

I really couldn't process all this information at the time. My medication dosage was quite high. I told Laurence that he would have to ask Andrew's mother, Eleanor, for money. She would have to keep us. But when he approached her, she almost went into shock because it turned out that Andrew had been supporting her for the previous years also. He had persuaded her to sell her three-storey four-bedroom Victorian redbrick on the Merrion Road and buy a cottage in Killiney. Andrew had promised her he was making good investments on her behalf. She had no idea that he had lost it all. At the time, he had told me that his mother was getting too old to manage a big house, and at the back of my mind I had thought that our money worries would be over when Eleanor died, because she had to be sitting on a large pile of cash. At the beginning of our financial woes, I had urged Andrew to go to Eleanor and borrow from her. I had thought he was too proud. In fact, he knew she had nothing except her cottage because he had gambled it all. All Eleanor now had was her pension. Finn and Rosie sent us a few cheques, but they reminded us (as if they needed to) that they had eight children to feed and that we must find a way to support ourselves. They got together with Eleanor to suggest that she might sell her cottage and move in with us. We have six bedrooms and so couldn't argue that we didn't have the room, but I made it clear that I would not countenance the idea. Eleanor took umbrage. Finn advised Laurence that we must sell Avalon immediately to free up the equity, but we couldn't do that: first, because it is the only home I have ever known, and second, because we could never take the risk of the new owners discovering what is buried beyond the kitchen window.

*

When Laurence eventually told me what he had discovered, I was astonished that he had put everything together in his head and come up with some correct answers. He knew the remains were Annie Doyle's. He even showed me the tarnished bracelet he had pulled from the hoover bag and all the newspaper reports he had kept. The poor boy had worried himself to shreds over it. Laurence held his father entirely responsible but insisted that we should go to the guards, so that the girl's family would finally have peace. He never suspected that I knew anything about it. He was so anxious telling me, he thought that the news would send me back to the psychiatric hospital. But I was a year out of it by then, and my wits had returned sufficiently. I feigned shock, horror and disbelief. I screamed and cried and grew hysterical. Fortunately, Laurence came to the conclusion that I would not be able for a scandal and the media attention that would follow. I suggested that he could move the body and leave it somewhere it could be discovered, but he convinced me that the horror of the job was too much for him and the risk of being caught too great. In fact, by then I liked having the girl in the pond – Diana had been buried in a plot in Deansgrange Cemetery, but I liked to imagine that she was right here in the old pond where I'd left her.

Eventually, at my request, Laurence paved over the flower bed and cemented the old bird bath on top of it. He planted a few shrubs around the edge of the raised platform. It still looked odd, like a sacrificial altar. Laurence averted his eyes from the kitchen window at all times. After a while, he installed a blind and kept it closed. The kitchen was gloomy now. We made more use of the dining room, which previously had only been used on special occasions. Laurence insisted that we sell Andrew's car. We got a shockingly low price for it and bought a small tin-can run-around. I taught Laurence to drive. He was a quick learner.

Before Andrew's death, the plan had always been that Laurence would study Law at Trinity College and then be apprenticed to Hyland & Goldblatt, the law firm that Daddy had founded in 1928 with Sam Goldblatt. Andrew worked there until he was appointed to the bench, but now most of Daddy's and Andrew's friends were either long since dead or had moved on and started their own practices. Besides, even if we could have availed of a student grant for Laurence, we would still have had no income.

Laurence took civil service exams after the Leaving Certificate. I had hoped that he might be recruited for the diplomatic corps, but it seemed that was impossible without a university education. He was given a choice of the motor tax office or an unemployment benefit office. I thought that the motor tax office might have more prospects, that perhaps they might train him as a tax accountant, but he did some investigation and found that would not be the case. I was horrified at the thought of his mixing with unemployed people, but he pointed out that *we* were both unemployed people.

'Women go to work now too, you know, Mum.' The notion of me getting a job was of course preposterous. I was trained for nothing and I have never mixed with outsiders. It was too late for me.

We survived on my widow's pension and Laurence's meagre wages, but as he was one of few men in his department, he was promoted quickly and steadily. Within four years he was in management, supervising a group of four or five. He made friends easily, and socialized after work on Fridays. I wondered at his ability to socialize. I never had it – not after the accident, anyway, but perhaps that is because I was home-schooled thereafter. I knew that Laurence did not enjoy his last schooldays, but that was all tied up with a sudden move to a new school, his father's death, exam pressure and discovering the body of that girl. He certainly retreated into his shell after that. Thankfully, that put paid to his relationship with the awful Helen girl. I knew Laurence would never commit to a girl like that, so when they split up I was relieved, although disturbed to discover that she had broken up with him, after cheating on him with another boy. Bizarrely, they even stayed in touch after that and she still called to the house from time to time. She was training to be a nurse. I was astonished that a girl like that would enter a caring profession, but she boasted about moving out of home and annoyed me by suggesting that Laurence should get a flat. Laurence did not want to move out, nor could he afford to keep two households, so thankfully it was out of the question.

Laurence started dating a girl from work, a quiet nervous mousy thing called Bridget. I could tell that she liked him more than he liked her, that the relationship was quite one-sided. She certainly phoned him more than he phoned her, and when I answered the phone, she whispered and said 'please' and 'thank you' more times than were called for. But he started to exercise and lose weight again, and I wondered if he was really doing it to impress this mouse. He showed me a photograph of her once. She was quite average-looking, and a heavy fringe covered her eyes. I relaxed more after that. He would not leave me for her. Still, I helped him with his diet.

Acquiring or giving birth to another baby was now out of the question. I knew that there was no possibility of it. I had passed fifty. Laurence was an adult now, no doubt about it, but I was secure enough to know that he would not leave me. Laurence knew that I could never manage on my own. He would stay with me here, in Avalon.

11. Laurence

I never spent more time in the kitchen than I had to, which was difficult considering my love of food, but I rearranged the cupboards and moved a lot of it into the pantry with the fridge. I wanted to brick up the window so that I wouldn't have to look out on that . . . tomb, but Mum wouldn't let me. The compromise was a blind that is permanently lowered. It admits low-level light. We cannot employ a gardener, and not just because we can't afford to, so I tend to the garden and the grave with great reluctance.

It is a terrible, terrible thing to live with, this knowledge of a murder – and the evidence right here – but now it is too late for us to do anything. It is five years since I discovered it. Since it can be established that I am the person who paved it and put the bird bath on top, I am implicated in the cover-up.

After I discovered Annie Doyle, I became fearful of everything. If I could not trust my own father, who could I trust? Not Helen. Helen dumped me the day after we got our Leaving Cert results. The circumstances were sordid. She had sex with the boy in my class who had bullied me the most. He made sure I knew about it. I didn't care that much by then. I didn't really care about anything. I was humiliated, but she was never the love of my life. I didn't think I would ever have a love life.

I didn't stick to Granny's diet and exercise regime. I became obese again, revolting and disgusting. I caught my reflection in shop windows sometimes and turned away, sickened by the sight.

Going to university was no longer an option for me, but it may have been a blessing. I liked working in the dole office. Apollo House was right in the heart of the city, surrounded by shops and offices and pubs. At first I shadowed others as they showed me how to go through the various application forms with the claimants and then how those claims were processed. There was an awful lot of paperwork involved. I didn't really get to process any actual claims for the first few months. I did a lot of carbon-copying, and delivering files from one section to the other, and fetching teas and coffees. At the end of the process, our office issued a giro, which could be cashed in the post office across the road. This was all tightly controlled and well managed. Every section of about eight staff handled about 500 claims. The section was made up of two clerical assistants and five clerical officers, one of whom was the supervisor. Our supervisor was middle-aged Brian, a widower with three grown-up children – he didn't appear to be very clever, although he was very nice to all of us.

In the beginning I was scared of the unemployed. I'd heard about them from my father, who had referred to them as layabouts and spongers. I had the impression that they were all criminals. Although a few of the people we dealt with were just out of prison, most were ordinary people who had lost jobs or were looking for them.

Unemployment rates were high and all kinds of people were turning up to sign on. Middle-class housewives abandoned by their husbands, college dropouts, winos and junkies. The father of a former classmate, and our old butcher, who had been put out of business by the new supermarket – they joined the type of people who had never been employed. Queuing up for a government cheque was the great leveller, and yet they didn't get to go for a drink together afterwards and discuss how their day had been. Unemployment was something they experienced on their own in their long empty days at home, or mooching around the park, drinking tea in cheap cafés and trying to make it last. I understood that loneliness without ever having experienced it.

The claimants were usually nice to me – I guess because they thought I was making the decision whether to give them money or not. We did have a little power, and if someone was particularly aggressive I learned there were ways of delaying a claim, or 'losing' the paperwork, if you were so inclined.

In a few months, I learned far more about the world than my years of schooling had given me. And I had real friends in a way I had never had before. Mum didn't understand that, and it was only when I was out in the world that I realized how unusual she was in that respect. She had no friends.

Work was good for me. My job was not difficult and my colleagues were very nice. I almost couldn't believe my luck. I got to go and spend every day with a bunch of people who didn't bully or demean me, doing work that didn't exactly tax me, and at the end of every week I got money for it. Not a lot of money, but I didn't have rent or a mortgage to pay, so there was almost enough to pay our household bills and have the occasional cinema trip and a few drinks after work most Friday nights before catching the last bus home. The section I worked on was made up of all kinds of people of all ages.

Dominic was a gum-chewing DJ at his soccer-club disco who couldn't say a sentence without the words 'know what I mean?' tacked on the end. He didn't want to be thirty, I think. He'd have preferred to be my age. Chinese Sally was a little older than me. She was actually half Korean, half Irish, but had grown up in Tralee. Everyone still referred to her as Chinese Sally and she had got bored with correcting them. Evelyn was the oldest of us all. She was a bitter, chain-smoking alcoholic with a line in filthy jokes and no-good ex-boyfriends. She had grown up in the inner city. Pretty Jane was my age. She was the first lesbian I had ever met. She wasn't at all what I expected. She had long hair, and wore skirts. Arnold was a 24-year-old father of three who didn't like children – 'I love my boys, right? I just can't stand them.' He was always broke and miserable. He was a grade above me, but clearly wasn't earning enough to keep a family of five.

We were a strange mix and yet we all got along. Not one person mentioned my weight. Everybody's quirks were accepted, though they did call me Posh Boy because of my south County Dublin accent, but in an affectionate way. It seemed to me that none of us had had a childhood dream of working in an unemployment benefit office. We had all just landed there from our different walks of life and would probably pass the time there until retirement.

In June 1982, even though I had only been in the job seven months, I was promoted from clerical assistant to clerical officer (now I was allowed to talk to claimants on my own!). There was a small pay increase. Sally was furious. 'Just because you're a man!' she said. She had been there for nearly two years without promotion, but I couldn't help my gender. Mum and I were just about keeping our heads above water.

There were girls in the office who were perfectly nice, and reasonable-looking, and while they didn't run screaming when I talked to them, neither did they give any hint of encouragement. I didn't feel romantically attracted to them at all. I was still in touch with Helen, who had a succession of boyfriends and was never stuck for company. Helen and I had a strange kind of friendship. As awfully obnoxious as she was, part of me liked her honesty, her ability to say what she thought without fear. If she'd discovered her dad had killed someone, she'd probably have beaten the shit out of him before she called the guards. She took a proprietorial interest in my sex life.

'Why don't you ask out a fat girl?' she said. It was her idea of being pragmatic. 'They probably feel as self-conscious as you do. You need to get into the dating game soon or you'll be stuck with your crazy mother for the rest of your life.'

I didn't like the way Helen always referred to my mother as unstable or mad. It wasn't fair.

'I'll tell you what's not fair,' insisted Helen, 'it's not fair that your mum has never suggested that you could move out on your own. She seems to expect you to look after her for the rest of her life. She could sell that fecking mansion and you could both get apartments and live your own lives. It's ridiculous the way you carry on – as if she's your wife rather than your mother!'

This was a sore point with me. Even people in work had said the same thing. They just didn't get it. I liked living at home. Avalon was huge. My mother and I got on well, and I wasn't heartless enough to leave her on her own. Mum wasn't like other women. She would have hated the idea of an apartment. There was no reason for me to change my domestic circumstances. Besides, I didn't want to leave her alone with the corpse beyond the kitchen window. Though, strangely, it seemed to bother me more than her. Maybe in the future, if I fell in love and wanted to get married, I might consider it, but that was extremely unlikely.

At the end of the summer of 1984, two things happened.

A new girl, Bridget Gough, had joined the office. I didn't notice her until Jane informed me that someone had a crush on me. Apparently, I had held the door open for Bridget one day, and another time I'd got up to give her a seat in the break room. Bridget was eighteen, and worked as a secretary to one of the managers, Mr Monroe. She had indirectly asked questions about me, Jane said – where I lived, if I was single. I was stunned. Somebody had a crush *on me*? Jane pointed out the girl to me. She was normal-looking with shoulder-length brown hair. She was a little overweight perhaps, and had a bad squint, but she was not a freak like me.

Jane and Sally were determined to play Cupid, and inveigled everyone else into their childish plot. It was mortifying. They invited her to Mulligan's with us one Friday, insisting that she should sit beside me. As soon as we'd had our first round, Arnold went to the bar and returned with drinks for Bridget and me only, as everyone else made excuses that they had to go, had things to do. I was convinced they were just going to decamp to the nearest pub. Bridget and I sat mutely. I tried to be polite.

'So, do you like the job so far?'

'Yes!' She beamed at me.

Silence.

'And Mr Monroe treats you well?'

'Yes!'

Silence.

'Do you have any hobbies?' I remembered writing a similar question to a German pen pal when I was ten.

'Yes! Photography,' she said, still grinning inanely at me with her good eye. Her bad eye looked at the nicotine-stained ceiling.

I think she realized that she needed to pull her weight in the conversation then. She spoke very fast, almost without taking a breath.

'I love taking photos of just ordinary things, you know? Leaves, raindrops on glass, the way a chair is positioned in a room, or a bin lorry at the end of the street. When I was fourteen, I won a camera in a school raffle. It was quite a good one and I've been taking photos ever since.'

'That's good.'

'You were the first person to speak to me in the office, you know. I'd been there two weeks and nobody apart from Mr Monroe and Geraldine had said anything to me, and they were just talking about work stuff, you know the way it is, and then on the fifth of June – I remember because it was my birthday – on the fifth of June, you came out of the gents and I came out of the ladies at the same time and you bumped into me and you said, "Excuse me." It was so nice of you. I really appreciated that.'

Bridget was clearly someone who'd never been the focus of much attention in her life.

'And then, one day in the break room, you offered me a seat beside Sally and then she started talking to me, and really, if it wasn't for you, nobody would have talked to me at all!'

I knew what it felt like to be ignored, but I wasn't sure what it felt like not to be noticed. I imagine they are very different experiences.

'Right. Well, I'm glad you're settling in. Do you live nearby?'

'Not too far. I'm in a flat in Rathmines. It's a bedsit really. I'm from Athlone.'

'Can I have your phone number?' It was the least I could do.

Bridget dived into her bag, took out a pen and scribbled her name and number on to a beer mat. Instead of a dot over the 'i' she'd drawn a little love heart.

'Thanks a million,' she said. If only needy were attractive. I made a show of putting the beer mat into my breast pocket. She leaned forward for a kiss on the cheek, but I deliberately misunderstood her and pulled her scarf up where it had slipped on her shoulder. I got up to leave, saying I'd call her. She gathered her bags and followed me to the door. She looked at me expectantly and I knew I was supposed to say *when* I'd call her, but I did the cowardly thing and waved goodbye.

Earlier that day, the other notable incident had happened. I was sitting at the Fresh Claims desk, going through all the forms with the new claimants, when a man sat down in the chair in front of me. I didn't look up, as I was noting something on a previous claimant's form, and asked him to bear with me for a moment. He handed his application form across the desk without saying anything. I finished with the previous form and filed it and then faced this new claimant. He was a heavyset man, and I didn't recognize him straight away. Even when I saw his name at the top of the form, it didn't immediately click with me, but when I looked him in the eye, I knew him. Gerry Doyle (Gerald on the application form and his documentation), father of Annie. How many times had I pored over those newspaper cuttings of the press conference? In the intervening years he had lost some hair, and what was left of it was silver. His face was ruddier and more bloated-looking than I recalled. I coughed and shifted in my chair. I excused myself and went out the back door of the office for a gulp of air. I wanted to throw up, but I forced myself to calm down and return to the desk. I noted all his details on the form. I imagined I could see the sorrow in him, the loss of Annie. He was separated from his wife, Pauline.

'Any dependants?' I asked.

He inhaled deeply and then said, 'No. Two daughters, all grown up, Annie and Karen.'

As I talked to him, I felt his sense of shame at being unemployed for the first time in his life. I did everything I could to put him at ease. 'It's not your fault,' I said with false confidence. 'It's just the way things are for the moment, but the economy will pick up again soon.'

He smiled at me. I got his P45, birth certificate, address, his tax ID number, his employment history. He needed help with the application form. He admitted he couldn't read or write very well and had always done manual labour. Gerry had been apprenticed as a baker in Fallon's in 1966 and had worked there ever since. Before that he'd been a road labourer for Dublin Corporation. Old Mr Fallon who owned the bakery had been losing money on the place for a long time, and with his failing health he could no longer work there himself. It couldn't be sold as a going concern as there were no buyers. Mr Fallon had relinquished the lease on the building and shut up shop. Gerry's wife had left him to live with her sister, and Gerry stayed on in the council-owned family home on Pearse Street, not far from our office. He had no savings. He had never earned a lot, and all of it had been spent on his home or his family. Since the separation, he had always given Pauline exactly half of his earnings. She had worked in a newsagent's until her moods forced her into early retirement.

'Her moods?' I asked.

'Yeah, she gets upset a lot.'

'I'm sorry to hear that.' I was genuinely sorry, and I knew well the source of Pauline Doyle's depression. I wanted to say something to him, to let him know that I understood something of his pain, but I said nothing.

When everything was done, he stood up and we shook hands. 'Thanks,' he said, 'for making this so easy. I've been dreading this day for months, you know.'

'I understand. Nobody *wants* to be here.'

As I left the pub that evening, instead of heading to the chip shop, I wandered down towards Pearse Street and stood for half an hour outside Gerry's address. I had memorized it from the claim form. It was a 1960s redbrick corporation house. Two bedrooms. As he was a single man living in a family home, technically he should have been rehoused, but I felt a responsibility to him so I had ticked the one-bedroom box on the form. Gerry had had enough upheaval in his life.

All the windows were grimy. Rubbish had been wind-whipped into the corner of the doorway. Nobody came or went. I'm not even sure he was in, but it unsettled me, to watch his home and imagine him inside, staring at his television, perhaps trying not to think about his lost daughter.

I headed for the bus stop, but realized that I really didn't want to go home. Not yet. I passed a phone box. Digging for change in my pocket, I took the beer mat out and dialled the number. It rang about nine times before it was answered. I quickly pushed Button A as the coins chinked their way into the machine.

'Yeah?' said a disembodied voice – older, female, but not Bridget.

'Is Bridget there, please?'

A long sigh. 'She's in Flat 4 at the top of the house. You'll have to wait.' The phone clanked as it was dropped on to a hard surface, and I heard footsteps trudging slowly up the stairs. I deposited another five pence into the slot and waited.

'Hello? Dad?' She sounded worried.

'Hi, Bridget. It's me, Laurence.'

Silence. I couldn't afford silences. Another coin into the slot.

'I was just wondering if you'd like me to come over.'

'Here? Now?' I could hear an edge of hysteria in her voice.

I looked at my watch. It was 10.30 p.m.

'Well, if it's too late . . .'

'No, of course not. Oh yes, do call over!'

'Only if you're sure?' I wondered if I'd get the address out of her before I had to drop in another coin.

I was forced to ask.

By the time I reached her front door twenty minutes later, I was completely single-minded. When she opened it, I kissed her on the mouth and pushed her into the hallway. I'm not sure what I would have done if she had resisted, but she seemed as eager as I was. We climbed the four flights of stairs to a tiny flat. Photos covered the walls, strange photos of a vagrant begging on the street, a child's hand, a signpost, the hubcap of a car. They made it all the more claustrophobic. There was a single bed in one corner, a fridge and hob in the other. I felt like a giant. As powerful as a giant. Seven minutes later, I came successfully inside her. Eyes squeezed tightly shut, trying not to think of Annie Doyle. And hating myself for it.

'Thanks a million!' she said.

I opened my eyes to the reality of naked Bridget. Her

complexion was heightened by the exertion, but her body felt smooth, her breasts full and firm, her long limbs entwined around my own lumpen flanks. She had met my enthusiasm with her own and seemed grateful for the experience. She covered herself immediately with a blanket. I hid under the sheet.

'I'm sorry I was so quick.'

'I take that as a compliment,' she said. 'I wasn't sure, you see, in the pub earlier – even after you asked for my number, I wasn't sure. But now I know you were thinking about me too.'

I tried to feel guilty, but where was the harm? We had both got what we wanted. She was sitting in profile, so all I could see was her good eye. In the light of the thirty-watt bulb there was something appealing about her vitality, her innocence, but mostly her sudden confidence. She picked up her camera, took a photo of my shoe.

I emerged from my trance-like state. I needed to go home. I picked up the clothes I had frenziedly abandoned, and turned away to put them on, feeling again the shame of my size that I'd felt in Helen's bedroom years earlier. Bridget walked up behind me and kissed my shoulder before reaching for her robe.

'Do you have to go?' she said, disappointed.

'Yes, my mum . . . she doesn't like . . .'

Bridget laughed. 'You're so funny!' she said. 'So sweet!'

I knew I wasn't either of those things.

As I reached for the door handle, she said, 'See you . . .?' leaving the question hanging.

'Monday,' I said. 'See you Monday.'

I didn't look back, but when I walked down the stairs

and out of the front door into the orange glow of lamplight, I could feel her uncertainty. I had no idea what had just happened. Was I sick in the head? What was going on between Bridget and me? Lust had led me to her door. Apart from that I wasn't sure of anything either.

The next morning I informed my mother that I was going on a diet and that I was going to take up regular exercise. I asked her to exclude bread, crisps, sweets and potatoes from the shopping list.

'Oh, Laurie, that is such a great idea,' she said enthusiastically. 'We can get some diet books from the library today and make a plan.' Then she paused for a moment. 'Are you trying to impress a girl?'

'I might be,' I said.

I was aware that Mum had some anxieties about my dating girls, but I wasn't sure if it was about me getting hurt or about her being left alone.

'Is it a girl from work?' she asked.

'Yes.'

I dusted down the weighing scales that sat on top of the bathroom cabinet and stood on them as gingerly as an almost-sixteen-stone man could. I had work to do.

I walked five miles that weekend, having barely walked the length of myself since Granny had moved out three years earlier. I even tried some press-ups, but ended up straining a muscle in my shoulder.

The next Friday night after drinks in Mulligan's, we had sex again in her dim and tidy bedsit, and though it was less fierce, less urgent, my eyes were still tightly shut as I refused to see Bridget smiling up at me. I used condoms that

Arnold had given me. I would have to source them myself after this, from my sleazy barber probably. In the following weeks, I sat with Bridget at break times and we sometimes had lunch together and went out at weekends. I didn't exactly keep my word about taking things slowly, but it seemed that Bridget didn't want me to either.

I also followed Gerry Doyle, waited outside his house, sussed out his watering hole, where he bought his daily groceries. The pub he went to, Scanlon's, was pretty close to our office. Over the course of a few weeks, I managed to make Scanlon's our new regular Friday-night spot. It was a traditional Dublin pub where the clientele were a mixed bunch of older locals who drank Guinness and smoked Major in packs of ten. They served toasted sandwiches, which was the latest fad, and that was quite a draw. Alcoholic Evelyn was the hardest to persuade. She was a creature of habit, and food would never be as big an attraction as a pub where she knew the owner, his father, his dog and when the wallpaper had last been replaced. She was resistant to change, and as she was our lead drinker it took a bit of work, but when she realized that she was about to turn into a solo drinker if she didn't come with us, she changed her tune. I saw Gerry in there from time to time and we nodded acknowledgement at each other, but I wanted to know more about him, I wanted to be in his company. The nods turned to salutations on my part, which he graciously returned, and when it was his signing-on day, I always volunteered to run that desk so that we could exchange a few words. Always courteous, always friendly. I felt I should do more for him, though, so I amended his claim to make it appear as if he had two dependent children and sent it to the Children's Allowance section. I used my forgery skills to make it look like Dominic's writing.

When Gerry spotted me in Scanlon's three weeks later, he asked for a quiet word. 'Someone gave me a rise,' he said.

I pretended not to know what he was talking about.

'I got an extra thirty pounds in my dole last week.'

'Did you? Well, our staff make mistakes all the time. If I was you, I'd keep that to myself.'

'Really? Will I not get into trouble over it, like?'

'Not at all, not if it was our fault. I'll be turning a blind eye anyway.' I winked at him and tapped my nose. He offered to buy me a pint, but I declined and rejoined Bridget and the others. I had done a small thing to make him happy. As he raised his glass to me from the corner of the bar, I felt good.

I stuck to my weight-loss programme, and gradually the chins began to disappear again and my feet came into view. At first, I had walked everywhere. Running was out of the question because I wasn't able for it and people would laugh at me. I did exercises in my bedroom and then Mum bought the Jane Fonda *Workout* book for me for Christmas, which was pleasing in many ways. After a short time, very strangely and without too much effort, my appetite nearly disappeared. I was suddenly a bundle of energy with too much vitality for sleep. I got up earlier and went to bed later. I can't explain what happened. It was as if a switch in my brain had flipped. I was eating a quarter of what I had been used to. Which was probably what a normal person should eat.

‘Is it my imagination, or are you thinner than you were when we got together?’ asked Bridget one Saturday morning, post-coital. I hadn’t told anyone in work of my weight-loss plans, though my reduced lunch portions had been noted. In the six months we had been dating, she had never once mentioned my weight. I appreciated that. It was as if she had never noticed. I was grateful.

I was delighted by her question. ‘Yes, I think I have,’ I said. ‘I’m trying to be healthier anyway.’

‘Well, I think you’re very handsome, no matter what you weigh.’

We weren’t the type of couple to be romantic with each other or to pay compliments like that, so I was a little taken aback. It dawned on me that I should then say something positive about her. ‘You’re pretty cute too.’

She beamed.

I had developed a sense of obligation to her and she could be good company sometimes, but I felt no genuine love for her, just a warmth and a fondness. I hoped it could become something more real.

Of course, one night we bumped into Helen when we came out of the cinema. She was on her way from the pub with a gang, quite drunk.

‘Well, for fuck’s sake, look who it is! Where’s the rest of you?’ she bellowed.

I introduced Bridget as my girlfriend.

‘Girlfriend?’ said Helen with an unnecessary degree of incredulity.

‘Yes,’ said Bridget confidently.

‘Riiight,’ she said, winking at me, ‘so you’re getting the ride, then? Sure, come on back to my flat, I’m having a party. I just graduated, I'm a fucking nurse! Can you believe it!'

I politely declined but she insisted on writing down her address and phone number in case we changed our minds, and then she ran off, roaring up the street after her friends.

'Who was that awful girl?' said Bridget.

'Just an old neighbour. She is awful, isn't she?'

We laughed and I kissed Bridget on the mouth, grateful that she was no Helen. Everything was going well between us. We were a solid couple.

Until I met Karen in August 1985.

12. Karen

I waited a few weeks after Yvonne told me what James had said about a murder suspect. I guess I was learning to accept the truth. It wasn't entirely a surprise, but thinking it and knowing it were two different things. Annie was dead.

O'Toole was still in the same job. My letter of complaint had been ignored all those years ago, or maybe they were never going to take seriously a complaint from the sister of a junkie prostitute. He knew about my letter though. He smiled broadly in my face when I went to see him.

'Well, there you are now. You just get prettier all the time.'

I smiled sweetly at him. I had gained confidence after a few months of modelling. I was prepared to use it.

'Declan' – I used his first name – 'I just wanted to check if there were any further developments in my sister's case.'

'Do you now? As I recall, you weren't too happy with us before. As I recall, you complained about how I made my enquiries.'

'I know, I'm sorry, it was a difficult time. I was on edge.'

'You sure were.'

'I was sorry to hear that Detective Mooney died.'

That seemed to touch him, and he passed a hand over his eyes.

'A very sad business. He was a good lad, young James.'

'He was. I believe he had a suspect in mind for my sister's murder?'

O'Toole leaned back in his chair. 'I don't know about that.'

'Yes, someone that you and he questioned.'

'And who told you that?'

I shook my head, not prepared to give away my source.

'That was all in Mooney's head. He had a big imagination.'

'I'd like to know who the suspect was. I heard he was a high-powered guy.'

'Ah, Karen, Karen, Karen, you'll have to stop this now. It's been what? Five years? There was never a suspect, just a few notions.'

'What about the car?'

'What about it?'

'The Jaguar car that was seen outside Annie's flat.'

'Yes?'

'Did you ever track it down?'

'No.'

'Will you tell me what type of Jaguar it was? What colour?'

He lifted his hands in the air, in a gesture that said he was not going to help me.

'You should never bite the hand that feeds you. You threw a drink in my face.'

My fixed smile faded now. He was enjoying this as if it was some game.

'Fuck you.'

He laughed. 'There's the little ginger alley cat now, hiding behind the perfect make-up and the hairdo. You don't look as cheap as you did, but I reckon I could still have you for less than twenty quid. High-class hooking is still hooking.'

I could hear him laughing at me as I walked away.

'He's dead anyway,' he shouted at me.

I turned back. 'Who?'

'The fella Mooney thought had done it. Died six weeks later. So I guess you're even.'

'Who was it?'

He leaned back in the chair again with his hands behind his head and nodded towards his crotch. 'That info will cost you.'

This time I kept walking until I was home and had shaken off the anger and fury I felt at our so-called justice system.

Even if he was dead, I still wanted to know the murderer's name. At home, I went to the heap of newspaper cuttings I had kept from the time of Annie's disappearance. Some of the reports mentioned the vintage car. I could start there. I rang the fella who serviced the vans for the dry-cleaner's and, without giving any reasons, asked him what he knew about vintage top-end cars. Nothing, as it turned out. But he had a friend who restored them. He'd ring him and see what he could find out.

Dessie came home, wanting to know why I'd been ringing his mechanic. News travelled fast, it seemed. I told him all that had happened, though I played down O'Toole's insults. Still, I thought Dessie would be angry too, to know that there was, or had been, a suspect. But he seemed to be pissed off by the news.

'Sure, that's only speculation, guesswork, like. Why

can't you just let it be? You're not feckin' Nancy Drew. If the cops couldn't find him, then what makes you think you can?'

'Because I want to know *why*, that's the difference.'

'Maybe the reason why is awful. Maybe you're better off not knowing.'

'I just need to find out who he was.'

'And what are you going to do, dig him up?'

I could scarcely believe that Dessie was being so mean. How could he not understand?

'I . . . I can't just forget about Annie. There was a suspect, a possible murderer out there, who could have done it before, destroyed somebody else's family!'

'And he's dead!'

'We don't even know that for sure. I don't trust O'Toole. He's an arsehole.'

'Would you listen to yourself? You are talking about going out to track down a dead murderer. Do you know how stupid that sounds?'

That was the biggest row we had ever had. I grabbed my bag and coat and went out, slamming the door behind me. I had to tell Ma and Da. They needed to know. I rang Ma in Mayo, but her sister said she was at Mass. This wasn't unusual. Since Annie had been taken from us, Ma had taken to churchgoing in an obsessed way, going to Mass two or three times a day and feeling guilty when she wasn't there, praying for Annie's return. I got the bus to Da's place.

Da had been laid off the previous summer and was now drinking away his dole money every night. I didn't think he was an alcoholic as such; he just went to the pub for company. He was lonely without workmates or family.

He used to bring the *Evening Press* with him and pretend to be reading it. He was fierce ashamed of not being able to read properly. I think that's why he was so hard on Annie when she was in school. He didn't want her to fail the same way he had.

When there was no answer at his door, it wasn't such a leap of the imagination to find him in Scanlon's. He was delighted to see me, or as delighted as three pints of Guinness on a Friday afternoon would allow him to be.

'My beautiful daughter,' he said, throwing an arm around me. 'Isn't she gorgeous?' he said to the barman, who nodded at me in embarrassment.

Maybe I should have waited until he was sober to tell him all that had happened. I hadn't told either of my parents about any of the developments since Yvonne's news about her son, but now I sat Da down at a corner table of the bar and told him all the latest information about Annie, leaving out O'Toole's lewd suggestions about me.

Da listened to it and said nothing for a moment, but then his shoulders started to shake and his eyes watered. 'It's all my fault. I should have let her keep the baby, kept them safe at home.'

We were interrupted by a young fella in a corduroy jacket. I was aware that he'd been sitting at a table near us with a few others.

'Is everything OK?' he said gently. I was flustered, embarrassed, and Da inhaled deeply to get his sobs under control.

'Thanks,' I said, 'we're fine, just some family business.'

Da put out his hand. 'I'm sorry, we're grand, just a

personal thing. Karen, this lad works at the dole office where I sign on just up the road. What's your name, son?'

'Laurence,' said the man. 'Sorry for interrupting. I just noticed you were upset.'

I was a bit annoyed by his interrupting, but when he offered a handshake and I looked in his face, I saw genuine concern.

'Laurence here has been very good to me, Karen. Karen is my daughter.'

'Hi.'

'Hi. Look, I'll leave you to it. Sorry.' He backed away and rejoined the table of what I assumed were his workmates.

'I'm sorry, love, it's just a shock. Even after all this time, I thought she might walk in here one day with that cheeky look on her face, wanting money off me. I suppose, deep down, I knew it. And O'Toole said yer man is dead? Well, that's something, I suppose.'

When Da put it like that, I realized that O'Toole must have been telling the truth about the suspect being dead. I knew from Yvonne that if James Mooney had good reason for suspicion, he would have followed up the case himself. Mooney had only died two years ago. The suspect had been dead five years, according to O'Toole. How did he die? Where was he buried, and more importantly, if he had murdered her, where was Annie's body?

'I don't think your mother will be able for it. Can you not tell her?'

Da was right. Ma had her faith to protect her, however misguided it might be. There was no reason to tell her. It wouldn't change anything.

*

I took Da back to his house and made him coffee. I asked him if I could stay the night in my old room. Our old room. Mine and Annie's. He raised his eyebrows.

'Everything all right with Dessie?'

'I don't want to talk about it.'

'Did he hurt you? If he laid a finger –'

'No, nothing like that. I'll go home tomorrow. I just need a bit of space.'

I found an old nightie of Ma's and went into the bedroom. I turned on the radio to stop myself from thinking about the way Annie had filled this room with her personality. They were playing that song again, 'Feed the World'. There had been a big concert a few weeks previously in London to raise money for famine victims in Ethiopia. The famine was all over the television news these days. They showed footage of tiny children with sticks for bones and bloated bellies full of air. We had done a charity fashion show to raise money. Some of the other models went to the Live Aid concert in London. I'd said to Dessie about trying to get tickets and going over for a weekend, but he went on again about saving money for a house and starting a family.

I'd got married too young. Yvonne was right. And it wasn't the age difference that was the problem between us. Dessie was suffocating me. He just wasn't the right guy for me. I'd known it for a long time, but hadn't wanted to admit it. Aside from the Annie thing, he wanted to know where all my modelling jobs were, what kind of venues, what type of clothes I'd be wearing. He demanded to see the Polaroids from the shoot immediately afterwards, and he wanted to meet Yvonne. So far, I had been able to put him off. I felt like it was too late to do anything about my marriage. Could I find a way to fall in love with my husband again?

I thought about ringing him to let him know where I was, but it would have meant getting up again and going downstairs to the phone in the hall, disturbing Da. As I pulled the curtains, I looked down into the street below and for a second I thought I saw that man from Da's dole office looking up at our house, but he soon moved off along the street.

I went home the next day. Dessie was furious. 'You could have rung me. I was worried sick. You should know, of all people, what it's like when someone goes missing!'

I had been prepared to be sorry, but this drove me up the wall. 'I did not "go missing". If you were really worried, you'd have rung my da. And Annie did not "go missing" either. She was murdered. And the guards have known it for years. They just didn't think it important enough to tell us.'

Dessie took hold of my shoulders to hug me, and I let him because there was nothing else I could do.

'I'm sorry, love.'

'It's OK, let's just forget about it,' I said, only I wasn't going to forget about it.

I had a few jobs over the following weeks that kept me fairly busy, but I tracked down and met one of the girls who had actually seen the old Jaguar. She had been living in the shared house with Annie. I remembered she worked in H. Williams on Baggot Street, so I found her there. She was frosty with me, and said she would never have stayed in the house if she had known what was going on there. She was referring to the prostitution, I assume. She had already told the guards everything she knew, she said. I had managed to charm some old car brochures out of a gamey old high-end car dealer, and I got her to look at them. We narrowed it down to the Jaguar Sedan brand produced between 1950 and 1960. She said she'd only spotted the driver twice but that he had looked 'prosperous', had worn a pinstripe suit and a trilby hat pulled low over his eyes. She couldn't recall anything else particular about him: he had been regular height, no beard or moustache that she could remember. She couldn't guess at his age as she hadn't seen his face. She said she'd seen the car parked around the corner from the house more times than she'd seen him, over a period of about six months. She'd seen him get out of it once, and the other time she'd seen him saying goodbye to Annie at the doorway. She had never seen him or the car since Annie's disappearance, though she had continued to live at that address for a year afterwards. I asked her if she had ever seen other men coming and going to Annie's flat and she said no, that she had assumed Annie conducted her 'business' elsewhere.

I chased up Dessie's mechanic about his friend who restored vintage cars, but he told me that Dessie had told him not to worry about it. Dessie was making decisions for me again. Without consulting Dessie, I insisted on getting the number of the man, who was called Frankie and had a garage out in Santry. I rang him to ask if I could meet him to ask a few questions, saying that I was looking for a particular car to use on a photo shoot. He wasn't as helpful as I'd hoped. He was too busy flirting with me. He guessed there were about twenty cars fitting that description in Dublin. He had only ever serviced two of those vehicles, one for a car museum and one for an octogenarian who lived in County Offaly. He gave me some names and numbers of other mechanics who specialized in old cars.

I had no further luck with those. One of them led me a merry dance, and neither of them had any helpful information. I was hitting a brick wall. Dessie was getting suspicious about where I was going and what I was doing, and I resented having to lie to him.

Early on a Saturday morning in September he reached for me in bed, and I realized that I couldn't stay with Dessie any longer. The previous evening he had quizzed me about numbers called on our itemized phone bill. I didn't even know our bill was itemized, and it would never have occurred to me to check it. I had lied, badly, and he confronted me with the news that he had rung the numbers and found out they were all mechanics and car dealers. There was a row, and again he had told me I was stupid and obsessed and ridiculous. For the sake of keeping the peace, I had apologized and backed down and we had kissed and made up. But the next morning, I woke up feeling angry. Angry at myself, mostly, for not standing my ground. I turned away from his kisses.

'It's not working, Dessie. Us, I mean.'

'Ah, Karen, don't be like that. Sure, I've forgotten all about it.'

'Yeah, until the next time. I'm sick of it. You're checking up on me all the time. Turning up out of the blue to collect me from jobs.'

He sat up and leaned on one arm.

'You're embarrassed by the van, is that it?'

'Christ, Dessie, that's not it at all. You don't even know how you're controlling me all the time. Checking my phone calls? For God's sake.'

'I wouldn't have to check if you were honest with me.'

I raised my voice now, my frustration levels growing. 'I'm not able to be honest with you, 'cos you go off the deep end. You have practically ordered me to forget about my sister!'

'Not this again. Jesus.'

He got out of bed and went into the bathroom, and I waited, listening to the long stream of piss, grateful for a moment to collect myself. By the time he came back, I had calmed myself for the storm I knew I had to face.

'I don't want to be married to you any more.'

It happened so fast that I didn't see it coming. There was just a brief flash of his hand towards my face. I felt the air whip past my cheek. He dropped his arm at the very last second so that no contact was made. Dessie was handy with his fists. If he had meant to hurt me, he could have. Dessie didn't want to hurt me. It was the opposite.

He cried and begged and apologized. He said he worshipped me and couldn't live without me. He was terrified that I'd go down the wrong route like Annie. While I'd been at the dry-cleaner's, he'd known where I was nine to five every day, he'd known who I was mixing with, but he was worried about me modelling, dressing up for strangers. He didn't know what kind of people I was meeting.

There were stories in the *Sun* about models and drug addiction, but he didn't understand that the Dublin scene was not London. I had heard about London supermodels using cocaine and champagne like it was going out of fashion, but Dublin might as well have been another planet, certainly an earlier decade. Most of the girls were middle-class types straight out of school, waiting for a husband, or earning their way through university. They were younger than me and hid the fact that they smoked from their parents. I had never been offered drugs. Or champagne for that matter. I had explained all this to Dessie, but it seemed he was as obsessed with Annie as I was, although in a different way. He was afraid that his wife was going to become a drug addict, prostitute and murder victim. He said divorce was illegal anyway, and I told him I didn't need a certificate to leave him.

That evening, I packed a bag and moved back home to Da's. My father was upset, but once I assured him that the break-up was my decision, I think he was secretly delighted to have me home.

'I'm not going back, Da.'

'And sure, why would you, with a perfectly good bedroom lying empty here?'

In the years since Annie had gone, my father had become a nicer person, albeit a nicer person with a potential drink problem.

Dessie phoned frequently and called to the house to try to have peace talks. but my overwhelming feeling, aside from guilt and fear for the future, was one of relief. I no longer had to account for my movements or my actions. I no longer had to make excuses as to why now wasn't a good time to get pregnant. I no longer had to hand over my earnings for the 'house fund'. Dessie could keep what I had already contributed. I didn't want anything from him. I just wanted our relationship to be over. Ma was very upset when I told her on the phone.

'You had a good lad there. Hasn't our family name been dragged through enough muck?' She thought I was having my head turned by the modelling, and no amount of talking could persuade her otherwise. 'He's been so good to you and you throw it back in his face. When I heard about this modelling lark, I knew there was going to be trouble.'

I got the train to Mayo to see her, but she spent most of the weekend in the church in Westport, praying for my immortal soul no doubt. When she did finally speak to me, she blamed herself for setting a bad example by leaving Da.

'It's nothing to do with you, Ma. Honestly!'

She rattled her rosary beads.

The arrangement of living back at home suited Da well, because I could contribute financially to the household and do some of the cleaning that men just don't notice needs doing. He told his friend in the dole office, but apparently Laurence was very understanding and said it wouldn't affect Da's payments. I was earning good money and could give Da a few extra bob now and then, even though I knew he'd probably end up spending it in Scanlon's. I made it clear to Da that I was only staying with him as a temporary measure. When the dust had settled, I was going to look for my own place to rent. But for now, I just needed to wallow a bit and think about my future and how I would continue to look for Annie's killer, even if he was dead. Da didn't like to talk about her. His guilt, I suppose.

I joined Da a few times in Scanlon's, and that guy Laurence from the dole office was often there with his girlfriend. He was very nice to Da, very courteous, like. The rest of his crowd didn't mix with us much and stayed up the other end of the bar, but Laurence always came over to say hello.

One night he introduced me to his girlfriend. I liked Bridget immediately. She was incredibly shy and nervous, and my heart always goes out to people like that because it's not so long since I was like that too. She had a bad squint in one eye, so she kept her head angled to one side. I remembered trying to hide my red hair when I was a child. Laurence said she was an amateur photographer, and we got into good conversations about fashion photography. I said I'd be happy to pose for her any time she liked if she wanted to build up a portfolio, but she laughed and said it was just a hobby. Laurence was really encouraging, though, and told her she should take up my offer. She kept saying she couldn't possibly, but I insisted on taking her number and said I'd ring her the following weekend. I liked the way he was really supportive of Bridget trying to make a career out of a hobby that she was passionate about. They just seemed to have a nice relaxed relationship, like the kind I wanted.

So on a sunny Sunday afternoon in April, I met Bridget in Stephen's Green and she used up three whole rolls of film. I liked what she was doing. She didn't have all the equipment of a professional photographer, and obviously she didn't have a studio, but she knew how to balance all the natural spring light that streamed through the trees and how to frame a swan as it glided into shot. She was much more confident behind the camera. She had asked me just to wear minimal make-up and white clothing. She brought with her a long piece of white gauze that she used to drape over my shoulders or as a veil. She knew what she wanted, and I was quite excited to see how her shots would turn out. Laurence came too. He brought along a picnic and helped Bridget with all her stuff, even lifting her on to his shoulders to get a better angle at times.

After all the photos were taken, we spread out the rug and ate apples and ham sandwiches and shared a flask of tea as we watched people walking through, taking advantage of a sunny evening. The whole day had been lovely, and then it was utterly spoiled.

I saw him approaching but didn't immediately identify him in jeans and a T-shirt. At all our previous encounters, he'd been wearing a suit. In front of Bridget and Laurence, he said in a loud voice, 'Well, well, well, if it isn't the ginger whinger.'

'O'Toole.'

'*Declan.* Doing threesomes now, are we?'

'I'm just trying to have a picnic with my friends. Don't you have any serious crimes to ignore?' I don't know where I got the nerve to be so sarcastic like that with him – perhaps it was because I felt I had backup.

Laurence detected the tone of hostility and stood up, interrupting. 'Can we help you?'

O'Toole looked at him. 'Where do I know you from?' And the way he said it was really intimidating, because Laurence just shrank down on to the grass again.

'What do you want?' I said.

'Just passing the time of day with a future inmate. I'm surprised you're not up by the canal on an evening like this. Business would be much better for you up there.'

'Piss off!' I roared at him.

He sauntered off then, whistling, delighted with himself.

'Who was that?' said Bridget.

I was absolutely mortified. I should not have tried to get the better of him. I felt the tears welling up and saw Laurence silently staring at me. Bridget moved to put her arm around me, and then the floodgates opened and the frustration of years poured out of me right there in a public park in front of these people I barely knew, not to mention all the strangers who looked around to see who was behind the sobbing. Bridget started to fold up the rug and said to Laurence, 'Take her to Neary's. I'll follow you when I've everything packed up.'

I followed him blindly out of the park on to Grafton Street. He took my arm and guided me gently towards the pub, asking no questions while I tried to compose myself. He gave me a freshly laundered handkerchief. In the pub, Laurence installed me in a corner and went to the bar. By the time he came back, Bridget had arrived.

'Who *was* he?' said Bridget.

'Karen doesn't have to say if she doesn't want to.'

'He . . . he's a detective who was supposed to be investigating my sister's disappearance, but he never gave a damn about her . . .'

Throughout my marriage to Dessie, we lived in a kind of a bubble. We hardly hung out with other people at all. We were content just being the two of us, and sometimes going for a drink with the couple next door. Dessie didn't like me to go and meet friends in town at night, because he didn't think it was safe, and on the rare occasions that

I did, he would collect me at ten o'clock, when the night was just getting going. So after a while, my friends stopped inviting me out. When I left him, I realized that I no longer had friends of my own. The girls I had been pally with in the dry-cleaner's still worked with Dessie, and I hadn't really kept in touch with them since I'd started working with Yvonne. That was my fault. So really, I had no one to talk to. But now, here in front of me in this pub were two people my own age who were good company and decent types. Laurence seemed a good bit grander than Bridget, but it obviously didn't bother him. She was just an ordinary girl like me, with an office job, hoping to make something out of her hobby. I felt that I could trust them, so I told them everything.

I watched their faces as I told them the story of Annie. Her learning difficulties in school, her pregnancy, and St Joseph's taking baby Marnie away from her, her drug addiction and prostitution, her disappearance and probable murder, O'Toole and his disgusting attitude, my investigation into the old car, and Mooney's impression that the murderer was a high-profile man who had died shortly afterwards.

Bridget was utterly horrified, her mouth hanging open and her eyes widening, but Laurence's reaction surprised me. At the beginning of my story he just stared into his pint, but as I continued my sorry tale his shoulders began to shake, and when he looked up at the end, his eyes were wet with tears.

'Oh my God, that is just awful!' Bridget said, hugging me. 'I've never heard anything so bad. I don't know how you can have coped all these years. Oh my God!'

Laurence simply said, 'I am so, so, sorry. It's . . . horrendous. I am so sorry.'

'Please,' I said, 'it's not your fault. It's a tragedy, but I can't let it go. The guards are not interested in helping me, so I have to do it myself.'

'Oh God, we'll help you, won't we, Laurence?' said Bridget. 'We have office phones, we can ring around all the other garages at lunchtimes, can't we? And, Laurence, you're always at the library – couldn't you find out how to look up newspaper archives and see what important people died in the weeks after Annie disappeared?'

I hadn't even thought of doing that. Laurence nodded and got up to go to the bar again.

'He's pretty sensitive, don't mind him. But we'll help you, I promise. I can't believe that detective spoke to you like that, as if you were . . .'

'A prostitute?'

'What an absolute bastard. You should complain about him, or write to the papers – something, you know?'

'I did at the time. He got promoted. And now my agent thinks it would be bad for my career if I were to go public about any of this, but if you two could help like you say, that would be amazing!'

'Of course we will.'

Laurence came back with drinks. I toasted Annie and they joined me. For the first time in a very long time, I felt like I had friends, allies.

13. Lydia

'He can't have recognized you. You were three stone heavier and five years younger then.'

'He couldn't place me, but he knew me, I know he did!'

Laurence had been keeping secrets from me. It was profoundly disturbing. He arrived home one night pale-faced and shaking, having been out with Bridget. He admitted that he had made a friend out of the dead whore's father and, worse, her sister, who, he insisted, was investigating Annie Doyle's disappearance herself. Laurence was petrified that she was close to the truth.

'She's going to find out it was Dad. She knows a lot of stuff already.'

He had left Bridget and the girl behind in the pub. I tried to ascertain what she knew. Laurence had just met the same detective, O'Toole, who had questioned him at the gate of Avalon all those years ago. It seems his side-kick, Mooney, had suspected Andrew but the whole matter had been dropped when Andrew died.

'But how did you even meet this girl, or her father? And why didn't you keep away from them? They are not the sort of people you should be mixing with.'

Laurence was taken aback, and I realized I had to check myself.

'Mum, don't you see? We should be doing everything we can to help Annie Doyle's family. Dad killed her and she is buried behind our kitchen wall and I put a concrete shelf and a bloody bird bath on top of her grave. I try to forget about it, and most of the time I'm fine, but over a year ago Annie's dad came to sign on in my office and I recognized him. I got to know him a little bit, and he's a decent man, Mum.'

I handed Laurence a glass of whiskey.

'Darling, you really should not consort with these people, drug addicts and prostitutes, they are beneath us. Do you understand?'

'And what about murderers? Are they beneath us?'

I would have loved to have explained to Laurence that his father was not just a common murderer, that he had merely made a mistake under pressure and that the girl was of no consequence. If she had lived, she would have made no contribution to the world. Her family were obviously layabouts too, if the father was on the dole. Of course I am not saying that she didn't deserve to live, I'm not saying that at all, but who really missed her?

'Laurence, whatever happened, you must remember that your father was a good man. I'm sure it was a silly accident that led to the death. I very much doubt that your father would ever have gone with a prostitute. He just wasn't the type, and he loved *me*, you know he did. You must not think of him as a murderer. Who knows what type of trouble that girl was involved in? Wasn't she a heroin addict? Heroin is a terrible, terrible drug. It is quite possible that your father was trying to help her. He often helped people but he kept his charity work very quiet. I'm sure he was only trying to help her when she died, perhaps of an overdose, and to avoid a scandal he just buried her here.'

Laurence sat looking at me. I know he was thinking that I was in denial, I know he didn't believe a word I was saying, but I also knew that he would go along with it for my sake.

'But this girl Karen, Annie's sister, she's not giving up, Mum. She's going to find out. And she is so –'

'You must find a way to stop her.'

'Bridget has said that we will *help* her.'

'Well then, you're in the perfect position to find false information and throw her off course.'

'Mum!'

I raised my voice in anger. It is something I do very seldom. 'Laurence. I am trying to protect you. If this gets out, you will go to jail.'

He shut up then, realizing I was right. I used softer tones.

'Darling, let us think about this. Annie Doyle has been missing for nearly six years?'

'Five and a half. Yes.'

'But there is absolutely no proof she is dead?'

'Not that I know of, but one of the guards thought that Dad –'

'Never mind about that. Did she have a bank account or a post office savings account, do you know?'

'I don't know. Why?'

'Because we can bring her back to life. Send the mother a letter from her.'

'What?'

Even as I said the words, an idea was forming. Annie was not dead. Perhaps she decided to clean up her life and get off drugs and move away where nobody would know her, start afresh. She was living a normal life down the country but did not want to be contacted and reminded of her old life. It was alarmingly simple. When Laurence calmed down enough, he saw the wisdom of the idea, although he said it was cruel. Not as cruel as what Annie Doyle had done to us.

'But, Laurie, won't it be so much better for them to think that she is alive? It will be such a huge relief to them. We will be giving them back their daughter. It's an act of mercy. She will write to them.'

I changed my mind about Laurence befriending the Doyles. Keep your enemies close, isn't that what they say? I encouraged him to engage with them, gain their trust, find out as much as he could about Annie before we put our plan into action, and in the meantime he could feed them misinformation. He had already agreed to look up death notices in the *Irish Times* office for the weeks after 14 November 1980. He could conveniently omit Andrew's name from the list of his findings. He should take control of Karen's investigation, be sympathetic, but not too enthusiastic. Perhaps he could pretend to develop a personal interest in Karen.

But he seemed uncomfortable at the suggestion.

'I can't do that. She's Bridget's friend. And Bridget keeps asking me when she's going to meet you, and when I'm going to Athlone to meet her parents.'

'Athlone? God help us.' And then it struck me. 'Actually, I think you should go. You can post the Annie letter from there! Athlone is perfect – a letter posted from there could have originated anywhere. It's slap bang in the middle of the country.'

He winced at this. I was terribly excited. This was a project that Laurence and I could work on together. It could only bring us closer.

Over the next few weeks, Laurence and Bridget and Karen met up regularly to go over all the information she had about Annie. I encouraged Laurence to bring home whatever he could so that we could combine our wits to decide how best to use it. As I suspected, Annie had no savings accounts in which money might have remained untouched if she was dead. There was no proof at all that she hadn't picked up her life and moved away. We had to make it look like she'd gone in a hurry. One of the most crucial things Laurence brought home was an old diary in her appalling, childlike, semi-literate handwriting. I could see Annie had entered the payments from Andrew, which she listed under J, presumably for Judge. The little bitch had probably known all along who he was. Karen had entrusted the diary to Laurence so that he could check out the addresses and phone numbers. There was a letter in it to a child that she gave up for adoption, and when I saw that, I lost any sympathy I might have had for her. She had been pregnant before, *by accident.* She knew Andrew and I were desperate and willing to pay for a baby, and she had already given one away. What a truly pathetic creature she was.

But that book gave us everything we needed to construct the new Annie Doyle. I started to write the letter from Annie, using her typing and grammatical errors, but found I couldn't get the shape of the words convincingly. With a heavy sigh, Laurence took the pen from my hand. Laurence was an excellent forger, it turns out. He said that

Karen referred to her mother as 'Ma', so assumed Annie must have done the same. I dictated the note.

Dear Ma,

I am really sorry if you wore wurried about me over the last few years but I got in a bit of trouble with a lone shark and druges and stuff and I had to get away in a hurry to a kwite place to start my life agan. I know the cops was loking for me and all but I was in a bit of trouble with them too. So I bin laying low for a few years now but I have my act together ma and im living a good life and youd be proued of me if you saw me. I was to sad after the baby and all and I tried to ferget about her but you now What it was like with da. he was ashamed. I hope hes all rite. Tell him not to worry about me now and that im sorry for all the basel. tell Karen I love her too. i love you all but my life is bettur her. dont come loking for me couse theres no pont. Im not coming back ma but im very happy here.

Love from your Annie

I have a diffarant name now.

Laurence baulked at some of it. He was dead set against the reference to her father's shame, but it had to be realistic. The loan shark references were my idea. It would suggest that the large sums of money noted in the diary were sums owed rather than payments to her from Andrew. The guards had apparently made lewd suggestions that a client could have paid her large amounts for perverted reasons. Laurence wanted the letter to be written to Karen, but that didn't make any sense to me. Every child is closer to his mother than to anyone else. He wanted more about Karen in the letter, but I pointed out how illiterate Annie was, how much of an effort writing must be. She wouldn't write a word more than she needed to. A declaration of love should be enough to satisfy the sister.

I could tell that Laurence was quite stressed by all of this. I reassured him and told him that we were doing a very kind thing and that he was a good man. He had turned into the most handsome young man one could ever see, like a younger version of his father. Everything was going to be fine, I told him. This was just another of life's hurdles that we would have to get over.

14. Laurence

I was in love. For the first time, head over heels in love. I will never know if it was because of her relationship to Annie. I'd like to think I would have loved Karen anyway. The very first time I saw her in Scanlon's with her father, I felt a lurch deep in my chest as if my heart had swung out of position. She did not at all resemble the girl I knew well from the press cuttings, hiding behind a veil of unkempt hair.

She was delivering bad news about Annie to her father, as it turned out. I was struck by the way she spoke to him so tenderly, concern in her eyes. I sat beside Bridget in the corner of the pub, watching this amazing woman, wondering who she was.

When Gerry introduced her as his daughter, my insides lurched again. How much suffering had my father caused her? She looked up at me and smiled, and I have no idea what we said to each other. That night I followed them home to Gerry's house and was nearly caught by Karen, staring up at her through a window.

Karen and Bridget quickly became close friends and that made it harder. I had constant news of Karen – where she was going, what she was doing. Bridget was incredibly flattered that Karen took an interest in her, and I was jealous. Of Bridget. I found it impossible not to compare the two women, and while I stayed with Bridget, the true reason was that, without her, I wouldn't have seen Karen. But I became short with Bridget, impatient with her, though never in front of Karen. When Karen was around, I was the perfect gentleman. I hung around them like a lapdog, knowing full well what caused flashes of pain to occasionally cross Karen's face. I understood her hidden grief; I recognized her loss.

I discovered from Bridget that Karen found her own modelling career faintly ridiculous. She was grateful for the income, but didn't feel beautiful. That was so strange to me. She was stunning. When Karen and Bridget were sitting side by side, I couldn't help thinking of Beauty and the Beast. Karen had no airs and graces about it at all. She had recently separated from her husband, Dessie, but still used her married name. I was surprised that a girl my own age could already have an ex-husband. According to Bridget, Karen thought she had married too young. She didn't resent her ex-husband, but wished he would stop calling her and trying to rekindle their relationship.

And then one day we had that picnic in the park after Bridget's photo shoot and Detective Sergeant O'Toole walked past and insulted her in front of us, and she told us the whole story about Annie, more than I had ever known before. Now I knew why the bracelet was inscribed 'Marnie'. Karen was dangerously close to the truth, and when Bridget promised her that we'd help her, I felt like throwing up. I panicked. I had to tell Mum.

My mother had solutions to all these problems. She was clearly in complete denial of what Dad had done, but Mum's primary focus was to protect me. Her plan to make

Karen and her family think that Annie was alive horrified me. It seemed so dishonest and cruel, but Mum was neither of those things and I hoped it would bring them some comfort. And that it would keep me out of jail.

My old forgery skills were put to good use. I couldn't tell Mum that I was in love with Karen. Social class meant so much to my mother. I'd never even brought Bridget to meet her.

The idea of posting the Annie letter from Athlone made sense, I suppose. If they went looking for Annie after receiving it, her family would have an extremely wide hinterland to search.

Bridget had given up asking me to come and meet her family, so when I was the one to suggest it, she was delighted. The preparations started weeks in advance. The date of the visit was coincidentally set for Annie's birthday in July. Bridget and her mother exchanged letters daily on the upcoming 'arrangements' to be made. Bridget had two younger sisters who both lived at home in their three-bedroom house. For my two-night visit, they would share a room while Bridget slept on the sofa downstairs and I would have Bridget's childhood bedroom. Bridget said we were to pretend to be virgins. Her mother was apparently in a knot of anxiety. Did I eat fish? Because they always had fish on Fridays. They were changing the curtains to fix the draught in the bedroom. Would I attend Mass with the family on Sunday morning? Would I go with Bridget to visit her granddad in the local nursing home? There were protocols being put in place. I was being treated like visiting royalty. I don't know what Bridget had told them, but it was clear that my impending arrival was the cause of much fuss. I hate fuss. I tried hard not to be irritated by Bridget's excitement.

My mother thought it unreasonable that I was going away for two nights.

'Two? In Athlone? What will you do there?'

'I don't know, Mum, but it would be rude to just arrive on Friday night and leave on Saturday.'

'I've never been to Athlone.'

'You've never been anywhere.'

She huffed a bit. 'All you have to do is post the letter. Get the early bus back on Sunday?'

'I'll try.'

'Bring an extra sweater. It's always cold down the country.' It was July. I suppose she must have been outside Dublin at some stage.

We set off for Athlone on the bus on Friday after work, together with all the other rural immigrants along that route to the midlands and further west to Galway, making their weekly pilgrimage home with bags of laundry over their shoulders. I had the letter in my inside pocket, ready to be posted at the first opportunity. Bridget had prepared sandwiches and bought sweets for our two-hour journey, and there was a scheduled toilet stop in Kinnegad. Her camera clicked away as we rolled out of the city, and she chattered excitedly.

'You know that, outside Dublin, dinner is called tea and lunch is called dinner? And you drink tea with every meal and between meals and before bed? Josephine is fourteen and very nosy, but you don't have to answer any of her questions, and Maureen is fanatical about reading, so she'll have her head in the books all weekend. Dad won't say much, but Mam is very religious and will want to know who your parish priest is and all that.'

Mum and I had stopped going to Mass after Dad died. We had always disliked going. Our parish priest had visited and asked us to return, and we swore we would but had somehow never quite managed it.

'Oh well, don't tell my mam that! She'd have a heart attack.'

When we disembarked in Athlone, a creature appeared out of the crowd at the station, wearing a headscarf and a buttoned-up-to-the-neck raincoat with a handbag (plastic) dangling over the crook of her elbow. She grabbed Bridget fiercely by the shoulders and hugged her close, then turned to me.

'You must be Laurence. We're delighted to have you, delighted, only delighted! I said to Bridget's father this morning, I said, isn't this only fabulous, getting to meet Bridget's young man at last? After all, you've been going steady for a good while now, a good while, I said to Bridget's father.'

She was nervous. I guessed that normally, in these situations, the young man in my position would have been the one on trial, but in this case she clearly felt she was the one being judged. Any nerves I had disappeared.

'It's very nice to meet you. I've heard a lot about you.' This was probably true, though I only remembered what Bridget had told me on the bus journey.

Mrs Gough apologized that it was a ten-minute walk to the house and whooped with admiration when I offered to carry Bridget's bag as well as my own. 'A real gentleman, that's what you are now, a real gentleman so you are.'

The house was a grey one in the middle of a terrace of other grey ones on a narrow street. A wooden front door stood sentry beside a single window, while two windows above looked down on us. Net curtains fronted every window, despite the fact there was nothing about the house that would make one curious enough to look inside.

The interior of Bridget's house did not improve my impression of the place. Drab, ordinary, colourless and cramped. I always knew I lived in a big house, but I didn't expect small houses to feel so, well, small. From the front door, I could see the back wall of the house. There was a front room and a back kitchen and a narrow stairway to the right. Bridget's photos were everywhere, framed in the sitting room, Sellotaped to the fridge door in the kitchen, tucked into the frame of the mirror on the wall. We left our bags at the foot of the stairs and were ushered into the kitchen, where the overwhelming smell of boiled cabbage threatened the egg sandwich that had been idling in my upper intestine since lunchtime. 'Get in there out of the cold, the kettle's not long boiled, you'll have a cup of tea.' It was a statement rather than an offer. I was compelled to sit in a straight-backed stained armchair beside an old range. It was clearly 'Father's chair'.

Two plain girls, Bridget's sisters, were sitting at the kitchen table peeling potatoes. Mr Gough was in Slaney's bar but would be home for his 'tea' at seven thirty. Tea was being delayed for our arrival.

The youngest sister took one look at me and said accusingly to Bridget, 'But he's quite good-looking. You said he was really fat!' Whereupon she was kicked in the ankle by Maureen. 'Josie! That's rude.'

'I used to be very fat,' I said to deflate the bubble of panic that had arisen.

'Yeah, you're a bit fat but not massive. I thought you'd be huge,' said Josie.

'Josie!' in chorus from Bridget, Maureen and Mrs Gough.

'I'm only saying what Bridget told us. She said he was very fat and very posh.'

Bridget looked mortified.

'You girls can go up and clean your room,' their mother said. They trooped off, complaining it was too cold upstairs to clean. 'Put on a jumper!' called Mrs Gough after them.

Bridget and I sat in the sauna of cabbage steam while Mrs Gough made conversation.

'So, Laurence, Bridget tells me you're very good at your job?'

I answered her questions courteously but a heat was rising within me. It seems that even though Bridget had never directly mentioned it, she too had defined me by my weight. She was supposed to care for me. She acted like she was in love with me. Yes, I had been obese when she first met me, but it was the primary thing her family knew about me. I felt shame. And also malice. Bridget was no oil painting. She was no Karen.

When Mr Gough came home at seven thirty on the dot, the meal was served. This was a traditional home. Mr Gough looked me up and down, shook my hand vigorously, then stared at his shoes and said very little. A white tablecloth now covered the kitchen table.

'We only have tablecloths at Christmas!' exclaimed Josie, and then 'Oww!' as she was kicked under the table.

For the first time in months, I was absolutely ravenous. I ate everything that was offered. When I was offered second helpings I ate those too, and third and fourth helpings. Mr Gough paid attention now as the last scoop of mashed potato was dolloped on to my plate and Mrs Gough got up to fry me an extra cod fillet. I pretended not to notice their astonishment. For dessert, I ate half a chocolate Swiss roll while the family shared the other half, and after all the plates were cleared away and tea was offered again, I enquired if there were any biscuits. Maureen was sent to the shop to buy some. Even Josie was shocked into silence. Now Bridget could talk about her fat boyfriend.

The chatter was inane. What did I like to watch on television, which newspaper did I read, which sport did I follow or play? All my answers were at odds with the family. The visit was not going well. The television was turned on to the *Nine O'Clock News* to avoid further embarrassing conversation. Certain parts of Ulster were still saying no to the Anglo-Irish Agreement. Prince Andrew had married a fat girl in England, and Chris de Burgh's 'Lady in Red' had broken some records. 'And some record players,' I laughed, but they looked baffled and didn't get the joke. After the news, Mrs Gough indicated that it was time for the rosary and the whole family got to their knees, clutching sets of rosary beads. Not wanting me to feel left out, Mr Gough handed me a 'spare' set made of dark wood. I mumbled the prayers along with the rest of the family, but I made it obvious that I was not accustomed to this ritual. Even when my father was alive, there had been no religiosity in our family outside of Sunday Mass. Ironically, I had no recollection of my father ever having gone to Confession. He, who had the most to confess.

In that moment, reminded of my dad, I compared my murdering, dishonest family to Bridget's, and instead of feeling superior I realized they were sweet and innocent, this family who prayed on their knees together, who welcomed a stranger into their home. I felt bad for how I had behaved, how little effort I had made. Bridget caught my eye and I flashed her a genuine smile.

When everyone retired to bed, we were left alone momentarily. 'Don't be long, now!' called Mrs Gough from the stairs, obviously terrified of what we might get up to if left unsupervised.

Bridget threw another sod of turf into the fireplace.

'Laurence, why . . . why were you like that with them? Why couldn't you just play along? Don't you want them to like you?'

'Bridget –'

'No, stop, why did you eat like that? I've never seen you eat that much before. Why did you do that? Didn't you see that there wasn't enough food left for my dad? I don't understand.' She was tearful now.

How could I explain this meanness that was inside me? That I had taken revenge on her for saying that I had been fat, for having a normal family, for not being Karen? Why was I so spiteful towards this girl who had done nothing bad to me, had been nothing but kind?

I shook my head. 'I'm sorry.'

'I . . . I love you. I wanted them to love you too.'

Poor Bridget. She loved me. Her good eye pierced me.

I reached out and smoothed her hair and kissed her on the mouth.

'Tomorrow, I'll try harder. I promise.'

I did not sleep well that night in Bridget's childhood bedroom. I worried about when I would get to slip away and post the letter by myself. My stomach was queasy and the eiderdown was lumpy in places. Maureen had since occupied the room, but it was clear that this was a family who had never known privilege or wealth. The furnishings were cheap and the new curtains thin. Everything in the room was functional, no room for decoration apart from a solitary snow globe atop a bookshelf, a gift from some Christmas past perhaps, and a few obligatory holy pictures. There were no radiators in this room, but it was directly above the front room so the residual heat from the fireplace downstairs took the bite from the chilled air, and Mrs Gough had thoughtfully provided a hot-water bottle. They had done everything to make me feel comfortable. I resolved to be a better boyfriend the next day.

Saturday started well. Mrs Gough piled my plate high with bacon and sausages for breakfast, but I quelled my appetite with two pints of water and didn't gorge myself like I had the previous evening. Bridget chatted about her new friend Karen and showed her mother some of the photos she had taken of her.

'Well, isn't she just a smashing-looking girl? That's good enough for a magazine, isn't it, Maureen?'

Indeed it was. It hadn't even been one of the posed shots, but it was the best of them. It was a close-up shot of Karen sitting on the blanket in Stephen's Green, unscrewing the cap of the flask. She had been laughing at something I'd said. Her beautiful hair contrasted with the spring green of the trees behind her, and she looked entirely natural and without blemish. It had been just before the detective's interruption. Bridget thought that she had lost one of the prints a week or two earlier. It was in a hole in the wall behind my writing desk at Avalon.

Mr Gough asked politely what our plans were for the day. Bridget said we were going to watch Josie play a camogie match and then visit her grandfather in a nursing home on the outskirts of town. I smiled broadly, as if there were nothing I would rather do. I could feel them all warming to me. It didn't take much. They were inclined to be generous and forgiving, but I realized that I wouldn't easily get a chance to run to a postbox on my own.

On the sidelines of a camogie pitch in the drizzle, I struggled to keep warm. The game was, as all sports are to me, unremarkable. Sweaty, red-faced, aggressive teenagers wielding sticks and running around in the mud. Afterwards, we took Josie to a café.

'You were the best, wasn't she, Laurence?'

'You were,' I agreed.

'Are you going to eat that much again tonight, because Mam has to go to the shops again if you do?'

'Josie!'

'I'm only asking.'

'No, I don't know what happened to me last night. I have a metabolism disorder, I think.'

'Meta . . . what?'

'Josie, now please leave Laurence alone.'

I made up some semi-truthful story about my body

being unable to process quantities, which meant that sometimes I was ravenously hungry, but assured her that it didn't happen often.

'God, you must be mortified that it happened on your first night here. Don't worry, I'll explain it to Mam later. She was just worried that the housekeeping money wouldn't last the week.'

'I really am sorry about that.'

Bridget was grateful.

Later, she and I walked half an hour out towards the Roscommon road to see her granddad, passing two postboxes on the way. I dared not stop. It was a grim place, a state-owned nursing home. Bridget's grandfather sat in a high-backed chair among all the other shells who had once been people. Bridget took photos of the liver spots on his hand and of the adjacent tea trolley. Granddad didn't know who Bridget was, but Bridget talked patiently to him, answering his endlessly repeated questions: 'Are you Peter? Where's Daddy? Are we going home now? Where's Peter?'

Bridget introduced me. 'Granddad, this is Laurence, my boyfriend.'

But Granddad never even turned his head to look at me until we were leaving and then, out of nowhere, he turned towards me, stared for a few seconds and then looked back at Bridget. 'I don't like him. There's something wrong with him.' A pause and then, 'Where's Peter? Are we going home now?'

Bridget laughed it off. 'He doesn't know what he's talking about.' Actually, he did.

Afterwards, I suggested taking a short tour of the town

myself, but Bridget insisted that her dad was going to give me the tour next morning, and slipped her arm through mine. There was no getting away.

That evening, at tea, or dinner, I chatted cordially and was careful about how much I ate. Everybody tried hard to hide their relief. They were relaxed enough to start asking more personal questions.

'Exactly how long have you been going out together?' asked Maureen.

'It'll be two years in September.' I was surprised when Bridget said that. Had it really been that long?

Josie started to hum 'Here Comes the Bride'. This time, everyone ignored her. Mr Gough went to the pub for his two routine Saturday-night pints and a game of darts, and the rest of us settled down to watch television with tea and biscuits. I restrained myself once again.

The next morning, we were woken early to go to Mass. This was treated like a big occasion. The girls had been up early doing their hair, and Mrs Gough was polishing all the shoes, including mine. She tried to hide her disappointment that I hadn't brought my suit, but I placated her by wearing one of Mr Gough's nylon ties. According to tradition, we weren't allowed to eat before Mass. By the time we got to church at 10.30 a.m., I was starving. And the journey to and from the church had been a group one. My mood deteriorated.

On the way home, the women of the family rushed off together and I was left with the taciturn Mr Gough, who offered to show me around the town. I could hardly refuse, but felt ambushed. We walked up and down the grey streets and across the Shannon while he pointed to things in between long silences. 'That's the library . . . that's the castle.' Mr Gough was not a natural conversationalist.

Having pointed out his local pub on the riverbank, he said, 'Is there anything in particular you'd like to ask me?'

'Sorry?'

He sighed heavily. 'Is there anything you want to ask me about Bridget?'

With horror, the realization dawned on me that he was expecting me to ask for Bridget's hand in marriage. They all were. I dissembled. 'When did you say the barracks was built?'

He ignored my feigned ignorance. 'Mrs Gough and I were married at your age.'

I never found out their first names. They consistently referred to each other as Mam and Dad or formally as Mr and Mrs.

'But I'm only twenty-three.'

'Still, if you find the right girl, you needn't hang about.'

Unsure how to answer, I opted to say nothing. We were standing by the lock gate at the weir. He kicked at the ground with both shoes for no apparent reason, scuffing the toes. I recall thinking that Mrs Gough's earnest shoe-polishing had been for nought.

'Bridget is an unusual-looking girl, and she's not the brightest, but she has a kind heart and a sweet nature. And she's my daughter. If you don't want to marry her, you should let her go, so she can find someone who will.'

He was surprisingly eloquent. I could feel his embarrassment as it stretched invisibly from his reddened face to my crimson one.

'I don't mean to hurt her, Mr Gough –' but he strode

ahead. He had said what he was primed to say, and the 'chat' and tour of the town were over. That would have been my opportunity to go off and post the letter, but I was so blind-sided by what had just happened that I scurried after him.

The atmosphere at dinner was awful. It was obvious that the women had been primed for celebration on our return. An ashen-faced Bridget claimed a headache and went upstairs to lie down. She didn't join us for food. Mr Gough was completely mute. I was starving and ate everything put in front of me. When Mrs Gough offered more, I took it, until there was nothing left. If nobody had been looking, I would have licked all of the plates.

'There's something wrong with his metasism,' said Josie helpfully.

Mrs Gough kept up the banter. 'Did you see Una Crawley at Mass? Wasn't her hair lovely? Though I don't like the way she goes up to the front pew. It's far from the front pew she was reared, and she only married into that family six months. They always thought they were better than they were. She'll want to be having a baby soon, the Farrells will be wanting a son to carry on the name in the town . . .'

Maureen interjected occasionally to point out how old-fashioned her mother's attitudes were, and Josie stared at my plate, nudging her sister every time I reloaded it.

It was almost time to go to the bus station. Mrs Gough went up to see if Bridget was all right, and I went to gather my things from my bedroom. I could hear Bridget sobbing through the thin walls and her mother talking to her sternly.

I waited in the kitchen until Mrs Gough appeared to say that Bridget wasn't feeling well and would stay at home for the time being. She apologized that she wouldn't accompany me to the bus stop this time, as she had visiting to do. She shook my hand but did not meet my eye while I thanked her for her hospitality. Maureen waved from the top of the stairs. Mr Gough's handshake was limp, but he mumbled a 'Goodbye and good luck now', relieved, I think, that his part in the drama was over.

Josie followed me out to the street. 'You're not good enough for her anyway!' she said, and then burst into tears and ran inside.

I posted the letter beside the bus stop and boarded the bus, grateful that the ordeal had come to an end.

When I got home that afternoon, there was a car in the driveway that I didn't recognize. I let myself into the house and saw Mum standing in the hall with a man.

'Hello, you must be Laurence.' Tall, late fifties, well dressed in a casual yacht-club style, he was debonair and confident.

Mum introduced him. She seemed upset. 'Laurence, meet Malcolm.'

There was something vaguely familiar about him, but I couldn't place him. I was courteous and polite, but it was awkward standing around in the hall. He left after five minutes' conversation about the weather and the Anglo-Irish Agreement.

'How was your weekend?'

'How was yours?'

'Fine, lovely, Malcolm and I went out to lunch.'

'Out?'

'Yes, well, it was very lonely here without you.'

'And how do you know Malcolm?'

'He . . . he's a friend. I met him in . . . St John of God's.'

'What?'

'He's a psychiatrist. He was here in a personal capacity, as a friend.'

That's why he looked familiar. I had met him once or twice when Mum was in the psychiatric hospital. I was reassured. She smiled one of her best fake smiles. She was clearly uncomfortable talking about him and diverted quickly.

'Did you post the letter?'

'Yes.'

'Did anyone see you?'

'No, it was fine.'

I went to the kitchen to turn on the kettle for tea and noticed the window blind was gone.

'We can't live in the dark for ever, darling. We must move on,' said Mum, standing behind me. She ruffled my hair fondly, like she used to when I was a boy.

'Your granny is coming for dinner. You should go and freshen up, darling. I can smell the turf fire on you. How primitive!'

The phone rang at about six o'clock. It was Bridget.

'I'm still in Athlone. I'm too embarrassed to see you.'

'Bridget, I'm so sorry. I had no idea you were expecting –'

'Please don't say it, I feel bad enough.'

'But we're so young, marriage hadn't even crossed my mind –'

'Why did you want to meet my family? You must have known what that meant to me?'

'I was . . .'

'What?'

'I don't love you.'

I could imagine her bad eye rolling up into her head.

'What do you mean?' Her voice was very high-pitched.

'I'm sorry.'

'What? Are you breaking up with me? I know things have been a little odd between us recently, you've been so busy helping Karen.'

'That's not it.'

'I just think you've got a bit, you know, emotionally involved, but I can tell her you need a break. You don't have to . . . we don't have to get married yet, but that's no reason –'

'Bridget, I can't –'

'Please don't dump me.'

'I'm sorry, Bridget, I really am, but you deserve better than me.'

I hung up the phone gently and went to get myself a drink. I joined Mum in the kitchen. The evening was bright. The bird bath was smothered in swallows.

'I just broke up with Bridget.'

'Oh dear, is she very upset?'

'Yes.'

'Poor Bridget.'

Indeed. I felt relief, but was also worried that seeing Karen would be awkward at the very least. She and Bridget were confidantes, I knew. I waited to see what would happen when the letter landed in Pearse Street.

15. Karen

I was absolutely raging with Annie. I couldn't believe that she could be that cruel. For nearly six years, me and Ma and Da had been half worried to death over what could have happened to her. Our worst fears haunted us, and all this time she'd been sitting on her arse somewhere down the country, living a new secret life and not giving a toss about us. She'd left us to rot. She'd broken up her parents' marriage and didn't even know or care.

I knew the handwriting on the envelope when I saw it, and even though it was addressed to Ma, I screamed for Da to come downstairs. He nearly passed out when I explained it was from Annie. Da was no good with reading. 'Open it,' he said.

What a betrayal. No address, no contact details, and she was apparently living under a different name so that we wouldn't find her. I knew that Annie could be wild and destructive, but I had never thought she could be that selfish.

Da cried and rang Ma. She arrived on the next train, tearful and delighted at the same time. 'At least she's OK!' she kept saying, but I found it impossible to find any comfort in this. I turned it over and over in my mind and, yes, I think I would have preferred if she'd been dead. That probably makes me a horrible person, but I loved her and she had shat on all of us. I had never been rejected before, but my own sister didn't want to know me.

We examined the envelope and the writing paper. They were unremarkable. The letter had been posted on Sunday the 20th of July, from Athlone. We went through the letter, line by badly spelled line. At least that hadn't changed. Da and me were devastated, but Ma felt justified. She said it proved that it was Da's fault and not hers. I didn't care about blame. I was hurt by the fact that I only got six words in the whole letter. It was like I was an afterthought. She had forgotten about me. We discussed whether we should take this to the guards, but Ma said no, because if she'd been in trouble with them before she left, there could still be charges pending against her.

'What will we do?' said Ma.

'Nothing. Leave her alone. She doesn't want us.' Da put on his jacket and we didn't have to guess where he was headed.

Ma stayed. I wondered if she and Da would reconcile now. I thought about ringing Dessie because I wanted someone to comfort me, but I knew he would feel smug and would point out that my search had been a wild goose chase. Ma slept in my room, in Annie's bed, that night. We heard Da falling up the stairs in the small hours of the morning. The next day, I cancelled work for a few days. Yvonne wanted to know why, but I didn't want to explain. The truth was too humiliating, and it made a fool out of her son. James had been wrong all along about the murder suspect. I claimed illness.

I rang Bridget at work, but she wasn't there, so I tried

Laurence. I told him what had happened. He was completely silent for a few moments. I suppose he was annoyed. He and Bridget had spent months tracking down death notices and old car registrations. I had wasted their time.

'Do you want to meet later?' he said.

'Maybe. Where's Bridget? I heard she wasn't at work today.'

'No, she's . . . in . . . Athlone with her folks. I'll see you in Kehoe's? About five thirty? You can tell me everything.'

I had forgotten that Bridget was from Athlone. But hearing the place name made me angry again. How could you, Annie? I rang the bus company to check the timetable. I packed a small bag and told Ma I was meeting a friend in Kehoe's and that I was going from there to get a bus to Athlone to find Annie.

'Karen, I don't know . . . she seemed certain . . . she doesn't want to be found.'

'And what about what we want? Don't you want to see her?'

'I do. Of course I do. But . . . maybe you're right. Wouldn't it be wonderful if we could all go and visit her?'

'Exactly. Well, I'm going to find her first.' I had the silver-framed photo of Annie from the sitting room on top of my bag.

'Be careful though, love. You don't want to give anyone the impression that she's in trouble. If she's living a good life now, she won't want to drag up her past.'

'I'm going to say that I found the photo and just want to return it to its owner.'

*

I met Laurence. I apologized profusely for all the time he had wasted looking for my sister's 'murderer'.

'Please, don't. At least she's alive. And happy.'

'And cruel and selfish.'

'But aren't you glad she's OK?'

The way he looked at me when he said it. I noticed again the kindness in his eyes. I tried not to cry and put my head down, but he put his arm gently around my neck and kissed the top of my head. I pulled away, reluctantly. I was momentarily confused, but before I had a chance to react, we were interrupted by Dessie. He caught me by the arm and physically pulled me off the stool, knocking it to the ground.

'Who the fuck are you?'

Laurence stood up and faced him. 'I'm her friend. Let her go.'

'Dessie, please, what are you doing here?' I shook him off.

'Your ma rang and told me what happened. She told me you'd be here with a *friend*. Is he why you left me?'

Everyone in the pub had stopped to stare.

'I think you should leave,' said Laurence.

'She's my wife.'

'Not any more,' I said.

'I was right about Annie all along. She was nothing but trouble and she never gave a shit about you. I'll wait for you outside.'

The barman was approaching to remove Dessie. He put his hands in the air to show he wanted no trouble and was escorted to the door.

'I'm sorry, I have to go talk to him.'

'Karen –'

'Laurence, can you give me Bridget's address in Athlone? I'm getting the seven o'clock bus.'

'You . . . what?'

'I have to find her. Is Bridget on holidays? Why is she in Athlone?'

'Find Annie? But didn't the letter say she wanted to be left alone?'

'Yeah, but she's not getting off the hook that easily. Can I have Bridget's address?'

He wrote it into my notebook. 'Karen, I'm so sorry.'

Outside, I confronted Dessie. I was livid. 'Don't you ever do that to me again. You are only embarrassing yourself. I am not your property. I left you, and now I know for sure I was right to do it. Laurence is a friend, a friend who understands about Annie. He has a girlfriend who also happens to be a friend of mine. There's nothing going on, and even if there was, it's none of your business.'

'It didn't look innocent from where I was standing. Do all your friends kiss you?'

I was shaking with stress and anger, but I managed to walk away.

It was only later, on the bus to Athlone, that I thought about that strange kiss and the way he had said he was sorry. I thought that Laurence really was genuinely sorry that Annie had abandoned me. Or maybe he was sorry that he had kissed me, even though he had done it so innocently. I didn't know what was meant by the kiss, if anything was meant at all, but I know I liked it. I liked the comfort of Laurence's arms around me. I liked his kind eyes. I felt that he understood me, particularly about Annie. He had really gone out of his way. On weekends he had gone to garages down the country, and he had illegally pulled files from social welfare records to see how much money Annie had got when she was on the dole, and tried to reconcile it with amounts marked in that notebook of hers. Of course Bridget helped too, but I don't think she was as interested. Laurence really cared. I felt bad for even thinking that way, betraying Bridget.

I got off the bus in Athlone late that Wednesday night and walked through the rain until I turned up at Bridget's door. I should have looked up her parents' phone number and called first. Her mother ushered me into the front room. She spoke in the exact same nervous, rushed way that Bridget did.

'I recognize you from the photo! You're Bridget's friend Karen. Come in out of the rain! Did she ring you with the news? You're very good to come. She's devastated! Hang on there now till I call her down. You'll have a cup of tea.' And then she disappeared and I heard her shouting up the stairs to Bridget.

I was utterly confused. What was she talking about? Why was Bridget devastated?

When Bridget appeared, her face was pale and her eyes were red-rimmed. She was very surprised to see me.

'Karen, what are you doing . . . how did you know?'

We exchanged our news and I realized why Laurence had avoided answering any of my questions about Bridget. He had broken up with her three nights previously. I tried to put the kiss to the back of my mind and comfort my friend. I explained that we'd had a letter from Annie postmarked Athlone.

'What? But I thought you said she was dead? We were looking for the guy who killed her.'

'I was wrong. She's here. Or somewhere nearby. I'm going to look for her tomorrow, but I should get going. I've booked a bed and breakfast place down the street.'

Mrs Gough bustled in with a tea tray. 'Mam, Karen can stay here, can't she? She's booked a B'n'B, but she can stay?'

'Of course you can. You'll be more than welcome, more than welcome. You are so good to come. We can make the same arrangement as the weekend – Maureen and Josie can share.'

'Oh no, please, I don't want you to go to any trouble.'

'Hush now, girl. Sure, it's no trouble at all. Oh, Bridget, she's even more beautiful in the flesh. And you're a model? Well, that's no surprise. Sure, we've never had a model in the house before. Are you hungry? You must be. I'll make you up a sandwich now. Bridget, light the fire for our guest. It's freezing in here. Sure, you wouldn't think it was the middle of summer at all at all.' And off she went, a whirlwind of nervous energy.

Bridget and I smiled at each other. I used the Goughs' phone to cancel the bed and breakfast.

'I never told my mam about Annie. She wouldn't understand – you know, about the drugs and . . . that, so she thinks you're here because Laurence dumped me.'

'It's OK, I understand. I won't mention her.'

She apologized that she couldn't help me look for Annie the next day, because the town was too small and her parents would find out and she didn't want to have to explain to them that I was the sister of a . . . she couldn't find a polite word. I felt more resentment towards Annie, and a little towards Bridget.

Bridget and me sat up late that night by the fire, talking about Annie initially, but the conversation kept coming back to Laurence. Bridget had booked a week off work because she wasn't ready to face him in the office. I wondered why Laurence had never moved out of home. It was a bit weird, though of course I was back living with Da. But I'd been out of the house for years until I left Dessie. I tried to ask about Laurence casually.

'Do you think Laurence has told *his* mum about Annie? His dad is dead, right? What's she like, his mum?'

'I've never met her. That should have been a sign, shouldn't it? I mean, if he had really been interested in me, he would have introduced me to his mam. I'm such a fool.'

It was strange that Laurence had never brought Bridget to see his mother after nearly two years.

'I think she has that disease – you know, the opposite of claustrophobia.' I had never heard of claustrophobia. Bridget explained. Mrs Fitzsimons apparently never went out.

'What? Never?'

'Well, she goes out to the shops and things, but she never leaves the house overnight. Never goes away for a weekend.'

'And what's the house like?'

'I've never been in it. That should have been a clue too, shouldn't it? He must have thought I wasn't good enough.

But I was curious, so I walked past it once. I couldn't even see it from the gate. There's a big avenue leading up to it. I'd say it must be huge.'

'Don't be silly, he didn't dump you because you're not good enough!'

'Well, he was acting weird for the last few months. Definitely. I mean, he's always been a little bit odd.'

'What do you mean?'

'When I first started dating him, he was really big – obese, you know? And then when he started losing weight, he got really fidgety. Even in the office, he's kind of jumpy all the time. When he stayed over with me, he only slept about three hours a night. And over time he got more and more jumpy, but the last few months he's just been . . .'

'What?'

'Hot and cold? And then he asked to come and meet my family. And I think after he met them, he thought that his mam would never approve.'

I had an uneasy feeling that Laurence may have dumped Bridget for an entirely different reason. I remembered the smell of his skin as he drew me in for that hug and the feeling of his lips on the crown of my head. I thought about all the times he had tagged along when Bridget and me were going to the cinema, or shopping. I'd felt like I was the gooseberry sometimes, but maybe it was Bridget who was the gooseberry.

Bridget burst into tears again. 'What am I going to do?' We talked it through. She didn't think Laurence would reconsider their relationship. He had been very insistent there was no going back in their final phone call. She had to be realistic, she said. She was going to apply for a transfer to a different office. She didn't want to have to see him every day.

I wanted to tell her that I'd met him earlier that evening, but something stopped me. There had been no real reason to meet. We could have had our conversation over the phone. I knew that by not telling her I was betraying our friendship. I knew that it was the start of something for me. And for Laurence.

The next morning I met the rest of Bridget's family. They were lovely. The youngest girl, Josie, asked for my autograph. 'I've never met anyone who's been in a magazine before,' she said.

I thanked them for their hospitality and hugged Bridget, arranging to meet her before I got the bus back home. I set off on my quest to find Annie. I told the shopkeepers, pub and café owners that I had found this silver-framed photo at the bus station and wondered if they knew the girl in the photo. It was the only story I could think of. Because of the harelip, people might remember Annie. Her photo hadn't featured in the press for more than a few days after the initial investigation. Other young women who had gone missing all over the country sparked annual appeals and renewed press coverage, but I guess that because of her background Annie's case was never reopened.

A few of the people I asked thought she looked familiar, 'except for the mouth', but most didn't recognize her at all. In a hairdresser's, I suggested that it was probably an old photograph, that she could have changed her hair colour. The salon owner looked at me suspiciously and I realized how weird my story sounded. The receptionist at the Prince of Wales Hotel advised that she could be from anywhere, as Athlone was a bus changeover spot for travellers from Cork, Limerick and the West.

Athlone was a pretty small town, and after four hours I had visited every single business premises, including the ones out on the Roscommon road and the Galway road. At a petrol station on the outskirts of town, I was showing the photo to people when one of them pointed out I'd already been into her jewellery shop with it that morning. 'You're going to an awful lot of trouble to track down a stranger,' she said with a hint of mistrust in her voice. At that stage I didn't care.

I went to the garda station and baldly asked if anyone knew the face in the photograph. The guards shrugged but insisted on keeping the framed photograph. The frame was worth something, they said, so whoever lost it would report it lost to them. That was stupid of me.

At three o'clock I met Bridget in a café.

'No luck?'

'None.'

'I'm sorry, but it's a needle-in-a-haystack situation. She could be living miles out of town in a quiet place, nearer to Mullingar or Ballinasloe. She could be anywhere.'

My fury with Annie had not abated. Hours of tramping around the rain-sodden streets, holding Annie's photo in my hands, had given me time to think about what I would say to her if I came face to face with her. I couldn't even imagine myself being pleased to see her, even if she was safe. I wanted to smack her for everything she had put us through.

I rang home from a phone box and told Ma and Da the bad news, but I said I was going to cover another part of the midlands next week. I'd cover the whole country if I had to. I was going to find Annie. She owed us an explanation.

When I got home that evening, I had dinner with my parents. None of us said much. Da was annoyed that the guards now had his silver photo frame. We had loads of photos of Annie. We'd had hundreds printed at the time of her disappearance. It was the frame that bothered him.

'I bought it specially, after she . . .'

'Ran away?' I suggested.

'Yeah.'

The next morning Yvonne rang in a state of high excitement.

'I hope you're feeling better. Because guess who's going to Rome?'

'I'm much better, thanks, but what's this about Rome?'

'It's a new perfume – Gilt. They want you as the face of Gilt!'

'Guilt? That's a weird name for a perfume.'

'It's Gilt. Without the "u". Gilt. And they want you in Rome next Saturday. I knew you were going to be the one. I knew it all along! Do you realize how big this is?'

It was exciting but I had planned to go to Mullingar. And then I realized how foolish I was being. I had the chance to go to Rome, and I was thinking about not going because of Annie? I could wait. Annie could wait. She'd waited six years to tell us she was still alive.

'That's fantastic!'

'Is your passport in order?'

Dessie and I had been to the Isle of Man the previous summer, so my passport was up to date. Yvonne said I should call to her office and collect all the details.

When I left there later that day with all the information, I had an urge to ring Bridget and tell her this great news, but maybe it would be rubbing her nose in it. I wanted to tell someone. I wanted to tell Laurence.

I rang him in the office. I updated him on the futile search for Annie. His voice was comforting, concerned. I told him about my trip to Rome.

'Wow! That's fantastic. Rome.'

'Have you been?'

'No, never. My mother doesn't like to travel, so we never did foreign holidays, or even domestic ones for that matter.'

I said it before I even realized it had come out of my mouth. 'Come with me.'

There was a slight pause and then he said, 'OK. I will.'

16. Lydia

Malcolm was one of my psychiatrists during my confinement in St John of God's. He had seen me at my very worst, semi-comatose and unresponsive. I had one-to-one sessions with him. He knew of my reluctance to mix with others, my miscarriages, and that I had been desperate to have another baby. He did not, of course, know how desperate. Even in my weakened, drug-induced state, I had never told him about Annie. It would have been a betrayal of Andrew. However, I trusted Malcolm. I think Daddy would have liked him. I had even told him about Diana and how I had drowned her on our ninth birthday. It's funny, because I had never told Andrew those details, just that she had tragically drowned. Malcolm insisted that I had been a child and that I should not feel responsible for something I could not have understood at that age. Malcolm could not accept that I had wanted to kill her. He wanted to believe the best of me.

So when I met him at the florist one afternoon four years later, he greeted me cautiously and remarked how well I looked and seemed. He invited me to go for a coffee. I'm sure it was against some patient/doctor rule, but I didn't mind. I like to be admired. And besides, he was no longer my doctor. Nowadays, I only saw my GP from time to time. Menopause had come and gone, and medication kept my moods stable and my thoughts calm.

Malcolm's German wife had died some years previously. We were both single. We started to date tentatively. He would make love to me and I would close my eyes and imagine that he was Andrew. He came to the house sometimes when Laurence was out. I wanted to keep him a secret from Laurence. I needed Laurence to know that there was nobody I loved as much as him.

But the problem with Malcolm was that he never stopped trying to fix me, even when I did not need to be fixed. Outside of our earlier therapy sessions I never spoke of Diana, and yet, when we were dating, Malcolm would bring it up from time to time. When he was in Avalon, after dinner one evening, he asked where the pond was. I thought my freezing silence would stop his curiosity, but he was oblivious to my iciness.

'You really are one of the most interesting cases I ever had. The fact that you kept all this guilt hidden away from your own husband for what, twenty-odd years? I think it's quite unhealthy to keep these things bottled up. You should be talking to someone about this. Not me now, obviously, but you would be amazed the difference it could make to your sense of freedom if you were able to talk about it. It might give you the liberty to leave the house overnight, to go on a holiday. I'm sure it's at the root of all your issues.'

'One of your cases? Is that all I am?' I said, trying to ignore his comments. I went to prepare a tray for coffee, but when I returned to the dining room, he wasn't there. The front door was wide open. I found him in the back garden.

'I can't find the pond,' he said.

I pointed to the raised paved area with the bird bath on top. 'Daddy filled it in afterwards. Come in and get your coffee while it's still hot.'

He took my arm and admired the shrubbery as we crossed into the house.

'You don't *have* to talk about it, Lydia, but I think it would do you some good.'

When Laurence was going to spend the weekend in Athlone, I knew I would be desperately lonely, so I invited Malcolm to stay with me on Saturday.

He arrived at lunchtime, bringing a surprise guest with him. She had aged badly, but I recognized her immediately. I have always kept myself in shape and taken pride in my appearance. We were the same age, she and I, but her hair was short and grey, her face wrinkled, her navy clothes shapeless. I noticed the crucifix around her neck and realized she was a nun.

'Amy Malone,' I said, and I clutched on to the sideboard in the hall and then my knees could no longer support my weight and I fell to the floor.

When I came round, Malcolm was waving a cushion over my face and Amy was still there.

'Have a cup of sugary tea, dear. I know it must be a terrible shock.'

Amy had watched me sit on my sister's chest and extinguish her life.

'Oh, Dr Mitchell, you should have warned her. I wouldn't have come if I thought you hadn't prepared her!'

I sat up and waved away their ministrations. 'Please.' When I was able, I sat on the sofa and drank a cup of sickly sweet tea.

'Now, Lydia, you remember Amy, of course you do. She is Sister Madeleine now, with the Loreto nuns. And I brought her along to talk to you.'

'Malcolm, how dare you? I don't want –'

'Sister Madeleine knows it wasn't your fault, don't you, Sister?'

I walked past them and went straight to the drinks cabinet while they babbled behind me in a blind panic.

'We were so young, Lydia. We were children. You couldn't have known that Diana was going to die. It was an accident and you were not to blame in any way. It was God's will. The Good Lord would never want you to feel guilty. You never intended her to die.'

'There, you see? I thought it would be a good idea to bring you two together so that you could talk about that day and lay old ghosts to rest.'

'It's not a day I'll ever forget, God bless her soul. It was a childish row that got out of hand. You couldn't have understood that she might die. It was just one of those things, Lydia, and you know I get down on my knees every night, and I pray for you and Diana.'

'Why don't I leave you to it for twenty minutes? And when I come back, perhaps Sister Madeleine could lead us in a prayer at the site of the old pond? What do you say, Lydia?'

I did not turn to face them but drained the glass of brandy and then refilled it.

'Please leave,' I said.

'But, Lydia, Sister Madeleine has come all the way from Sligo to see you –'

'Leave.'

'I'm so dreadfully sorry, Lydia. I had no idea this was

going to be a surprise for you. Dr Mitchell, please take me back to the station.'

'There's no need –'

Amy and I both turned on him then, and they left together in a burst of embarrassment.

Malcolm telephoned later but I hung up on him. I drank the rest of the bottle of brandy and wondered how Laurence was, and if he was missing me. I wondered what Bridget's family home would be like, and knew that it couldn't possibly compare to ours. I raised the blind in the kitchen and looked out at Diana's grave. I knew it was Annie's, but I liked to think it was Diana out there, and that she was sitting on the edge of the pond, waving at me, beckoning me to come and join her outside. I raised my hand and waved. I climbed up on to a stool and tore down the blind. I put back the original curtains. Laurence would have to get used to it.

Malcolm came to Avalon the next day to apologize. I didn't let him past the hall, but I allowed him to think he might some day be forgiven, and fortunately Laurence came home and interrupted us. Malcolm made small talk and then left. Laurence's mission had been successful. The letter had been safely posted.

In the evening, Laurence received a phone call and then reported that he had just broken off his relationship with Bridget. I knew it would never last. I was surprised it had gone on so long, but I assumed that seeing the drab little lives of others had opened his eyes. He must have realized that he could never be with someone like Bridget. Things would settle down now.

My mother-in-law, Eleanor, came for dinner. She was irritatingly punctual. If she was invited for seven, she would arrive early and hover on the porch outside until the grandfather clock in the hall chimed before she rang the doorbell. After Andrew died, she had insisted on coming once a month whether I invited her or not, so in the end I was forced to make the last Sunday of the month a regular fixture. I always made sure Laurence was there. After all, she hadn't come to see me.

She was very pleased that Laurence had been able to keep weight off for over a year, as if he had achieved it on his own. I could see that she was fond of him, but he was still quite wary of her. He told me how she had treated him when I was in the clinic. He certainly did not love her as much as he loved me. I wasn't going to tell her about Malcolm, obviously. Each time she visited, she stopped and looked at every single photograph of Andrew on the mantelpiece. After Laurence had 'found out' about Annie, he had wanted to put away all those photos, but I insisted they stay. Eleanor often made comments about the big old draughty house we lived in, implying that it was way too big for the two of us. She often talked about how lonely I must be and how boring it must be to spend days by myself. It was perfectly clear she wanted to move in. She had been increasingly frail recently, and I think she felt the cottage in Killiney was a little too remote.

'And Laurence will be moving out sometime. Won't you, dear?'

'I hope so,' said Laurence.

'Maybe you will be planning a family of your own. When am I going to meet this Bridget girl?'

I could see Laurence squirming with embarrassment.

'I don't know.'

'Do you like her, Lydia? Is she good enough for our handsome Laurence?'

'Nobody's good enough for our Laurence,' I said, and changed the subject to spare his blushes.

I thought that the letter would be enough, that it would put a stop to things. It infuriated me that her family could not just leave things be. Laurence had done an excellent job of throwing the Doyle family off course. He pretended to help Annie's sister, and took over the really crucial parts of her search. He told her that there was no record of Andrew's car, that it must be a red herring. I told him that he should find photographs of people of note who wore trilby hats, but Laurence would not countenance putting anybody else in the frame of suspicion. The letter was supposed to put an end to all the subterfuge. But now, Annie Doyle's sister was furious with her and wanted to track her down to confront her. How ridiculous.

And then Laurence announced out of the blue that he was going to Rome for a holiday in three days' time. He had once been on a school rugby trip to Marseilles when he was in Carmichael Abbey but had never expressed a desire to leave the country before. I told him that it was a ridiculous idea and that we couldn't afford it, but he sharply reminded me that he was earning our income. Laurence was by then in management in the dole office. The cream rises to the top. Still, his salary wasn't even a third of what Andrew's had been. I could not understand why he had made this sudden decision, and why Rome?

'I just need a break.'

'Are you going alone?'

A slight pause. 'Yes.'

'But why, and for how long?'

'A week.'

'A whole week.' I was feeling quite hysterical now. I had never been on my own for a week before.

'I'll come with you.'

'Mum, no, you hate travelling, you hate leaving the house. Why would you want to come to Rome?'

'What will I do here on my own?'

'What you always do.'

'On my own?' I couldn't believe he was being so selfish.

'Mum,' he tried to use a soothing voice with me, 'Mum . . . I think sometimes . . . that you have always lived a very sheltered life. You have always had someone to take care of you, but the world has moved on. Most women are out in the world now, holding down jobs and fighting for their rights, but it seems as if you don't want any independence. You are not bad . . . or wrong at all, you're just . . . unusual.'

'Old-fashioned?'

'A little. You don't have to change if you don't want to, but I live in the new reality and I like it.' He paused. 'You could ring your friend Malcolm. I'm sure he'd like to keep you company.'

I turned my face away.

'It's OK, Mum, for you to have a . . . friend. He seems like a very nice man.'

'We . . . it's not like that.'

'Well, why don't you ask Granny to come and stay for a few days? I'm sure she'd love to be invited. She's always hinting at it.'

'Oh, Laurence, if Granny came, we'd never get rid of her. She doesn't even like me.'

'Mum, I will move out sometime. I can't live with you for the rest of my life. It might be an idea to think about Granny moving in, for company, like. If she were to sell the cottage, the proceeds would probably be shared between you and Uncle Finn. Think about it.'

I had already thought about it. I had talked to Eleanor about the cottage and what might happen to it if she died. She and I had an understanding. I had been of the opinion that Laurence understood too, that he would stay with me always, like I had stayed with my father. There was absolutely no need for him to move out. This whole recent business about Annie Doyle and Laurence's involvement with her family was a huge mistake. I was beginning to think that Laurence no longer trusted me.

He made his travel plans regardless. He left the phone number of the hotel he was staying in. He urged me to call Malcolm, Finn and Rosie, or Eleanor if I was lonely. Two nights before his departure, his old girlfriend Helen turned up at dinner time.

'How'r'ye, Mrs F!' she said in her usual uncouth manner. 'Laurence said you'd be on your own next week, so I'm going to call over and check you out while he's away.'

I looked at Laurence in horror. 'Check me out?'

Laurence looked at his knees and didn't dare meet my eyes.

'Yeah, you know I'm a nurse now? Might be useful.'

Helen seemed to be pleased to hear that Laurence and Bridget had ended their little friendship. 'She never suited you, Lar. I don't know how you put up with her wonky eye.'

'Her . . .?'

'Did you never meet her, Mrs F? You never knew if she was talking to you or the ceiling. Hilarious.'

It disturbed me that Laurence had been dating a girl who was disfigured. How could he? He should have known how important aesthetics were to me. Had I not set him a good example?

Helen prattled on. 'I mean, when you started going out with her, you were a fat bastard, so you were even, like. But fair play to you for losing the weight. You look normal now.'

I shuddered at the girl's vulgarity, but she was being coy in her compliment to Laurence. He looked fantastic. Like his father. I saw no reason to tell Laurence that I had assisted his weight loss. When he began his training programme eighteen months previously in earnest, I thought I could help him out and crushed the pills into his food. Phentermine. They had been prescribed to me when I was in the clinic to lift me out of my lethargy, but the side effect had been a suppression of appetite and bursts of energy. When I began to see Malcolm, it was no problem to acquire a pad of prescription papers and fill them in whatever way we needed. I had withheld the tablets from Laurence in the week before he went to Athlone: I thought food would be his reward for carrying out my wishes regarding the Annie letter. It wouldn't matter what the Bridget family thought of him. I wondered how he would be in Rome. It was I that was keeping Laurence slim. Let him gorge himself in Rome. It might teach him a lesson.

I warmed to Helen. She could be my ally, and I might be able to use her in the future.

The night before Laurence left for Rome, he came home with a bloodied nose and scraped knuckles. My first thought was one of relief. He claimed to have been a victim of a mugging, but curiously he still had his wallet and his grandfather's watch. And he refused to call the guards. He cleaned himself up and rang Helen for medical advice, but I could tell his face would be bruised. He wrapped ice in a tea towel and applied it to his eyes.

'What a shame, darling. I know you were so looking forward to this holiday.'

'What do you mean?'

'I'm sure you can get a refund under the circumstances.'

'I'm still going.'

'But, darling –'

'Mum, I'm going. I'm fine.'

Why Rome? Why now? Who had struck my son and why? Why was Laurence keeping secrets from me?

17. Laurence

At the departure gate, I tried to read the newspaper but the headlines about the death of Monsignor Horan, and the Spanish fishermen lost at sea, meant nothing to me. I reread them again and again, trying to stop my brain from going over the shock of the previous evening.

He had been waiting for me outside the office at the staff entrance. He grabbed me by the collar and slammed me up against the wall.

'She's my fucking wife. Stay away from her. This is your only warning.'

He punched me straight in the face, but I managed to turn my head by a fraction just in time so he didn't manage to actually break my nose or cheekbone. I could tell that Dessie wasn't entirely satisfied by the contact, but thankfully he thought he had made his point and walked away. Sally picked me up. She wanted to call the guards, but I insisted I was OK. There was no way I could ever be connected with Karen's family by the guards in case it rang bells with someone who might have been around when my father was a suspect in Annie's murder.

'What was that about?'

'I haven't a clue!' I said. But now I was more determined than ever. Karen was never going back to such a brute. Even if nothing ever happened between us, I would protect her from men like him, like my father.

As the tannoy in the airport announced delays, I noticed a certain charge in the atmosphere as people around me sat up straighter and turned their heads. Distracted, I looked up to see what they were gazing at. Karen was walking slowly towards me. She was even more beautiful than the last time I'd seen her. None of us could avert our eyes as she glided forward, fresh-faced, wearing a simple white shirt and a tiered sky-blue silk skirt. She wore a linked gold chain around one ankle. And she was coming to sit beside me.

'Laurence?'

'Hi.'

'What happened to your face?'

'A silly accident in work. A shelf of ledgers fell on top of me. You look great.' Understatement of the century. I could actually feel the jealousy radiating from the other men sitting nearby. The women too were watching.

'Did you tell Bridget you were coming to Rome with me?' she said.

'No.'

'Me neither.'

She looked at me and I wanted to reach out and touch her face, but I stopped myself. I needed her to feel safe around me. More than anything, I wanted her to feel safe.

'Karen, you've been through so much, and I need a holiday. Let's just put everything behind us and enjoy Rome.'

She smiled. 'Let's not mention Annie, or Dessie.'

'Or Bridget.'

Her face clouded 'She's my friend. I feel like I'm betraying her.'

I feigned innocent motives. 'We're not doing anything. I've never been to Rome. I've always wanted to go. It just seems like a good opportunity.'

She was embarrassed. 'You're right. We're not doing anything wrong.'

My horrors fizzled away and Karen was beside me, chatting, laughing, touching my arm, as if we had always been very dear friends. When we boarded the flight, she dazzled the air hostess into agreeing to let me change seats so that we could sit together in first class. Karen was on an all-expenses-paid trip and was being accommodated in a five-star hotel. I was on a very tight budget. My hotel was starless. She ordered us gin and tonics, even though it was 10 a.m.

Karen was going to be in Rome for three days for a shoot for an Italian fashion magazine. She clearly loved her work, if you could call it that – it sounded like one long holiday to me.

'But you've no idea!' she said, laughing. 'All the hanging around, and the posing in really uncomfortable positions, in clothes that you are sewn into, in the heat, or in freezing temperatures. Try doing a summer collection shoot on an Irish beach in January, and then tell me how glamorous it is.'

When she asked about my work and my living circumstances, I avoided talking much about living at home and instead talked up my management job.

'Pretty boring really,' I said apologetically.

'But things are going well for you? You must be fairly senior if you can afford foreign holidays.'

I had taken out a bank loan.

It turns out that Karen did not have to work until the next day, so she was free for the whole day in Rome when we landed. It was as if some long-held fantasy was coming true.

'I hate travelling on my own. The crew I'm working with are Italian, and I don't know them at all. Will we spend the day together? I've never been to Rome either, so let's go sightseeing.' She put her hand on my arm to encourage my agreement. As if I needed encouragement.

When we had retrieved our suitcases from the carousel and stepped outside, a wall of heat hit me that I had never experienced before. Karen hailed a taxi. 'I'll put it on my expense account,' she said, to my relief, as I'd planned to get a bus. We agreed to go straight to my hotel to drop off my bags and then to hers, which was more central. The taxi journey was a revelation. Around every corner there was a monument or a building or a statue straight out of my history books. It was almost alarming to see them still standing among the flocks of tourists.

We stopped at my 'hotel', in a semi-derelict area behind Termini station. It was a doorway in a run-down street, which had two flights of steep stairs up to a tiny reception area. I quickly dumped my suitcase in my nondescript room, ran into the bathroom at the end of a sloping corridor, swabbed my armpits, applied four long blasts of aerosol deodorant and changed into my best shirt, short-sleeved and linen.

I checked myself in the mirror and for a shocking moment I saw my father looking back at me. There was a photo of him at home on the sideboard, with his rugby team at a dinner dance, slicked-back hair and chiselled jaw. He too had a bruise under his left eye, acquired through the rough and tumble of contact sport. I was as good-looking as he had been. Visually, at least, Karen and I were not such an odd-looking couple. For a split second I was sorry that my father hadn't lived to see me like this, but I refused to ruin this moment by thinking about him and put the notion out of my head. Karen was waiting in the taxi. I practically threw the key at the receptionist, Mario, on my way out. Mario halted me. 'Your mamma telephoned,' he said, sounding like a character in a pizza ad.

'My mamma?' I said, embarrassed.

'Yes, you must call her now, yes?'

'Thank you. Later, I will later.'

'Not now?' He was disappointed in me.

'Later,' I said, backing away towards the staircase.

He shook his head, disapprovingly. I worried. It was just Mum being Mum. Damn her, couldn't she let me go for one day? Was she going to ring me *every* day? Long-distance calls would cost a fortune. I would ring her tomorrow. Right now, I was going to enjoy a day sightseeing in Rome with my friend Karen the model.

She surprised me. I guess I had just assumed that a working-class girl would have no interest in culture. She knew a lot about art history and we set off to see a couple of Caravaggio paintings in the Augustinian church of Santa Maria off the Piazza del Popolo. I had not taken art as a subject in school and knew nothing of art history or artists, but she was able to talk with enthusiasm and insight, pointing out his use of light and shade. I tried to see these things through her prism, and even though these works were undeniably beautiful even to my uneducated eye, her passion gave them added excitement and importance. I bought postcard images of the work I had seen, and regretted that I had not brought a camera. Bridget had put me off the idea of photography permanently. Karen was surprised I hadn't brought a camera but spent so much time in front of one that she was glad to be free of it. Later, I regretted that I had no photograph of Karen and I together in Rome.

The museums and galleries were thankfully cool. Outdoors, the sun was merciless. I thanked God that I had not made this trip before I'd lost weight. I would not have been able to cope with the heat or the walking around. Sitting on the Spanish Steps, we snacked on street food, washed down with ice-cold beer in the afternoon, and stopped in all of the beautiful churches on the Via del Corso with their incredibly ornate side-chapels. At the end of that street a large structure rose in front of us. It was only as we got close that I realized its monumental scale. 'What is that?' I said.

Consulting the guidebook, Karen explained it was the Victor Emmanuel II Monument at the foot of the Capitoline Hill. 'Isn't it crazy?' she said. 'The Romans are mortified by it. They think it's too big and gaudy. All that white marble! Isn't it fabulous?'

By seven o'clock, we were both exhausted. We went back to her hotel, and I waited in the heavily ornate rococo lobby while she went to freshen up. The beer I had while I waited cost several thousand more lira than I'd expected.

When she stepped out of the elevator, everyone stopped to look. Her hair was piled high on her head, like Minerva in the frescoes at the Villa Medici we had seen earlier. She wore a long simple straight dress made of dark blue silk, cinched at the waist with a rope-style belt. She looked like she had just stepped down from a plinth and become flesh. Rome, I had noted, was full of beautiful and shapely women, but Karen stood out with her freckles and red glossy hair and piercing green eyes. No wonder they wanted her in their magazines. Nobody here looked like Karen.

'You look beautiful,' I said, but she brushed the compliment aside easily. She was used to it. She looked at me curiously, and then took a small compact out of her purse and delicately dabbed a pink sponge under my eye.

'I'm not hurting you, am I?'

Far from it. She turned the mirror towards me and the redness of the bruise had all but disappeared under the make-up.

We stepped outside into the bustle of a Rome evening, just slightly cooler now, passing groups of American tourists following a green umbrella; ice-cream salesmen; hawkers of mostly religious souvenirs; and small gatherings of Italians, all well groomed and speaking with their hands and their mouths at the same time.

We wandered down the street towards the Piazza Navona and passed several restaurants packed with tourists, but Karen led me further away from the main drag, down a side alley to an anonymous door in the wall.

'The concierge in the hotel told me to come here!' she said, as I looked unconvinced at the door that displayed no restaurant name but just a painted ceramic tile with a number on it. Through the door, we found ourselves in a large leafy atrium. Tall umbrella pines surrounded three circular fountains, every one as ornate as a miniature Trevi, which we had been rushed past amidst a throng earlier in the day. Water poured from the mouths of dead-eyed stone gargoyles. Bougainvillea leaves glistened with the spray of water from the fountains.

A small man with badly dyed hair came from nowhere and greeted us.

'*Prego*.' He pointed us in the direction of one corner, and as we followed him a vaulted colonnade appeared behind the trees, open to the courtyard on one side and open to a busy kitchen on the other. Simple wooden tables dressed in paper tablecloths lined this colonnade, mostly occupied by older people, all Italian. We were the only tourists, but while they could have resented me, they were clearly taken by Karen and acknowledged us kindly with a nod. Beauty is an international passport to acceptance. I used my phrase book to decipher the menu, which included pizza and pasta, as one might expect, but also aubergine, mozzarella and artichokes, exotic to me.

I had an overwhelming urge to devour everything on the menu but fought to eat delicately in front of Karen. She, of course, ate like you might expect a model to eat, picking at her food like a bird, but bemoaning the fact. She would love to eat more, she admitted, but didn't dare put on an ounce as she was on a diet. I groaned inside as her half-full plates were removed. I resolved to find more street food later when I was on my own.

I couldn't remember a better day in my entire life. We talked easily to each other. It didn't matter that we had few shared interests. She listened to my opinions on current affairs and books, and I learned more about pop stars and actors and fashion than I had ever known, but we were able to engage each other. Inevitably, though, the conversation turned to Annie.

'I'm not going to give up until I find her. Even if I have to go to the press, even if it upsets whatever new life she has now. She owes it to us to make proper contact. One lousy letter after six years of trauma isn't good enough. She nearly destroyed us.'

I was tentative. 'What would happen if you just let it go? Stopped looking, forgot about her?'

Karen's eyes glistened 'I can't. I loved her. I know that she loved me. There's something not right about it. I can't help feeling she is being kept against her will. It doesn't make sense.'

I didn't know what to say, so I said nothing.

'I'm sorry, I've ruined our day. It's been perfect, hasn't it?'

'Yes.'

I paid the bill and tried not to panic about how I would survive for the rest of the week.

At ten o'clock, she stifled a yawn and I offered to walk her back to her hotel.

As we meandered slowly through the streets, I wondered if I should take her hand. She held her hand loosely beside mine as we walked, just centimetres away. Was it an invitation? Emboldened by the wine at dinner, I thought maybe there was a chance, but just as I was about to make a move, she turned suddenly.

'Have breakfast with me tomorrow! I'm not being picked up until eleven.' I readily agreed. We parted with a peck on the cheek. I sensed for a second that we might have kissed properly, but I was the one who hesitated.

Why did I? There was nothing I would have liked more than to follow her up the grand staircase of her hotel, but something stopped me.

'See you in the morning,' she said, trailing her fingers away from my shoulder.

I made my way back to my hotel slowly, wondering what was wrong with me. I stopped at a small pizzeria and ate my way through a very large pizza on my own. The proprietor baulked at my capacity, and I worried that my old appetite was returning.

The streets and alleyways behind Termini that had seemed so lively earlier now took on a sinister glow and I thought, at first, that it was my malign thoughts that had brought this change in atmosphere, but then I noticed the girls. Lounging in groups of two or three, dressed inappropriately for their age in very short miniskirts and skimpy T-shirts and the highest of heels. The girls whistled at me as I approached, and I realized that they were for sale. A dangerous-looking man in a leather jacket sat in a Mercedes nearby, surveying his wares. He was clearly the pimp. The girls catcalled, hissed and followed me for a few yards. They tried several languages, including English, but I kept my head down and my hands stuffed into my trouser pockets. I knew that I didn't look prosperous enough to mug, and I passed unscathed.

The encounter unnerved me. All I could think of was Annie. Selling her body as if it was ice cream to the nearest buyer. I wondered about the man in the Mercedes. Was he there to mind them? Would he treat them well? Or beat them, kill them?

*

When I got back to my hotel, Mario was still on duty.

'You telephone your mamma now, yes? She call four times.' Christ. 'I place call for you, yes?'

'Thank you, but I will telephone in the morning.'

'Not now?'

'No. It is late. Tomorrow.'

He heaved a deep sigh. I suspected he would never have made his mother wait for a return call.

'There is another message. A lady. Is name Helen.'

'Helen? When?'

He seemed reluctant to tell me.

'An half-hour ago.'

Oh God, something was wrong.

'I'm going to my room. Can you place a call to Dublin for me in five minutes?'

'Yes. Helen or Mamma?'

I did not answer him, but took the stairs two at a time, dreading the news I was going to receive.

In my room, I picked up the receiver with a shaking hand. I was not in the humour for Mario's impertinence and barked my home number to him. He put me through without delay. Helen answered.

'Helen! What are you doing there? Is Mum OK?' I heard her say 'It's him', and then there was a grappling sound as somebody else took the phone, while voices babbled in the background.

'Oh, Laurence, where have you been? We've been trying to get hold of you all day!' My mother, breathless and excited.

'What is it? What is so important?'

'Try not to be upset, dear, but it's your grandmother.

She died this morning. Your Uncle Finn and Aunt Rosie are here. It's all so awful. Such a lot has happened. It's up to you of course, but I really think you ought to come home.'

Shit. Shit. Shit.

'Yes, I will.'

'Oh, that's great, darling. I knew you would. Helen went to the travel agent and booked your ticket for first thing tomorrow morning.'

'She . . . what?'

'She's been an enormous help. Would you like to speak to her? . . . Helen!' Mum dropped the receiver and Helen took it up again.

'Sorry about your granny, Lar. I know she was a fierce wagon like, but she was still your granny.'

'Thanks. So what time is my flight tomorrow?'

'It's at 9.20 a.m. You can collect the ticket at the airport. Is that OK?'

I rang Mario and asked for an alarm call in the morning. I told him that I would be checking out. He was incensed that I was cancelling my week-long stay, but when I told him I had to go home to my mother because my grandmother had died, he understood immediately. I asked him to place a call to Karen's hotel. The receptionist there refused to put me through, insisting that Karen had asked not to be disturbed. I guess 'beauty sleep' is a real thing. I left a message with the receptionist, apologizing for not being able to keep our breakfast appointment, explaining I had to return to Ireland.

I lay back on my bed, considering the last forty-eight hours of my life. Yesterday, Granny was alive and Karen's husband physically attacked me, and now here I lay after spending the day with her in Rome. I was genuinely sad about Granny Fitz. Despite her rudeness, I think she did always have my best interests at heart. When I was a boy, she doted on me in a way that made Mum jealous.

I knew that I would not be coming back to Rome after the funeral. The flights were too expensive.

Thankfully, Mario wasn't on duty in the morning. A silent girl served me strong coffee with chocolate powder in it and a croissant, and hailed a taxi on the street to take me to the airport.

My mother greeted me tearfully when I arrived home. Helen had stayed the night in one of the spare rooms to keep her company.

'Jesus, Lar, what happened to your face?'

I had forgotten about my bruise.

'Laurence was mugged by some hoodlums,' said my mother.

Later, Helen grilled me about the 'mugging'. She couldn't understand why they hadn't taken my watch or wallet.

'Come on, Lar, what really happened?'

'I walked into a shelf at work.'

She hooted with laughter.

'You're some eejit. Why does your mum think you were mugged?'

'If I tell her the truth, she'll ban me from going to work. You know what she's like.'

'Are you going to sue them? The office?'

'What? No.'

Helen shrugged. 'I would.'

No doubt she would.

Helen grabbed me and gave me a hug. 'Fuck's sake,' she whispered, 'I thought your granny would live for ever. She was made of steel!'

Helen stayed all day, helping my mother. She even did some light housework before she came to say goodbye.

'That'll be twenty quid, please, Lar.'

It was easier to pay her than to fight about it.

Granny had been found by a neighbour. It was a heart attack. Probably the same congenital failure that had killed my father, although the stress of killing somebody was no doubt a contributing factor in his case. Mum was in stoic form, despite the tears. She and Uncle Finn and Aunt Rosie were coordinating the funeral arrangements. Aunt Rosie said something about every funeral you go to reminds you of all the other funerals you've ever been to. I'd only been to one.

'You know, I hardly remember a thing about your father's. I was in such a state!' said Mum.

Before the funeral, out of respect for Granny, I asked Rosie to help me put make-up on my bruise. Rosie wanted to know all about the mugging. The funeral car arrived to take us to the church before I had to do too much explaining.

We stood at the top of the church as Granny's friends and acquaintances shook our hands, mumbling their condolences. Granny's coffin was closed. Apparently she had made her wishes known in case someone dressed her inappropriately. Mum said they'd given the undertakers

Granny's tweed skirt and mink stole. That seemed inappropriate to me. Being buried with an animal that was already dead was worse than wearing it, in my opinion.

After the obligatory shuffle around Uncle Finn and Aunt Rosie's chaotic, sandwich-laden home, made worse by throngs of elderly people in various stages of decrepitude, shot through with their eight rowdy offspring, I drove Mum home.

'What a day!' she said, but she was almost cheerful. She'd got what she wanted. Her interfering mother-in-law was out of the way and her son was home, back where he belonged. She didn't try to fake her sorrow that my holiday had been aborted almost before it had even begun. She didn't ask me how I had spent my twenty-four hours in Rome. My day with Karen was something I could keep to myself. She didn't notice my mood, or if she did, she probably thought it was because I was missing my holiday or my grandmother. She was in good form, gossiping about what the mourners were wearing, which of Dad's friends had come, how well Aunt Rosie had coped with having 'all those people' in her house. She fixed us both drinks.

'I think we're going to be all right now,' she said.

I didn't know what she meant. 'What?'

'Financially. Eleanor told me last year that she had changed her will to look after us. I just told Finn. He was furious about it. I don't know exactly what she did, but she definitely said we'd be taken care of.' Mum was quite gleeful about this. I had never realized before how mercenary she could be. We did OK on my management salary and her widow's pension, but it was nothing like the scale my father used to earn, so even though we could cover our bills, there were no extras like the old days. No fine dining and designer clothing like Mum was used to. I didn't miss that kind of thing, but my mother yearned for it.

'Mum?'

'Yes, darling?'

'Annie's family is not going to give up on looking for her. Her sister has been to Athlone looking for her and she's going back to the midlands to continue the search as soon as she can.'

'Oh, for God's sake, are they stupid?' My mother was irritated and I was astonished by her callousness. 'It's ridiculous. Why can't they just drop it?'

'If I disappeared, would you stop looking for me?'

'Darling! Of course not! I am just trying to protect you and the memory of your father. Send her another letter.'

'What?'

'The sister. What's her name? Send her a direct letter from Annie, something that will stop her. We'll compose it together. You'll have to go back to Athlone to post it.'

My mother was being so practical and unemotional about this cover-up of her husband's murderous history. It horrified me. And yet what could I do? She was right. It had to be done. And it also gave me the chance to give comfort to Karen.

'Karen. Her name is Karen.'

18. Karen

Ma and Da were sort of back together. He was so grateful to have her back, he smartened up, stayed out of the pub and went looking for a job in earnest. He had really missed her and was determined to keep her home. Dessie was trying to get me to come home too, and my mother was doing her best to help him. She was at me all the time. 'Don't make a mistake you'll regret for the rest of your life. Dessie Fenlon is a good man and sure, doesn't he love the bones of you?'

Dessie had doorstepped me shortly after Rome, but when I'd ignored him, he shouted down the street after me, 'I sorted your man in the dole office, he won't go near you now.'

I wheeled around. 'You did what?'

'Gave him the hiding he deserved.'

I remembered the bruise under Laurence's eye and his explanation of the ledgers falling on top of him at work. 'You stupid bastard,' I said. 'He's only a friend.'

'Yeah, well, he won't be anything more than that after I've finished with him.' And Dessie sauntered away, hands in his pockets and head up, as if he'd just had a good day at the dog track.

In my head, I was reliving my day in Rome with Laurence. It had been such a brilliant time and a real shame that it had to be cut short. When I got back, he explained about his granny dying, but I found myself thinking about him all the time. I felt terrible about Bridget. Laurence could have kissed me any time that day, he could have taken my hand, made some gesture of affection, but he didn't. I thought I had been misreading the signals, but I felt like he and I were involved in some way. And yet any time I had tried to reach a higher level of friendship with him, he had gently turned me away – like when I'd asked for his home phone number, he had mumbled that I could always get him in the office. It struck me now that Dessie had scared him off. Or maybe Laurence just didn't like me in that way. Maybe the modelling business had given me too much confidence.

I rang Laurence at work and asked him straight out if Dessie had assaulted him. He sheepishly confirmed it.

'But why didn't you tell me?'

'It would have ruined our trip.'

'I'm so sorry, Laurence.'

'Don't be. It's not your fault, but do me a favour and don't go back to him.'

'I . . . I won't.'

'Good.'

Mixed messages again. Laurence didn't want me to get back with my husband.

I was still looking for Annie, but I was looking for a flat too. Yvonne told me my shoot in Rome had been a huge success, and I had more money than I'd ever had and more offers of work in Milan and Paris. Yvonne was worried that I'd move to London and change agent, and maybe I would have if I hadn't still been looking for

Annie. Also, I felt a loyalty to Yvonne. I would still have been in the dry-cleaner's and living with Dessie if she hadn't taken me under her wing. I hadn't told her that Annie was still alive. I didn't want her to know that her son had been wrong.

The weekend after I got back from Rome, Bridget rang to tell me that she'd got an office transfer to Mullingar in the meantime and that I should come see her there and stay in her new flat to continue my search for Annie. I agreed to go, and on the first Friday night of my visit, I admired her new home. It was a shared house on a new housing estate just outside the town. She shared with two other girls, who were watching *Blind Date* on TV. We took a bottle of wine up to her room, where she had a pull-out mattress for me on the floor. I drank too much and told her that Laurence had come to Rome with me. I immediately regretted it.

'He . . . what?'

'I was going anyway, and he said he needed a holiday, so he just booked the same flight as me. It made sense. I should have told you before, but I didn't want you jumping to conclusions. I mean, we met for a drink one night after you split up . . .' With every word, I was making it worse, over-explaining everything. 'But there's nothing going on, I promise. You believe me, don't you?'

I didn't know until then that it was possible to tell the truth and still feel like a liar. She was distant with me for the rest of the weekend. She said she had a cold the next day, so I went around the town on my own, showing Annie's photo, asking if anyone had seen her. I got more or less the same response as I'd had in Athlone. Annie looked like someone they used to know. What was wrong with her mouth? Why was I looking for her? Had I reported it to the guards? This time I didn't go into any explanations.

I went back to Bridget's house wet, cold and disheartened. She spoke little to me that evening. Eventually, I broached the subject of Laurence again.

'I should have known,' she said. 'I can't believe I've been so stupid. He was always so much nicer when you were around. And he spent so much time and effort trying to find your sister's murderer. I always thought it was ridiculous. Like you were playing at being detectives.'

'It isn't a game!'

'The two of you have made a fool out of me. You can lie to yourself that he's not interested in you, but look at us.' She pointed to the mirror behind us. 'Who would you choose if you were him?'

'Please, Bridget, he's never made a move on me, I swear –'

'Give him time, he's just waiting. God knows, he wouldn't want to do anything inappropriate. You're a married woman.' There was a bitterness to her tone.

The next morning I returned to Dublin utterly miserable. I told Ma and Da that I was going to be moving into my own place. Ma cried and said I should be moving back in with my husband, but Da understood. I warned Ma not to give Dessie any more information about me or my friends. My new apartment was on Appian Way.

'But sure, we don't know anyone who lives around there,' said Ma. She was uncomfortable with the idea of me living where I didn't belong.

'I'll get the keys soon and then you can come over for dinner, Ma. You'll love it.'

I was woken early the following week when Ma came into my room. Her hands were shaking. 'There's another letter, with a parcel. From Annie. It's for you.'

I turned the package over in my hands. The postmark was Athlone. The wrapping on the parcel was torn on one corner and, without ripping the paper away, I could see it was a set of oil paints in a clear plastic case.

Dear Karen

I wrote to ma a few weeks ago and im sure you probabley herd about it. i bin thinking about you a lot and I know I should have writen to you and da as well. i know I done a terrible thing running away and leaving you all to worrie about me and i keep tinking about that art set i never got you like i said i would. im never going to be able to make it up to you for the trouble I cosed but I hope youll get to use these paints some time. the thing is I herd that someones bin loking for me and I think its you. if you love me your to leave me alone don't worrie about me im safe and happy and even thow I miss all of youss even da I know he never ment to be croull to me.

Its bette that you let me do my owen thing. One day I mite surprise you and pae a viset but please don't look for me. ill come to you when im readie.

Love your Annie.

I passed the letter to Ma, who read it out to Da. He looked at the shapes of the letters and said for the first time that I could recall, 'I wish I could read.'

'Amn't I forever offering to teach you?' said Ma. 'But you were always too proud.'

'Not any more,' he said.

They held each other and it was as if they were losing Annie all over again, but they'd found each other. I left them alone and went to my room.

She was in Mullingar, or thereabouts. She had to be. Someone I showed the photo to had recognized her and reported back. I wondered if it was the shifty-looking fella in the betting shop. He had been really uncomfortable about the whole thing. I wondered why she wouldn't let me into her life. I knew from the letter to Ma that she had a new name, so she had probably made up a history for herself that didn't match the truth and, when I thought about it, it made sense.

I rang Bridget. I expected her to be frosty with me, but she sounded more relaxed. I told her about the letter.

'She's in Mullingar, or somewhere around there. Do you still have the photo I left? Will you keep an eye out for her?'

'Yeah, of course I will. I'm glad you're a bit closer to finding her.'

'I'll probably leave her alone now. She doesn't want to know me, but I'm sort of less annoyed with her now, if that makes any sense?'

'Yeah.'

There was a pause.

'Have you seen Laurence?'

I could answer honestly: 'No, haven't seen him since I last talked to you.'

'Right.'

'Why?'

'I think . . . I'm sorry I was suspicious of you two.'

'It's OK, it must have seemed weird.'

'Yeah, it's just that I think he wants to get back with me.'

I inhaled deeply. 'Yeah?'

'Josie spotted him down the town in Athlone on Saturday. I think he was probably thinking of coming to my house, but he lost his nerve. He probably didn't know I'd moved to Mullingar.' Bridget was breathless with excitement.

'But he never went to your folks' house?'

'No, you know how nervous he can get, and after what happened last time I don't blame him. I rang him last night and left a message, but the bitch of a mother probably never passed it on. I'll ring him in work tomorrow.'

I tried to keep the disappointment out of my voice. 'Great, that's great. I'm really pleased for you. Honestly,' I said, dishonestly.

I didn't ring Laurence and he didn't ring me. I moved into my new apartment, and as I unpacked my boxes and suitcases and surveyed my new home, I looked at the set of paints, posted with Annie's letter from Athlone. They were oil paints. Annie had forgotten that I hated using oils. I took out the letter again. I had saved all the parcel wrapping. I looked at the clear plastic package that the paints had come in. It was a far cry from the antique box that had sat in Clarks's window, but maybe she was only buying what she could afford. I looked at the postmark again. Athlone, dated Saturday three weeks ago. Something bothered me. Hadn't Laurence . . .?

As I went over the details in my mind, I felt a fever develop until I thought my head might explode. The question was suddenly painfully obvious. Had Laurence sent the letter – not just this one, but the first one too? Had he copied Annie's handwriting from the notebook I'd let him borrow? I remembered him telling me and Bridget about being forced to forge other boys' school reports back in the day. He was really good at it. He must have taken note of every detail I had told him about her and used them all to convince me that Annie was still alive. I phoned him at the office.

'Laurence?'

'Hi!'

'Hi.'

'Are you OK?'

'Yes, I just need to ask you something, and I need you to be really honest with me, OK? I mean, if the answer is yes, well, that's fine, but I just need to know.'

There was silence on the other end of the line.

'Laurence?'

'Yeah.'

'Did you write those letters pretending to be my sister?'

19. Laurence

I allowed my mother to think that she was dictating the second Annie letter, but hers was too impersonal, too callous for what I knew of Annie's temperament, so I tore it up and wrote another one later, using the words I thought Karen needed to hear. I remembered Karen saying something about a set of paints that Annie had been going to buy her before she disappeared, so I bought a set and included them in the package. I knew it would give an air of authenticity to Annie's story. Karen would be reassured that Annie still loved her. That was important to me.

I got the bus to Athlone that Saturday, knowing from Mr Monroe that Bridget had been transferred to Mullingar so there was no chance of my bumping into her. It was a simple task: get off the bus, go straight to the post office and then back to the station to catch the same bus returning to Dublin.

Mum was waiting eagerly for my return. She had some news. She had been shopping and bought herself a whole new wardrobe. There were expensive wine in the drinks cabinet and smoked salmon in the fridge.

'We got the cottage!' she exclaimed. Apparently, Granny had left her cottage to us. The contents, which included some nice pieces of antique furniture and noteworthy paintings, had been left to Uncle Finn and Aunt Rosie.

Eight years previously, my father had encouraged his mother to sell her four-bedroom Victorian house in Ballsbridge and buy an isolated cottage up on top of a cliff in Killiney. He had invested the balance in those disastrous Paddy Carey deals that came to nothing. Mum planned to sell the cottage and pocket the proceeds to spend on luxuries we had not been able to afford for a long time. I was again dismayed by her apparent glee. The counterfeit letters were of no consequence to her. She didn't even ask about my journey.

Some days later, Uncle Finn came to the house with Aunt Rosie. I welcomed them courteously, but Uncle Finn was in no mood for niceties.

'My mother's will. I'm hoping you'll do the decent thing,' he said, addressing himself to me.

Mum intervened. 'It was Eleanor's wishes. You aren't suggesting that she was of unsound mind?'

'No, but you must see how unfair it is. Andrew was the one who lost our inheritance, and you are the only one to profit from what's left.'

'She left the contents to you. It's not as if you got nothing.' My mother was trying to be reasonable.

Aunt Rosie glowered at me. 'You owe us.'

Why were they looking at me? Mum breezily dismissed them. 'You are not going to contest it, are you, Finn? Drag us through the courts and make a public spectacle of the family?'

'Of course not, but Laurence is old enough to decide for himself what happens.'

I didn't understand. 'Me? Why me?'

Uncle Finn glared at my mother. 'You haven't even

told him the full truth, have you?' He turned to me. 'My mother left her cottage to you, Laurence. Not to Lydia, just to you. For your independence, she said.'

Mum was defiant. 'Yes, and Laurence sees no reason why he should share the proceeds with you.'

Aunt Rosie was furious. 'You might have told him, Lydia. Well, what do you think, Laurence? Are you going to sell up and keep the money for yourself or are you going to share it with us, like a decent person?'

Mum stood behind me and put her hands on my shoulders. 'I think it's appalling the way you are trying to bully my son. I must ask you to leave. Right now.'

Mum saw them to the door.

'The nerve of them! Who do they think they are, trying to tell us what we can do with our inheritance? Your father would be livid if he could see how things were turning out. Don't mind them, Laurie. That cottage is ours and we'll do what we want with it.'

'Mine. The cottage is mine,' I corrected her.

'Of course, darling,' she said, flashing her most dazzling smile. She continued to rant about Uncle Finn and Aunt Rosie.

'How could you not tell me about this, Mum?'

'Don't make such a fuss, Laurence. How does it make any difference?'

'But, Mum, it isn't fair. They should get at least half the value of the cottage.'

'Why? Why should they get anything? Eleanor knew exactly what she was doing. Finn and Rosie can afford their eight children, and if they can't, well then, they shouldn't have had so many.'

My mother tried to hide her jealousy of Aunt Rosie's ability to successfully bear eight children.

'We have struggled. You know I never liked to complain, but I would like us to live in the manner to which we were accustomed. Back when your father died, everyone was trying to get me to sell this house and move into a nasty little flat, and I know it's been a big responsibility for you to keep us here but now we can relax a bit. You have earned it, darling.'

Helen dropped in later that evening. Mum and she were on good terms now, since Helen had been so 'helpful' around the time of Granny's funeral. I even got the impression that Mum would quite like us to rekindle our teenage romance. She made a point of leaving us on our own.

'Granny left me her cottage in her will.'

'Wow! Seriously? That's cool. Your own home!'

'Not really, Mum is selling it.'

'Wait now, *who* did your granny leave the cottage to?'

It hadn't occurred to me till now. Earlier, I had thought that we really should sell the place and split the proceeds with Uncle Finn, but Helen alerted me to the possibilities.

'Your own place. Rent free! What's it like?'

As I described it, I gradually realized it was perfect, exactly what I needed. Granny had specified that it was for *my* independence.

'It's quite isolated, up a laneway off a tree-lined avenue in Killiney. One large bedroom that stands out over a cliff. There's a big sitting room with views out to Dalkey Island and the bay. The kitchen is a bit old-fashioned. No neighbours. It backs on to the train tracks on one side, and beyond that, the cliffs and the sea.'

'Party in your place!' said Helen, missing the point entirely.

In Rome, Karen had told me she was moving out of her da's place. I'd been impressed by her ambition to live freely and independently. It was time I did the same thing. I was surprised that Karen hadn't rung me since she got the letter, but I was busy making plans for our future, hers and mine.

That evening, I told Mum that I was moving out to the cottage at the end of the week. I didn't dance around the issue. I was quite matter-of-fact and told her that I needed to live as an independent adult and that she would soon see that it would be good for her too. I explained that I would still cover all her bills and expenses and that I would call to see her at least once a week. She would be free to entertain Malcolm whenever she wanted. I was sure that he would be more comfortable in the house if I wasn't there.

Mum cried and begged me to stay, but I didn't rush to comfort her. I felt awful, but I couldn't give in to her again. I needed to be allowed to grow up. She went to her room and remained there for the evening.

About 11 p.m., I knocked on her door to say goodnight. There was no response. I pushed the door open. She was sprawled across the bed, fully clothed.

'Mum?' And then I saw the two empty pill bottles.

I shouted at her, pulled her head up. She was breathing but the breaths were uneven and shallow.

'Jesus! Mum! What –' But I knew exactly what she had done, and I knew why.

'Leave me alone,' she mumbled, 'I just want to sleep.' I

dragged her out to the bathroom, opened all the windows and positioned her on the floor. I held her jaw open with one hand and used a toothbrush to poke at the back of her throat until she began to retch. I pulled her over to the toilet as she started to vomit.

'Mum, I have to call an ambulance.'

Between retches she screamed, 'You can't, you can't! They'll send me back there!'

I knew she meant St John of God's, and I knew she was right. I left her there throwing up, and belted downstairs and dialled.

'Hello?'

'Helen, it's me, Laurence.'

'Well, what the fuck time –'

'Can you come to my house? Right now? It's an emergency.'

'Why, what's happened?'

'Can you come? Please. My mother has taken some pills, a lot of pills!'

She finally got the urgency of my tone. 'Is she conscious?'

'Yes, she's throwing up now.'

'Good, that's good. OK, yeah, I'll be there in ten minutes.'

Helen was fantastic. Once I explained what my mother had done, Helen took over. She ignored my mother's protestations and eventually put her to bed, not before removing all of the medications from the bedroom and bathroom. We stayed with my mother until she fell asleep, then we went downstairs.

'Don't worry, she won't try anything else tonight, she'll be out cold for at least twelve hours. Why did she do it?'

'I told her I was moving out.'

Helen looked at me with genuine sympathy.

'You should have called an ambulance.'

'They'll only take her back to St John of God's.'

'Well, maybe that's where she needs to be.'

I couldn't help it then: the tears came to my eyes and I began to sob. I don't cry gracefully. I heave my shoulders and it's noisy and ugly. Helen went to the drinks cabinet and poured me a large whiskey.

I took it gratefully and drank half of it in one go, feeling the welcome heat coursing through me.

'I promised her she wouldn't have to go back there.'

'For fuck's sake, Laurence, that is a promise you can't keep.'

'I have to.'

'You don't.'

'Helen, you don't understand. She doesn't have anybody else. It's my duty to look after her.'

'And what about your duty to yourself? What about living your own life? Are you going to live at home for the rest of your life to stop your mother from topping herself?'

'I didn't think she'd take it so badly. I knew she was upset, but I thought she'd see in the end that it was for the best. She's been quite stable for a few years now. She has a boyfriend –'

'Will he look after her? Is he kind to her? Like, will he marry her and move in? Is it even a possibility?'

'I don't know. I don't know him. He's a psychiatrist.'

Helen began to laugh, and in the emotion and horror of what had just happened, I began to laugh too. And it was like loosening an air-pressure valve. The hilarity subsided.

'What am I going to do?'

Helen was thoughtful for a minute or two.

'You definitely don't want her to go back into psychiatric care?'

'No. Besides, we can't afford it.'

'Can you afford to hire me?'

'You? What do you mean? You have a job in St Vincent's . . . don't you?'

'Not any more. They fired me last week. They found out I'd nicked a load of Valium.'

Why was I not surprised?

'Helen! Why?'

'I don't know. It was stupid really. I should have nicked amphetamines or something that gives you a bit of a buzz. Fuck's sake. Valium are just downers. I was at a party a month ago and everyone was asking for them, but the fucking eejits got greedy and took them like Smarties. Nearly everyone fell asleep. Disaster!'

'So what are you going to do?'

'I don't know. I was lucky they didn't take me off the register. I was going to apply for some nursing-home jobs, but I could work here, couldn't I?'

'What?'

'Just for a few weeks, until she stabilizes, like. I still have the Valium. That's probably all she'll need for a while, and I could monitor the dosage –'

'Helen, my mother doesn't even like you very much.'

'Yeah, well, she likes me a lot better than she used to. And what option does she have? Are you going to give up work and nurse her, watch her?'

It seemed like a drastic solution but Helen was right. I didn't have a lot of choices.

'You're not moving in. Just watch her while I'm at work.'

'Fine.'

We sat up till 3 a.m. We negotiated a fee. She actually charged a lot less than I expected. 'Mates' rates. For cash, like,' she said.

I told her about work. We talked about our disastrous relationship in the past, and she admitted that she had been unnecessarily cruel to me. I admitted that I hadn't been attracted to her.

'Wanker,' she said. She told me about the nine different boyfriends she'd had over the previous six years. 'You weren't the only gobshite I dated.' She complimented my weight loss. I let my guard down and told her about my break-up with Bridget and the non-proposal. As expected, Helen thought this was hilarious. Helen convinced me that I must move out, that I had to live independently.

'It will be good for you. And her. Get the Malcolm fella on board.'

I was incredibly grateful to Helen for her company that night.

I stayed off work the next day and carefully explained to Mum that Helen was going to mind her for the next few weeks and reassured her that I would not move out until she was more stable. She was tearful and ashamed. She apologized over and over.

'I'm so, so sorry. Why am I so useless? Why am I like this?'

'You're not useless, Mum, far from it. You're just not ready for me to move away yet. I should have let you get used to the idea for a while.'

'Please don't go!'

'We'll talk about it again when you're stronger. Would you like me to ring Malcolm?'

'No! Don't tell him. He'd just – don't tell him.'

'OK, I won't. But, Mum, why are you . . . Is he married, is that it?'

She was taken aback. 'No, of course not.'

'You never talk about him. You never have him around to the house when I'm here . . . but when you're better, I'd like to meet him properly, OK?'

She nodded. 'Malcolm is . . . he's . . . I just want to keep him separate, away from the rest of my life.'

'But why?'

'He knows me . . . too well.'

'Don't you . . . *like* him? Do you want to go on seeing him?'

'I do, he's a good man. It's just that . . . he knows.'

'About Annie Doyle?'

'No, of course not, I'd never tell anyone about that, it's just . . .' She trailed off.

I had no idea what she was talking about but speculated that she might feel she had compromised her privacy with him. If that was the case, though, why did she continue to see him? It hardly made sense, but further questions increased her unease so I let the matter drop.

I recalled how Helen had behaved around my parents

before with her couldn't-care-less attitude, and I worried that it was a big mistake to have her looking after Mum, but she was completely different when she was in nursing mode: courteous, respectful and caring. I came home from work one evening to find her repotting plants with Mum at the kitchen table. She spoke softly and gently held Mum's arm steady when the pot threatened to fall from her hands. If only she could be like that all the time. I said so to Helen later.

'Yeah, well, I'm a good actor, aren't I? I should get a fucking Oscar.'

Mum and Helen bonded over those few short weeks. Who would have ever thought it? Helen said Malcolm rang a few times, but Mum refused to talk to him. He sounded concerned, apparently.

'Should we tell him what happened?' I asked Helen.

'No. It's her business. She doesn't have to see him if she doesn't want to.'

'But he obviously cares about her.'

'Yeah, but does she care about him?'

At work, I was the subject of some office gossip. The girls held me responsible for driving Bridget out of her job. Evelyn and Sally wondered why I hadn't been the one to apply for a transfer. I tried to explain that Bridget wanted to be closer to home, but they had talked to her and knew that I had broken up with her.

'She was really good for you,' said Jane. 'Look at how you started eating healthily when you began going out with her. You couldn't have done that on your own.'

I protested that I *had* done it on my own. They accused

me of being ungrateful. I pulled rank and sent them back to their desks. Bridget rang me at home, and in the office several times, hopeful of a reconciliation. She told me that Josie had seen me in Athlone. I point-blank denied it. I told her that Josie must have been mistaken. She rang back later that afternoon. She had double-checked and Josie was absolutely sure it had been me.

'Jesus, Bridget, just drop it, will you? We are not getting back together. I did not go to Athlone. I do not love you.' I hung up to see Jane watching me through the open door of my office. She shook her head in disgust.

Some days later, Malcolm called to the house an hour after I'd got home. Mum was upstairs, resting.

He didn't want to come in, but stood awkwardly on the doorstep. 'I'm very sorry, I just wanted to . . . I was worried about her,' he said by way of explanation. 'She hasn't returned my calls and I thought that maybe I'd offended her in some way.' He seemed genuinely upset.

'No, I can assure you it's nothing to do with you. She just needs some time out.'

'Has she . . . is she seeing a doctor?'

'She is in excellent hands.' This was true.

'Laurence, I . . . I never intend to take your father's place, you know that, don't you? I would never come between a mother and her son.'

'Of course not, I understand. When she's up to it, we will all have dinner together.'

'Really? I'd like that very much. I'm very fond of her.'

I could see that was true. I assured him that I would call him in a few weeks. He seemed relieved.

My mother got better. She treated her overdose as a minor aberration – 'It was a very silly thing to do' – but insisted that it would never happen again and that she had overreacted to my talk of moving out. 'It's just that I've never been on my own before . . .' She still didn't want me to go.

I had finally begun to resent my mother. Her emotional blackmail had me trapped. Helen had been good company, and though we'd agreed to keep in touch, I missed her around the place when she left. There was nothing romantic between us at all, but, unlikely as it seemed, she had turned out to be a good friend in a crisis.

Nevertheless, Karen had been constantly on my mind as I wondered what her reaction to the second Annie letter had been, and then she rang me one day in the office.

'Did you write those letters pretending to be my sister?'

I stalled for time as I tried to anticipate the consequences of any answer I might give, but I was sick of the subterfuge, sick of the deception, exhausted from lying. What I wanted was the best for Karen. If she was now to discover that my father had murdered her sister, that Annie was buried in my back garden, that her search was over, would it bring her peace? Would it bring me peace?

'Yes,' I replied.

She exhaled, and then said the most unexpected thing. 'I think I love you too.'

20. Lydia

Laurence told me he was leaving home. I could not let that happen. His place would always be here with me. He thought I was unhinged. I could see it in the way he talked to me sometimes, as if I were a child. I decided to use his opinion of my instability for our benefit. He had been pulling away from me for some time, and he was secretive and suspicious. Covering up the whole Annie Doyle business had taken its toll on him. I told him that he must put the matter out of his mind, but he was really preoccupied with it.

Damn Eleanor, she'd got the better of me with her last will and testament. She had told me that she was going to look after us, but she excluded me and looked after Laurence alone. She had always adored him and frequently criticized my parenting skills, but even when I heard the words from her lawyer – 'for his independence' – I still never thought that Laurence would leave me. The only struggle I had anticipated was with Rosie and Finn, who wanted their 'fair share' because they had been greedy enough to have eight children. I had planned to go clothes shopping in the boutiques where they still knew me by name. I was going to take Laurence out to introduce him to the rudiments of fine dining and a good wine list. The silk curtains in our drawing room needed replacing, as did the carpets in the hall, stairs and landing. A crack had appeared on the wall above the mantelpiece, and the enamel was wearing through in my bathroom. Daddy would never have stood for such imperfections. We finally had the means to restore everything, but Laurence intended to defy me.

The suicide attempt was a desperate measure, but I had to do something. I didn't actually take any of the pills, but I had drunk plenty of water so that I would have something to throw up when he found me, which I knew he would. I knew Laurence would never send me to St John of God's, and thankfully he kept his cool and called on Helen. I began to see Helen in a new light after that. It was clear that Helen adored Avalon. She didn't need much of an excuse to turn up. She had been useful before, when Eleanor died. She could be vulgar and uncivilized, but she was entertaining and wonderfully indiscreet, and at least she had a name. Her mother, Angela d'Arcy, was a poet of repute. She did not write anything to my taste, and of course she was horribly bohemian. It was hardly surprising that Helen had grown up wild like a weed, but it was she who told me the full story of Laurence's visit to Bridget's family in Athlone. It was laughable that that silly girl had actually thought my Laurence would marry her, a girl of no breeding or background. I thought it useful to keep Helen around, as Laurence was obviously confiding in her more than me.

Unfortunately, the 'overdose' only deterred Laurence temporarily. He was determined to go ahead with his plans to occupy Eleanor's cottage. He tried to prepare me for his departure by inviting Malcolm over more regularly, as if Malcolm could ever replace Andrew, or Laurence.

Malcolm and I had not spoken of the Amy Malone

incident since it happened. I told him in no uncertain terms that if we were to continue our relationship, he must never mention Diana's name again. Laurence did not tell him about the pills, but Malcolm suspected there had been some setback to my mental health and urged me to go and see somebody professionally. I insisted that I had had a bad case of the flu. He and Laurence got on well and I asked Malcolm to intercede and ask Laurence not to move out.

'Lydia, he is twenty-three years old. Do you think he will stay here for ever?'

'Well, why wouldn't he? Everything he needs is here in Avalon.'

'Except his freedom.'

'I don't know what you mean.'

'A young man like that, he should be able to entertain his girlfriends without his mother looking over his shoulder.'

'But he hasn't got a girlfriend. Not that I know of.'

'That's exactly my point. He's a good-looking young man. If he doesn't, he will soon, and didn't you say that you never met the last girl? Bridget, was it?'

'It was Laurence's decision not to bring her home. I certainly never banned her from the house. Helen comes and goes as much as she likes.'

'I'm amazed that you put up with her. She can be so ill mannered. I'm astonished that Laurence ever dated her.'

'Helen is actually good for Laurence. You see, you don't know a thing about him.'

'I know that he wants to grow up and leave home, and I think it would be a positive thing for you if he did. I live just ten minutes away. I can be here whenever you need me.'

I didn't *need* Malcolm at all, but I was too polite to say so. I had another plan to keep Laurence at home. It meant an almighty financial sacrifice, but we wouldn't lose everything.

I went out one evening to visit my brother-in-law. Finn's welcome was not effusive.

'Lydia, what do you want?' The disrespect in his tone was quite unforgivable, but I buried my dislike and got down to business.

'Finn, I've been thinking about things and I can see now that I was wrong to think we should keep the cottage. I would like to do what you suggested and put it up for sale and split the proceeds.'

He restrained himself from dancing a jig right there and then. He called Rosie and I was invited to stay for dinner. What a spectacle that was. Yes, I had always wanted more children, but my children would have been raised well. Five of the eight children were present, two of whom were teenagers who seemed to be competing to see who could be the most sullen. Laurence was never like that, not until he was forced to move schools, and that was Andrew's fault. The smaller children climbed over and under the table and flicked peas at each other like savages. In addition to the peas, dinner consisted of fish fingers and potato waffles, a whole new experience for me. Rosie was unapologetic. After the plates and the children were cleared from the room, she said, 'I'm so glad you've made this decision, Lydia. With eight children, it's quite a struggle, you know? We could really do with the money. The school fees are killing us.'

'Yes, well, when we had to make sacrifices, Laurence had to go to a state school.'

'Oh yes, of course I know, but it was Andrew who gambled the money. Finn had nothing to do –'

'Let's just put all that behind us,' interrupted Finn, who must have noted my brittle tone.

'There's just one tiny problem,' I said. 'Laurence has become quite attached to the idea of living in the cottage himself, and as you know, the legacy is in his name. I have tried to make him see that the best thing, the *fairest* thing, would be for him to live at home.'

Finn and Rosie exchanged a look.

'What exactly are you saying, Lydia?'

'Well, just that I do not want to fall out with my son, so I'm hoping that you two could apply pressure without involving me.'

'Oh, for Christ's sake!' said Rosie.

'Rosie,' warned Finn.

'It's outrageous!' Rosie ignored him. 'You should have sold that mausoleum of yours years ago. There isn't even a mortgage to be paid on it! There would be plenty of money available for you and Laurence to buy perfectly decent homes. You stressed Andrew so much with all of your whims and demands about the upkeep of Avalon, and now Laurence has had enough of it too. It isn't right that a young man like that should have to support his idle mother in her mansion. He wants out, and you are using us to get him to stay.'

'Rosie!' Finn raised his voice.

I ignored her completely and addressed myself to him. 'If you can persuade him, we will both get what we want.'

Rosie flounced out of the room, slamming the door behind her.

Finn spoke quietly, deliberately. 'My wife is right, you know. Andrew worshipped you. He thought you were the most beautiful creature he had ever seen. He even tolerated your phobias because it meant that he could mostly keep you to himself. He tried so hard to give you every damn thing you wanted, whether it was a diamond ring, or a fur coat, or lunch in the Mirabeau, but it was never enough for you, was it, Lydia? Even though I didn't agree with it, my mother knew exactly what she was doing when she left the cottage to Laurence. Andrew would never have taken all those financial risks if it weren't for you pushing him all the time. My mother was trying to save Laurence from you. If we didn't need that money so badly, I wouldn't think twice about letting Laurence have the cottage, but I will talk to him. You'll get your own way again, Lydia, you always do.'

I had retrieved my bag and coat while he made his little speech. He had followed me out to the hall and down the front steps of their dilapidated house. I kept walking.

As it turned out, Finn and Rosie were not successful in persuading Laurence to give up the cottage. I suspect that they didn't even try that hard. They had decided I was some kind of monster. My darling boy was now desperate to move out. And then Malcolm made everything considerably worse for me.

Laurence had not yet moved out, but he was coming home later and later, sometimes staying away overnight, without offering any explanation. I was careful not to ask questions, but I was sure he was sleeping around. On those nights, he ensured that Malcolm was there, but one night he arrived home at about nine o'clock and I could see from his face that something had happened. He found me in the kitchen.

'Tell me about Diana,' he said softly.

'What?'

He took her framed photograph from behind his back and set it on the table between us. 'Tell me about the day she drowned.' He led me to a chair and gestured for me to sit down.

'Why? I don't want . . . What are you talking about?'

'I remember when I was a child and I asked Dad about her, and he said that she'd drowned at the beach. He said that I must never ask you, because it upset you so much.'

'He was right. I don't want to talk about it.' I made to get up, but Laurence blocked the doorway.

'I've just had dinner with Malcolm. I can't believe you have kept this secret from me for my whole life. He says I should ask you. It could really help you to talk about it. Tell me about the day Diana drowned.'

'I don't remember, I was just a child.'

'He says you do remember, he says you can never forget it. He says she drowned, and that you blame yourself.'

For a stupid moment, I allowed myself to think that perhaps Malcolm was right. Perhaps sharing the story of the accident would bring Laurence closer to me. It had been quite a while since he had talked to me so tenderly. Everyone had always insisted it wasn't my fault, and Laurence loved me. Maybe *his* forgiveness was what I needed.

'After Diana died, I was sent away to an aunt in the countryside. I didn't know if I would ever be allowed to come home again. I was lonely and terrified. I've never been so frightened. Even now, when I go to the shops, I cannot wait to get home. The feeling of banishment was torture to me. It was only ten months, but to a child it was an eternity.'

'Mum,' Laurence exhaled, and a little light entered my soul. I could feel it. Forgiveness was coming. 'Go on, you can tell me. I won't judge you, I won't interrupt.'

'It was after Mummy left. She didn't die when we were babies like I told you. It would have been better if she had. Daddy married beneath him. Mummy was not like any of our friends' mothers. She was loud and brash and wore scarlet lipstick.'

I was transported backwards to a different time, in this house, in its glory days. In my head, I heard Mummy and Daddy bickering in the hall.

'Daddy spent so much time trying to teach Mummy how to behave in society, but she would come to our school sports day and get drunk and flirt with the other fathers. She always let us down. Diana was ashamed of her, but I loved my mother. And then she ran away with a plumber and I never saw her again. She left us. But I still loved her, stupid me. I could never quite accept that she didn't love us enough to stay. After she went, everything was just . . . harder. All the softness disappeared from the house. Diana said she was glad that Mummy was gone. Daddy and Diana were always together, and I was left out. For two years, everything was awful and I was so sad all the time, and then one day Daddy said we could have a party for our ninth birthday. We got new dresses made of peacock silk. Our maid, Hannah, and Tom, the handyman, decorated the garden. It looked so beautiful. The cherry trees were in full blossom. There was a banquet laid out, and bunting was strung from tree to tree. We were so excited, I'm sure we didn't sleep a wink coming up to the day. Diana and I had invited all the girls from our class, but . . .' I choked up at the memory. '. . . only Amy Malone showed up. She told us that the others weren't allowed to come because our mother was a tart.'

Laurence was staring intently. I couldn't bear for that tenderness to disappear, so I tempered my story, just a little.

'I didn't understand what she meant, and Diana said that Mummy had ruined everything and that I was just like her, that I was common, just like Mummy. She called me a hussy and we fought. I pushed her into the water, and she . . . hit her head. I felt dreadful. I still do. Everyone said that I must forgive myself, but –'

Laurence looked confused. 'In the bath?'

'No, darling, in the pond.'

'Where Dad buried Annie Doyle?'

I was momentarily distracted as I wrenched myself forward in decades. 'Yes, it was the most suitable place I could think of at the time, we were in such a panic that night . . .'

Laurence's eyes opened wide and he stared at me, and I realized what I had just said. I stopped, checked myself, turned to face the sink and the darkened garden beyond. But it was too late.

'You *chose* to bury Annie Doyle right there?' He pointed out of the window into the darkness. 'You *knew*?'

'What? Sorry, I'm confused. We were talking about Diana . . .'

'You just said that it was the most suitable place *you* could think of.' Laurence leaped out of his chair. 'You knew about it. Oh God!'

'Laurence, you mustn't . . .'

'Did you kill her?'

'No!'

'You killed her and Dad covered it up? Is that what happened?'

'Laurence, please calm down, you are being so melodramatic! I was talking about Diana and you confused me . . .'

He roared at me then: 'Stop lying to me! Oh God, I can't look at you.'

'She deserved it! She was a thief and a liar. She betrayed us!'

He flew out of the room.

Daddy hadn't been able to look at me after Mummy left, and after Diana died. I looked in the mirror above the kitchen table. I was still beautiful, I knew it, and yet nobody wanted to look at me. I heard Laurence throwing things around upstairs and then he ran downstairs with a suitcase in his hand and I met him in the hall.

'Don't go,' I pleaded with him, 'I'll die.'

He stopped for a moment and I thought I had him, but his eyes filled with tears. He turned away and slammed the front door. I heard the car engine screeching into reverse. He drove away from me as if his life depended on it.

21. Karen

Being with Laurence was different to being with Dessie. Laurence made me feel like I was a person of my own, rather than Annie's sister or someone's property or baby maker. He didn't expect me to be available when it suited him. He borrowed art books he thought that I might be interested in from the library. He drove me to the airport and wished me well when I went off on jobs, and greeted me with flowers on my return. I realized quickly that he was not as well off as I had supposed, but it had never been his wealth or class that I was interested in. He introduced me to his workmates, most of whom I'd met on those Friday pub nights when he was with Bridget. Some were OK with me and others were distinctly rude. 'Some friend you turned out to be,' said Evelyn on one of my first nights out with them as Laurence's girlfriend, but I swore to her that I hadn't ever wanted to hurt Bridget and that we hadn't cheated on her.

Laurence defended me. 'It's nothing to do with Karen,' he insisted. 'I split up with Bridget for lots of reasons.'

The older guy, Dominic, said, 'Jayzis, Lar, you're punching above your weight there, you know what I mean? Weight, get it?' and proceeded to tell me that Laurence used to be obese. I remembered Bridget saying the same thing. It didn't matter to me. I had changed too. I used to be eaten up by thoughts of justice and revenge, but love had fixed me. I wouldn't have thought it possible.

Laurence stayed over in my apartment some nights and was about to move into a cottage he inherited, but he told me about his mother's fragile mental health and how attached to him she was. I insisted he should take his time moving out, and make sure that she was OK first. He was trying to ensure that his mother's boyfriend, Malcolm, would be there for her when he left. And there was some legal wrangling over the cottage to do with his uncle, but Laurence insisted he was keeping it. We went to see it a few times. It was a beautiful whitewashed fairy-tale house, although the roof was slated rather than thatched. I looked forward to visiting him there, walking on the beach, cosying up by the fire and watching the sunset over the bay.

As I might have guessed, somebody in Laurence's office told Bridget about us. I should have had the courage to tell her myself, but in the last conversation we had, she was sure that he was trying to get back with her, and I just took the coward's way out and didn't contact her. When she discovered the truth about us, she rang me and screamed and cried down the phone.

'You were supposed to be my friend! I told you everything. I can't believe you would do this to me!'

'Bridget, I'm really sorry, we never planned it –'

'Was this going on behind my back? You're some bitch, after everything I did for you. You even came to my parents' house, and all the time you were seeing him behind my –'

'But I wasn't, I swear. We didn't get together until much later. I never wanted to hurt you, I know it seems wrong, but –'

She slammed the phone down. The trust between us was broken and could never be repaired. I felt guilty because, whatever way you look at it, I had betrayed a friend. But she took her revenge out on Laurence in a really cruel way, and I didn't feel sorry for her after that. Laurence didn't tell me about it at first. His friend Jane told me in the pub. Bridget had posted photographs of Laurence to his friends in the office. Photos that had been taken when he was at his heaviest, photos taken while he was naked and asleep. He played it down in the pub, but I could see he was mortified. He told me about it later when we were alone.

'She took photos all the time, but I never knew she was taking photos of me when I was asleep. Some of the junior ones in the office were laughing at me behind my back and passing comments. I didn't know what it was all about until Sally told me.'

Evelyn had gathered up all the photos and binned them. She had also rung Bridget in Mullingar and torn strips off her.

Laurence tried to make a joke out of it all, and I could tell that his co-workers liked him. He was a good boss and very fair. Privately, he was upset about it, but we got on with things and moved on as a team. He wrote Bridget a cross letter, letting her know that all of her friends had been disgusted by what she'd done. We didn't hear from her again after that.

Da was really surprised that I was going out with Laurence. He didn't know that Lar had split up with Bridget. 'It makes sense now,' he said. 'He was always asking about you in a roundabout way.' Da had always liked him, and he'd started his new hospital porter job in the Mater, so he wasn't signing on at Laurence's office any more. 'No conflict of interest,' he said, chuckling. I didn't dare tell my parents that Laurence had written the Annie letters. I don't think they would have understood that he did it for me. He had done more work to find her killer than anyone. He knew he was hitting a blank wall, and he just wanted the heartache to stop for us. It was the most considerate, generous thing anyone has ever done for me. Da was prepared to let it go now that he'd been let off the hook in the second letter.

'Didn't she say she'll get in touch one day? I hope it's soon,' he said, and I knew that the forgiveness and hope were enough to keep him going, even though Annie was never going to walk in the door.

Ma had already accepted everything when she got the first letter. She had agreed with Dessie that we shouldn't look for Annie. She agreed with Dessie about everything. She was very upset that I was seeing Laurence. 'It's cheating,' she said. 'In the eyes of God, you are still married and always will be. That man was nothing but good to you. Look at me and your father, back together again. Why don't you give him another chance, love? This Laurence fella, you'll end up hurt, I know you will, there's something about him I don't trust. Why would the likes of him, from a big mansion so you tell me, be interested in the likes of you? He's only after a bit of fun. It's only because you're a model now. He wouldn't have bothered with you if you were still in the dry-cleaner's.'

'Hush now, Pauline, leave her be. He's a nice fella, that Laurence. Very good to me so he was, before he even met Karen.'

My mother's words were hurtful and I did wonder if they might be partly true, but Laurence was proud to have me on his arm and introduced me everywhere as his girlfriend. He never treated me like I was his bit of fluff.

Except for when it came to his mother. I knew Bridget had never met her, and I knew that Laurence and me were in the early days of our relationship, but even though it was unspoken, I felt there was a commitment between us. I was still married to Dessie, and the divorce referendum had just been beaten earlier that year, so marriage wasn't even an option, but the way he talked about the cottage, it was as if he meant it to be our home, and he mentioned us travelling in the future. He found out about fine-art courses I could enrol in. This was definitely not going to be a fly-by-night romance, and yet he never suggested I meet his mother. He had talked about her various phobias and her difficulty with strangers, but I figured that if she was well enough to go to the supermarket, she might be able for me. I wanted to ask him if he had told her about me, but I was afraid I'd be disappointed by the answer. If Bridget got the impression that her family wasn't good enough for Laurence's mother, then I was in the same boat. Socially, Bridget and me were on the same rung of the ladder. If anything, I was lower because I had left my husband, and that made me a loose woman.

Work was going well. I travelled a bit, and without Dessie watching my every move and checking up on me, Yvonne was freer to accept the jobs he would not have approved of. I still didn't want to do sexy lingerie shoots, but there was a swimwear shoot at Cap d'Antibes for British *Vogue*. I was so nervous about that one because the other girls were English, Sri Lankan and Ethiopian. My skin was pale blue compared with their peachy, coffee and ebony tones, but the director of the shoot insisted that was what he wanted. It was all done very tastefully, and an army of stylists made me look good and with the help of some careful padding increased the size of my bust. Laurence thought that was funny. Dessie would have been apoplectic.

Every time I went home to Ma and Da's, there'd be a letter from Dessie waiting for me. In the beginning, they were full of apologies and begging me to give the marriage another go. Then, after a while, they were more about practical matters, like how the bill had come in for getting the boiler fixed, and as I'd lived there at the time he felt it only fair that I contribute. Even though he still had total control of the house fund that I'd paid into every week, I sent him a postal order to keep the peace, and to keep him off my back. Then the letters became abusive. I had made a fool out of him. He was going to get his revenge. Everyone at the dry-cleaner's was laughing at me when they saw me in magazines, and thought I had notions about myself. He was my husband and I had no right to walk away from him. And then they got nastier. I was a stupid slut like my sister, and I'd end up a prostitute just like her. He wouldn't be surprised if I got murdered one day for flashing myself in public. He threatened to sell a story on me to the tabloids about my junkie whore sister, and I began to get genuinely scared of what he could do to my career. I knew he'd been talking to my ma, so I showed her the letters and I warned her again not to give him any details about me or where I was living. She was shocked then and felt guilty about taking his side. Then later, she met Laurence and was charmed by his good looks and fine manners. She put on her telephone voice when she was speaking to him until Da and I ribbed her about it.

My relationship with Laurence was easy from the start. There was no need to make a big effort with him, to dress to please him or to talk a certain way to impress him. He told me I was beautiful many times, but he also told me that I was clever and interesting and funny, and I felt the same way about him. Our dates were pretty ordinary, I guess. The cinema, music gigs in pubs, dinner out occasionally, but we never ran out of things to say to each other, and I knew I would never get tired of his handsome face.

Everything was going pretty well for us, and then Laurence rang me one night out of the blue to say he had moved into the cottage that night. He seemed upset but didn't want to discuss it. I was surprised because it was barely furnished at the time. He said he'd see me during the week, but when I called his office to leave a message they said he was sick, so I took the train out to Killiney and walked up the hill to the cottage that weekend. Laurence had been full of plans about how he was going to do it up. It was a pretty place. The windows were diamond-paned, ivy grew up the walls, and rose bushes stood on either side of the front door. I rapped the brass knocker. There was no reply. I knocked again and eventually heard a shuffling behind the door and it opened a crack.

'Laurence, it's me.'

He pulled the door open reluctantly.

'They said you were sick. Are you OK?'

'Yeah.' He opened the door wider to let me in. He was clearly unwell, still in his dressing gown and unshaven. I followed him into the bare sitting room. The curtains were closed, blocking the amazing views of the bay, and the air was sour.

'You look terrible. Have you seen a doctor?'

'I'm fine.'

He was clearly not fine. There was a single mattress and a duvet on the floor in front of a muted television, and it was surrounded by crisp packets, cereal bowls, cake boxes and empty brandy bottles.

'Laurence, what's going on?'

He pulled me towards him, rested his head on my shoulder and began to cry. I was alarmed.

'What is it?' I embraced him and tried to squeeze his pain away.

'I can't . . . my mother . . .' he sobbed. I could smell alcohol and stale sweat.

'You should take a shower, clean yourself up. I'll put the kettle on.'

He nodded and headed towards the bathroom. I rummaged through a suitcase on the floor and found a clean towel, which I hung on the towel rail amidst the rising steam. I went into the kitchen, which was laden with dirty dishes and empty food containers. I began to wash up and clean the place as best I could. He had clearly moved in a hurry, because there were no cloths or scourers and only a handful of old chipped plates and crockery, left over from his granny's time.

I always knew that Laurence was sensitive and could be emotional, but I wondered what could have happened to cause this sudden collapse.

He emerged clean-shaven, and I gave him a fresh set of clothes. He turned away from me as he dressed, as if ashamed.

'Lar, whatever has happened, you know I love you, right? That still means something.'

'I'm so, so tired,' he said. 'I just want to sleep.'

'You mentioned your mother . . . ?'

'I can't talk about it. I don't want to see her. Ever.'

'But she loves you. You always said she loved you too much.'

'Please don't ask me about her, please? I just can't.'

'Will you come and stay with me for a few days? For as long as you like.'

He bowed his head. 'I don't deserve you, I really don't deserve you.'

Laurence let me drive – he wasn't sober enough – and when we got back to my apartment, he went straight to bed and slept for twelve hours.

He never told me what the row with his mother was about, but it certainly affected him deeply. I couldn't imagine what had caused the upset, but some part of me felt relief, I must admit. He had been attached to her in a way that even his work colleagues found odd. They joked about it, and he had always been mildly embarrassed about living at home. He stayed with me for a week and then went back to work. He had a friend, Helen, who retrieved some stuff he needed from his mother's house while I flew off to Milan for a lipstick shoot. When I returned, he had moved into the cottage permanently. He had been to Avalon and used a rental van to take beds, ancient sofas, odd chairs, tables, rugs, curtains and a dinner service, all things he said were never used and wouldn't be missed. He said the attic of his house had been covered in dust sheets for years. I helped him unpack boxes of books and records and hang pictures and curtains. I met his friend Helen when she delivered other bits and pieces one day. Laurence had gone to the hardware shop for paint.

'So you're the one.'

'Pardon?'

'I mean, don't get me wrong, he should have moved out years ago, but his mum is very vulnerable at the moment.'

I thought we'd got off on the wrong foot. 'Hi, I'm Karen.'

'Helen. I was his first girlfriend.' She seemed pushy and mean, and barged past me into the sitting room. She took a look around.

'I knew his granny you know, who owned this cottage? She was a right battleaxe.'

'Would you like a cup of tea?'

'Have you moved in already?'

I was embarrassed. I was trying to be polite, but I realized I sounded as if I owned the place.

'Oh no, I'm just helping Laurence – but the kettle's just boiled.'

'Grand so.' She dumped her boxes in front of the TV and sat in Laurence's armchair.

I made an effort to be mannerly. 'So, about his mum? I

know they had an argument, but I don't know what it was about.'

Helen's eyes narrowed. 'He didn't tell you? Me neither, but I'm assuming it's because he moved out. His mother is insane, but I really think he should still talk to her at least. He could pick up the phone. I'm around there every other day. Laurence pays me to keep an eye on her, but she isn't eating and barely sleeping. She is refusing to talk to Malcolm. You've heard about Malcolm? The psychiatrist? He says she'll have to be sectioned if something doesn't change soon.'

'Oh God, I had no idea she was that bad.'

'She's sleeping in his bed, for Christ's sake. Laurence really needs to go and see her. He won't listen to me. Yeah, she's mad as a brush, but he's being unfair to her. She just keeps crying and saying that he's all she has. A visit even once a week shouldn't be too much.'

'He was upset too, about the argument, really upset.'

'And you have no idea what it was about?'

'Not a clue.'

'It could have been about you.'

'Me?'

'Yeah, him choosing you over her. You should tell him to go visit her.'

'Nobody is making him *choose*. I will tell him to visit.'

She leaned back in the armchair. 'So how long have you been going out with Lar?'

'A few months.'

'Yeah? How did you meet him?'

Her questions were rude and nosy, but I wasn't going to pretend. 'My dad used to sign on in his office.'

Helen smirked. 'Lydia's not going to like that.'

'Lydia?'

'His mum. She's a pathological snob.'

'She's not going to like that I'm separated from my husband either.'

'Fuck's sake! Really? No wonder they had a row.'

Helen hung around for a bit longer, waiting for Laurence to arrive. We chatted cordially enough, but I could tell she didn't like me very much. Eventually, she had to go.

'No harm to you, you seem all right and you're pretty and all, but it's never going to work, you and Laurence. You come from different worlds.'

'I don't think that's any of your business.'

'I've known him a lot longer than you.'

'He loves me.'

'Touché. But it's not enough. Good luck.' She swanned out the door, brazenly swiping a bottle of wine off the table as she left. 'He owes me.'

I was deeply unsettled. When Laurence came home, I quizzed him about Helen and what she had said.

'Ignore her. She's jealous. You and I? We were thrown together in the most bizarre circumstances, but we were the good to come out of it. We can't let others interfere.'

I didn't think that Da signing on in his office was so bizarre, but I was comforted by his words. 'What took you so long at the hardware shop?'

'I tried to walk there, but I got so tired, I had to get the bus and I had to wait ages. I'm so tired and hungry all the time. I'm trying to stop eating. I don't understand why I suddenly crave food all the time, like I used to.' He flopped down on to the sofa and put his feet up, turning the television on.

I hadn't commented on it, but Laurence had been looking increasingly bloated over the last few weeks. I was sure it was just a phase, something that would correct itself when he resolved this row with his mother. He hadn't been his usual attentive self. He seemed moody and depressed.

'Maybe Helen is right and you should go see her.'

'Who?'

'You know who. Your mum.'

Sometimes when Laurence didn't want to discuss something, his eyes sort of blanked, as if he was shutting down.

'No.'

'Look, I already know she's not going to approve of me. Helen told me as much. But if she's really suffering, you should make the effort, Lar. She *is* your mother.'

'No.'

'Laurence –'

'Just shut up about her, will you?'

That was the first time Laurence had ever raised his voice and snapped at me. He reminded me of Dessie in that moment. Bullying me into submission. I hadn't expected Laurence to be like that. I wondered for the first time if I'd made a terrible mistake. Of course he apologized later, and was extra kind to me – exactly like Dessie. But I had convinced myself that Laurence was better than that. I needed him to prove me right, but I was helpless as I watched him slide further and further into himself.

22. Laurence

My mother. I tried to get back to work, get back to loving Karen, get back to being normal, but I couldn't get my mother out of my head. As a nine-year-old, she had killed her twin sister, and yet she had been able to compartmentalize that, to put the fact to one side and carry on as if it had never happened. Maybe it was a genuine accident, but if there had been no intention, why had she never talked about it? And now that I knew she had been involved in Annie's death, I felt like I had been living with some kind of version of my mother. I knew her better than anyone. And yet I hadn't a clue who she was or what she might be capable of. She could turn on the flip of a coin from an emotional wreck to a sort of robot – clinical, callous and detached. Malcolm, of course, had always wanted to see the best in her, so he was inclined to give her the benefit of the doubt about Diana, but he didn't know anything about Annie Doyle.

I questioned every conversation I'd ever had with her about Annie's body and why my father may have killed her. I analysed all the ways she had manipulated me, and recalled how she had spoken to my father in the few months prior to his death. She had been the strong one. He had gone to pieces. They were complicit in Annie's murder, and I knew that if it had been a straightforward accident, there would have been no need to cover it up. I couldn't guess what had driven her or them to kill a vulnerable young girl, but I couldn't stop my mind from imagining all the possible scenarios and seeing Karen in Annie's place. It tormented me. My mother was as monstrous as my father, perhaps worse because she had been so well able to lie and pretend for so long. I tried to get my head around it. My sweet, frail, vulnerable mother had killed one if not two people. It explained her neuroses, her snobbery, her fear of leaving the house. And it terrified me. Because if my parents were capable of murder, was I?

Karen was bewildered by my change of mood. Things had been so good between us, and she didn't deserve the way I had snapped at her. If only bloody Helen hadn't tried to interfere. I could see the trust fade from Karen's eyes. I attempted desperately to repair the damage, and we tried to get back to normal, but I found it hard to control my moods, and after years of being relatively stable I found it hard to control my weight too. I was permanently starving. I tried to exercise to counter the increased food intake, but I was exhausted by the slightest exertion. Karen said I was depressed. She didn't mention my ballooning stomach, but I caught her looks of surprise and dismay when I took off my shirt. I felt that old shame again, and when we made love it was different from before, until I began to avoid it for fear of further increasing my shame.

For a month, Karen put up with it all. She put up with my bad temper and my dark moods and my increasing girth, but she stopped talking about us as a couple, and I knew I was losing her. On some level, I was relieved.

I didn't deserve her, because of what my family had done to hers. I couldn't be sure that I wouldn't one day really hurt her. But I also knew that if she left me, I would be bereft.

Three weeks before Christmas we had endured another evening of awkward silences. I had more or less abandoned any interest in decorating the cottage. Dried-out paintbrushes stood in stiffened paint pots, and wallpaper hung half-ripped from one wall. Without saying anything, she began to collect the few items she had left around the cottage, her toothbrush, a few T-shirts, some make-up in the bathroom. She put them into a bag, leaving the gifts I had given her behind. I should have expected it. We hadn't had sex in weeks, and apart from going to work I had barely left the house. Maybe my mother's neurosis was hereditary.

'You're leaving me.' It was a statement rather than a question.

Tears glistened in her eyes. 'I thought you loved me.'

'I do, you have no idea how much.'

'So what has changed?'

'I . . .' How could I begin to explain?

'Here's the thing, Lar. I don't care whether your mother likes me or not. It's what you think that's important to me. I don't ever have to see her, but you do. Unless you go and make peace with her, it's over between us. You can have her *and* me in your life. It's not an either/or situation. Go and see her.'

'You don't understand what you're asking. It isn't about you.'

'Of course it's about me. Don't treat me like a fool. Go

and see her. Tell her we're together, but that you will continue to see her once a week. Tell her she never has to meet me, but don't cut her off. For both your sakes. She's not going to be around for ever. She's on her own. You always said she had nobody else. You can make room for both of us. You don't have to choose.'

Karen is the kindest person I have ever met. Even though she had no idea why, she knew my mother despised her, and yet she was willing to share me with her, because she couldn't bear to see me suffering or to hear of my mother's suffering. I couldn't refuse the ultimatum, and so that afternoon I arranged to go and see my mother. It was six weeks since we had spoken, the longest time I had been apart from her in my entire life.

23. Lydia

I knew he would come back eventually. He had to. Laurence and I are bonded. I gave birth to him, and therefore he is mine.

I ate very little during the six weeks of his absence, knowing that Helen would be reporting everything back to him. I was genuinely distraught, especially when our estrangement went on so long, but I knew he was paying Helen to watch me, so it was not as if he had stopped caring. He loved me really.

I cursed Malcolm's stupidity and indiscretion. The Hippocratic oath clearly meant nothing to him. I would never have told Laurence or Andrew about Diana. There was never any need for Laurence to know anything about that, but when I was forced to, I misspoke when talking about the pond. My son thought that Andrew and I had murdered that girl together. He may have been correct, but he could not possibly know why, and I knew that if I could just talk to him, I could make him understand.

I slept and wept in his bed, trying to hang on to the essence of him. It was my bedroom when I was a girl. And when I pulled back the writing desk, I found my old hiding place in the wall. There, I found photographs of the girl who I assumed was Laurence's new lover. I was taken aback by how beautiful she was. They were studied, professional photographs. She could have been a film star. And then I really worried because this girl had something that I could not compete with. Beauty, yes, but youth too. I did not want her in our lives. Also, I found the identity bracelet and newspaper cuttings about Annie Doyle's disappearance, and disturbing handwritten fantasies about him dating Annie Doyle and having sex with her. When had he written these? Why had he kept hold of these items? Why could he not let go of the past?

I tried to call him, but he would not take my calls at work and hung up when I called the cottage. A week after he had left, he came to the house with a hired van and began to remove furniture without speaking to me or looking at me. He trooped through the house seven or eight times and refused to acknowledge my cries and pleas. I contemplated another overdose. Helen had confiscated my medication and was doling it out to me as if I were a child. She also found the phentermine.

'Why are you taking these?' she said.

I lied that Malcolm had prescribed them.

'Idiot,' she said, and flushed them down the toilet.

Helen was always insightful. I still had one of Malcolm's prescription pads and could get any drugs I wanted, but I decided to wait, and the longer I waited, the more my anger towards Laurence increased.

But when after six weeks he telephoned and said he was coming to Avalon to talk to me, I heaved a huge sigh of relief that my son was finally coming home. I filled the prescription for him.

I was shocked by his appearance, and I think he was shocked by mine. For every pound in weight I had lost, he had gained three. He was closer to the obese boy I had been able to control. This pleased me. Because it could not have been attractive to her.

I had sent Helen home and prepared his favourite meal. I had dressed carefully and washed my hair for him and laid the table in the dining room. I chattered about the weather and programmes on television while I piled his plate high.

He was reluctant to talk in the beginning, but I soon coaxed him into conversation.

'Darling, it's so good to see you. I'm so glad you came back.'

'I'm just visiting.'

'Of course, and how is Granny's cottage? Draughty, I imagine, with those big windows?'

'It's fine.'

'But aren't you lonely there?'

'No.'

'Do you have friends coming to see you there? Because if you liked, you could have your friends visit here. I would stay in my room –'

'Just one friend, my girlfriend.'

'Oh, you have a new girlfriend? How sweet.' I feigned ignorance. I did not want to talk about *her*. I changed the subject. 'Darling, about Annie . . .'

He passed his hand over his eyes. 'I don't want to talk –'

'But we must, otherwise you will spend your whole life thinking that your father and I are monsters, and we aren't. It was an accident, just like Diana –'

'Mum, please . . .'

'Annie Doyle was hired by your father to do a job.'

His curiosity got the better of him. 'What job?'

'You know how desperate I was to have a baby, a little brother or sister for you? You remember, don't you?'

He said nothing but he watched me, watched my mouth as I spoke.

'Your father, I . . . we hired Annie . . . to get pregnant.'

'What?'

'It was my idea. Your father was to get her pregnant and she was to give us the baby.'

'But . . . that's ridiculous! Dad would –'

'She was to provide a service, darling. I didn't know she was a prostitute. Your father didn't know either. He was never a kerb crawler, my Andrew. He had to be so discreet. He caught her picking his pocket one day, but he felt sorry for her. He could have had her arrested, but instead he helped her. And then later he asked her to help us. She was handsomely paid for her services, and after only three or four attempts she told him she was pregnant.'

'This is crazy! It's illegal for a start, and . . . oh my God, poor Dad.'

'I know, poor Andrew didn't want anything to do with it, but I was desperate, I begged him, and even though he tried to persuade me it was a terrible idea, I convinced him. I needed that baby. You were growing up. What was I going to do without you?'

'Mum, do you have any idea how insane you sound?'

I struggled to remain calm. 'Don't. Don't you say that. I always wanted to fill this house with children, with life. It isn't insane to want to be a mother. I had no mother growing up, I needed someone of my own. I had no sister because she was dead.'

'But, Mum –'

I didn't want any interruption. 'And I had so much love within me to give. Every miscarriage ate away at my soul. You will never know what that was like for me, time after time, the life being torn out of me. I need family.'

Laurence sat perfectly still. 'So what happened to Annie?'

'She lied to us. She demanded more and more money. She refused to get a doctor's note to confirm her pregnancy, and I began to doubt that she was pregnant at all. And then, on . . . that . . . last night, I told your father I wanted to see her. He had . . . *dealt* with her, made the arrangements . . . impregnated her, or so he thought. I had kept away, but I was worried. We had so little money and he was paying her month after month. I needed proof that she was pregnant, so when she was supposed to be about five months gone, Andrew got into a row with her because she had figured out who he was and she admitted that she wasn't pregnant at all. She tried to blackmail him. She said she was going to the papers. He lost his temper.'

'And?'

'He lost his temper. It wasn't his fault. He was under so much pressure financially, and she had stolen from us. She was a common thief, Laurence. She had used us and defrauded us and your dad . . . lost his temper.'

Laurence pushed his empty plate away and rose from the table. I needed Laurence to see that the girl was the victim of her own misfortune. I had to bend the truth a little.

'He killed her.'

'Yes, but he didn't mean to. It was an accident. She

pulled a knife on him. She was a nasty guttersnipe. It was self-defence. He strangled her. He was dreadfully upset. He really didn't intend to kill her.'

'Oh God. I was right all along. He murdered her, but you are as much to blame.'

'Me?'

'I can't believe you forced Dad into such an outrageous plan. No wonder he died so soon after. The stress of it all killed him.'

Tears welled up in my eyes. I needed Laurence to understand.

'I miss him every day. That girl, she was so evil. She tried to stab him! She pushed him to the limit.'

'*You* pushed him to the limit. And yet you've been able to carry on as if nothing has happened, just like after Diana . . . drowned.'

'Life throws hurdles at us, darling. We must get over them.'

'Annie was a hurdle? Diana was a hurdle?' Laurence's voice was breaking.

'Please don't be dramatic about this. What is done is done, and we are both implicated.'

I could feel his anger. 'You involved me. You knew what had happened, and you involved me. I poured cement over her grave!'

'Yes, but we have to just forget about it all now, get back to normal.'

'You have no idea what normal is.'

'I'll do anything you want, I can change.'

'You can't.'

'But I will –'

'Mum, I am never, ever coming back to live with you. Ever.'

'I see.'

I was perfectly calm, set a smile on my face.

'I can't live in a graveyard.'

I used the only thing I had. 'Darling, I can make you slim again – look how you have ballooned since you left this house.'

I knew that I had thrown him with this statement. He sighed heavily and pinched the top of his nose between his thumb and forefinger.

'What are you talking about?'

'I had you on phentermine. It's a drug prescribed for lethargy and depression, but the side effect is weight loss.' I explained how I'd got the drug, how I had crushed it into his meals. I went to the kitchen and took the bottle of tablets out from behind the vanilla essence and showed him. 'Here, you can keep them. They work really well. I didn't tell you because I didn't want you to feel self-conscious about it. I wanted you to think you'd lost the weight by yourself.'

Laurence began to cry, and I took him in my arms and placed the tablet bottle in his pocket, but he aggressively shook me off and stood in the opposite corner of the room.

'This is so screwed up. I can't believe it.'

'Everything I do is for you, darling.'

'Please, just stop.'

I stopped then because everything I said seemed to make things worse. He threw open the window and inhaled deeply. Freezing December air stole into the room. The silence between us grew in length, and the atmosphere plummeted with the temperature. When he turned back to face me, his tears had dried and he pushed his thumb under his chin the way Andrew used to when he was going to make an announcement. He spoke without emotion.

'For now, I will support you financially as far as I am able. Once a month, I will come for dinner.'

My heart lifted. It was something. I could work on him to make it once a week.

'But there is one condition. I have a girlfriend. You must accept her, she will come with me. I'm only here now because she forced me to come.'

'Oh, but, Laurence, can't it be just us? You are my only relative. She would feel like an intruder.'

'Mum, I will not be living here, and she will only feel like an intruder if you make her feel like one. And . . . there's something I have to tell you about her.'

His forehead glistened with sweat, and I wondered what could possibly make him so nervous.

'She is Annie Doyle's sister. It's Karen. Karen Doyle is my girlfriend.'

I was utterly stunned.

'The prostitute's sister?'

'I think you should refer to Annie as the murder victim. Karen is not a thief or an addict or a prostitute. She is sweet and kind and generous, and really beautiful. If you gave her a chance, you would really like her. She is modelling at the moment, but she's going to study art, and she is quite well travelled. You might even have seen her in magazines . . .'

He babbled on and his eyes shone as he spoke of her, but I tried not to listen because my head began to pound, although it didn't stop me from hearing him say, 'I love her, Mum.'

The treacherous bastard.

Somehow I kept it together and managed not to show signs of the electrical storm fizzing in my head. Laurence asked if he could bring the girl to dinner. I smiled and nodded.

'Are you sure?' he said. 'Do you need more time to get used to the idea? Of course, she doesn't know anything about what happened to Annie. We won't even mention Annie. I think she might be uncomfortable if she knew . . . that you knew about her sister. Are you really sure it will be OK?'

'I'm sure, darling.'

He looked at me with uncertainty. 'I think I'm glad I know the truth now. About Dad and Annie. I think I can understand why he did what he did, but it really is unforgivable. And, Mum, I really think you need to get help, psychiatric help. Obviously, you can't tell Malcolm about Annie, but you should see somebody, professionally. I think you have invested too much of your life in me, and you need to let go now.'

I agreed with everything he said, and smiled benignly at his suggestions while waves of red-hot anger surged backwards and forwards between my temples.

After Laurence left, I went upstairs and carefully applied the very last of Mummy's scarlet lipstick.

24. Laurence

Knowing the truth has finally given me some . . . I'm not quite sure what the word is. Relief? Not peace of mind, because that is a different thing altogether. I am deeply disturbed by my mother's mental state and her role in Annie's life and death. I can't stop thinking of what my father did. I am sickened that I must keep this secret from Karen for the rest of my life, but Mum has agreed to see a psychiatrist and has finally accepted that I have moved out of home. I think telling the truth may have helped her. Despite everything, she is my mother. She did love and nurture me, and I am in some way obligated to her. I will not throw her to the wolves, and maybe these disclosures might bring her some peace and stability. She has no more secrets, nothing more to hide.

With hindsight and a little distance, I can see how obsessed she has been with me for my whole life, and I wonder when that love became deranged. I'm inclined to believe that it happened after Dad died, when she knew for sure that she would never have another child. Helen was right about Mum all along. But I feel sorry for her, for both of us, because I was never enough for her. I wonder would things have been different if she'd had another child, or if she simply always wanted a relationship as close as the one she must have shared with Diana.

My mother has been at least indirectly responsible for

the deaths of two people, not including my father. Living with that knowledge is my albatross, but I cannot put her through a murder trial. It would most certainly kill her, and there has been enough death.

After Christmas, I am going to see a specialist about my weight. I have been drugged for two years. I suppose Mum thought she was helping me, and maybe I should be grateful, but I am angry with her for not telling me. She was so determined to control me. I am back to taking the tablets to get my weight down as soon as possible. Consequently, I am buzzing with energy again and rarely sleep. I'm only doing this for the short term, just until I can see a dietician. Karen is delighted that I am in better form, that I am out running every morning before work and that I cycle halfway to and from the office. She hasn't ever mentioned my size, but it cannot be attractive and I don't want to give her any further reason to question our relationship. Last Friday, in the pub, Dominic nudged her and pointed at me, saying 'Beauty and the Beast, know what I mean?'

We are going to dinner together at Mum's for the first time next week. I have rung Mum several times to make sure that she hasn't changed her mind and that she will not be weird with Karen. I dared not tell Mum that Karen is married. One step at a time. But Mum's mood is much improved too. She says that she is looking forward to the dinner and that she has been poring over recipe books to make sure that the meal is perfect. I'm trying not to let Karen know how nervous I am about this meeting. They will either get on or they won't, but the truth is if Mum forces me to choose, I will choose Karen.

25. Karen

When Laurence told me that his mother had invited me for dinner, I knew that it was a big deal for him. And it was a big deal for me too. I was terrified of a woman I had never met, but Laurence seemed a lot better after that visit to his ma. I was so glad that I made him go. He started exercising again, dumped the junk food and suddenly he was more energetic, cleaning up the cottage and making proper plans for its renovation. He lifted out of his depression quickly, and I wondered if this was how it was going to be between us. If Laurence was prone to bouts of depression, I decided that I would be willing to stand by him. Nobody understood me like Laurence did. He had my best interests at heart. Laurence was supportive of whatever decisions I made. He was not jealous or small-minded. He made me a better version of myself. I wanted to make him happy. In bed on the morning of the dinner, I very tentatively asked Laurence if he thought it would be a good idea if I moved in with him. I stumbled over the words, knowing that, traditionally, it would be the man who asks this question, but I wanted to demonstrate my commitment to him.

He grinned at me.

'Yes! Yes, of course. I was going to ask you, but I was afraid that I'd scared you off. That's what I want too, to live with you officially. I'd marry you if divorce was legal –'

He stopped, shy suddenly. 'I mean, if you said yes, obviously.'

'I'd say yes.' I moved my head on to his pillow and kissed his mouth, and he kissed me back with a slow sweet passion and that turned into a kind of lovemaking that was more tender than ever before.

Later, as we prepared to go to his mother's house, I dressed very carefully. It was cold, early December. I had received a big cheque during the week from Yvonne with a note attached, advising me of a designer's sample sale in the Westbury Hotel. I arranged to meet her there. She knew a little about my relationship with Laurence. She hadn't met him, but when I told her of his mother's dinner invitation to Avalon and her address, she seemed pleased but sounded a warning.

'If I can give you any advice, dear, I would suggest that you should not go where you don't belong. It rarely works out.'

I laughed at her. 'But it's worked out for you.'

'My life is a pretence. I would not recommend it for everyone, and I've grown fond of you,' she said, lighting a long cigarette.

There was a touch of sadness about the way she said it, and I thought of her poor dead son and the fact that she had never mentioned him since the day we discussed Annie's murder.

At the sale, she picked a silk and wool-mix dress in a shade of emerald green for me. I pointed to my hair. She threw her eyes up to heaven in an exaggerated look of exasperation. Yvonne was not a devotee of the 'red and green should never be seen' idea which had most fashion houses dressing me in whites, blues and russet tones.

'Nonsense. Try it on.' And I did and it was perfect.

Laurence answered his door and said, 'Wow.'

'Do you think she'll approve?'

'It doesn't matter whether she does or not.'

I hoped it was true. We had arranged to go to Avalon together. Laurence drove. He was quiet on the journey.

'Well, at least give me some dos and don'ts,' I said.

'Nope. I don't want you to have to pretend, but try not to say "fuck",' he said, smiling.

'Like Helen?' We laughed.

When we drove up the long driveway to the house, I caught my breath. It was a mansion from the front, but as we drove around the side of the house to park beside a garage, I could see that it was twice as long as it was wide.

'Oh my God.'

'It's just a house.' He squeezed my hand.

'But it's –'

'Just a house,' he whispered, and put a finger to my lips. I kissed it.

I could see a shape through the windows and it moved as we walked around the outside to the front door. She got there before us and held the door wide open.

'Welcome, welcome!'

She was extremely classy-looking. I had come across some older models of around Laurence's mum's age on assignments, but the years had touched Mrs Fitzsimons very lightly, with just a few strands of grey at her temples and some faint lines around her bright blue eyes. She was tall and very slim, and only slightly stooped in the shoulders. She had dressed simply in a black cashmere dress and a long string of pearls.

She smiled at me broadly. 'I am so glad to finally meet you, Karen. You are as pretty as a picture!'

Even though Laurence was directly behind me, I could sense his relief.

'Very pleased to meet you, Mrs Fitzsimons.' I handed her a box of Milk Tray.

'Oh, thank you, darling, but please, call me Lydia. Laurence, you told me she was beautiful, but you are stunning, my dear, simply stunning.'

'Hi, Mum.'

She hugged Laurence first and then embraced me warmly, though her limbs were thin and bony, and swept us into the house. I had never been in a house like it in my life. I had been to a stately home on a job, and Avalon reminded me of that. A crystal chandelier hung beside a central staircase, and although the house showed a few signs of wear and tear, it was far grander than I had imagined. I tried to think of what Ma and Da would say if they were here. I didn't think they could ever be relaxed in such surroundings. I wondered how Lydia might receive them, but she was perfectly sweet to me, complimenting my hair and my dress as she poured me a gin and tonic. I was grateful for the drink because, despite Lydia's kind welcome, I knew I might have to answer uncomfortable questions about my background. Laurence had told me to be honest, though he admitted that he hadn't revealed that I was married. 'Keep that one for another day, eh?'

She and Laurence talked about his work and plans for the cottage, which she approved of wholeheartedly. She told him how well he looked, and congratulated him on his renewed exercise programme. She nodded in my direction. 'Clearly, Karen is a great influence.'

When she headed towards the kitchen, I offered to come and help but she put her hands up. 'Not at all, I have everything under control, don't worry about me. Maybe Laurence will give you a tour of the house?'

And so Laurence showed me out of the drawing room, across the hall and into the dining room, the breakfast room, the playroom, the pantry, the cloakroom and the library before taking my hand and leading me up the stairs.

'One day, all this will be ours . . .' he whispered.

I nudged him and we laughed. I saw the bedroom he had slept in for most of his life, a man's bedroom, sparse and functional despite the corniced ceiling and grand fireplace. I looked out at the view down the avenue through the barren trees and tried to imagine what it must be like to grow up in this luxury. Would Annie still have grown wild? I put the thought out of my head.

An old rocking horse stood on the corner of the landing. 'I was never allowed to play with that, I can't remember why. Perhaps it was too delicate,' he said.

Out of respect for her privacy, we didn't enter his mother's room, but the other three bedrooms and a box room – 'that's where the maid used to sleep in Mum's day' – were structurally beautiful, though old broken furniture and books and boxes lay scattered around the rooms, covered in dust. A large empty room with a mirrored wall and a ballet barre was next door to Lydia's bedroom. I couldn't hide my astonishment.

'Yeah, Mum did ballet when she was younger. She still practises every day.'

No wonder she was in such great shape.

'Will you show me the garden?' I asked, peering through a window, trying to see beyond my own reflection.

'Another time, maybe. It's too cold and dark now.'

Lydia called up to us from the hall to say that dinner was ready. Laurence grabbed me and kissed me on the lips before we ran downstairs.

The table layout in the dining room freaked me out. All the settings were at one end of a long table, so that Lydia would sit at the head of the table between Laurence and me. I had done etiquette lessons for Yvonne, but there were too many forks and knives and I couldn't remember which side plate was mine. Laurence saw my confusion and mouthed, 'Watch me.'

Lydia and I sat down as she asked Laurence to carve the shoulder of lamb.

'It's totally out of season of course, so it's out of the supermarket freezer, I'm afraid. I hope you like lamb, Karen?'

'Oh yes, I'm sure it will be delicious.'

As dinner progressed, I could see Laurence becoming more relaxed. I didn't sense any snobbery from Lydia at all, and saw no sign of her infamous neurosis. She was sweet and charming and chatty throughout. Maybe I had got her on a good day, or maybe Laurence's recent spat with her had made him more wary. Maybe he had totally exaggerated her condition and her attitudes, because she was very nice to me.

'And I believe you met because your dad signed on in Laurence's office? Well, at least that's interesting. From what I can see on the television, everybody meets nowadays in tawdry nightclubs.'

'Karen doesn't like nightclubs very much,' said Laurence.

'Very sensible,' she said, smiling.

'My dad isn't signing on any more. He got a job a few months ago.'

'Isn't that just wonderful? Where is the new job?'

'He's a hospital porter.'

I could see Laurence stiffen.

'Is he? He must be a very kind, caring man to do that kind of work. I think it's admirable, don't you, Laurence?'

'He's a very nice man, Mum. You'll meet him sometime.' Laurence smiled at his mother and she put her hand on his, I think to reassure him.

While she filled our wine glasses and cleared the plates away into the kitchen, refusing any help, I said to Laurence, 'I don't know what you were worried about, she's lovely.'

'I know, I can't believe it. She's certainly on her best behaviour.'

Lydia re-entered the room. 'I am so silly. I forgot to get another bottle of wine. It was on my shopping list and I've just realized that I never crossed it off. I'm so sorry.'

'Don't worry, Mum. We've had enough.'

'Oh, but I wanted us to relax in the drawing room and hear all about Karen's travels. I wanted to buy Italian wine to remind you both of Rome.'

Laurence and I exchanged a quick glance.

'I'm not stupid, darling. Anyway, Karen might just inspire me to jet off somewhere.'

I offered to pop out to the nearest off-licence, but Lydia wouldn't hear of it. I suggested that Laurence should go, but he was reluctant. 'Please, Laurence, I'd love to tell your mum about Paris and Milan. I think she'd love Paris in particular.'

He looked uncertain, but agreed. 'I'll be as quick as I can.'

His mum looked at him, smiling broadly. 'Darling, you needn't worry, I adore her! And try to get a Chianti?'

After Laurence had left, she allowed me to help her a little in the kitchen. We chatted as I dried some serving dishes.

'Look out there, can you see? There used to be an ornamental pond there when I was a girl.'

I put my face up against the glass and could just see a raised stone platform on the grass with a small stone structure on top. 'What's that?' I asked.

'It's the old bird bath that used to be in the pond. About five or six years ago, Laurence took a notion that he was going to build up a platform and cement over it. I don't know what got into him. He never showed any interest in the garden before that, but nothing could stop him that time – and it was winter too, around this time of year, I think. Doesn't it look odd?'

I laughed, agreeing it did look odd. 'And do you know that from the day it was finished, he hardly ever set foot in the back garden?'

We went into the drawing room and sat in the glow of

the fireplace in upholstered armchairs, slightly frayed at the corners, though you could tell the fabric had been expensive.

'Would you like to see photos of Laurence as a child?'

I readily agreed, and she came and sat on the arm of my chair with leather-bound photo albums. She turned the pages and pointed out what an adorable baby he was, and indeed he was extremely cute, waving his spoon at the camera, crawling out from under a table. There was a photograph of him at about five years old, wearing a hat that was way too big for him.

'That was his grandfather's trilby. You know, Laurence wore it all the time, even when he grew up. He was very attached to it. I must ask him what happened to it. I haven't seen it in about six years now. But I suppose it is very unfashionable these days.'

Lydia turned more pages and I gasped at a photo of Laurence, quite obese, standing with Lydia beside a navy vintage Jaguar. I knew every make and model of Jaguar from that era. I kept my voice steady. 'Where was that taken? Who owns the car?'

'That was my husband's. A 1957 Jaguar Sedan. God knows, he poured so much money into keeping it on the road for Laurence.'

'For Laurence?'

'Oh yes, Laurence begged Andrew to teach him to drive when he was seventeen years old. Laurence was absolutely obsessed by that old car. They had terrible rows about it. Laurence didn't even have a driving licence at the time. Didn't he tell you about it? One day, after Andrew died, he sold it, just like that, as if it had never mattered.

I should warn you, Laurence is adorable but he does have his peculiarities!' She grinned at me. 'If you could have seen him, driving around in that car wearing his grandfather's old hat. Hilarious!'

I had only had a glass of wine after my gin and tonic, but I felt hot and cold and confused and sick. Lydia noticed.

'Are you all right, dear? You are very pale. Shall I fetch you a glass of water?'

These things are perfectly normal, I told myself. Of course Laurence would never have told me that he had driven that car or worn a hat like that. He knew it would have upset me. I regained my composure. Lydia returned with a glass of water and a cardboard box.

'Here you are, drink up, you poor thing. Are you sure you're all right?'

'I'm fine. Just a passing headache, thank you.'

'By the way, I found this stuff in an old hidey hole in Laurence's bedroom. It's probably just old junk, but he may want to take it to the cottage.' She placed the box on my lap and exited the room again to fill the coal scuttle.

There were photographs face downwards, and I gingerly turned them over to find that they were photographs of me. I felt better. I shouldn't have, but I delved into the box again and found pictures of me cut from magazines, and then underneath there were yellowing newspaper cuttings. I lifted them out and opened them up. They were dizzily familiar. The cuttings were dated November and December 1980. All of the reports about my sister's disappearance. Laurence was certainly dedicated in his search. But then I stopped and thought how could he have got these? I'd only met him last year. It didn't make sense. There was something else. A matchbox wrapped in tissue paper. My hands shook as I pulled it open, all regard for Laurence's privacy gone.

I turned the broken identity bracelet over in my hands. The engraving was there: *Marnie*. One end of it was broken, but I could see that the clasp was stained crimson red where Annie had picked it up before her nail varnish had dried on the day I had given it to her.

I jumped up from my seat, knocking the items on to the floor. I tried to rationalize all the thoughts that were zooming around my head, but there was no way Laurence could have got that bracelet from anyone except Annie. He had the car; he had the hat, the bracelet; he had cut out newspaper reports about her. The cogs turned in my head as Lydia returned, but I couldn't hear what she was saying, couldn't believe all the evidence that surrounded me. I tried to remember how he had come into our lives, Dad telling me that this guy in the dole office had taken special care of him, long before I met Laurence. He hadn't written the Annie letters to comfort us, but to throw us off track.

Annie's killer wasn't dead. Laurence killed her. Laurence killed my sister. I ran, pushing past Lydia, ran for the front door, down the driveway to the gate. As I reached the gate, Laurence drove in. I stopped dead in my tracks.

'Where are you going? What's happened? Are you OK?'

And then I began to run again, as fast as I could. He jumped out of the car, calling after me, and then he began to run too, but he was still quite heavy and I outran him. I ran and ran until he was out of sight, and then I ducked into the nearest phone box and dialled 999.

26. Lydia

Laurence threw me across the room. I never knew he had such a temper. Though I suppose he must have inherited it from Andrew.

He came storming into the house, winded and red in the face. I had cleaned up the spillings of the box and put them away, together with the photo album.

'What did you do? What did you say to her?'

'I should warn you, Laurence, that you are probably going to be arrested very soon.'

'What? What are you talking about? Karen is terrified! She ran away from me. What happened?'

'You should not have betrayed me. I gave you every opportunity to come home, and still you chose that tart's sister over me.'

He was apoplectic, and through gritted teeth he snarled at me, 'What did you say to her?'

'I didn't say anything directly, but I presented her with the evidence.'

'What evidence?'

'The evidence that you murdered her sister.'

'You . . . but it was Dad . . . and you.' He shook his head. 'You wouldn't do that. That doesn't even make sense. She would never believe that.'

'You killed Annie Doyle. I have tried to protect you, but I cannot stand by you any longer.'

'Oh my God, you are more insane than ever!'

'It's all here. Karen has seen all the evidence.'

'Why are you being like this? What twisted game are you playing now?'

'It's not a game. Motherhood was never a game. You rejected me. Even though you knew how much that hurt me. You chose her over me. I can do what I want with you, and now I choose to send you to jail.'

'For Christ's sake, Mum, you're talking in riddles. What exactly did you say to her?'

'I showed her the photo of you standing beside Dad's old car. I told her you were driving it at seventeen.'

'But I wasn't. You taught me to drive years later.'

'You are so forgetful, darling. Your father taught you to drive, in the Jaguar. You insisted.'

Laurence pulled at his shirt collar and leaned on the piano to hold himself up.

'And the photo of you as a baby, wearing Granddad's hat? I told her how you were very attached to that hat until . . . let's see . . . about six years ago, when it suddenly vanished.'

'That's a lie! I never wore it!'

'You choose not to remember what doesn't suit you. I gave her all the cuttings and vile scribblings and the tatty cheap bracelet you kept hidden in the hole behind your writing desk. Karen recognized it straight away. And while you were gone, I showed her the tomb in the back garden that you so kindly built.'

He lost his temper and came at me, spitting and red-faced. He physically threw me across the room. The coffee table broke my fall, but I could tell immediately that my wrist was injured. And then we heard the sirens. I glared at him, this ungrateful brat in whom I had invested my life.

I kept my voice very low. 'You should have obeyed me. I'll probably marry Malcolm now. You have left me no choice. We will make each other miserable, but he will never leave me. He is not the type.'

And then everything dissolved into slow motion and it was as if I was going back in time. Laurence's colour was very high, his breathing came in rasps and his eyes stared wildly about him. He clutched at his chest and then fell to the ground. Just like his father. There was a blue flashing light beyond the window and a hammering at the door. I let the guards in and I screamed at them to get an ambulance. But Laurence's eyes had rolled up into his head, like Annie's, and his body went limp, like Diana's. I was hysterical. I had taken it too far, just like with Diana.

When the ambulance came, I was allowed to travel with Laurence to the hospital. As I was being helped up the steep step, I saw Karen weeping in the back seat of one of the garda cars that were scattered all over our lawn.

In the end, I got what I wanted. My boy will be home with me for ever. He will never argue and he will do as he is told. The heart attack he suffered cut off the supply of oxygen to the brain. This means he is mentally a child, and physically he is slightly damaged. His mouth hangs open and his feet turn inwards. The staff in the rehabilitation centre, knowing of his crime, were inclined to treat him cruelly. I was the person that made sure he did his daily exercises. I control every single thing about him, and he does not question me.

He is my child again, so there was no need for me to marry Malcolm, as I will not be alone. Laurence had inherited his father's and grandmother's weak blood vessels, though the medics later said that the levels of Phentermine in his system and his rapid weight gain and loss were also contributing factors to his cardiac arrest.

The guards invaded my home and I was questioned for hour upon hour. They found all of the evidence that incriminated Laurence, and they dug up the pond as I might have predicted, and found the remains of Annie Doyle. I was not allowed into my home as forensic investigators went through everything, but I spent my days in the hospital and my nights at Malcolm's as a media storm began to gather:

'Prostitute murdered by schoolboy'.

'Murder suspect has heart attack when arrested'.

'Top model Karen Fenlon was well known to the man suspected of her sister's murder'.

Her name was Fenlon. Her *married* name. She never even had any right to my Laurence. The audacity of her to think she could bewitch my son, with her uncouth accent and appalling table manners. All of her magazine photos were reproduced alongside headlines that screamed 'Sister of murdered prostitute'.

Because of Laurence's medical condition, there was no possibility of his standing trial. So the newspapers could never name him, though Dublin being such a small city, anybody who was anybody knew within days that Laurence was the suspect. I had to keep my wits about me during this time. I detested the publicity, but I knew that if I ended up back in the clinic, if I was sectioned, Finn and Rosie would get power of attorney and sell Avalon, so I had to stay focused and clear-headed. Malcolm held me up.

Everybody was shocked. None of Laurence's workmates ever suspected him of being capable of such a thing. Helen, surprisingly, was inconsolable. She visited me several times, trying to figure out how he had hidden it from her, trying to find an excuse for him. I wept bitter tears with her, but claimed that sometimes Laurence had been prone to violent outbursts. My wrist had been broken in our final confrontation, so I had sufficient evidence. Helen worked out that she had been dating Laurence at the time of Annie's disappearance. She never realized that she was his alibi, because nobody could ever pin down the exact time and date of Annie's death.

Apparently, Karen Fenlon abandoned her modelling career and returned to her husband, who was foolish enough to take her back.

Three months after Laurence's heart attack, I was allowed to return to Avalon. I spent days erasing all traces of the garda investigation in my home. Malcolm came and filled in the pond again and planted rose bushes. Then Laurence was released into my custody. He was only semi-verbal, but extremely docile. He would never be able to read or write again, would never be able to take care of himself. He needed some help with feeding but could manage the toilet and most of his dressing. He babbled senselessly, but he knew the word 'Mum' and could point at things he needed.

Malcolm hung around for months, trying to console me, but thankfully, although he dealt with mental instability on a daily basis, he found mental disability more difficult to cope with, and eventually he drifted out of our lives, except when I needed him about the house for some manly task.

Legally, as Laurence was no longer capable, I managed to get the cottage registered in my name. I sold it immediately. We would have to live on the proceeds for some considerable time. We would have to make the money last. The government provided a disability payment for Laurence, and with my widow's pension it meant that we would not starve. After a certain period, Helen was our only visitor, apart from an occasional social worker. But mostly, it is just Laurence and I. I don't think he understands anything much, but often, very often, I find him standing in the kitchen, looking out of the window. I ask him what he is looking at, but he doesn't respond and stares vacantly.

PART 3

2016

27. Karen

At the time, I was so distraught that I couldn't trust my own judgement. I had been wrong about everything. Dessie was incredibly kind to me. He offered a solid shoulder and assured me that everything would be OK. Ma and Da were shocked. Laurence had fooled them too, especially Da. Ma thinks that Laurence probably intended to kill me too, but we'll never know now.

When I think of the nights I shared with him, I want to pull clumps of hair from my head. Sometimes, I do. The guards warned us to stay away from Avalon after Laurence got out of hospital. I didn't want to go near the place, but Da badly wanted to beat the living daylights out of him. I am still so angry that he got off scot-free. Laurence murdered my sister and I never got to know how or why, and even if he is brain-damaged, I don't think that is enough punishment because he doesn't have to live with himself in the way I do.

Because I had some kind of public profile then, Yvonne could do nothing about protecting me from the media. Ma and Da's house was besieged, and somehow they found my flat. They couldn't name Laurence, but they could name me and Annie, and reprint photographs of me alongside lurid headlines. Dessie offered me a place to stay and I went home with him. I drank myself into oblivion in those first few weeks. I was a mess. The police interrogations seemed endless. Detective Mooney had been wrong about the murderer being dead, though they couldn't rule out the possibility that Laurence's father had helped him, despite Lydia apparently insisting that he would never have done such a thing. Poor Lydia. This time, the guards were taking it seriously, now that there was a middle-class Cabinteely man involved.

It was three days after I had called the guards from the phone box that I realized the significance of the garden monument that Laurence had built. My suspicions proved to be true. The guards had sealed off the house and were searching through everything. They found some essays in Laurence's handwriting about dating Annie and having sex with her. I still feel sick at the thought of it.

I never intended to get back with Dessie, not then, but he was so rock steady and so ready to forgive. I thought if we got back together, I could make things right and turn back the clock to when we'd been happy. Yvonne thought that the notoriety would die down after a while, and that I could resume my career, as I was still in demand in Europe, but the whole modelling scene seemed so stupid and trivial to me. Dessie said the money would be handy, but he let me make my own decision. Eventually, I got a job in Arnotts' shoe department. Dessie was as protective as ever, but that was what I needed back then. He tried not to comment on my drinking in the beginning.

We have a house in Lucan and two children, Debbie and Stevie. I should be happy. I should be able to let go of the past. And I should never have gone back to Dessie. After a while his protective ways turned into full-scale intimidation and bullying. He has never raised a hand to me again, but he doesn't have to because he knows that I am afraid to ever leave him. Our daughter drives him up the wall. She was wild like Annie when she was a teenager, and he blamed me. I drank more wine and blocked it all out. Stevie is a good boy. He's a lorry driver, getting married this year. I don't have much of a relationship with him. Dessie and Stevie stick together. Debbie and Stevie stick together. Nobody sticks to me.

When the news scandals broke in the 1990s about the Mother and Baby homes, I thought about looking for Marnie, but Dessie went ballistic when I mentioned it.

'Jesus Christ, Karen. Remember how your last search went? Are you stupid or what?'

I am stupid. A fool.

The only person I see on an occasional basis is Helen. I'm not sure why we still meet up, but we do. Every six months or year or so, we'll go to a pub and rehash the whole story, as if we were old soldiers reliving our days at the front together. Helen is now a pharmaceutical sales rep on her second husband, a lab technician. She never had children. We still don't like each other very much, but we are somehow bonded by our experiences of Laurence Fitzsimons.

She still visits Avalon. I didn't understand why she bothered, but she said that in the beginning Lydia paid her to do shopping and cleaning and to help with caring for Laurence. Helen says it's hard to see Laurence as a murderer when she is giving him a bath and spoon-feeding him his dinner. I can't see him as anything else. In the last few years, Laurence and his mother have lived in just three rooms downstairs. Lydia has run out of money, anything left of any value has been sold off, and she can no longer pay Helen.

'So why are you still helping them?' I asked recently.

'For the house!' she said triumphantly.

She admitted that she had had papers drawn up. About ten years ago, she came to an arrangement with Lydia. She got Lydia to make a will, leaving the house to her, as long as Helen comes once a week with shopping and anything they might need. The arrangement is that Lydia can stay there until she dies. Lydia and Laurence never leave the house at all. Helen says Avalon is worth millions now, even though it's in bad repair, and I don't doubt it.

I feel sorry for myself a lot of the time, and I really need to stop drinking soon, but the person I feel most sorry for is Lydia. How must it feel to be the mother and full-time carer of a killer? She must be well over eighty years old. Helen says she has dementia now. I think that must be a blessing.

28. Lydia

I can't remember if I fed Laurence today. He is crying a lot and we are very cold.

When those boys came and threw stones at our windows and smashed them, when was that? I went to call that man, the one who adores me, but I don't think the telephone is working. Daddy will be very cross when he comes home and finds glass everywhere.

I lie on the sofa under a rug, but the broken spring is hurting my ribs.

The girl . . . Helen . . . that's her name, I remember! She's not a girl any more, but her, the one who always came. She brings coal sometimes when she comes with shopping in her car. But today we are very cold and I cannot find the matches. Diana took them from me. She says we mustn't play with matches.

Andrew says I must stop Laurence from crying. Maybe he is teething. I have pushed him out into the garden and tied him to the drainpipe to stop him wandering.

Mummy is calling me to come in for dinner. I love the smell of her perfume. I follow it indoors.

It is dark outside. I can still hear him crying.

Acknowledgements

Thank you to my agents: Marianne Gunn O'Connor for her loyalty and loveliness, and Vicki Satlow for carefully placing me into the best international hands.

Thank you to my editor, Patricia Deevy, for her sound judgement and for steering me away from the cliff edge. Thank you to my homies at Penguin Ireland – Michael McLoughlin, Cliona Lewis, Patricia McVeigh, Brian Walker, Carrie Anderson and Aimée Johnston – who all ensured that this book made it into your hands.

Thank you to the amazing team at Penguin UK – Stephenie Naulls, Rose Poole, Keith Taylor, Holly Kate Donmall and Sam Fanaken – who made me look literate and for making sure you heard about the book. Thank you to Caroline Pretty for her gimlet eye to detail and chronology. Thank you to Leo Nickolls for the stunning cover design. Thank you to Catherine Ryan Howard for being my social media maven.

Sincere thanks to the Irish Writers' Centre and the Tyrone Guthrie Centre for support in the form of the Jack Harte Bursary, which afforded me the time and space to work on this novel. A royal thank you also to Judith Gantley at the Princess Grace Irish Library in Monaco for treating me in the manner to which I would like to be accustomed.

For specialist help, many thanks to: Dr Marie Cassidy, state pathologist, for advice on a decomposing corpse(!);

Anne O'Neill, pharmacist, for medicinal advice; my sister Dr Mary Nugent, educational psychologist, and my brothers Peter Nugent and Michael Nugent, solicitors, for information on dyslexia and legal matters respectively; Eileen Conway, PhD, who wrote the book (thesis) on adoption; Yvonne Woods, communications officer at the Free Legal Aid Centre; Richard Walsh, consultant neurologist; Peter Daly, FCA, accountant, and Joe McGloin at the Department of Social Protection; and finally Barry McGovern and Donna Dent for bringing Oliver and Moya to life.

For their expertise in other areas: Gillian Comyn, Benjamin Dreyer, Rachel O'Flanagan, Isibéal O'Connell, Declan Paul Reynolds, Finian Reilly and Donald Clarke.

For their professional encouragement: Sam Eades, Rhian Davies, Rick O'Shea, Maureen Kennelly, Sophie Hannah, Marian Keyes, Sinead Gleeson, Sinead Desmond, Sue Leonard, Martina Devlin, Claire Hennessy, Aifric McGlinchey, Victoria Kennefick, Bert Wright, David Torrans, Frank McGuinness, Ryan Tubridy, Sarah Webb, Vanessa O'Loughlin, Declan Burke, Kilkenny Arts Festival, Roundstone Culture Night, Belfast Book Festival, Mountains to Sea Festival, Airfield Writers Group, Dromineer Literary Festival, Sunday Miscellany, Skibbereen Arts Festival, Dalkey Book Festival, Hay Festival Kells, International Literature Festival of Dublin.

For having to listen to all this endless guff about me: Mum, Dad, Peter, Grainne, Michael, Lucy, Paddy, Monica, Mary, Matt, James, Fiona, Jennifer, Gary, Elaine, Colm, Joanne, Alan, Davy, Jennifer, Julie, Patrick, Julie and John.

Also, big love to my ever expanding coven, which

includes but is not limited to: Brid, Maria, Rachel, Olivia, Grainne, Mike, Susie, Al, Aingeala, Frank, Philip, Margaret, Anne O', Anne M, Beta, Katherine, Susan, Nuala, Deirdre, Claudia, Clelia, Vanessa, Sinead M, Sinead C, Jane, Karen, Paul, Donna, Marian, Tara, Louise, Kate, Martina, Hilary, Lise-Ann, Jen, Angie, Alexia, Gillian, Megan, Fiona, Paraic, Donal, Tania and Grace.

For their warmth and welcome, thanks to the fantastic community of readers, writers, librarians, booksellers and bloggers who know that there will always, always be room for more stories.

Last, but by no means least, to the writers of the future: Sophie Nugent, Robert Nugent and Mia Creamer.

If you loved *Lying in Wait* you'll also love Liz Nugent's award-winning bestselling debut, *Unravelling Oliver* . . .

'I expected more of a reaction the first time I hit her.'

Alice and Oliver Ryan seem blessed, both in their happy marriage and their successful working partnership. Their shared life is one of enviable privilege and ease. Enviable until, one evening after supper, Oliver attacks Alice and puts her into a coma.

Afterwards, as everyone tries to make sense of his astonishing act of savagery, Oliver tells his story. So do those whose paths he has crossed over five decades.

It turns out that there is more to Oliver than Alice ever saw. But only he knows what he has done to get the life to which he felt entitled. And even he is in for a shock when his past catches up with him.

'Compelling, clever and dark, unlike any other psychological thriller you will have read before, you'll gobble it up in one go'
Heat

'Truly excellent, beautifully written . . . strongly recommended' Sophie Hannah

'A book that truly deserves the overused accolade of "page-turner"' *Sunday Times*

'A superbly paced and shocking story' *Sunday Mirror*

'A compelling "whydunnit"' *Daily Mail*

'An extraordinary read' BBC Radio 2 Book Club

Please turn the page to read the first chapter of *Unravelling Oliver*!

1. Oliver

I expected more of a reaction the first time I hit her. She just lay on the floor holding her jaw. Staring at me. Silent. She didn't even seem to be surprised.

I was surprised. I hadn't planned to do it. Usually when you hear about this kind of thing, it is the 1950s, and the husband comes home drunk to his slovenly wife from the pub and finds that his dinner is cold. On the contrary, it was 12 November 2011, a wintry Saturday evening on a south Dublin avenue, and Alice had prepared a delicious meal: lamb tagine, served on a bed of couscous, with pitta bread and a side dish of mint yoghurt. Though the lamb was a tad lukewarm by the time she presented it, I really couldn't fault it. I had washed the meal down with two glasses of Sancerre, while Alice prepared the raspberry roulade for serving. I certainly wasn't drunk.

But now, here she lay; the lower half of her body nearly hidden behind the legs of our mahogany dining table, her arms, head and torso curled inwards like a question mark. How had she fallen into that shape? There must have been considerable force behind my closed fist. If the glass had been in my hand, would I have stopped and put it down before I hit her? Or would I have smashed it into her face? Would it have shattered on contact and torn her pale skin? Could I have scarred her for life? It's very hard to know.

The words that come to mind are 'circumstances beyond our control'. I emphasize the word 'our', because, although I should not have done it, she really should not have provoked me.

The phone rang. Maybe I should have ignored it, but it might have been important.

'Hello?'

'Oliver. It's Moya. How are things?'

These rhetorical questions irritate me. 'How are things?', indeed.

Sorry, Moya, I've just punched Alice in the face and she's lying on the floor. And we've had a marvellous dinner.

Of course, I didn't say that. I made some ham-fisted attempt at an excuse and bade her farewell. I waited for the reciprocal adieu.

There was a moment's silence and then:

'Don't you want to know how I am? Where I am?'

I was short and to the point. 'No.'

Another silence. And then, whispered, 'Oh right, OK, is Alice there?'

Go away, you stupid irritating woman.

I didn't say that either. I told her that now was not a good time. She tried to inveigle me into a conversation, prattling about her new life in France. Even amid the turmoil, I could tell that she wanted me to be jealous. Bloody Moya. I ended the conversation politely but firmly.

I thought that the decent thing to do was for me to leave the house immediately. Not permanently, you understand. I thought there was more chance of Alice getting up off the floor if I wasn't looming over her. I went to get my coat from its peg in the hall. It was a little difficult to do up the buttons. My hands suddenly seemed to be too large for my gloves.

Two hours later, I was on my third brandy in Nash's. Nervously, I buttoned and unbuttoned my shirt cuffs. It is a habit from childhood, a thing I do when I am distressed. Even John-Joe commented on my rattled demeanour when he served me. Brandy would not have been my normal tipple. But I had had a shock, you see. Now I *was* drunk.

I wanted to phone Alice to see if she was all right, but I had left my mobile behind and I thought that perhaps borrowing somebody's phone would make a bigger deal of the situation than it warranted. Don't get me wrong, I knew it was serious. A significant error of judgement had been made. She should not have ended up on the floor.

I am aware that I am not the easiest of people. Alice has told me so. I have no friends, for example. I used to, many years ago, but that really didn't work out. We drifted apart and I let them go – voluntarily, I suppose. Friends are just people who remind you of your failings. I have several acquaintances. I have no family either to speak of. Not in the sense that matters.

Over the years, Alice has never pried, has never been too curious. In fact, I would describe her as habitually obedient with just an occasional rebellion. I am not, have never been, violent.

I went to the bar and bought a packet of cigarettes. Strong ones. I was worried that my hands were still unsteady. Isn't brandy supposed to help at a time like this? Or is that an old wives' tale? Old wives.

Outside in the 'beer garden' (a yard with half a roof beside the front door), I lit my first cigarette in years. Barney Dwyer, a neighbour from the Villas, approached from the public bar. Barney spent more time in the beer garden than inside the pub.

'Thought you were off them?' he said.

'I am.'

'Jaysus,' said he, a swagger in his voice and sucking on a Rothmans, 'they couldn't break me.'

Here we go. Barney prided himself on his forty-a-day habit. When the smoking ban was introduced, most of us did our best to quit. I am proud to say that I was the first to succeed. I became known as the man with a 'will of iron'. Barney, on the other hand, made no such attempt. If Barney had never smoked, he would have started the day the ban was introduced. A contrary bugger if ever there was one. Thin head, big ears.

'Welcome back,' he said.

'I'm not *back*, I'm just having the one. It's been a bad day.'

'Jaysus, Oliver, it's never just the one. You're back on the fags. Face it.'

I threw my almost smoked cigarette on the ground. Stamped on it. Tossed the packet containing nineteen cigarettes at Barney.

'Keep them,' I said. 'Go on, kill yourself.'

My wife had finally brought out the worst in me. It was most unexpected. I had always been fond of her, in my way. She was a marvellous cook, for example, after all the gourmet cuisine courses I made sure she attended. Also, she could be very athletic in bed, which was nice. It is terribly sad to think of such things now, considering her current state.

We met at the launch of a book she had illustrated back in 1982. My agent wanted me to meet her with a view to her doing the illustrations for a children's book I had written that he was pushing around to publishers. I resisted the idea of illustrations initially. They would just distract from my text, I thought, but my agent, I admit it, was right. The drawings made my books far more marketable. We were introduced and I like to think there was an immediate . . . something. Spark is not the right word, but an acknowledgement of sorts. Some people call that love at first sight. I am not so naïve.

Neither of us was in the first flush of youth. Both in our late twenties, I think. But she was lovely in a soft way. I liked her quietness and she made few or no demands on me. She just accepted whatever attention I gave her, and then withdrew into the background without complaint when I did not require her presence.

The wedding happened very quickly. There was nothing to be gained by hanging about. Her frail mother and half-witted brother stood behind us at the altar. No family on my side, of course. We didn't bother with the palaver of a hotel reception. We had a rowdy meal in a city-centre bistro owned by a former college friend, Michael. Barney was there. Back then I quite liked him. He was very emotional at the wedding, more than anybody else. One couldn't blame him, I suppose.

We rented a spacious flat in Merrion Square for a few years. I insisted on a big place because I needed privacy to write. I can only write behind a locked door.

Those were good times. We made a bit of money when nobody else did. It made financial sense that we would collaborate on what was becoming quite a successful series. During the day we would retreat to our separate corners to work. Me, producing my books. She, cleverly matching pictures to my words. She was good at it too. Her work flattered mine appropriately.

I became quite well known as a critic and occasional scribe for the weekend newspapers and for an infrequent guest spot on televised chat shows. In those days, everyone was more discreet and low key about their achievements, their successes. Not like current times – I can't tell you how often in the last decade I was approached about partaking in a 'reality' show. Heaven forbid. Alice avoided all of that, which suited me really. She did not like the limelight and she underestimated her own contribution to the success of my books, insisting that my work was more important, that she was just a doodler. She was timid and didn't even want it known that we were a husband and wife team in case she would be 'forced on to the telly'. Rather sweet, and it meant that for a lot of the time I could continue my life as a seemingly single man. It had its rewards. Truthfully, she could not have been a better helpmate.

Alice's mother died suddenly in 1986, at the end of our fourth year of marriage. Thanks be to God. I can't stand old people. Can't stand it even more now that I am getting to be one.

I used to make excuses to avoid visiting her and her doily-draped furniture. Used to pretend to be too busy to eat with them when she came to visit us. It was never pleasant to witness her struggling with her dentures, the half-wit dribbling by her side. Her death was a mixed blessing. We got the house. But we also got Alice's imbecilic brother. The house is quite a pile on Pembroke Avenue. The brother goes by the name of Eugene.

Alice begged me to let her keep him. Until now, that was the biggest upset in our marriage. Bad enough to have a child, but this was a 27-year-old, fifteen-stone dolt we were talking about. Eventually, I had him accommodated in a home for the 'mentally handicapped', or those with 'special needs', or whatever they are calling them this year, at considerable personal expense.

When we got engaged, I made it very clear that children were not on the agenda. Well, I said I didn't want children, and she agreed. I should have got that in writing. She must have been extraordinarily besotted with me to sacrifice something so fundamental to her in order to marry me. Maybe she thought I would change my mind, because it seems that lots of men do. Or maybe she knew that if I didn't marry her, I'd marry the next quiet one that came along.

Of course, five years into our marriage, Alice began to whinge, and grew more shrill with each passing month. I reminded her of our agreement. She claimed that at the time, that was what she had wanted too, but now she desperately wanted a child. I am nothing if not a man of my word.

I couldn't depend on her to protect herself, so I took control. I made a ritual of bedtime cocoa with a little crushed pill as an added extra. Alice thought that was so romantic.

I haven't exactly been a saint within our marriage. Women, by and large, are attracted to me and I do not like to disappoint them. Women you would never expect. Even Moya, for God's sake. I eventually resent the ones who try to cling.

In later years, I had begun to satisfy myself with some tarts that operated near the canal. I never objected to them, even before I became a client. They were objects of curiosity. They were cheaper and more desperate, mostly addicts with raddled bodies and ropey veins, but perfectly adequate for my needs. I would order them into a shower before any congress was allowed and I always provided a new toothbrush. Some of them took it for a gift. Pathetic. They are usually too emaciated to be good-looking. One would think that they might make an effort to make themselves attractive. Alas, they were only selling their various orifices; the packaging was immaterial. But still, they held a fascination for me. After all, my mother was one, or so my father said.

Returning to the house on the night Alice pushed me too far, I fumbled with the key in the door. I stepped into the dining room. She wasn't on the floor, thank God. She was sitting in the kitchen, nursing a mug of tea. Her hand rubbed at her face. She looked at me without affection. I noticed that her jaw was quite red on the right-hand side. No bruise. Yet. I looked at her. Smiled.

The wooden box in which I had locked away my darkest secrets lay open on the table in the hall, its lid agape, lock smashed, contents violated.

'Liar!' she said, her voice breaking.

It was clear that she intended to ruin me.

The second time I hit Alice, I just couldn't stop. I am very sorry about that indeed. I have been in control of my life since I was eighteen years old, and to lose control is a failing. Needless to say, I am not allowed to visit her in hospital. It is silly really. It is February 2012, so it's been three months now. In her condition, she wouldn't know if I was there or not.

It turns out that I am a violent man after all. It comes as a shock to me. I have been psychologically assessed. I decided to tell them almost everything. Apparently, I have been harbouring bitterness, resentment and frustration since my childhood. Now, there's a surprise.

What will the neighbours think? What will anybody think?

I really couldn't care less.